The Phoenix Rising

Destiny Calls

By
Phenice Arielle

~~

This book is dedicated to my mother the journalist, to my father the activist, and to my aunt the teacher—who I know would've loved this book.
I am one-third each of you, and everything you instilled to help me believe this was possible.
Thank you.

~~

CONTENTS

Destiny:
(Timing is everything.)

Preface

"What do you remember?"

I could barely make out the unfamiliar voice through the blinding light. I could barely even catch my breath, before being shoved back down into the piercingly cold water—a hand over my face—my arms and legs strapped down in the clear water-filled contraption.

I gasped for dear life when the hand finally let me come back up for air. The voice wanted to know something I couldn't remember. I was going to be killed for something I couldn't remember. And, I had a feeling, it was something I didn't *want* to remember.

But my life was at stake. "Nanyamka, *please* remember!" I screamed at myself inside of my head.

Boom!

The explosion sent two guards flying. I knew I should help, but it was my only way out—my only way back—back to the land that I once called home.

So I took my advantage and made a dash for the door. But it had found me even here.

I thought I should run—again—but the low warning roar stopped me. There was no time left. I quickly turned around, and took out the ivory-white dagger that was handed down to me. There was no tribe—and no crown—but I braced myself for the battle that was upon me. Because I had made my choice—destiny or not.

I then prepared for the worst, and hoped my loved ones knew—that no matter the outcome; when the sun had set, and the wounds had healed, the phoenix would rise, and I would return again.

PART 1

1. Passport

I've never been diagnosed, but I've suffered from night terrors ever since I was eight. By now, I should either be used to it—or insane.

Still, I frantically checked my body for burns or any other signs of trauma—none physical. The only trauma suffered seemed to be the mental one caused by these stupid, repetitive dreams.

And though I've never enjoyed waking up in a dripping cold sweat, I had to admit that lately, something undeniable was happening.

Because for the past year my little experiences were becoming more and more real to me each time; the sunlit jungle—the roaring lion—the explosion—the screams. Actually, what it was becoming was *exhausting*.

My roommate at least didn't seem disturbed by anything I might have said in my sleep. I looked over at her enviously. Beth was in her own little dream world, and I couldn't be sure, but it looked like she was smiling.

I secretly wondered if there was some way I could talk her into trading dreams with me. Probably not.

It was 6:23 A.M. according to the clock radio on the nightstand by my bed. I didn't have to be to my first class until 10:00 A.M., but I knew there was no way I was getting back to sleep now.

So, after throwing back the cheap navy blue covers I'd bought two weeks ago for the start of the new semester, I half-heartedly patted around the bed for my glasses. I'd left them on top of the equally inexpensive blue comforter sometime before falling asleep last night.

I don't know why, but there was something about reading the school newspaper before bed, that helped ease the anxiety of knowing what I'd see when I closed my eyes at night.

Glasses in hand, I swung both legs over the side of the bed and cautiously tiptoed across the creaky, wooden floor. When I reached the dresser on the opposite side of the room, I checked to make sure I hadn't woken Beth before I opened the bottom drawer. This time, she snorted softly—still smiling—but didn't wake up. Must be that George Clooney dream again.

I pulled out the very first thing I touched in that bottom drawer. It was a light grey cotton hoodie with dark purple writing on it. I'd won it last year in one of those silly yet secretly fun potato sack races during sophomore orientation.

Already in the white tank top and sweatpants I'd fallen asleep in, I pulled the light grey hoodie over my head, and softly walked into our small university style bathroom. It was plain-looking, and practically the same size as our closet, but at least it was clean—I shuddered when I thought about what the inside of a boy's bathroom might look like.

Commanding myself to refocus, I stretched and looked straight forward into the large, rectangular mirror embedded into the bathroom wall. There, I read the acronym formed by the purple painted letters on my chest. They read: NYU.

I smiled. At least, I did until I caught a glimpse of my *more* than slightly disheveled hair. Then I frowned. If I weren't going to have any more peaceful nights of sleep, I at least shouldn't have to look like it when I woke up.

I leaned back into the mirror. My body was still warm from the intense dream session, and my cheeks were slightly flushed. I couldn't help but tilt my head. Here I was, a junior in college, and I was still surprised whenever I saw pink showing through my golden brown skin.

Beth was always telling me how beautiful I was—actually, everyone did. But for some reason I never really saw it. Still, today I was going to take Beth's word for it because today was the day my passport arrived in the mail—and I was in way too good of a mood to spend time focusing on my flaws right now.

It took me a minute to get my elastic headband from around my wrist and onto my head, but once I did, I splashed some cool water on my face and decided to go for a jog.

I've always thought New York is at its most magical when it isn't so full of hurrying people. In fact, my favorite part of getting up so early is when the sidewalks are empty, and the streets are quiet. You can be alone with your thoughts in one of the most crowded cities in the world.

I don't know what it is, but there's something that makes my skin tingle knowing that while my heart's pumping with my feet, millions of people are still asleep. And, for the 30 minutes that it takes me to jog to

Washington Square Park and back, I feel as if I'm the only person in the world—and those nightmares I have—are just a figment of my imagination.

Thankfully, I wasn't the only person in the world. The stores I passed were evidence of that. And yet somehow, I couldn't believe what I saw as I jogged by.

Storefronts already had Christmas decorations in their windows. We'd completely bypassed Halloween *and* Thanksgiving, and had fast-forwarded straight to the most profitable holiday of the year.

I didn't like the rush, but part of me understood it. The lights—the unity—the sense of peace—all contribute to why there truly is nothing like being in New York during Christmastime.

But I wouldn't be here this Christmas.

So as I jogged past yet another snow-can covered window, I tried to allow myself time to enjoy the magic of a peace-giving New York during September.

Of course, as soon as I turned down Bleecker Street, I saw him. And I suddenly remembered why I stopped jogging this route—so I wouldn't run head-on into the past.

"Quick! Get me someone from the mayor's office!" I remember it was sophomore year; two weeks before everyone would leave for Christmas break. The final student newspaper was going to print in less than two hours, and I'd had it on good authority that an investigation was going to be launched to determine whether the mayor violated election laws during his last campaign.

I took a quick look around for the long-haired blonde with the ponytail who'd just joined the student newspaper staff. "Beth!" I yelled from across the room, "Do we have someone on the line yet?"

"I'm being transferred to the press secretary now mate," she said in her thick Australian accent.

I was about to break the story before the *New York Times*, the *Daily Challenge* and even *USA Today*. If I could pull this off—without any errors of course—the *Sunday Times* would have to choose me for the apprenticeship in South Africa. They'd just have to!

Caught in the frenzy, I barely heard him through the frantic bustling of the student newsroom.

"Excuse me, does anyone know where the registrar's office is?"

I was still waiting for Beth to get off hold so I could get a usable comment from the mayor's office. That's why I didn't pay attention to the low voice coming from the doorway. Someone else would attend to him.

"Beth, they're stalling! Hang up and call them again, and *keep* calling until someone gives you something we can work with!" I was going to get a quote from them if it killed me.

The deep voice cleared his throat and spoke louder. "Um, excuse me, is this the registrar's office?"

"Does this *look* like the registrar's office?" I didn't look up, and I didn't mean to be rude, but sometimes I was less than polite when I was in the middle of breaking a story.

"Oh." The deep voice was startled, but spoke again. "I need to pre-register for the winter semester. Do you happen to know where I can do that at?"

This guy obviously wasn't going away, so I finally looked up. And when I did, for a moment at least, I forgot where I was.

We both stood there—silent. And I don't know why, but I had the feeling that our expressions mirrored each other's—though we couldn't possibly have been thinking the same thing.

Yet, I really don't know *what* I was thinking. My thoughts had begun racing. A million different images were swirling by so fast that I couldn't make any individual one out.

It was like my body was working overtime—the way it does sometimes when it's trying to remember something from a dream—I was *desperately* trying to remember something from a dream.

The somehow familiar stranger took half a step forward. He was captivating, and his beautiful almond shaped eyes—among other things—caught me off guard.

"I'm sorry," he continued, "I know you're in the middle of something but..." He seemed to lose his train of thought for a moment. And if I'd been just crazy enough, I would've sworn that he was looking for something, and that what he was looking for he was trying to find...in me.

We continued to stand—both of us frozen in place. I tried to remember where I thought I had seen him before, and if I *had* seen him before, why I didn't recall feeling like...this. But before I could reflect on it any further, he took two more steps through the doorway, which immediately interrupted my thoughts.

"I could really use your help." For some reason, he was speaking in a whisper as if he were afraid that if he spoke too loudly or made any sudden movements, I'd run off, and he'd never see me again.

But that's crazy—that this stranger would care if he ever saw me again. The images continued to swirl around in my head. The jungle—the lion—the explosion—the screams—the...the what? There was always a fifth element of the dream that I couldn't remember. *Why* couldn't I remember?

I shook my head and came back to reality.

"Down the hall; two lefts and a right."

"Thanks," said the incredibly handsome co-ed. The usual noise of the newsroom returned then, and even though I expected him to leave and to never look back, he kept his eyes locked on mine. And if possible—I mean, if not just made up in my mind—it seemed as if he were trying to force himself to leave. Was there something *he* was trying to remember as well?

Beth brought me back from my trance. "The press secretary's on the line mate. Line 2."

I couldn't believe that was almost a year ago. Moreover, I couldn't believe how completely soaked in sweat I was by the time I got back to the dorm. I couldn't tell if it was because of the jog or because I saw... Don't think about it Kay.

Seeing him in the middle of my jog had unhinged me a bit, but I still felt energized enough by the jog itself to start the day.

So as quickly as I could, I ran up the stairs to my room on the second floor, and didn't think twice before peeling off my college sweat suit. Beth had already gone to class.

"Pump it! Louder! Pump it! Louder!" I turned on the radio to full volume, and The Black Eyed Peas were on. That made me even more amped for the day ahead. That is, until I checked the mirror. Great, from bedhead to windblown hair.

It was so much easier when I decided to wear my hair in braids all freshman year, but I tired of the style I'd worn on and off most of my life, and decided to blow out my long, dark brown hair for my junior year. It was easier this way—for now.

I leaned back through the bathroom doorway to double-check the time. It was 7:40 A.M. I would have plenty of time to stop by the mail center before class.

So after I showered, I dried off and put on my glasses. I could see pretty well without them, but for someone with a nose for a good story, I unfortunately didn't have an eye for good direction. I once got so lost trying to read the downtown street signs that two homeless gentlemen offered to walk me home that night.

Ever since then we decided… Ugh. I've *got* to stop referring to myself in the plural sense. It's just that, I have so much going on in my head these days that sometimes it *feels* like a "we" in there. Beth, the eternal comedian, said there was a term for feeling like there's a "we" inside my head, and that she learned that term in her psychology class. Psychology or not, I decided that I should probably start wearing my glasses more often, just to be safe.

Towel on, I decided to dress up—which to me just meant a fancy top over jeans. I looked back in that bottom drawer from earlier and pulled out a silk, lavender tank top. I decided not to wear a hat, but I did put on my brand new, beige trench coat as I anxiously exited the dorm room for the main building. That's where all my mail was sent.

I wasn't sure which housing unit I'd be in when I applied for my passport four weeks ago, so I gave them the university address. I just didn't want my passport going to my parents' house, even though they lived right where we always have—mere minutes away from the very university I was now attending.

My mom—though I love her immensely, is a total worry wart; and my dad isn't much better.

Still, I was hugely fortunate to have parents who loved me so much that they'd made enormous financial sacrifices to be able to send me to sleep away camp when I was younger. So you'd think with them having practice being away from me during all those childhood summers that they'd be reasonable about me spending the holidays in another continent—but no. If they'd seen a passport come in the mail, it would've been interrogation season all summer. But I vehemently, and I mean *vehemently* decided against that.

When I arrived at the main building, I walked to the mail center with my head held high. I really enjoyed being an upperclassman. For some reason, I always felt like fresh meat when I was a freshman and even still when I was a sophomore. But I was a junior now, and there were big things for me on the horizon.

I turned the corner and immediately walked up to one of the work-study students behind the mail desk. "Hey, is there anything for a Morowa back there?"

"Hold on, let me check." The tall, lanky male student turned around and disappeared into the back. He returned about 30 seconds later with a bulky envelope in his hand. He looked at the name that the envelope was addressed to, and seemed as if he were about to say something, but then changed his mind. "Morowa. Yep, here you go." He handed me the envelope and had me sign a piece of paper.

"Thanks!" I probably said it with a little too much enthusiasm, because he backed up as if he were afraid I'd jump over the counter and hug him or something. To be honest, I probably could have. But first things first. I ripped open the sealed envelope like I was a kid on Christmas morning. Paper cuts be darned, it was a risk I was willing to take.

And there it was—my ticket to becoming a world renowned news reporter—the key to my limitless future—the holy grail of all international travel—my passport.

I lifted it up and slowly opened the small, dark blue, texturized booklet I'd been waiting for. I held it in my hands as if it could break my heart and disappear at any moment.

At the top on the inside, was a picture of the American flag. Next to it was a picture of the bald eagle. And of course, underneath all the insignia was a photo of me— with a smile so wide it could've scared the Snuggle bear back into the drier.

Aside from some basic demographic information, and the passport's expiration date, there was only one thing left to be found—my ridiculously hard to pronounce name. But there it was, plain as day. It read: Nanyamka Apiyo Morowa.

No one ever called me that; mostly because they didn't know *how* to call me that. Most introductions were followed by a short pause, with the person finally saying o… kayyyy… Then I would casually joke for them to just call me kay for short. And what do you know? It stuck.

"There you are Kay!"

I didn't have to turn around to know who it was. Beth and I had become best friends last year while working together on the school paper. In fact, we grew so close that we each put in requests to be roommates this year.

"You were up *awfully* early this morning." Beth was right beside me now and had tossed her backpack on the mail counter in front of us. She was about to say something else, but instead put both hands on her hips and looked at me with a tilted head. "Aye, what are you laughing at?"

I didn't mean to, but I'd let out a slight giggle. I couldn't help but laugh every time Beth said a word that started with a vowel—I blame watching too many hours of Crocodile Hunter on TV. Steve Irwin was pretty much my only introduction to Australia, which is probably why I half expected him to jump out and say "Crikey" every time Beth got excited about something.

Gosh I miss watching Steve Irwin.

"I'm sorry Beth," I said with a chuckle.

"Oh I know you can't help it. Poor New Yorker." Beth smiled.

All junior year we'd been perfecting our banter, and now I was going to miss these conversations when I left. Beth was just so easy to talk to, and was really one of the only people I trusted.

I don't know why, but ever since I can remember, I've been guarded—as if I've been protecting myself from something, even though I didn't know what that something was—yet.

It seemed like the only time I didn't feel that way lately was around Beth. And I remembered the time that I used to feel that way around... him.

"Excuse me. Sorry. Oomph. Pardon me," I recalled yelling behind me as I blindly tried to make my way down Washington Square. I could barely see over the excessively tall stack of books I was trying to balance as I pushed passed some upperclassmen into the Bobst Library. Ugh, four more months until junior year Kay. I tried to keep myself motivated.

Exactly five months had passed since my big scoop about the investigation into the mayor's alleged campaign violations. It'd also been exactly five months since the one and only time I saw the handsome co-ed with the beautiful almond shaped eyes—the eyes I was almost sure I'd seen somewhere before.

It was nearly summer when sophomore finals were upon us. And I'd been putting in serious overtime when it came to studying. Unfortunately, not every subject was as exciting as my Armed Robbers & Smoking Guns: Intro to Crime Drama class. So from time to time when studying alone at night in my dorm room, I'd doze off in the middle of a textbook and wake up with a pulse rate that would make even a NASCAR driver jealous—all from the very unwanted, involuntary journeys I went on in my dreams.

But thankfully, Beth and I were becoming good friends. We'd been spending loads of time working on the copy for the student newspaper together. Plus, we were both journalism majors. So I gave Beth a call and asked her if she wanted to get together and study for our Media Law final in the school library—instead of in my dorm room—where the nightmares happened.

"I can't believe we're going to be juniors next year! Where did all the time go?" Beth transferred here from

Australia last fall and had been feeling a bit nostalgic all spring.

I, on the other hand, didn't think the time was going by fast enough. Because aside from being super wigged out by the unspeakable nightly occurrences, there was something else weighing pretty heavily on me.

After a year of declining party invites for extra studying time on the weekends, volunteering as a tutor in both my Media Law *and* Biochemistry and Molecular Biology classes, breaking three major local news stories on the student run school newspaper, and scoring an almost perfect 4.0 GPA, I *still* hadn't heard back from the *Sunday Times* about the junior year media apprenticeship. It had me literally biting my nails.

"Are you kidding me? I didn't think this semester would *ever* be over!" I shut closed the somewhat ragged textbook I'd been highlighting in and moved it to the side. There, it joined a rising collection of carelessly discarded hardcovers.

"When did they say they would let you know?" Beth sounded genuinely sympathetic. She knew how much the apprenticeship meant to me—though I think part of her was worried what I might do if I wasn't chosen. I could be pretty erratic at times in the student newsroom. But it was mostly because I was pulling double duty as both editor *and* student reporter.

"They just said chosen applicants would be notified before the end of Spring Semester," which of course just about killed me when I read it. I practically exploded. "How could they be so vague?? We're aspiring reporters! I need cold hard facts—who, what, when, where, why's and how's. Not don't call me's—I'll call you's." I dramatically flung out my arms and threw my head to the table.

"Aw, cheer up mate. They'd be drongos not to pick ya." Beth made sure to over enunciate. We'd only known each other for a few months, but she already knew how much I got a kick out of the accent.

I raised my head and smiled. "Thanks Beth."

"No worries."

We sat there for about another hour or so and underlined in more textbooks. After that I began to feel a little restless, so I told Beth that I was going to stretch my legs a bit and that I'd be right back.

I thought I knew where all the vending machines were in all of the NYU buildings, but for some reason, it seemed that they had all been moved. Luckily, I was able to find my way to the main elevator and took it up one floor to four.

Several upperclassmen in purple and white letterman jackets were giving each other high fives in front of the elevator when the doors opened. I politely excused myself and squeezed past the rowdy group when I heard a faint thud on the floor behind me. I turned around, and just as the elevator doors closed, I looked to discover a tattered black and white book on the floor.

I picked it up—realizing one of the juniors who'd just gotten on the elevator must've dropped it. I read the title on the dusty cover: "Psychology 102: Dreams and Nightmares." I carefully turned the page and read the first few sentences. "Dreams are a normal part of childhood up to age 10."

I wish someone had told my parents that when I was younger. Because every night when I ran into my parents room when I was eight, it was because of these odd dreams that no one could explain. I would describe this beautiful place I would go to in my sleep—a lush jungle with rivers and waterfalls. But I don't think that's why my parents took me to see a shrink.

I suspect the real reason was because every night in my young dreamland—in the serene paradise in my head, I would be forced to fight for my life—to the death—every—single—night. I shivered.

I had completely forgotten what those particular dreams were about until just now. No wonder my parents made me get therapy.

Unfortunately, all the counseling went to waste. I continued to have the same dreams for almost a year after the sessions ended. But because I stopped waking up screaming and crying, my parents assumed that the nightmares had stopped. Hence, they stopped making me lie on the strange woman's couch.

But a new nightmare had begun exactly five months ago, and I had no idea why. I turned another page in the textbook as I walked over to a nearby study table. I continued to read.

"Dr. Jennie Parker believes that nightmares help the brain 'rehearse' distressing and disturbing events that one is likely to encounter in the future." I re-read the end of the sentence to make sure I had read it right; "events that one is likely to encounter in the *future*." Well that's interesting. I turned the page.

"Her work has identified at least three distinct types of nightmare, all of which may allow the brain to rehearse its reaction to a distressing or dangerous situation. One involves being chased or hunted. Another involves the loss of a parent, child or partner. The third involves weird and new environments."

Life was a weird and new environment as far as I was concerned.

I closed the book and laid it on the table that I'd stopped at, when another book caught my eye. This book had a thick material cover to it—all black, with gold cursive writing on it. It read: "Destiny Calls."

Intrigued, I opened up the aging book to one of its first yellowing pages. There, inside, was the most beautiful illustration of a rising phoenix.

I recognized it immediately because my mother used to wear a silver pendant with the symbol of the phoenix on it. But she stopped wearing it very suddenly one day when I was eight, and I never did ask her why.

Still, I'll never forget what she told me the phoenix represents. The mythical bird, which every 500 years engulfs itself in fire, rises from the flames anew—stronger and better than before, triumphing over all past tribulations.

Looking at the black ink drawing, I began to outline it with my fingers. And although the book was barely held together by its loosening bound—gently as I could, I turned the page and read the fading, printed ink on the inside page.

"Destiny is that which is inevitable. It is something that *must* and will occur, regardless of an individual's will or desire for it to happen."

I'd gotten so absorbed in the book that I became totally oblivious to my surroundings, which is probably why I almost jumped out of my skin with fright when I walked head on into another student.

"Oh!" The book fell to the ground as I reflexively held my hand to my head—to stop any future arising knot. It stung a little, but I was too busy apologizing for my carelessness to really feel any pain.

"I'm so, *so* sorry." My eyes were still trying to focus, but I imagined the other student was feeling it a little as well. Oh man. I must've slammed into the person harder than I thought because all I could see was a Tetris style cluster of colors in front of me.

Suddenly, I felt a pair of hands—*big* hands—holding both of my arms. "Are you okay?" The deep voice seemed genuinely concerned. I realized that the voice had come from above me. That meant that whoever I slammed into was tall.

I stepped back to see that the vivid swirl of colors I beheld was actually a blue and white plaid shirt. I looked up to see who was in it.

I suppose I should have been at least a little surprised to see who it was, but I wasn't—not even a little. In fact, I felt relieved, as if part of me had been waiting to see him again.

"Hey there." He said it as if he'd also been expecting to see me—as if we were old friends who often crossed paths right at this very spot.

The handsome co-ed spoke again. "Oh. Sorry. You probably don't remember me. We sort of met a few months ago when... Hey, are you feeling okay?"

I could feel what I knew he was seeing—the distant look on my face. My head was facing downward, and I'd put a hand up to hold on to the wall beside me. I was having the oddest feeling—one that I'd only had in the student newsroom once before. It was a feeling like I was simultaneously in and out of consciousness—like I was here, but trying to remember something from someplace else.

What brought me firmly back was when I felt his hand cupping the back of my neck—the inside of his palm acted like a pillow. His other hand held the opposite side of my face, and now there was nowhere to look but directly at him—not that I would have wanted to look anywhere else.

He was the most attractive man I'd ever seen. And even though his almond shaped eyes were the same ones I remembered from before, they still wouldn't let me go. They were so full of expression, and his smile—it was a kind smile that I hadn't appreciated before.

His tall build was lean and athletic, and I bet he was just as solid as the column we were standing next to. At first glance, I would've guessed captain of the football team, but there was something incredibly humble about him—something that told me he'd earned his muscles working in a steel mill, or volunteering lifting boxes at a local food bank or something. Whatever it was, I got the feeling the jock thing wasn't his style.

Strange, he seemed to be studying me the same way I was studying him. I watched his eyes tracing my hands—the palms of my hands—my face...my lips. And I don't know that he realized it, but his face had moved in just inches away from mine. Similarly, I don't know when *I* realized it, but I was no longer standing flat on my feet. I was on my toes—practically weightless.

This handsome man was holding the entirety of my weight in his arms—and I trusted him to do so, because for the first time in a long time, I felt completely safe.

We became like magnets as he lowered his face to mine; as he lowered his face to…

"Dude!" The elevator doors opened without either of us noticing. It was the group of upperclassmen jocks from earlier. "Dude, which way did we come from?"

"Uh, from the left I think." I heard footsteps going the opposite direction.

"No, no. Your *other* left." They started laughing.

I was now planted back firmly on my feet—to my disappointment, when all of the sudden, we heard another shout.

"There you are Kay! I was looking all over for you!"

Beth was storm trooping my way. She began yelling half a dozen yards before she even reached me.

"Hey! I took a break to check the news line, and we got one in from Professor Edmonds. Did you hear me Kay? It's a real-time lead mate! Zap Kay, come on!"

Beth had reached me now and was pulling me away. I tried to look back for him, but the group of jocks blocked my view.

All I could see was one of them picking up the Destiny book while the next thing I saw was the elevator doors close in front of me.

That evening, I fought the inevitable for as long as I could—even though I had never once won the battle. Still, when I finally fell asleep, I was too soon kissing the handsome man goodbye, and waking up at the part where the explosion happened—no lion—no jungle—no fight to the death.

The dream was cut short this time, or maybe I just didn't remember having the rest of it by the time I woke up.

Oh my gosh! That's it!

The guy in the newsroom—in the library—those eyes... That's where I'd seen him before—in my dreams!

But—no. That would be impossible. I didn't even meet him for the first time until the day *after* I started having the dreams again—for the first time since I was eight.

I suddenly remembered the books I found earlier in the library. Kay *try* to remember. What did they say? Something about the future...destiny...must...will occur.

I remembered how we weren't surprised to see each other. How I wasn't just unsurprised. I was *relieved*. Could it be possible to dream about someone you'd never met before? Someone you'd never seen before? No. No, Kay. Don't be ridiculous. I laughed at myself inside my head.

Calmly, I checked the time on my cellphone. It was 3:21 A.M. I yawned and rolled over—softly saying each numeral aloud. "Three... Two... One..."

"And??"

I snapped back to the present. For a moment, I thought Beth was irritated because I'd gotten lost in my thoughts while looking over my brand new passport. But then I remembered that Beth was the only person I'd ever met that could develop an entire dialogue in her head, and be surprised every single time that you weren't already in on the conversation.

I sighed as we started to make our way out the mail center. "And what Beth?" I put the passport back in the envelope that the work-study student had handed it to me in.

Beth continued in that brilliant Aussie accent of hers, "Are you ever going to tell me what really happened??"

"What are you talking about Beth?"

She whispered and nodded her head in someone's direction. "Not what. *Who.*"

My heart skipped a beat. Yes, I did know who she was talking about. And part of me *did* want to tell her everything that happened over the summer.

No. I *desperately* wanted to tell her, someone, anyone, why my pulse raced 100 miles an hour at the very thought of him. I wanted to tell her why every night before I have that stupid repetitive dream, I cry myself to sleep.

Most of all, I wanted to tell *him* why I jogged five blocks out of my way this morning just so I wouldn't have to run into him. Instead, I gave her the exact same answer as before.

"Nothing happened."

Beth huffed. "*Something* happened Kay. Every time he looks at you, he looks like he's lost his best friend. Actually..." Beth wasn't going to relent, "it's not just when he looks at you. He kind of just looks that way in general—ever since you two got back."

My heart sank. I didn't have to look around to know he was near. Beth wouldn't have brought him up if he weren't. The worst part was that I wanted to see him so badly it hurt. But I didn't dare look up.

"Beth," I could barely whisper her name. She knew she'd said too much. My eyes were welling up, and I wanted to get out of there before anyone saw me lose composure.

"I'm sorry Kay." She didn't try to press it any further. Instead, she did what all best friends do—when they don't have any idea what else to do. She put her arm around me, and rested her chin on my shoulder; right before she gave me a light squeeze that for a moment, made me feel like I wasn't going to cry.

2. Countdown

It was 9:59 A.M. by the time I gathered myself together from the close encounter in the mailroom. And now Beth and I were right on time for our 10:00 A.M. class.

But as we walked through the classroom doors, we were surprised to find that our Art History professor Dr. Stevens had been replaced by an extremely statuesque woman that we'd never seen before.

The young new professor was shockingly beautiful—regal even. And there was something about the way she carried herself that demanded respect.

I tried not to stare as I walked past her, but I couldn't help but to admire the professor's finely braided hair. It was in the same style that I used to wear, except that hers reached down almost to her waist. Gold beads and silver cowry shells accented each braid and shimmered on her perfectly flawless skin—which was the color of mahogany.

I stopped gawking long enough to see that Beth had already made her way to our usual area of the stadium-style classroom. I wasn't far behind her, but for some reason—every few steps—I looked behind me. And each time I did, I would catch the unusually beautiful professor *staring* at me.

I nervously quickened my pace and plopped down in my seat. Beth already had her notebook out and was clicking the little push button at the top of her pen. I soon found myself mimicking the same action.

Satisfied, however, that everyone had settled in, the new instructor turned to face the blackboard and began to draw. I wondered whether or not the rest of the class had realized that we'd already begun because most of the students were still talking amongst themselves in low voices.

I didn't join the chatter.

I couldn't take my eyes off the intricate piece of art she was creating. It was as if the drawing were speaking to me even in its unfinished form.

Only a few more minutes had passed before the professor finally put down the chalk and turned around.

Complete silence.

Dr. Steven's replacement had the undivided attention of every single student in the classroom, and as she looked over her fresh, eagerly awaiting subjects, the instructor settled her eyes on me—again, slowly stepping to the side to reveal the completed masterpiece.

It was an ivory dagger.

And although the abstract drawing was to me, clearly defined, to Dylan, Beth's sleazy ex-boyfriend, the sketch was somewhat of a mystery.

Dylan was sitting behind me now and had begun tapping his fingers on the desk. Finally, when he couldn't take the suspense anymore, Dylan raised his hand.

"So…what exactly is it?"

"It's a symbol." The professor spoke softly, but I was still able to make out her distinct African accent. I raised my hand.

"Yes Nanyamka?"

Wow. She knew my name. Even Dr. Stevens never bothered to learn my *real* first name. I stopped being impressed long enough to remember why I originally put my hand in the air.

I cleared my throat.

"Um, what is it a symbol of?"

The regalness slowly left the professor's face as she smiled and answered, "Death."

Beth had opened up her Art History book to the same page that we'd left off on last week. She was saying something to me about the assignment, but I couldn't hear her over whoever was banging on the increasingly loud drums.

I suppose that should've been the first clue.

But it wasn't until the classroom doors swung open, and I could feel the heat of the blazing fire that filled the hallway that I finally realized what was happening.

I expected everyone to run—to scream—but no one noticed.

Nor should they. Because I was the only one in danger.

The fire suddenly broke off into a straight line that rushed towards me, flames set on destruction.

Instinctively, I looked to the new professor to be told what to do, but when I looked into her eyes I saw nothing there that wanted to help me. She just stared. And there was something in her unrelenting glare that made me afraid.

I wanted to scream, and I could feel it gathering in my stomach and creeping up my throat—but I didn't let out a sound. Because at that very moment, I saw him as he walked through the fire to get to me.

"I will find you." His almond shaped eyes stared into my soul. He wanted me to go with him somewhere. But as soon as he extended his hand, the woman I'd been dreading appeared and stood between us.

I couldn't make out her face, but I recognized her voice. "It's time Nanyamka." She too extended her hand, and I knew I had no choice but to take it. Only, I couldn't. The new professor stopped me.

In the professor's hand was the ivory dagger she had drawn on the board.

And with it, she charged at me. Swipe! Swoosh! Swipe!

The dagger would have cut through me like butter, but I deflected each one of her swings with my forearm.

Thud! It was the sound her body made after she lunged at me—when I lifted her over one of the desks and watched as the professor I was supposed to be able to trust, fell to the ground from the force of her own momentum.

The impact caused the flames around us to explode even higher—which is why I didn't see my adversary when she regained her ground. It was why I didn't see her when she plunged the ivory dagger into my stomach. Only then did I finally scream myself awake.

My outburst was so loud that it startled the entire Art History class. Dr. Stevens turned around to determine the source of the interruption, but everything appeared normal—except that everyone in the room was now staring at me. He mustn't have noticed because he just shrugged and turned back around to write the final assignment on the shiny new dry-erase board.

"Are you *okay*?" Beth looked slightly wigged out.

"I'm fine." She didn't seem to believe me at first, but I tried to reassure her as I took off my glasses to wipe my watering eyes. I quickly put them back on, of course, and took in a deep breath. I exhaled.

It was getting worse. I was having the nightmare during the day now. But what was really weird, was that I wasn't even tired. It was as if I were *forced* asleep somehow. Still, that's not what upset me.

What really bothered me—what had me still trembling in my seat, was the fact that something had changed.

I'd been able to predict exactly what I'd see every night when I closed my eyes for almost a year now. And, as disturbing as the dreams were, their predictability offered me the teeniest form of comfort.

But today, in the middle of class, that had all changed. Why?

I could feel that my entire body was tense, so I raised both of my arms in an elongated stretch, simultaneously spreading out my right hand—which was cramped from the tense ball it had formed during the dream. At that moment, the passport I'd been tightly clutching dropped to the floor.

I picked it up and looked at it longer than any passport warranted looking at.

That night, I had the exact same dream I'd had in class—and I had it again every single night for the next three months.

When the snow finally began to fall in December, I could almost hear a buzzing sound as every single cell in my body began to vibrate with excitement.

In just two days, with my new passport in tow—I'd be on a plane from New York City to Cape Town, South Africa. I'd have two days to lie on one of the beautiful beaches and soak up the sun before heading over to Johannesburg, to start my co-op media apprenticeship.

I saved up quite a bit of money over the summer because I knew that having those two days before the start of my apprenticeship would give me some time to unwind from my freakishly weird dreams. Though it suddenly occurred to me that nightmares—and now *daymares*—didn't need permission to tag along on vacation, no matter how far you traveled.

Bummer.

Wink, wink. Beth didn't have to silently send hints for long. After just a year-long friendship, we could have entire conversations with just facial expressions—which drove the people around us crazy.

I knew exactly what she was thinking right now. "Pizza," I said.

"Pizza," she said.

The thing I loved about Beth was that she always had food on the brain. I think it's one of the reasons we bonded so quickly.

We briskly walked out of the freezing December air and into our favorite warm pizzeria. We were at Famiglia so often that the silver-haired gentleman with the Italian accent stopped asking us our order, and routinely began telling it to us.

"Three plain slices. One for the blonde. Two for the brunette. Am I right?"

"You always are." We said it in unison.

After we graciously paid for our pizzas, we settled down into our seats, but not before three average height girls walked in.

I knew each of them. Natalia, Becky and Victoria. As usual, they were discussing someone who'd done something—or nothing—to get them chattering. I was just about certain that put together, the three of those girls could supply the gossip needs of an entire superficial nation.

"Hey Kay! Hey Beth!" Natalia ran over as soon as she spotted us.

I smiled, but didn't offer the same amount of enthusiasm in return. I just never felt the same about the trio ever since the day I heard them making fun of Beth, just because of her unique style of wardrobe. "Dorkanista," I believe they called her. I remember that day because it irked me even more than the time they didn't know I was standing behind them in the hallway, and overheard the not so nice things they had to say about me.

"She's an overachieving wannabe upperclassman," I believe they said after I finished a Media Law presentation that scored me a solid A. To be honest, it didn't really bother me *that* much, especially if that was the worst they had to say about me.

Besides, I worked hard for my grades.

"Hi Natalia." My voice was flat and as unanimated as the expression on my face. "Victoria. Becky." I politely if unenthusiastically acknowledged the gang who were currently making themselves at home at the table Beth and I were sitting at.

Naturally, they had started up about someone before they were even settled into their seats. "Seriously, she *must* be getting dressed in the dark. I don't know *what* she was thinking." The trio laughed.

I sighed. The group's mean-spiritedness was one of the reasons I distanced myself from them last year. We actually used to hang out quite a bit when we were on the Social Activities committee together. But after a while, I tired of listening to them gossip, and moved on to greener pastures in the friends department—though we remained cordial.

I always tried to be amicable with everyone, even if I disagreed with them. Still, it made me sad to wonder what had to be missing from their own lives—that had them so constantly focused on everyone else's.

I gently patted the grease off my pizza with a napkin, and tuned back in when I finally heard a lull in the conversation.

I tried to think of a way to change the topic.

"Hey, we're gonna have some pretty cool bands at the Winter Send-off tonight. I hope you guys can make it."

I actually really meant it.

Somehow I got stuck being in charge of this year's junior social. I'd done a fluff piece on the venue's owner last year to fill up space in the student paper. It was during one of the slower news months. So when the Student Activities committee was having a hard time getting permission to use the Roseland Ballroom in midtown, they asked me to call in a favor—despite the fact that I was no longer on the committee. It was just yet another one of the many things I'd let myself get talked into sometimes.

Our pizzas were still piping hot—much to Beth and my delight—when the gossip trio left. So we didn't waste any more time before digging in. And, with every bite, I became more and more certain that pizza was the total answer to all the world's problems.

I chewed and thought about mine.

"Aye mate, sorry again 'bout yesterday." It was nearly the end of sophomore year—the day after my unintentional rendezvous in the library with the man in my dreams—well, the man *maybe* in my dreams. I still wasn't sure yet, especially since I hadn't been remembering all of them too clearly. Waking up at 3:21 A.M. didn't do anything for my clarity either, which is partly why I wasn't fully lucid when Beth called me in my dorm room at 7:50 A.M.

"Hunh," I said over the phone without having opened my eyes yet.

"Yesterday," Beth reminded me, "when I grabbed ya to go after that news lead Professor Edmonds emailed us about. I was dead cert we'd get to the news conference in time to get a few questions in."

"Oh, yeah." I rubbed my eyes and finally sat up.

"Aye! I meant to ask ya. Did you know that gorgeous bloke who was standing near ya in the library? There was a bunch of blokes actually—but this one was one *tall* drink of water. I couldn't tell if he was with the lot of them—with their letterman jackets and all. Do you think he's on our football team?"

"Um, I don't know. I don't think so." I wanted to get off the phone in a hurry now. It was too early in the morning to start thinking about him again—him or that old book with the yellowing pages.

"Hmm," Beth seemed to contemplate something for a moment. "Well, maybe I'll pop in on a game one day just to make sure." She laughed.

"Hey Beth, I'm gonna try to get a few more minutes of sleep and then get up. Can I call you later?"

"No worries mate. Get some shut eye. I'll see you around the newsroom." She hung up.

I closed my eyes and tried to get back to sleep, but the sun was beaming through my window. I sighed and sat up again.

There were still a few more books I wanted to check out in the library to help me with a few of my final papers. So I thought about skipping breakfast and going straight there, but part of me wanted to see the handsome *bloke* again. And it was early evening when I saw him yesterday outside of the stacks. I considered waiting until this evening to make a trip there. But who was I kidding?

I was near ridiculous last night when I thought I'd been dreaming about this guy before we'd even ever met. So I probably shouldn't push the crazy any further by giving the whole thing another thought.

It was that Destiny book that put that silly idea in your head, not you Kay. I tried to reassure myself.

I threw back the pink flowery covers I was tucked into and looked at my bed set as I got up. My parents had bought the set for me freshman year. But I was starting to think it might be time for something a little more mature. Maybe I'll get that navy blue bed set I saw in the window on 125th Street. Yeah, I'll definitely get those for junior year.

I took a shower and decided to have some breakfast after all. I also did some quick research online to find out how one would go about getting an actual passport. I was determined to be picked for the media apprenticeship in South Africa—the one Professor Edmonds recommended I apply for. And I wanted to have all my ducks in a row for the day they called me. They just *had* to call me.

Because the only thing I wanted to be more than a ballerina when I was younger, was Oprah Winfrey or Barbara Walters. I wanted to travel the world like Ann Curry and meet new people—learn all about their stories and share those stories with the world.

So I clicked the star on my taskbar and added the passport website to my favorites list. I then grabbed my student ID and made my way over to the Bobst.

When I arrived at the library's revolving glass doors, I saw a notice on the side wall that said the third floor of the library was closing early due to emergency construction. Of course, that was the very floor I needed, so it was a good thing I didn't wait until later to stop by like I originally planned to.

I followed the revolving doors in their automated circle and went straight to the third floor. As soon as I got off the elevator I tossed my bag onto one of the study tables and went to work.

But soon I was having trouble believing exactly how much time had passed with my nose buried so deep in textbooks. It was already 4 P.M. and security was making the rounds to announce that the third floor was now closed. I hurriedly took down my last few notes from the book I'd pulled from the archives and rare books section—one of those gigantic books the library wouldn't allow you to leave the building with.

I was actually a huge fan of that rule because the truth was, I could spend all day in a library. The smell of the old books, the centuries worth of history—it all went straight to my head, and never failed to make me a little light-headed—in a good way—the same way the scent of a really subtle cologne did on an extremely cute guy.

And although I never knew why, in high school, while most girls were fantasizing about those exact said crushes, my fantasies mostly involved pulling all-nighters to study for exams while getting lost in the book stacks. Only to come across some 1,000-year-old book that no one ever knew was there, and end up having to spend the entire night in the library with this amazing artifact because the facilities crew didn't know I was still in the building when it closed.

Admittedly, I had some odd fantasies—and even weirder dreams—but there was a whole entire world I wanted to see. And I had a feeling that somewhere in this voluminous stack of books was the key to that future.

Though the third floor was now closed, the rest of the library was still open. So I found myself wandering my literary wonderland on and off of the elevator and via the stairs. I turned the corner to go deeper into the stacks on one of the upper floors. And I hadn't realized it, but my eyes were closed as I breathed in the pages of the old books that surrounded me. The aroma of ancient history was merrily floating through the air when, "Ow!"

You'd think I was speed racing the way I kept crashing into people. First yesterday, and now today.

"Are you okay?"

I recognized the voice immediately—though I tried not to visibly express the immense joy I was feeling being near him again. I still answered.

"I'm okay."

"Good." He sounded relieved—pausing before extending his hand.

"I'm Callum by the way."

"Kay," I returned.

"Okay Kay." He smiled at the alliteration. "You know, one of these days you're gonna get a ticket."

"For what," I asked, confused.

"For speed racing."

"Hey, I was *just* thinking that!"

"Yeah?" The gorgeous giant flashed a knee-buckling grin. "So, where were you heading?"

I thought about it for a moment. "Nowhere really. I was just…walking."

"With your eyes closed?"

"Yeah, sorry. I guess I was sort of in my own world."

"And what world is that?"

I couldn't believe I was about to admit it. "The world where I daydream about being inside of a library."

"You daydream about being inside of a library—*inside* of a library?"

I laughed. "Good point. I guess I'm not very creative."

"I don't believe that."

"Thanks."

I was unaware that anyone else was on the floor with

us, so I was slightly startled when I heard a group of freshmen laughing and walking towards us. I probably should've moved since I was directly blocking the path to the only elevator, but I suddenly couldn't force myself to even take a step.

That's when I felt his hand on my back, guiding me away from the elevator—and closer towards him. I held my breath as his touch set everything in me to slow motion. When I finally managed to blink, gradually regaining my bearings, I saw that I was no longer in front of him but by his side.

The handsome Callum extended his arms past my waist and then wrapped them around me. And when he did, my heart practically skipped five spaces and passed go. Though it didn't take long for me to realize that he was just acting as a buffer between me and our freshmen guests.

When the jocks got on the elevator, and the elevator doors closed, Callum let me go—much to my disappointment.

But he didn't look disappointed at all. Actually, he seemed nervous, which is why I was surprised when he moved from around my side and stood directly in front of me.

"Kay, I know we just met but..." He stopped. "Actually, we met five months ago—not, not that I've been counting. I mean, what I'm trying to say is..." Callum cut himself short again, and shook his head as if he had messed up something that he'd been practicing. Finally, Callum took in a deep breath, and although I wasn't sure he was ever going to let it out, at last he did— and with it, what he'd been trying to say. "Kay, would you ever consider going out on a date with me?"

I was floored. First of all, that had to be a rhetorical question. I mean, Beth was practically drooling over him on the phone. And the only reason *I* wasn't acting completely gaga was because I was too busy standing there looking dumbstruck. Oh no, I could feel it on my face—I looked dumbstruck.

Callum took my hand then, and my thoughts quieted down. "Kay, I haven't been able to get you out of my head. Not just since yesterday, but ever since that day in the newsroom. I'm sure you don't remember, but I've thought about it every day since."

My face went numb again.

Callum went on. "I told myself yesterday that if I ever saw you again, I wouldn't let you leave without finding the courage to ask you out. And well, I'm not sure that I've found it yet, but I'm asking you anyway. Please go out with me Kay."

This gorgeous, incredible man was baring his soul to me, and all I could say was, "Why?"

He thought about it for a moment, then turned my hand over in his, and looked at it as if it would help him to remember something.

"Kay, I really don't know how to explain this—not in a way that would make any sense anyway, but I just know I wouldn't have any rest unless I asked you out. I wouldn't *want* any rest. Because I want to know you. I want to have a reason to not feel so crazy when I'm thinking about you all the time."

So I wasn't the only one.

The mention of him not getting any rest made me think about my crazy dreams—the ones that hadn't allowed me *one* peaceful night's sleep—the ones that started exactly five months...

"Kay, I know how I sound right now, but please—please go out with me. What about tomorrow? Say four?"

I looked into his eyes. He was no longer smiling. His beautiful almond shaped eyes were pleading with me now. And somehow—even though I didn't know why—I knew that my answer would change our lives forever.

I bit my lip—anxious. "Could we make it a little earlier?"

Callum didn't hesitate to oblige. "Sure, yeah, any time. Um...what time would you prefer?"

I happened to notice a rectangular, digital clock on the wall above him. It had stopped at 3:21, which was the same time that Beth had woken me up this morning. Odd. "3:21," I said to myself—not realizing I'd spoken loud enough for Callum to hear.

He looked at me curiously—but before I could explain, Callum was softly repeating each individual numeral aloud.

"You and I. At three...two...one."

3. The Truth

As Beth and I left the pizza parlor, I smiled at the memory of Callum before intentionally putting it away. And I was thankful when the rest of the day flew by, despite Beth and I having to take two major finals in the afternoon. Which is why the second that we made our way back to the dorm room, Beth hung up her coat, and I turned on the radio to our favorite station. It was already time to get ready for the Winter Send-off, and I was kind of surprised by how much I was looking forward to it.

My last big shindig before leaving New York—I thought to myself, which *should* be cause for celebration. Yet, no matter how hard I tried, I couldn't shake the tiny few stubborn butterflies that were still floating around in my stomach.

What would I do if I saw him tonight? I'd been in a stealth-like avoidance of Callum for the past six months, and if I could stay away from him for just two more days I'd be in the clear.

But I couldn't stay away. That was part of the problem—and the reason—that I was more convinced than ever before that I'd made the right decision.

Part of me had been having second thoughts about going tonight just so I wouldn't be tempted. But there was another part of me—a part I couldn't control—that *had* to see him one last time before I left.

I was dressed much faster than expected, and was now styling some soft waves in my hair with the curling iron. After I finished, I smoothed out my party outfit, and stepped back from the mirror to get a better look at what I was wearing.

Skinny jeans—I think that's what they're called. Mine were a purposefully faded black. I also had on a silver, glittery party top that I'd only worn once before back in high school.

Though I loved dressing up, I just didn't have occasion to do it often. Being a journalism major meant being ready to hit the ground running—sometimes quite literally—whenever our Breaking News professor would send word of a potential news story. Thankfully, Beth and I passed that class last year with flying colors.

Still, I put on my finest pair of stilettoes tonight just to make Carrie Bradshaw proud; and hoped that they would help me to bid a temporary adieu to the lovely city I'd grown up in.

Not much time had passed when I noticed that aside from the radio on in the background, it was pretty quiet in here. *Too* quiet. Beth hadn't said anything the whole time we were getting ready.

"Beth," I asked, "Is everything okay?"

She was sitting on the edge of the tub with her hands folded together—very uncharacteristic of my favorite upbeat Aussie.

"Kay," Beth spoke softly. "Tell me the truth okay; do

you think I'm pretty?"

The question threw me for a loop. Since when did Beth have self-esteem issues? I made sure the curling iron was off before moving it to the side of the sink.

"What do you mean? Of course you're pretty."

In the short year that we'd know each other, we'd become practically like sisters. So when I detected an unfamiliar sadness in her voice, I moved pass confused and made my way over to concerned.

Beth tried to explain. "You're so pretty Kay—and lucky. The way Callum looks at you as if you're the only person in the whole entire world to him. What I wouldn't give to have what you and he have."

Had—I corrected her in my head.

"Guys never look twice at me. The only bloke who ever noticed me only noticed me until he noticed someone else."

My heart sank. I'd been so caught up in trying to score that apprenticeship—not to mention so caught up in all things Callum—that I never really stopped to think about whether or not Beth was happy here, so far away from home.

Even after her break-up with that slime ball Dylan, Beth just still always seemed so cheerful that I never really questioned it.

Beth went on. "Kay, I try *so* hard—but I can't help it. I know there are more important things in life, and I know I'm not supposed to let some bloke define me. But sometimes I feel like..." Beth bit her lip. I knew she didn't want to say it, but I also knew that she needed to let it out. "Kay, some days I wake up and wonder whether or not I actually *exist*. I mean, most days I don't think anyone ever notices that I *do* exist. No matter what I do it's like I'm invisible; as if I'm some sort of accident that wasn't supposed to be here; like every single bloke wishes that I wasn't."

"Beth." I said it with tears in my eyes. I had no idea Beth felt that way—*thought* that way. I gathered my thoughts and then sat down on the tub beside her.

"Beth, you listen to me okay? You—are—beautiful. And don't *ever* let anyone make you feel like you're not. Not because you think someone doesn't notice you, and not because you think you're not worth noticing. You are perfect. You are the best friend a girl could ask for. You're fun, you're smart, and you have a sense of humor I would kill for.

So if some *bloke* can't see that, then please, please Beth—just have patience that someone else will; someone who deserves you and everything that you have to offer because you're amazing Beth. Don't ever settle for thinking that you're not. And don't ever settle for accepting anyone who doesn't see that you *are*."

Beth started to cry—a happy cry. And it wasn't long before tears began welling over in my eyes as well. Because Beth was right earlier. I did have someone who saw all those things in me—someone whom I never, ever wanted to be away from. Someone who I knew I had no choice but to *run* away from.

Still, deep down I knew, it didn't matter what continent I was on. It didn't matter what plane I took. Some part of Callum would travel with me. So I made a mental note, and added it to the list of things a person can't escape when travelling.

One: dreams, and two: your heart.

It was only 7:30 P.M. when our cry fest ended, and we still had a full hour before the party started. After Beth and I had dried our eyes, I walked back into the common area and turned up the radio. What do you know? Our favorite song was on.

"GREAT PARTY!" Beth had to yell over the bass in the club mix that the DJ was spinning. The bands that were booked were going on soon, and the DJ wanted to make sure that everyone in the ballroom stayed amped until show time.

"I still can't believe you got this place!" Beth maintained her level of excitement but didn't have to yell quite as loud this time since we'd made our way towards the entrance. The owner agreed to let us set up a donation table for the Salvation Army. I volunteered to man the tables for the 10:00 P.M. to midnight shift. Beth was kind enough to help out as well.

Everything was going great. Natalia, Becky and Victoria arrived around the same time as Derek, Cassie, Thomas and Louis—four of my classmates from my Economics class. All-in-all, just about the entire junior class came out.

Now we hadn't done a final count yet, but it looked like we would definitely reach our goal of raising enough money to help out at least one hundred families for the holidays. Beth and I exchanged high-fives to celebrate.

I checked my watch. It was almost midnight, and I'd made it through the entire shift without seeing—well, the one person I really wanted to see—but knew I shouldn't.

I was organizing the cash in the lock box for the volunteers who were on the next shift, when suddenly my heart started to race. I hadn't even looked all the way up when I noticed him. I could tell it was him just by the way he was standing, even though his back was to me.

I shut the lock box closed, put it under the table, and made my way as quickly as I could to the stairs that led to the mezzanine. I prayed that he wouldn't follow me. There was no way I could look into those beautiful brown eyes and still make myself get on that plane tomorrow.

But just as my foot landed on the last step to the mezzanine, I heard a baritone-like voice calling my name. I tried to get some distance between us, but he grabbed me and turned me around. It was the photographer I hired for the event tonight. "Oh, it's you Lenny." I was both relieved—and not.

"Hey baby. Where you running off to? I haven't gotten any photos of you all night."

"Really," I replied, "I don't feel like taking any pictures tonight."

"But you're the star of the show." Flash. "You put this whole thing together." Flash. "You're gonna want memories…" Flash.

I asked him again to stop, but Lenny kept pressing the shutter button as I tried to cover my face with my hands. The next time the flash went off I heard it—but didn't see it. Callum had his hand wrapped around the camera, and was standing—towering over the photographer.

"She asked you to stop." I closed my eyes and breathed out a sigh of relief. It was a sigh of relief for so many reasons—even though I knew it shouldn't be.

Lenny didn't seem deterred. "Let me guess, high school sweethearts?" Flash. "No? Let me guess, the boy next door?" Flash. "No? Come on, work with me."

Lenny continued to snap photos of us, and it took

both of us a minute to decide whether or not to try to stop him. Because I think we were both thinking the same thing; that these photos might be the only way we could be together. That if we continued to let his flash go off we could actually live happily ever after, somewhere out there in the universe—if only in a picture.

"Okay, I've got it!" Lenny began exaggerating his gestures in a way that reminded me of an old drama school teacher. "Destiny is calling," Lenny shouted, "but you're not allowed to answer the call. She's the woman you can't get off your mind, and he's the man you can't stop dreaming about. You'll never love another, but you'll never be together—tortured to your last days—by the regret of what could have been..." Flash. Flash. Flash.

I froze.

"Hey, get in there!" Lenny put his hand on my back to push me closer into his envisioned frame—but Callum grabbed his hand.

"I think that's enough." Callum was far from quick tempered, but something that Lenny said made him unusually ruffled tonight. I could tell because even after Lenny put the camera down, Callum still wouldn't let him go.

"Callum," I whispered. I reached my hand to his shoulder. I could feel his muscles moving throughout his body with the deep breaths he was taking to calm himself down. People were staring—more because of the incessant flashing than because of Callum, but I still didn't want it to become any more of a scene than it already was.

"I'm sorry." Callum apologized to the overzealous photographer. Lenny smiled nervously before walking away, rubbing his wrist.

Callum turned around, facing me—his expression as full of guilt as it was concern. "Are you okay?"

"I'm fine." I said it even though I wasn't. I kept my gaze looking downward so I wouldn't have to meet his emotion-filled eyes. "They were just photos Callum," I lied trying to convince him as absolutely as I was trying to convince myself.

Callum wasn't buying it. Still, he spoke in his most nonchalant tone. "I know," Callum replied. "I just know how much you hate that."

He was right actually. For someone who grew up in such a large city, I had serious personal space issues. I loved New York—the energy—the opportunities, but there's always been a part of me that never quite felt that I belonged here; like my body was in New York, but my spirit or something was somewhere else—somewhere quiet and peaceful, yet wild and free.

I sighed, finally allowing myself to make eye contact. "Well, I guess you're my knight in shining armor tonight." No matter how resolute I was, no matter how hard I tried to stay away from him, once I looked into his gorgeous almond brown eyes, I was always a goner.

"May I?" Callum gestured to the dance floor. I followed him where he led, and stopped when he raised our hands, interlocking our fingers.

From that point on, we didn't take our eyes away from one another—not once—as we swayed to the melody of the love song that the band was playing in the background.

I smiled as his touch gave me a feeling similar to the one we shared that day in the park.

"I'll race you to the bridge!" I remember not even waiting for him to answer. Besides, I'd already given myself a pretty good head start—which I didn't consider cheating because his legs were twice as long as mine. He beat me anyway.

"I win!" Callum winked at me as he passed the imaginary finish line.

It was the day after our second crash collision in the library—and I still couldn't believe that Callum actually agreed to meet me here at 3:21 P.M. After all, I only said it out loud by accident. But Callum wasn't a minute early or a minute late. And I was kind of shocked that neither was I.

I tried on a dozen different outfits while I was getting ready that morning. But in the end, I just put on a grey cotton t-shirt, and as usual, another pair of jeans. I was glad I didn't go with the flowery shorts I first pulled out because it was still pretty cool for April, and Central Park was getting quite a strong breeze off the reservoir. I was especially glad because I didn't want to remember my first date with Callum having ended with me catching a cold.

I did want to put *some* effort into my appearance however, so I had made a thin French braid along the front side of my hair, leaving the rest of my hair out curly. I even used one of those fancy bobby pins with the rhinestones on the end.

"Have I told you how beautiful you look today?" The way Callum said it, it was as if we were two young-hearted elders who had already spent a lifetime together, and he wanted to make sure he didn't miss a day in telling me how beautiful he thought I was. It was reassuring somehow, to get a glimpse of what our future could be like.

As we walked off the reservoir path and under the stone jogger's bridge, Callum put his arm around me. It took me a moment to wipe the silly grin off my face before I finally responded. "I'm in a t-shirt and jeans Callum. And I'm pretty sure the wind has done atrocious things to my hair by now."

Callum quickly ran his fingers through my hair—tucking away a stray strand behind my ear. "Nope—still perfect."

We were only forty-nine minutes and 27 seconds into our first date—not that I was counting—and I was already more comfortable with him than I'd been with anyone my entire life.

"Okay, I've got one." Callum jumped in front of me and began walking backwards. "Favorite guilty pleasure?"

"Easy," I said. "Television wrestling. You?"

"*Lifetime* movie specials."

I raised an eyebrow. "This seems oddly backwards."

We laughed together as we continued to play the favorites game we'd been playing since we first entered the park.

Callum pulled me closer to him as a couple of joggers decided to sprint by.

After a while, we walked out from under the second stone bridge with the beautiful arch. And as we did, Callum lifted my hand and spun me around like a ballerina. Being with him just about as easy as breathing.

"So let me get this straight," I said. "You've lived in Wisconsin, Virginia, Florida, Georgia, Alabama, Washington and…"

Callum finished the sentence before I could. "And now New York."

"Wow. Talk about commitment issues."

Callum chuckled. "No, it's nothing like that. I only moved around so much because I was sort of an army brat. My uncle was a specialist in the Marines."

"Your uncle?"

"Yeah…" I noticed that Callum's grip around my waist tightened as if he were bracing himself for a difficult memory. "My uncle took me in when I was little—after my parents died."

I stopped short. "Callum. I'm so sorry."

"It's alright. It was a long time ago."

"Would you mind if I asked—what happened?"

Callum seemed to become lost in thought, and for the first time today he looked away from me. My heartbeat dragged along with every silent moment before he spoke.

"My mom was sick for a long time—a really, really long time. She passed away when I was eight. My dad died shortly after. The doctors said his heart just gave out."

Callum turned away even further as he fought back the tears. He wiped one away before facing me again. "Kay, can I ask you something?"

"Of course." I put on my best brave face for him.

"Do you think someone can actually die from a broken heart?"

"I…I don't know." The question caught me off guard. I'd read studies that talked about it—about the stress of losing a loved one, a soul mate so to speak. I just wasn't sure if now was the time to talk about it. I tried to think about the one thing that mattered most. "It sounds like your father loved your mother very much."

Callum took in another deep breath, looking back towards the reservoir.

"He did. He really did."

It started to drizzle. I was just about to rub my hands on my arms to keep warm when Callum took off his faded tan jacket and put it around my shoulders.

"Thanks."

Callum had the faintest smile on his face. But I didn't think his smile had anything to do with me. I think he must've thought of a memory he'd put away long ago. One that brought him joy to remember now—one about his parents perhaps. But just as soon as the joy had come to his face, it had left. He seemed to have another sad thought.

"Um, do you have...family Kay?"

The way Callum said it, it sounded as if he were almost afraid of the answer. I swiftly tried to put his mind at ease. "Yes Callum. I do. My mom and my dad. They actually don't live far from campus."

"Oh good." Callum exhaled.

"So, do you look more like your mom or your dad?" Callum waited for me to answer as he guided us on a right turn along the path—still holding my hand.

"People say my mom and I look alike. Sometimes I see it. Sometimes I don't. I think we're more alike in personality than in looks."

Callum laughed, and I was glad he was in good spirits again.

"So..." I hesitated. I didn't want to seem like I wasn't enjoying the day so far—because I absolutely was, but I was still curious. "Are we going anywhere in particular?"

When Callum asked me to meet him on the northern end of Central Park today, I didn't have any clue as to where we were heading. I thought he might've at least given me a hint when he called me that morning to make sure we were still on.

But instead, Callum asked me about all the places I'd been to in the city. He said he wanted to make sure he took me somewhere that I'd never been to before. I told him that would be pretty tough because I've lived here all my life. Still, I thought it was cute that he apparently thought I'd never been to the park before.

Callum smirked before responding. "Oh, you know— we're just walking. Like, with our eyes closed." Callum closed his eyes and pretended to crash into me—a clear imitation—and unfair reenactment I might add, of our first couple of meetings. I laughed.

"Very funny Callum." I asked him if he would mind if we stopped at one of the refreshment stands to get a couple of hot dogs, but he said there was food where we were heading.

That stumped me. I knew there was that little café not too far from the carousel, but that was about 30 blocks in the opposite direction. I thought about Tavern on the Green, but that had closed a long time ago. Plus, that would've been a bit extravagant for a first date.

The only other park restaurant I knew about was the Boathouse, but I told him I'd already gone there for a friend's wedding last year. And as he wanted to take me somewhere I hadn't been before, that couldn't be on the list.

I finally stopped trying to guess at it when Callum let go of my hand for a moment to fix the jacket that was now sliding off of my shoulders. When he had finished, and his fingers touched against mine again, I stopped worrying about our final destination. We could've been going to Mars for all I cared.

As we continued to walk, we greeted a few joggers who passed by us—some singles, some couples. It was such a beautiful day. But we hadn't walked much further when I noticed less and less people walking along the pathway.

Stubbornly, and disappointedly, my journalistic curiosity managed to get the better of me again. "Callum, are you sure we're going in the right direction?"

"I'm sure."

We walked another few yards. "Callum, I don't think there's anything this way. Where exactly are you trying to go?"

Callum kept his eyes forward. "Can't you hear it?"

"Hear *what* Callum?" I probably should've told him earlier, but I never did enjoy surprises. However, I could hear over the phone how badly he wanted to do something for me, so I decided to be a good sport about it. Plus, I wasn't passing up a chance to see him again.

We soon approached a group of trees so close together that I couldn't see past or even through them. Callum stepped out ahead to pull back one of their long, abundantly-leaved branches, and extended his hand in the cluster's direction.

"Do you hear it now?"

I looked at him, still confused. All I could hear were the faint sounds of cars honking on their way to the highway. After all, this *was* New York City. Even in the park there was never total peace to be found.

As I walked past the tree Callum was standing beside, my mouth dropped, and I realized immediately why I had been wrong about not finding peace in the city.

Callum casually strolled to my side, completely smug, and rightfully so. With his arm around my waist, Callum watched me as *I* watched the waterfall I couldn't believe we were looking at.

I was breathless. "Callum."

Callum gave me a light squeeze. "So you said you've been to the carousel. You've been fishing in the Harlem Meer. And although much to my disappointment—because I kind of wanted to check it out—you've even already partied at the Boathouse. But..." Callum hopped in front of me, proud to have surprised me. "You said the one thing you would love to do one day, is to have a picnic by a waterfall—and something about 'too bad there weren't any waterfalls in the concrete jungle.'"

"Callum! You found me a waterfall!" I still couldn't believe it.

"Well, it's *technically* a mini-fall. There's a more impressive one further out, but I was sort of pressed for time."

"Callum, I truly couldn't be any more impressed than I am right now. I had no *idea* this was here."

I'd lived in New York City my whole entire life, and it took a guy who'd moved here just five months ago to show me the best part of my city—our city now. I smiled.

Callum bent down and whispered in my ear. "Close your eyes."

I closed them. I wasn't questioning him anymore. I heard some rustling parallel to where I was standing, accompanied with the sound that Tupperware makes when you pull the plastic tops off; and before long, I heard him shout from a somewhat further distance away.

"Open them!"

I opened my eyes. Callum was standing about ten feet up on one of the large rocks that enclosed the mini waterfall. I had to blink to be sure—though I suppose I could've just taken out my glasses and put them on. But I was right in what I saw. Callum stood amongst a carefully laid out smorgasbord.

There was a beige wool blanket laid out on the rock above. On it was a large wicker basket with a red and white cloth sticking out of it—the kind I'd always seen in the movies. Next to the basket was a tall, green glass bottle of some form of refreshment. *And* to the sides of that, were what looked to be plates of tapas, antipasti, samosas and even shish kebobs. Well, he wasn't kidding when he said there would be food here. There was—*lots* of it.

To top it all off—as if Callum wasn't sure whether or not he'd already done enough, Callum stood there amongst it all while holding a single, red, thorn less, long-stem rose.

"So how'd I do?"

I didn't answer. I was in shock.

Callum had wanted nothing more than to give me an experience that I'd never had before. That's what all the questions were about before our date today. I couldn't believe how incredibly attentive he was, and how this surprising romantic gesture—of a somewhat shy co-ed, who just yesterday couldn't explain to me how he felt— "not in a way that would make any sense anyway"— today, showed me how much he'd been thinking about me all day long.

I walked up the jagged rocks that were stacked on top of each other. Callum handed me the rose, and I kissed him on the cheek. "This is incredible Callum. I don't know how you did all this, but thank you."

Callum's face brimmed with a smile. He was pleased— not with himself, but with my happiness; for which was the only reason he had done all of this in the first place.

This entire day was like a dream—a metaphorical one I mean, not the actual ones that had been driving me to the point of insanity.

I wondered what he would say if I told him what I'd been experiencing these past few months. That I'd been engaging in battles to the death in explosive fires, while being stalked by a familiar looking woman and a snarling lion; or that a man with almond shaped eyes that looked *a lot* like Callum pulled me out of the fire every night.

I wondered what Callum's reaction would be. That is, I wondered until I remembered that my own parents sent me to therapy for them when I was eight—concerned they said for my mental well-being.

Callum might think I was just as crazy. Then again, maybe he wouldn't. Maybe there was a reason that despite our incredibly brief meeting five months ago, Callum hadn't been able to get me out of his head, just as genuinely as I hadn't been able to get him out of mine.

I suppose there was only one way to find out.

"Callum," I began. Callum put down the plate he was holding and gave me his undivided attention. He always gave me his undivided attention. "There's something I've been wondering if I should tell you." I wanted to tell him everything. But just as I was about to speak, the prettiest little bird I ever saw flew down and landed on the basket between us.

"Callum look!" As a city girl, I always got a little overexcited whenever I saw something that wasn't made of concrete—or that didn't leave huge heaps of poop on said concrete.

I took out my cellphone and tried to snap a photo of the tiny yellow creature, but the low battery signal came up, and the beep nearly scared the little bird away. "Aw man, my battery's dead." I shook my cellphone in multiple directions, somehow hoping I could jar it back to power.

"I'll get it." Callum reached his hand into his pocket but turned up empty. "Shoot. I must've dropped my phone somewhere back on the path. Would you be alright here if I ran back and took a quick look for it?"

"I can go with you," I quickly replied.

Callum stood up and patted himself down again to be sure it wasn't on him, turning his pockets inside out just in case. "No, no. You stay here. If it's not somewhere nearby, then I'll just look out for it on our way back." Callum shrugged. "It might be gone already anyway."

I frowned. I didn't want him to leave, but I did want him to find his phone if it was still out there.

Callum went back through the trees as I cooed the little bird that had visited in the hopes that it would hang around until Callum got back.

And though my feathery friend did stick around, I was still surprised by how uneasy I felt with Callum gone. A breeze entered the picnic area, causing the small bird to fly over to a nearby tree.

Instinctively, I got up and followed it. I figured I

should keep myself entertained until Callum returned. But before I knew it, I could feel him gently touching my back. And I was almost embarrassed by how happy I became that he'd returned so quickly. "That was fast!" I turned around to give him a gigantic hug—but it wasn't him.

It was a woman. "Oh." I was slightly taken aback. "Sorry, I was expecting someone else." The woman didn't respond. Instead, she stood there—silent. I wondered if she were alright. She wasn't exactly dressed in normal New York attire.

The white cloak that she wore was covered in what appeared to be black butterfly symbols—African prints it looked like. The matching material that she wore across her top and across her lower half—though beautiful— exposed her arms and legs from underneath the hooded garment. I thought this was odd, as it wasn't quite warm enough for what she had on.

But what was also unusual were the gold, ruby and emerald jewels she wore around her neck. I tried to figure out who would dress like this and then go for a walk in Central Park.

"Are you lost?" I hoped I sounded as polite as I meant to be, but I was starting to get that uneasy feeling again— the one I had gotten the second Callum left. Still, silence.

The strange woman had long, wild hair that covered her face, so I couldn't quite make out any facial features. The only thing I noticed about her was that her skin was the same complexion as mine, and we were very similar in build. The strange woman took several steps towards me.

I took several steps back.

"Nanyamka!"

A startled gasp escaped me. "I'm sorry...do I know you?"

"Nanyamka!" She repeated—louder.

"It is time!"

At that moment, a violent gust of wind blew around us, blowing back the long, dark brown hair away from the eerie woman's face. And when it did, I almost fainted.

The face that the woman had...it was *mine*.

I don't think I'd ever been so panic-stricken in all my life. You're dreaming I told myself. This isn't really happening.

"You're not real!"

I screamed it at the image walking towards me.

"You're not real. You're not real." I said it over and over, but she still wouldn't go away.

I suddenly realized that this was the woman who always came between Callum and me in my dreams. She wanted to take me away somewhere—somewhere away from my family, away from my friends. But she wasn't the only one that I feared. There was another.

I looked behind me, and there, exactly where I expected her to be, was the lady with the ivory dagger. She stood beside a deathly fearsome lion—the one with the low warning growl.

"Go away! *Please!*" I continued inching backwards, trying to manage an escape, but I was running out of ledge over the waterfall. Finally, there was nowhere else I could turn.

When the mahogany skinned woman with the gold decorated braids realized she had me cornered, she lifted up the dagger—and lunged.

I screamed as I began to lose my balance. Oh no. I'd taken one step back too many. I felt the edge of the rock that was under the very tips of my toes.

No—no I didn't feel it anymore.

The very last part of my foot slipped off the rock, and I could feel my body rapidly descending to the bottom of the waterfall.

It felt as if my heart relocated to my throat on the way down. And I tried not to think about the crack I would feel on my skull as I would surely hit one of the rocks below.

Tears ran down my face as I continued to fall.

Splash!

I was still screaming and flailing my legs as Callum held me and tried to calm me down. He had jumped into the ravine and caught me just seconds before my head would have hit the monstrous rocks below.

"Kay! Kay! It's alright. You're okay."

I cried even harder when I realized it was truly him.

"Shh...Shh..." Callum held me close to his chest, putting his chin to the side of my cheek. "I've got you Kay. You're okay. You're safe." He spoke softly, stroking my hair.

When I finally quieted down, Callum stood me on my feet, but wouldn't let me go.

"Kay, what happened? I heard you screaming and I ran back as fast as I could."

I frantically pointed towards the direction I'd fallen from. "Didn't you see?? There! She... I was there!" I continued to point, but there was nothing. I was pointing toward empty trees in a city park.

Still, Callum dutifully surveyed the area. "I'm sorry Kay…I don't see anything."

My sobs grew louder. "Callum…Callum I think I'm going crazy." I cried into his thermal shirt, and expected him to peel me off of him.

Instead, Callum held my face in his hands, vigorously shaking his head. "No—no don't say that Kay. We'll figure this out. I believe you." Callum pulled me closer and kissed my forehead. I looked up at him, expecting his face to reveal what he really thought—that I should be committed to an asylum. But all I saw in his eyes was genuine care. "Whatever it is Kay—you can tell me anything." And I knew then that I could.

When the love song that the band was playing was over, we stopped swaying to the music, but as usual, Callum didn't let me go. The rest of the junior class clapped as the DJ played a filler song until the next set.

But Callum didn't clap. He didn't even seem to notice that the song was over. He just lowered himself a little and rested his face against mine. "I don't understand," he breathed into my ear. "Why are you doing this to me? What did I do Kay? Tell me and I'll fix it." Callum was in complete tears now. "Please Kay—I miss you so much—it's like…it's like I can't even breathe."

The soft exhale of his last words floated towards me. And at that moment, I could feel the entirety of his weight. Not his physical one, of course, but the other. It sat on top of his shoulders and waited for me to remove the burden.

"I can't…" I said it through tears of my own—ones that were building in the corners of my eyes as I tried to force myself away. It took every single ounce of my strength to do it—not just because he was holding me so tightly—but because I held onto *him* even tighter.

But I finally managed to break free. So I pushed my way through the crowd of people, and was thankful that the loud music covered the choked back sobs that got away from me.

I didn't waste any time once I reached the exit doors. I ran straight ahead to the subway and tried to clear my head long enough to think about where to go next. I didn't want to risk Callum showing up at my dorm, so I got on the C train and went to the only place I could think of—the only place in New York where I felt truly safe.

When I arrived at my destination, I knocked on the door, and hoped that someone would open. But I rang the doorbell and knocked half a dozen times before the light even came on.

When she finally opened the door, I was so relieved that I started crying again. I said the only thing I could manage at that point. "Mom," I whispered, "can I stay here tonight?"

"Of course honey." She opened the door wider and stepped aside. I saw my dad turning around on the couch in the living room, but I didn't stop to speak.

I ran straight into my old room and climbed right into the bed that I'd slept in most of my life. It was ironic that I sought comfort here, being that it was in this very bed that my frightening night terrors had begun. But what I had been experiencing lately was something that would have put my eight-year-old nightmares to shame.

So I tried to stop thinking about it as I drew the cover over my eyes and hoped for a better tomorrow.

When I awoke the next morning to the smell of banana walnut pancakes, it was like waking up to the smell of not having a care in the world. I smiled and stretched my arms before slowly sitting up. I wished I could wake up this peacefully every morning.

I was just about to swing my legs over the bed when I noticed a familiar looking material hanging over the footboard. I leaned forward and picked up the white woven throw with the black printed symbols on it. I couldn't put my finger on where I'd seen the butterfly-like pattern before, but then again, I couldn't really think past the sweet aroma of banana walnut in the air.

I walked out my bedroom and into the hallway. And as I made my way to the kitchen, I admired all the framed achievements on the walls. I suddenly remembered that I did come from a long line of over-achievers—as the gossip trio would have pointed out.

These particular certificates were equally divided—a third of them being Deans List and other Academic Achievement awards that I had earned while in high school and in college.

A second third of the awards were plaques my dad had received for his pro-bono work as an advocate for children in foster care.

The final third of the frames were media honors that my mom had received. She was an award-winning journalist, and was the main reason I became a journalism major in college.

She used to tell me so many wild stories about her travels on assignments, but she stopped travelling after I was born to stay home and raise me.

Still, Mom never fully gave up on her goals and dreams, and started an on-line news site that generated enough extra income for her to begin her own personal African art collection. Now our house was full of incredibly beautiful bronze masks and gold sculptures—pieces that were more magnificent than anything I'd ever seen in any museum.

My mom and I both love art and have so many other things in common as well. She truly is my best friend in the whole world—and is unquestionably the only person who knows me inside and out.

So after everything that had happened last night, I couldn't imagine being anywhere else right now.

Because I remember when I had my first heartache, she didn't ask me who broke my heart. She didn't try to make me talk about it. She simply turned on the television and sat with me—both of us staring at the screen but not actually watching anything. She could always tell when I wanted to talk, and when I needed not to.

When I finally got to the kitchen, Mom was flipping over her famous mixed pancakes.

"Morning baby!" I could be 40 and she would still call me baby. I walked over and gave her a hug and a kiss.

"Morning Mom," I said as I bent over and took in a whiff of the perfectly browning batter in the pan.

"Careful Nanya! I don't want you to burn yourself."

My mom started calling me Nanya for short when I was little because even I couldn't say Nanyamka growing up. I would get to the first few letters and then make some sort of gargled sound at the end.

She thought it was hilarious. But she always made up for laughing at me with pancakes. And now, by the looks and smell of things, breakfast was just about ready. So after I washed my hands in the sink—and simultaneously remembered how much Mom hated when I did that—I walked over to the dish dryer and pulled out three plates.

Soon I was making my way into the dining area and just as quickly setting the table. Moments later, Dad walked in from the living room with his newspaper and coffee in hand.

"Hey princess. I thought I heard you up and about."

"Morning Dad." I pulled out a chair for him as Mom called out from the kitchen.

"Two pancakes or three?"

"Two and a half please!" Dad and I yelled it at the same time, and were thrilled that it was less than a minute before the finished batch was ready and everyone was sitting down to eat. Mom said grace as usual, and in no time we were all digging in, complimenting her on how delicious everything was—as always.

"So, this is a nice surprise." Dad folded his newspaper and placed it on the chair underneath the table. "I'm glad we got to see our little princess before you headed off."

Mouth full, I tried to force down the overstuffed bite I was chewing so I could speak. "Really—I wasn't going all the way to South Africa without coming to see you Dad."

"Of course not honey." Dad looked out the window while I washed the fluffy pancakes down with a glass of Mom's freshly squeezed orange juice. "Oh Mom, that's delicious."

She smiled, but didn't respond.

I returned my focus to Dad.

And I was just about to ask him how work was going when I noticed that he was no longer looking out the window. He was staring at the wall as if he were contemplating something. "Um, *ahem.*" I sarcastically cleared my throat.

No response.

I searched the table and picked up the orange juice glass, clinking it with a fork as if it were a wedding reception. The noise finally recaptured his attention.

"I'm sorry princess. Did you say something?"

"I was just going to ask you how work was going."

Dad drifted again. "Oh that's good honey. Good for you."

Okay, something was definitely up.

I looked to Mom, whose intense stare was focused on Dad—her eyes darting at his every twitch and movement. Whatever was going on, I didn't like the feel of it.

"Hey. What's going on with you two? Is there some secret that I'm not in on?" Both of them stopped chewing. Their eyes flitted to me, and then to each other. Mom shook her head frantically at Dad. He glanced at her apologetically in return.

"Princess," Dad begun, "there's something we need to tell you, and it's not something we're proud of."

"No!" Mom jumped out of her seat, quickly collecting our dishes—even though no one was finished yet. She scraped the leftovers into one plate.

"Nanya, get your coat. I'll ride with you back to campus."

Mom was panicking. I could tell. I'd never seen her lose composure like this before, and I didn't know where it was coming from.

It scared me.

"Elizabeth, it's time."

"No!" Mom was practically yelling now. "Richard, why are you doing this to me? This isn't fair!"

As Dad stood up, he put both of his hands on the table, then leaned in as calmly as he could. "Liz, you said we were going to tell her when she was six; then when she was sixteen...eighteen. My gosh Elizabeth—how much longer are you going to wait? Nanyamka has a right to know the truth!"

I had no idea what they were talking about, and I was beginning to think that maybe I didn't *want* to know. I suddenly got a horrible feeling in the pit of my stomach.

"Mom? Dad?"

My mom burst into tears. My dad hung his head—a feeling of guilt overcoming his expression.

"Nanyamka, there's something we need to tell you—something you need to know."

4. Truth Hurts

I felt sick. I was so angry I was actually sick—and crying. I was so angry I'd somehow skipped an emotion and was involuntarily crying. So much so that I didn't even notice the cars coming toward me until I heard the blaring honks.

The alarming sounds finally brought me back from my daze, and it was then—when I turned down Bleecker Street—that I realized my body had automatically taken me from my parents' house straight to Callum's dorm. I stopped.

I thought about it; being able to run into his arms; tell him everything they'd just told me. But then I remembered that I was the one who had ended things, and that I couldn't go to him. Not now.

People in the street kept coming up to me, asking if I were okay. Some just looked—probably wondering what could make someone fall apart this way.

They had no idea why I slumped onto the nearest park bench and let every single emotion flow through me until there was nothing left inside. But I knew. So I sat there on the sidewalk's long wooden seat, and replayed everything that transpired less than an hour ago.

"Adopted??" I couldn't wrap my mind around it. I felt as if I were having an outer body experience—except it was real.

Adopted. I repeated it in my head. I thought maybe there it would make sense, but it didn't. None of it did.

"Riots? Fires? Village? Embassy?" The room was spinning.

"I know we waited a long time princess—too long, but we thought you should know before you go back." My father was walking towards me now, but I felt too much as if I were being cornered to stay in my current position. I retreated to the other side of the room.

Wait. "Back?" I shook my head. "What do you mean *back*?"

"To South Africa honey. You should know that it won't be your first time there."

I didn't understand. But what I didn't understand most was how the two people I trusted more than anyone else in the *whole* world could have lied to me for so many years.

My mother... I paused at the word. The woman who'd been my best friend my entire life had kept a secret from me that she had no right to keep. And my father—my own flesh and blood. I laughed. I guess I can't use *that* expression anymore.

"Nanya, please...let me explain." She could see me fuming, but was still in tears from when she begged Dad not to tell me the truth. I was thankful when she turned and walked into the living room. Yet, even though everything in me was telling me to leave, I followed her in there.

Mom sat on the couch and tried to regain her

composure. "It was chaos Nanya."

"*What* was chaos?" I folded my arms as she looked out the window. Then I waited for her to wipe her eyes and to blow her nose before speaking again.

"When De Klerk announced that Mandela would be freed, it was the story of a lifetime. I couldn't think about anything other than getting to Cape Town to be a part of history. But things became complicated."

I cut her off. "I'm sorry. What does Nelson Mandela have to do with the reason you felt the need to lie to me all these years?" The man I called Father sat down on the couch with her. He patted one of the cushions while looking me in the eyes.

"Please princess, just hear your mother out. She's doing the best she can right now."

I let out another sarcastic laugh, but sat down on the edge of the couch anyway.

Mom—I mean Elizabeth continued.

"I was ecstatic when my editor approved the assignment, but he was worried that I wouldn't have anyone to travel with. I hadn't met your father yet, and I knew when I applied for the assignment in Cape Town that apartheid wasn't yet over. So my editor and several others on the staff flew with me, just in case I ran into any trouble out there."

I tried to remember everything that I had learned about apartheid in school, and tried to picture my mom being bullied, assaulted or worse—any place she went just because of the color of her skin. I wanted to ask her about it, but remembered there was another topic at hand.

"You see Nanya, I was on my way to Paarl—to Victor

Verster prison with the other journalists to cover Mandela's release—when a young girl ran out in front of our van. It was terrifying. We stopped just inches away from her tiny little face.

The poor little girl was frantic. 'Please! Please! Help! Please!' The moment I got out of the van she began tugging on my pant leg and pointing in the opposite direction. I tried to ask her why she needed help so badly, but she was so small, I don't think she knew any other words. No—there were two others. 'Langa! Fire!'

I knew then that something was terribly wrong, so I got back into the van where everyone else had stayed, and told them that we needed to help. But if we did, we would of course risk police attention, and police during that time did awful, *awful* things to people of color.

That's why the rest of my news team didn't want to get involved. They were older than I, and remembered the evil in America much clearer than I did. Being in Cape Town during that time brought back painful memories for my editor—memories of growing up in the South. And even though I knew that deep down he wanted to help that frightened, little girl, at his age, there wouldn't have been much he could do for her anyway.

So I told the crew to go on to Verster without me, and that I would find a way to meet them there later. But before they left, I went into the back of the trunk and grabbed the fire extinguisher that Eddy—my editor— kept next to the emergency kit.

I had no idea what I was going to do when I got there, but I took the little girl's hand and ran as fast as we could to the place called Langa."

"Langa?" I had never heard of it before.

"Yes honey. Back then, townships were established to enforce segregation in South Africa. One of them was called Langa."

"Oh." I leaned back against the couch, but then quickly sat back up. "Wait, you said you went to South Africa to cover Mandela's release. That was in 1990." I remembered that much from my textbooks.

"Yes Nanya," Mom replied. "Unfortunately, the evil of apartheid still existed even to the day you were born."

I was shocked. I'd been baffled in school when we learned that segregation and discrimination was still lawful in America even into the sixties. But I was completely thrown to know that the largely Dutch and other European run South African government condoned that kind of behavior even until the nineties.

"The little girl and I were lucky that we didn't get into any confrontations on our way there, but we weren't so lucky when we finally reached Langa.

Smoke billowed from the walls and from the rooftop of one of the shacks. Dozens of people were coughing in the street.

I clutched the little girl's hand as we ran to the very shack that was on fire, but just as we got there, a woman jumped out through the door and dropped to her knees. She collapsed practically lifeless onto the street. Yet, her arms never unfolded. I had to kneel down to see what the woman was grasping onto so dearly, and when I did, I saw that what she held so tightly in her arms was a tiny, precious baby girl. And that precious baby girl Nanya, was you."

My hands flew to my mouth. So this was my story.

"Your mother fought so hard for air, but her lungs

were too filled with the black smoke that had consumed her. Still, people began to surround us. They were shouting, 'She saved us! She saved us! Help her please!'

The little girl who had brought me there shouted the loudest. She yelled for the woman until her little lungs gave out. Finally, the young girl kneeled beside the woman who whispered something into her ear. I remembered the child nodded, and then just walked away.

To this day I don't know exactly what happened. But as the woman lay there on the ground, she begged me to take you from her—to take you away from that burning village. She handed you to me in a woven blanket with beautiful black butterflies on it."

I looked towards my room. I knew that blanket. It was now only big enough to be a throw, but it lay across the foot of my bed in my bedroom.

"Your birthmother continued to cough and to gasp for air, but she fought to tell me your name. She said you were to be called Nanyamka, and that I must promise to always take care of you."

"And then what happened?" I begged for more information.

"When I promised her, she took off the silver necklace she was wearing and raised it to the sky. I'll never forget how the silver pendant shimmered in the sunlight, even through all of that smoke."

I remembered that pendant. It was the one with the phoenix on it. Mom wore it every day until I was eight. I suddenly became angry that she never told me it was my birthmother's necklace.

"She fought you know, until the end. And I stayed with her. But then she said something to me that changed everything. 'Ubaba,' the woman whispered.

I didn't know what it meant at first, but she handed me a little piece of paper with your name on it. Above it was a picture of a silver-haired gentleman.

It took some asking around, but finally we were led to Tokai—to the U.S. Consulate in Cape Town. I was so afraid I would be stopped with you on my way there, but I wasn't."

Dad took her hand, rubbing the rest of her fingers with his own.

"Nanya, I had no idea what I was doing. I didn't know anything about children, and I didn't know what I would say when I arrived at the Consulate. So when the soldiers asked me where I was going, I just showed them the little piece of paper your birthmother had given me. And when I did, the guards quickly escorted me inside.

I assumed someone would take you, and that I would go back to meet the crew that I abandoned."

I couldn't believe what I was hearing.

"You were just going to *leave* me there?"

"Nanya, within a matter of hours I had gone from being on my very first international news assignment to caring for a living, breathing, human *being*. I hadn't even had time to take it all in, when the man your birthmother sent me to find came out to where I was waiting.

No one said anything at first. Even you had been so quiet throughout the whole ordeal that I had to check to make sure you were still breathing.

But suddenly, when this silver-haired man with his beautiful chestnut skin came and stood over you, you giggled. It was the first time I heard you make a sound all day. And oh Nanya, it was the prettiest little sound I ever heard.

The kind, older gentleman placed his hand on the top of your head, and started to chant something I couldn't understand. I think it was a prayer. When he finished, he walked back into his office—still not having said a word to me—and walked right back out with the most handsome man I'd ever seen." She looked at Dad with a twinkle in her eyes.

He picked up for her where she had left off. "Inkosi Ubaba was a very well respected man in the community. He was my supervisor, and he told me there was an urgent matter I must attend to right away. So I dropped everything and immediately followed him out the office. That's when I saw her."

The way Richard looked at Elizabeth, it made me unsure if they even remembered I was still in the room— until he went on.

My father told me the story of how they got back to America—how Dad was instructed by Ubaba to only get Elizabeth and I to a certain point—but that once he did, he wouldn't leave us to make the rest of the journey here alone.

Dad said that while they were waiting for all of the paperwork to get me home, Elizabeth would sing to me to keep me entertained—and that I would play with the shiny, silver pendant she wore then in my little hands.

"The phoenix," I said. "You stopped wearing it."

"Yes honey, when you started having those nightmares."

Suddenly a flood of memories came back to me—and they weren't good ones. I remembered the year she made me spend in therapy when I was eight. I remembered how she always told me that the fires I dreamed about being surrounded by were all in my mind—but they weren't.

I jumped up from the couch—furious.

"You knew what I was trying to remember—and you tried to hide it from me by making me think I was crazy!"

Mom jumped up with me. "No, Nanya. That's not true. It's not even possible. You were just a few months old then. There's no *way* you could have remembered any of that."

"You put me in therapy!"

"We didn't want you to keep having those horrible nightmares." Dad had risen from the couch and was now standing by Elizabeth's side.

I backed up and tried to calm myself, but ended up breathing through my teeth. "You should have told me the truth."

"Princess…"

"Don't! You didn't say anything—*anything*—all those nights I woke up screaming. You just let me think that there was something wrong with me—that I was some kind of…*freak*."

"That's not what we meant to do. We just wanted to protect you."

"From *what?*" I tried to imagine what kind of darkness they thought they were shielding me from—but I also knew there would be no satisfying response.

"Nanya, we did what we thought was best."

I wished she had said it more convincingly. Because I wanted to forgive her. I wanted to forgive both of them. But for years they let me believe that I was crazy, when all I was doing was remembering the secrets they'd chosen to keep.

I walked back into the dining room and picked up my coat. I put it on and walked over to the living room door.

Elizabeth spoke softly. "Sweetheart, I love you."

I didn't respond. I didn't turn around. I reached for the door, opened it, and let it slam closed behind me.

When I finally got up from the park bench, I was calmer than I had been when I initially sat down. Thankfully, it didn't take me long to regain my bearings once I located the street sign that spelled out my location. It also didn't take me long to remember that I'd left my coat at the Winter Send-off last night, which is why I was shivering so profusely—because I didn't keep a change of clothes at...*their* house.

Still, despite the cold, I slowly dragged my feet all the way back to the dorms.

That was the first night in an entire year that I didn't have the dreams.

The next morning I thought about everything that had happened the night before. And even though I'd always been an early riser, right now I just couldn't seem to find the courage to face the day. So I stayed in bed and pretended to be asleep until Beth left for the cafeteria.

But just as I was trying to decide if I would *ever* get out of bed, the room phone rang. Slightly annoyed, I threw back the covers and walked over to the side of the room where we kept the landline.

It was facilities. They said I was the only number associated with the student newsroom, and that they needed someone to strip it down so they could clean for us over the holiday break. Well, so much for wallowing in my despair until departure time.

I hung up the phone after I told the guy on the other end that I'd have it done by this afternoon. He asked me if I was sure, because if so, he could schedule a cleaning for this evening. I told him yes, and let him know that I had a 5:00 P.M. flight tonight anyway.

I checked one last time to make sure that I had everything in my luggage packed securely. Then I cleaned out the bathroom and stripped the bed.

Beth and I would have the same dorm room next semester, so we didn't have to worry about taking anything with us over the holidays. However, everything in the room still needed to be put away so that it could be as thoroughly cleaned as the newsroom would be.

After I did my final checks, I went over to Beth's work desk and borrowed a pen, along with one of her artistically colorful sticky notes.

Dear Beth, I'll miss you lots. Really wish you were going with me, but I'll see you soon. XOXO ~Kay

I stuck the note to her laptop. I would have plenty of time to come back to the dorm room before I'd have to head to the airport, but Beth would want to know why I didn't come back after leaving the Winter Send-off, and I didn't have the energy to discuss life changing events right now.

Once I arrived at the student newsroom, I put my luggage on one of the desks, and got to work pulling down laminated articles from the walls.

The time went by pretty quickly—though I had to switch staple removers a couple of times to get the really stubborn ones out of the wall. Still, I was down to the last three newspaper articles when he knocked on the door.

"Kay?"

I didn't turn around. I had been hoping to get out of dodge without having to do this with him. Maybe—*maybe* I could have handled seeing him today without all of the revelations from last night, but now I was just left on empty.

"Kay, don't you think it's time we talked?"

No. I didn't. "I'm sorry Callum. I'm pretty busy right now." I moved the chair that I was standing on slightly to the left so that I could reach the last few articles nearest the ceiling.

Callum was all packed for the holiday break, and he had placed his uncle's army bag—the one he used sometimes to pack his clothes in when he traveled—on the floor, right by the chair that I was standing on. I could tell Callum didn't plan on going anywhere anytime soon.

He began again. "Kay, I don't know what I did...but I think I at least deserve a reason."

"Please, not now Callum." I couldn't handle another emotional exploration this week. Three was my limit. I ripped the last article from its staple in the wall—and with such a force that I lost my balance and slipped off the chair. Thankfully, Callum caught me.

"Thanks."

He put me down. "No problem. Now can we talk?"

"About what Callum?" I was desperate to avoid this conversation. But at that moment, I don't think I'd ever seen him so confused before. And though I tried to ignore it, I could feel the wave of guilt about to come crashing down on me.

"Kay, do you even remember the last time we were together?"

I did, but I was hoping he wouldn't make me think of

it again—*ever* again. He had no idea what he was asking me to remember. And I knew he didn't know—because I was the one who had kept it from him.

It was a secret I'd kept ever since that day at Coney Island.

"Here, take a bite." I was still woozy from the tea cup ride when Callum held a pink and blue swirl of cotton candy to my lips. But when I went to bite down, he swiped it across my nose instead and laughed.

"Hey!" I picked cotton candy bits out of the bottom of my hair while still chewing on the part I was able to chomp on anyway. Callum thought it was hilarious— probably just as hilarious as I thought it was when I dabbed my soft serve ice cream cone on his chin.

Callum and I had spent every second of every day together since our first date. We shared our biggest fears with each other, our goals in life, and our deepest secrets—except that there was one thing I wasn't ready to talk about yet—the daymares.

"So we should do something to celebrate." Callum swung my hand in his as we walked down the Coney Island Boardwalk.

I looked around. "Like what?"

"Oh I don't know. What do you do when you beat out a thousand other students for an all-expense paid apprenticeship to South Africa?"

I skipped once and shouted. "We all go to Disney World!"

Callum picked me up, my feet now in the air, and twirled me in an enormous circle. But we almost hit an elderly couple so we decided to stop goofing around a bit.

We giggled.

As we continued to walk down the boardwalk, I thought about travelling the world—specifically, I thought about travelling with Callum. "Hey, so out of all the places you moved to as an army brat, which one of them was your favorite place to live?"

Callum pondered it for a moment. "Well, Alabama had great food, and Washington had good fishing."

"And Wisconsin?"

"Oh of course—great cheese."

I rubbed my stomach. "Mmmm. Cheese."

Callum laughed. "But it's no comparison. Here is definitely the only place that feels like home to me." Callum stopped to lift a stray piece of cotton candy from my hair. We watched it float away in the wind.

"Well, I've lived here all my life and can attest, New York does have a certain way of capturing the heart."

"It's not New York that has my heart Kay."

I blushed—fumbling for words to respond. "But it'll still keep you good company while I'm gone."

"Or," Callum leaned in even closer, "I could just go to South Africa *with* you."

"You mean, you would travel all that way—for *me*?"

"Kay, I would follow you anywhere. You should know that by now."

And I did.

Callum and I continued our peaceful stroll along the boardwalk as the sun began to set. We were enjoying the smell of salt water in the air and of hot dogs being roasted when not very much later—still hand-in-hand—Callum nodded to someone off in the distance. He guided me in the direction of the baseball cap wearing stranger.

"Callum, what's going on? Do you know that man?"

Callum didn't answer. Instead, he just continued nudging me forward, all the while keeping his hand on the small of my back. We walked until there were fewer and fewer people surrounding us, finally reaching the fellow Callum had acknowledged several yards prior to our arrival.

"Okay, you know the drill." Callum took his hand off my lower back and stood in front of me.

"Drill?"

Callum huffed.

I suddenly remembered our first date in the park, and how fond Callum was of surprises. I knew what he was going to ask me to do next. "Close your eyes," said the preemptively smug co-ed with something up his sleeve.

I couldn't resist rolling them before closing them because Callum knew how much I *didn't* like surprises—but as soon as they were tightly shut, Callum picked me up and lifted me over the boardwalk's wooden railing.

I became curious when I realized he had carried me across quite a stretch of sand before placing me back on my feet.

"Okay, you can open them."

I did as requested. And there, on the crowded Brooklyn beach, was an entirely sequestered, private patch of land with a white cloth covered table on it. On top of the table were candles, flowers and dinner plates. The beautifully thought out dining experience came complete with a man in a waiter's tuxedo, and a woman playing the violin. I shook my head. Callum never ceased to amaze me.

"Do I even want to know?"

Callum nodded at his friend with the baseball cap who waved before getting inside of the green Parks

Department truck, and again before driving off. I caught a quick glimpse of the guy's army pants and wondered on which of the many army bases Callum had first met him at.

I turned my focus back to the man of the hour. "Callum I *truly* don't know what to say. I can't believe you did all of this just for our first holiday together."

Callum pulled my chair out and gently pushed me in once I was seated. He then turned and asked the waiter for the sparkling cider, pouring a glass first for me, and then one full glass for his self. Callum moved the centerpiece slightly to the right before speaking again.

"Do you even know what holiday this is?"

I rolled my eyes, not believing he was serious. I answered anyway.

"The Fourth of July Callum. Duh."

Callum shook his head. I thought about taking his temperature because it was undeniably July 4th, so I wondered if Callum were feeling alright.

I kept a close eye on him while unrolling my cloth napkin and laying it across my lap.

"You may not remember as well as I do," Callum began, "but our first date was *exactly* three months ago. It's our three month anniversary Kay."

"Our *what?*"

Callum laughed as I scratched my head. "Callum, I don't think there's such a thing as a three month anniversary."

"Well, there is now."

The waiter brought out our first course as we lifted up our glasses and toasted to the beautiful evening. And, as the hours drifted away, the violinist and the waiter quietly went home while Callum laid out two large towels for us to relax on. We sat there on the sand and waited for the fireworks show to begin.

Not much time had passed before Callum got off his towel and moved over to mine. And when he did, I noticed that we'd somehow managed some company.

"Hey! It's a lighting bug!" I jumped up to my knees, immensely excited as I hadn't seen any all summer.

We watched it flutter about until Callum extended his lengthy, muscular arms into the air, and gently cusped the beautiful creature in his slightly ajar hands. Its glowing light blinked on and off in front of our joyous, appreciative eyes.

"It's so beautiful," I murmured.

"Here." Callum placed his hands on top of mine and didn't let go until I had a firm grasp on the transfer of the mesmerizing gift. I made a peep hole between my thumbs, causing its blinks to seem brighter in the hollow of my hands.

"Did you know that fireflies blink their lights to either warn another firefly or to give off a mating signal?" I mentioned this without taking my eyes off the beautiful glow. "I wonder which one it's doing now."

Callum tilted his head.

"Well, if it's giving off a mating signal, I'm definitely going to have to challenge it to a duel."

"Hmm, I wonder who would win?"

Callum peered into my hands. "Let's see. He's definitely got spunk—a little feisty too I imagine." Callum shrugged. "It'd probably be a tie."

I exhaled as if I'd been holding my breath. "Oh good, nobody gets hurt." We both nodded very seriously.

"Listen Kay, there's something I've been trying to figure out a way to tell you."

"Yes?" I let go of the little firefly and watched it dance away.

"Well, it's just that I've never felt this close to anyone before. You know, with all the moving around. I've never really had someone that I could talk to, the way you and I do—who I get along so completely with. The truth is I've just never met anyone who is quite like you." And I him.

"It's as if my whole life I've been waiting for something—something I couldn't explain, but ever since the day I met you, I don't have that feeling anymore. It's as if whatever puzzle this was—that now here with you—it's finally complete. And now you're my *very* first thought in the morning, and you're the last thought I have before I go to sleep at night. So I guess what I'm trying to say is," Callum sat up straight—perfectly at attention, "I'm completely and utterly in love with you Kay, and I hope you don't mind me saying it."

How could I? He'd already shown me a hundred times.

Still, my heart fluttered as if it were a lighting bug of its own—just unable to display its beaming glow on the outside. But then again, maybe it was able to after all. Maybe that's what Callum saw as he leaned in and kissed me—right at the same time the fireworks went off in the beautiful, starry night sky.

I was on cloud nine, and there was absolutely nothing in the world that could've convinced me that I hadn't been floating the entire time Callum walked me home that night.

I only came back down to earth when we stopped in front of my parents' door.

Callum continued to walk towards me until he was just inches away from my face. And, as he'd done many times that night, he took my hand in his and kissed it before lowering it down.

"I hope today was okay."

"Callum, today was perfect."

"So—I'll see you tomorrow?"

I didn't have to answer. Because from now on, it would be rhetorical. I'd go out with him tomorrow, and the day after that, and the day after that, and the day after... His kiss gladly interrupted my thoughts.

Callum's hands slid down my shoulders, only to slowly linger on their way back up; passionately running themselves through my hair—our bodies fiercely wrapped around each other; my hands tightly gripping his waist.

I was still on my tippy toes—eyes closed, when Callum slowly ended the kiss. I was in a daze. Callum bent down one last time to put his lips near my ear, and to whisper those three beautiful words one last time. "I love you." Then he kissed me on the forehead and walked down the street.

That night changed everything. That was the night we officially became a couple. That was the night Callum finally said I love you. And that was the night I held his lifeless body in my arms as he died.

5. Now Boarding

Why did he have to make me remember—when I would have given anything to forget? Callum's unmoving chest, his colorless lips, the blank stare of his eyes; for months that's all I could think about.

I wanted to be angry with him for dredging it up, but I knew he didn't come to the newsroom today to make me remember.

Because of all the wishes, of all the goals, of all the future hopes and dreams that we shared over the summer, the one thing I never once told him about was the heart-wrenching terror I couldn't help but to believe.

When I finally walked through the door of my parents' house, still floating like a firefly from Callum's kiss, it didn't take my mom long to figure out the reason.

"Well this is new." Mom loved teasing me. She was sitting on the couch, inspecting my face from a distance.

"What?" I tried to play coy, but I knew it would be pointless. My mom *was* an investigative reporter after all.

"Richard, you have to come see this!" Mom yelled for Dad, who promptly leaned in through the doorway, eager to be part of some mischief.

"My, my. What an enormous smile you have."

"The bigger to have a crush on someone with," said Mom, as if she were reading from a children's book.

"And oh my, are you *actually* walking on sunshine?" Dad winked at my mother.

"Mom! Dad!" I covered my face, totally embarrassed.

"So what's his name?" Mom patiently waited for an answer, while Dad lay down on the couch, pretending to twirl his imaginary hair like a teenager waiting for gossip.

I ignored them both, and instead calculated how quickly I could get to my bedroom without further interrogation.

Eight point five seconds, that's all I'd need. *"Goodnight!"* I leaped towards the stairs and made a beeline for the bedroom. I closed the door as quickly as I could, but not before letting out an extremely girlish giggle that could've put to shame the youngest of schoolgirl crushes.

Mom was right. I'd never been so ecstatically happy before. It *was* new.

After thoroughly washing my face, and somehow managing to get all of the left over sand out of my hair, I turned off the bathroom light and got ready for bed. And, for the first time ever—I went to sleep with absolutely no fears of what I would see when I closed my eyes at night.

But I should have.

Because after I had the usual dream—the one with the fire, and the stalking lion in the jungle, I had the second dream. A new one. The one that ended everything—my hopes, my joy. The one that let me know that Callum and I could never, ever be together.

Because the moment I closed my eyes, that's when I saw the beautiful white Boathouse Callum once spoke so fondly of. The soft light from the flickering lanterns; our friends, our family—they were all there.

I remember the rings that we placed on each other's fingers before we each said "I do." I even remember the chimes of the nearby church bells as they rang in the dancing wind.

But the last thing I remember is the one part I've tried so hard to forget.

It was when the candles blew out, and everything went dark. Suddenly Callum and I were on the ground and I was weeping, shaking, cradling Callum's lifeless body. I had been left alone; begging Callum to wake up—only to discover that he wasn't asleep. He was dead.

When I awoke from the horror, I was numb. Gasping for air, I stepped out the bed and collapsed to the floor. I was sobbing so hard I threw up. And even though I knew I'd been dreaming, I couldn't shake the feeling that what I had experienced was real.

My mind raced. It was trying to tell me something I already knew. Then, I remembered the words I read that day in the library.

"Nightmares help the brain 'rehearse' distressing and disturbing events that one is likely to encounter in the future."

I repeated it over and over, but it wouldn't sink in. How could your mind know what you're going to encounter in the *future*? I started to tremble.

What if I hadn't been having dreams after all? What if I'd been experiencing something *else* all together? No. No Kay. You're not some carnival freak. You don't have *visions* into the future, so don't go running out to buy some mystic ball. There has to be another explanation.

91

Any other explanation.

At least, that's what I'd been telling myself ever since I was eight—ever since my parents put me in therapy for all of my horrible dreams. But what they didn't know— what I never told them, was that sometimes they—my dreams—came true. Sometimes, if I dreamed about someone I'd never met, I'd meet them the next day—in oh, for instance, a library let's say.

But I'd always chalked it up to coincidence. It couldn't be the actual person I dreamed about. It had to be someone that just *looked* like them. Still, no matter how much I wanted to remain in denial, was I willing to be in denial with Callum's life?

Still shaking, I managed to peel myself from the floor and stumbled my way to my bedroom desk. I found a loose piece of stationery on the tabletop and began to write.

Dear Callum, I need some time alone. Please don't try to contact me. I just don't think this is going to work out.

I put the pen down and ran my fingers through my hair. I needed time—time to figure out what this all meant.

Why is it that the day I met Callum, I started having those frightening dreams again from when I was eight? The ones in the fire. The ones fighting for my life in the middle of some jungle.

Why is it that after all these years, I finally meet the man of my dreams, and yet those same dreams are telling me that we can never be together? That the day we profess our love in front of our friends, in front of our family; the love of my life will surely die.

I felt faint again, so I allowed myself a minute to

breathe. I stared down at the cryptic note I'd written, and flinched as it stared eerily back.

But eventually I forced myself out the chair and booked the first flight I could afford to L.A. I spent the rest of the summer there with my aunt, and refused every phone call, text and email Callum sent. I felt awful about it, but I just didn't know what else to do.

That's why I understood the confusion in Callum's eyes as they pleaded with me here in the student newsroom—in the very city that I was once again about to leave him in.

"Kay, I told you I loved you, and then I never heard from you again. I didn't understand. I thought maybe you just needed things to slow down—that maybe I shouldn't have told you I loved you so quickly. So I tried to do what you asked—not to contact you, to give you space. But you have no idea how hard it's been—not seeing you, not being able to laugh with you, not being able to hear your voice or to hold you after a long day. I've been trying to keep it together. I've been trying not to go insane, but I feel like I've lost a *part* of me."

Callum hung his head and sighed as if he were ready to accept a provisional defeat. "Kay, don't you think I at least deserve a reason why?"

I did. But I knew there was nothing I could do for him—not even when I thought about our magical day with the firefly, and the passionate kiss by the boardwalk underneath the fireworks.

"Kay, I went to see you the next day, after the beach, only for your parents to tell me you'd left town. Just like that—no explanation; just a flimsy letter saying you didn't want to see me anymore. Do you have any idea what that was like for me? I felt like someone had ripped my heart out my chest without even the good grace to tell me why."

Callum slumped down into one of the chairs and buried his somber face into his fiercely strong hands. I watched as his tall broad shoulders rose with the inhale of the exhausted breath he'd taken, and restrained myself from running over to console him. But just as suddenly as Callum had sat down, he immediately jumped back up and kicked back into full gear.

"You know what? I don't care anymore if I rushed things—if maybe I shouldn't have confessed so soon my feelings for you. Because the truth is, I never felt that way before. I've never felt *this* way. And it's killing me how you can pretend that you don't feel exactly the same. So I don't care what it takes, but I'm not leaving until you tell me exactly what it is that I did wrong."

I didn't know what to tell him. If I stood here after all this time that's passed, and told him the reason I ruined what we had was because I had some ominous dream about the end of the world—the end of *our* world anyway, it would probably come out sounding exactly as crazy as it did in my head.

Because who would give up on everything that we shared, over a stupid dream? No. I couldn't tell him that. He deserved a better reason—something that made more sense.

I myself had learned to come to terms with our future—or rather lack thereof—while I was in L.A. Because I was right. Away from Callum I was able to think.

And I realized that I'd gotten so caught up in my

feelings for Callum that I'd forgotten all about the goals and dreams I once had for myself. Before I met him, all I could think about was becoming a world renowned news reporter with a top notch career.

But the day I met Callum, time seemed to have stopped, and I would have been perfectly content to have never left Callum's side—no matter what that meant for my own future. Suddenly, the little girl who wanted to be just like her mother when she grew up, resented herself for being so eagerly willing to trade in her dreams.

I looked up into Callum's beautiful brown eyes, and though I knew he sought comfort, I had none to offer. All I had left for him was the final tear that would complete the break he confessed I had caused in his heart.

It was then that I remembered the question Callum asked me that day in the park.

"Kay, do you think someone can actually die from a broken heart?" He was talking about his father then, but with what I was about to say, I desperately hoped that it didn't turn out to be Callum who would find out the answer today.

"Callum," I made sure to look directly into his eyes. I didn't want him to doubt what I was about to say. Maybe at least this could be a clean break. "I know this may be hard for you to hear, but I meant everything I said in that letter. I don't think it would work out between us. We're different Callum. We have different goals and dreams, and frankly, being with you was holding me back from mine."

Callum stumbled back as if someone had punched him in the stomach.

"That's not true Kay. I want whatever you want."

No clean break. I balled up my hand into a fist and prepared to go for the throat.

I sighed nonchalantly. "That's the problem. I don't need two of me. I didn't then, and I don't now. So will you please just leave me alone?"

I was desperately trying to keep it together, but if he pushed any further, I knew I would give in. I waited for his response.

Callum walked towards me—slowly, but I hesitantly stepped back, and I didn't stop until I felt the cold hard plaster of the newsroom wall against my back. It contrasted against the rising temperature of my nervous body. I put up a hand, hoping he would stop, but Callum came even closer. He didn't stop walking towards me until there was nothing—not even air between us.

With less than a centimeter between our bodies, I could feel the soft caress of his warm breath on the cusp of my cheek as he lowered his face to mine; his lips practically already touching my own. Callum carefully took his time as he lowered down, and picked up his uncle's army bag with all of his belongings inside. "Fine."

Callum slung his bag over his shoulder and walked out the room. No. He didn't just walk out the room. He walked out my life—and rightfully so—forever.

Night came then, and when I arrived at the airport, I was nervous about the month ahead. So many things had changed in just the past few days alone, and that was exactly how I was beginning to feel—alone.

My apprenticeship in South Africa was supposed to be an experience that I would never forget. But with everything that had happened this week, I had lost some of my zeal for it.

I just felt that I was leaving New York with so much undone. And I didn't know how to deal with the turmoil inside of me.

Coincidentally, two of the sources of that turmoil were causing my phone to vibrate now. My parents had been calling me non-stop ever since I stormed out last night, but I'd been ignoring their calls.

I still hadn't come to terms with the fact that the two people I trusted most in the world, had been lying to me my entire life—that the secret they had kept had begun in the very part of the world I was travelling to now.

I also couldn't believe that the nightmares my parents sent me to *therapy* for when I was eight, weren't just the disturbed creations of a young child's wild imagination—as my parents led me to believe. They were memories; memories of being carried out of a blazing fire by my birthmother, in a place called Langa, sometime during apartheid, on the same day Nelson Mandela was released from prison.

My head started to spin. I knew that I would eventually have to sit down and process it all, but right now, I just didn't have the time—or space left in my head.

I waited and let the call go to voicemail before lifting up my boarding pass to check which gate I needed. But before I could place myself, I heard someone call out my name.

I raised my head, not being able to imagine who it could be, but didn't see anyone nearby. I shrugged and lifted up the boarding pass again. But this time I heard my name even louder.

I spun around, looking out towards the payphones. No

one. Was I hearing things?

I stepped out a little further from where I was standing to survey the busy terminal. Finally, I spotted the individual who had been calling me.

In the back of the airport, in front of the enormous floor to ceiling window that let the soon to be passengers see the arriving planes, was an incredibly old man with long, silver dreadlocks. He was smiling at me.

The somewhat elderly sir stood up and waved. He didn't seem familiar, so I assumed he had been calling someone else's name that just sounded like mine. Still, the old man continued to try to get my attention.

Confused, I smiled awkwardly and waved back—hoping he'd realize I wasn't the person that he thought I was.

It didn't work.

In fact, the grandfatherly gentleman became *certain* it was me that he'd been waiting for, and practically began jumping up and down, using both of his hands to beckon me towards him.

I figured maybe I should go over before the old man gave himself a heart attack, but then it occurred to me. He must've been waving to someone *behind* me, and my big head was probably blocking the intended interaction.

Curious, I turned around to see exactly who I'd been blocking all this time, but there was no one behind me. Now I was genuinely perplexed. I swiveled back to face the silver-haired gentleman, only to see that he had disappeared.

Odd.

Oh well. I glanced back down at my boarding pass and started making my way towards the gate—that is, until I almost bumped right into the elusive, well-aged stranger. Wait. How in the world did he reach me so quickly?

"Oh, excuse me sir." I said it in part apology, and part attempt to get around him. The old man bowed, but didn't move—or speak. I frowned.

"I'm sorry sir, but are you waiting for someone?" The old man titled his head and stared at me blankly. It was as if I'd asked a rhetorical question.

"It's you," he finally spoke. "You're here. But you're supposed to be there."

"Um, okay." Was this part of an early welcoming committee or something? The silver-haired elder seemed frustrated that I didn't understand.

"I came to warn you," he offered.

"Ah," I said as it finally started to sink in—this guy was a kook.

I tried to decide what would be the best way to get rid of him. Maybe he'd leave if I just indulged him for a few moments.

I gave him my best drama school smile. "Okay. Warn me about what sir?" To my surprise, the old man became even more frustrated.

"Not what! Who!"

"Oh, of course," I replied as I slowly started backing away. "Warn me about *whom?*" I emphasized the corrected grammar.

The elderly gentleman ignored my sarcasm and pointed behind me. "I came to warn you about *her.*"

I looked over my shoulder and immediately dropped my bags. I couldn't believe it was happening again.

Not here.

Not now.

It was the woman with the ivory dagger. She was smiling sadistically over the wild-haired woman from the park—the wild-haired woman with *my* face—the one with the crown and the jewels upon it.

The ivory dagger that my attacker raised above me glimmered in the light. I lurched forward, desperate to stop the attack, but I knew there was nothing I could do. I'd seen this all before, and I knew how it ended.

I die.

Suddenly someone grabbed me from behind, and I screamed.

"*Whoa* mate, what's the fuss?"

"Beth?" I was in complete shock.

"Who else mate? I've been calling you since the security checks. Didn't you hear me?"

No. I was too busy hallucinating.

"Beth, what in the world are you doing... *here?*"

Beth smiled as she put her hands on her hips in her favorite Superwoman pose. "Aw, come on! You didn't think you were gonna shake me that easy? You should know me better than that by now."

"Well Ms. Thomas, I see you've caught up with Ms. Morowa after all." I knew that voice. It was Mrs. Liu, our Media Law professor.

"Professor Liu?? Beth?? What are you two doing here?"

"It's good to see you as well Ms. Morowa." Professor Liu chuckled under her breath.

I tried to wipe the shock off my face by shaking my head. "I'm sorry. I'm just..."

Beth cut in. "Stunned, awed and surprised?"

I nodded.

Professor Liu smiled as she motioned us in the direction of the gate that I needed.

How did she know which gate I needed?

We were all headed in the same direction when my curiosity finally got the best of me. "Uh, Beth? Not that I'm not happy to see you or anything, but what exactly is going on?"

Beth was practically hopping with excitement. "Haven't you figured it out mate? I'm going with you!"

I wasn't sure I heard correctly. "You're coming...to South Africa?"

"Can you believe it? Professor Liu has a timeshare on one of the beaches in Cape Town."

Professor Liu shrugged it off, nodding at a few open seats in our gate's waiting area. "It's nothing much. Just somewhere to relax."

Apparently Beth disagreed because she almost jumped out of her seat. "Are you kidding me? I looked it up online Kay. It has six rooms, three bathrooms, an indoor *and* an outdoor pool, a personal gym, marble floors and best of all, 24 hour room service!"

Wow. Professor Liu had an intriguing definition of *nothing much.* Then again, maybe it wasn't much to her after all.

Professor Liu was always extremely well dressed. Almost *too* well dressed—for a professor anyway. She often wore extravagant looking furs during the winter and didn't hide her affinity for incredibly expensive jewelry.

In fact, just a few weeks ago, I walked in early to class only to overhear the professor on her cellphone negotiating something to be added to a "certain collection," I believe she said. I remembered her using the words "right price" and "ivory." But of course, I didn't know exactly what that meant—not that it was any of my business anyway.

Professor Liu took out a newspaper while we waited by our gate, and was catching up on some light reading when I turned my attention back to Beth. "So—this is for *real*? I mean, you're *really* coming to Cape Town?"

Beth nodded and waited for the impending scream. Within seconds, Beth and I were jumping up and down doing our secret handshake slash happy dance. I was ecstatic. If there were anything I needed to take with me on this trip, it was a friend.

"Beth, I can't believe it! This is gonna be awesome! We're gonna have so much fun!"

And I would make sure that we did. I would put all of my problems aside, and make sure to enjoy myself—I ordered myself in my head.

The plane was almost at the gate when everyone began standing in line. Beth and I got our bags ready. "So how in the world did you work this out?" I was genuinely curious.

"Oh I didn't. Professor Liu did," Beth explained. "There's some sort of media convention going on in Johannesburg, and her assistant cancelled on her just two hours before she had to leave for the airport! Well, *apparently* Professor Liu asked Professor Edmonds for our dorm number to see if I would tag along. I guess I must've mentioned I was staying in the dorms over the holidays. Anyway, she said all she needed was someone who could take notes and transcribe the press conferences while she's there—all in exchange for a mini-vacation in her Cape Town timeshare before the convention! Well naturally mate, I zapped to volunteer."

Professor Liu had just finished reading her newspaper when our gate announced that it was time to start boarding. I guessed that Professor Liu would be boarding first as she was probably flying first class.

I was right.

"Okay ladies, looks like I'll see you in Cape Town, although I'll probably take a couple of walks through the aircraft to stretch my legs, and of course to check on you two troublemakers before we get there."

Beth grinned. "Aw Professor, we promise not to cause *too* much trouble on the way."

Beth and I made our way to the back of the boarding line to wait for our zone to be called, but as we stood on line, I couldn't help but to think about my earlier episode.

My thoughts were interrupted when I heard the click of the airport PA system. "We're now boarding zone 3. Now boarding. Zone 3."

I took in a deep breath and looked over at Beth. Both of our eyes widened—but probably for different reasons. Beth was the first to speak.

"I can't believe by this time tomorrow, we'll be lying on one of the most beautiful beaches in the world! I know the first thing I'm gonna do is to order one of those fruity drinks out of one of those cleverly designed twisty glasses with the little umbrellas on the side." The pitch of her voice suddenly went up two octaves. "I can't believe this is really happening!"

I was equally psyched. So as we stuffed our carry-on items into the overhead compartments, I tried to visualize the trip ahead.

I wondered how long Beth would stay in Cape Town

and then in Johannesburg with Professor Liu. I was about to ask her when the flight safety video came on. Beth and I paid super close attention in case anything happened during the 15-hour flight before us.

Naturally, as soon as the video ended, all of the lights went out. And within seconds I was feeling the intense vibration of the engine revving up, and the deep slant of the airplane taking off as it flew up…up…and away.

Beth was totally knocked out in the seat next to me by the time the midnight sky started to blend in with the dark blue Atlantic Ocean. So I turned on the little overhead light, and rummaged through the airline provided reading materials in the mesh pocket attached to the seats in front of us.

There were a few trade magazines—mostly technology based, but there was one other magazine in particular that caught my eye.

It was from July, and the feature highlighted on the cover read: *Happy Birthday Nelson Mandela.* The name immediately brought back memories from the other night.

I started to put the magazine back, but something wouldn't let me. I held it in my hand and stared at the cover. In less than 12 hours, I would be in the very country I was taken from as a child. The thought lingered in my mind. I wondered if I would feel anything when I arrived there.

Still in deep contemplation, I reached under the airplane seat and pulled out my carry-on canvas messenger bag. I opened the latch and took out my glasses—putting them on before opening the magazine to the contents page. Finally, I skipped ahead to the page that the story was featured on.

Happy Birthday Madiba!

This month we celebrate Rolihlahla "Nelson" Mandela—or as those who adore him know him as, Madiba—his Xhosa clan name. Around the world however, the man whom we call Madiba, is more commonly known by the English name his teacher gave him on the first day of school—Nelson.

Before attending Fort Hare University to study for his Bachelor of Arts, Nelson attended Healdtown Comprehensive School, which is where the majority of Thembu royalty attended school.

Ah yes. Madiba, or Nelson Mandela if you prefer, was born to a father who served as chief of the Mvezo village that Madiba was born in.

At birth, Madiba was given the name Rolihlahla, which can be translated as meaning troublemaker. It is this moniker that perhaps foretold his destiny.

Rolihlahla "Nelson" Mandela would grow up in times of unthinkable acts of horror inflicted on man by his fellow man. A system of segregation called apartheid was put into practice at this time by the government representing the British and Dutch immigrants—and their descendants, who settled in South Africa to claim South Africans' land as their own.

The settlers had come with the belief that their skin was superior in some way to the skin of other colors—and that they were entitled to steal, beat and kill for what they wanted. It is an entitlement thought process still used by many terrorists not just in South Africa, but by terrorist groups around the world—such as the KKK in America.

Over the years, Mandela would try various peaceful methods to stop the evil being done in South Africa. But when the descendants of the conquest seekers only increased their vile acts, Mandela turned to non-peaceful methods of resistance in the anti-apartheid movement.

However, because of his response to violence with violence, Mandela was arrested and jailed in 1964, where he would spend the next 27 years.

Outside, those years were tumultuous, to say the least, with much blood being shed. One of the most notable illustrations of this is the 1976 Soweto Uprising.

It began as a peaceful march by high school students in protest of white languages being instituted as the primary language used for instruction in South African schools (which many black South Africans did not speak as a primary language). However, the protest was cut short when police opened fire on thousands of black South African high school students. One of the students killed by the police was Hector Pietersen. He was thirteen-years-old.

Amazingly, students fought back with mere stones and sticks—anything they could get their hands on, and outnumbering the police, forced those particular, immoral officers to flee to regroup. Still, too many children were killed that day.

Nelson Mandela continued to fight apartheid from jail, famously becoming president of South Africa four years after his release in 1990. But long before that, during the opening of Mandela's trial on charges of sabotage [to the government and apartheid system], he gave a statement of which the following lines are often quoted:

"During my lifetime I have dedicated myself to this struggle of the African people. I have fought against white domination, and I have fought against black domination. I have cherished the ideal of a democratic and free society in which all persons live together in harmony and with equal opportunities. It is an ideal which I hope to live for and to achieve. But if needs be, it is an ideal for which I am prepared to die."

Whoa. I hadn't been prepared for such heavy reading on the plane ride to Cape Town.

By the time I closed the magazine, I could feel the increasing turbulence of the plane walls around me.

So I closed my eyes and braced myself.

Because even though I didn't know just *what* was about to happen next, I did have a feeling it was going to be a bumpy ride.

6. Into the Lion's Den

"Mayday! Mayday! We're going down!"

The left engine gave out—and then the right. I could feel my heart pounding as the plane jolted to the side, and as the oxygen masks dropped from the ceiling. I jumped with the rest of the passengers as we all screamed. Finally, I couldn't take anymore, so I stopped watching. Whoever picked this movie as our inflight entertainment had a sick sense of humor.

And though I preferred not to see the multitude of possibilities that could go wrong while I was tens of thousands of feet in the sky, it wasn't just the scary movie that was the reason for the uneasy feeling I was having in the pit of my stomach.

It was the same feeling I had hoped would have disappeared during the connecting three-hour flight to Cape Town from Johannesburg. But of course, as soon as we landed, the feeling only began to intensify.

"Ladies, there you are. Did you enjoy the flights?"

Professor Liu was smoothing down her all black business dress as she waited for us on the tarmac at the bottom of the plane.

"Oh the flights were fine Professor—except for the bit of turbulence there towards the end. I did get some interesting reading done during the first flight."

"That's good... Good to hear..." Professor Liu's response was somewhat vacant. But I didn't think much of it as she politely held the door for us so that Beth and I could enter the landing gate. "Listen girls, why don't you two head over to the baggage claim and wait for me there? I have a bit of an important call I need to make before we head over to the timeshare."

Beth stood at attention. "Aye, aye Professor!"

As Beth and I walked away, I saw Professor Liu unzipping what appeared to be an incredibly expensive, red leather purse. Once it was open, she pulled out her cellphone and began to dial. Her quick keying movements caused a glimmer to bounce off the rather large diamond on her pointer finger. I was surprised I hadn't noticed it earlier. I also seemed to have missed the matching diamond earrings that hung as teardrops from her ears.

And although I didn't mean to stare, *something* was beginning to nag at me; something I couldn't put my finger on.

There was something that just didn't feel quite right.

"Beth," I began, "do you think it's normal for an instructor to dress the way Professor Liu does?"

Beth gave it some thought. "Hmm, I don't know. Why?"

"Well, I was just wondering how she's able to afford such expensive jewelry, and own an international four-star timeshare on her salary."

Beth shrugged. "She probably does alright for herself.

That or she has some super-secret side gig we don't know about." Beth laughed.

As we approached the international baggage hall, there was such a commotion that we thought something might be wrong. It was totally flooded with people. Well, actually, it was totally flooded with girls—screaming girls.

Beth pushed her way through the crowd to get a better view. I was able to get a spot beside her, just in time to see Beth's eyes light up.

There were about a dozen male South African models standing around the baggage carousel—I assume trying to get their luggage, but being accosted by an unrelenting group of screaming girls asking for autographs instead.

I blinked at the barrage of flashes going off.

By the time my eyes adjusted enough to fully open them, I saw that Beth was already in the middle of the crowd with her arm around the shoulders of one of the models. She'd even given her camera to someone to take their picture—a picture that I knew would go straight on our dorm room wall when we got back to New York.

Oh well, at least I didn't have to worry about whether or not Beth would enjoy herself in Cape Town. And after that heartbreaking breakup she had with that sleazy Dylan from campus, I figured she deserved a little distraction from her woes.

I could tell we'd be here a while, so I leaned against one of the columns and tried to enjoy the show. And I did—until one of the models turned around—one who looked like he could be twin brothers with Callum.

I took in a heavy breath and sighed it out. I wondered what he was doing right now. I wondered how he was planning on spending the holidays. But mostly, I wondered if I would ever stop wondering about a guy I couldn't be with.

Probably not. Because even though Callum was almost eight thousand miles away, I absolutely felt like he was still with me.

And he was.

But the hollow place in my chest that he stayed with me at was beginning to ache.

Eventually the male models left, and we were finally able to get to our luggage. But as Beth and I turned around to see if Professor Liu was ready yet to start our adventure, two extremely handsome men approached us, greeting us in a language we didn't understand.

"Sanibonani," said the first one. He directed it to the both of us. I wondered if he were asking directions. Beth immediately assumed he was flirting. The gentleman was Beth's complexion, but extremely tall. His long, white shirt appeared custom made, and his black slacks had a super crisp pleat in the middle. Some sort of business professional I assumed—or possibly a grad student.

The second gentleman, not much older than I, had skin that was slightly tanner than mine, but his eyes were crystal blue. He had short cropped curly hair, and a jawline that would make any man jealous. His perfectly fitting light grey suit didn't make him any less envy-worthy either.

I realized that the gentleman must've noticed me staring because he smiled at me in a way that almost made me blush. Still, it wasn't long before the mysterious stranger lifted my hand and kissed it. "Sawubona," he softly whispered.

I knew this time I wasn't being asked for directions,

but I still wasn't quite sure what to say in response. The admittedly attractive suitor could tell he was going to have to break it down for me.

He began.

"Saw…"

I repeated.

"Saw…"

"oo…"

"oo…"

"bo…"

"bo…"

"na."

"na."

I put it all together. "Sawubona!"

He laughed and I felt like I was on Sesame Street.

The confusion of what had just occurred was probably still on my face, so he finally took pity.

"Don't worry beautiful, I speak many languages, including English."

I was immediately relieved.

"That was just hello in isiZulu," he informed me, "but please, where are my manners? I am D'marco Ibo," said the well-dressed linguist as he placed his hand over the breast pocket of his silk grey suit. He then gestured to the towering man standing next to him. "This is my associate Zuri Dyakov."

Zuri smiled.

The two of them asked us what we were doing in Cape Town, and I explained to them about the apprenticeship—and also about how we scored a stay in a four-star timeshare with our professor.

D'marco seemed genuinely interested—especially by

the last part.

But about a few minutes into the conversation, I happened to look up, and could see Professor Liu pacing. She'd been on her cellphone this whole time—visibly flustered.

When the professor finally ended the call, she just stood there with a blank expression on her face. I wondered if she were okay until oddly, without any warning, she started for the street exit. Okay, now she was *running* towards the street exit.

Did she forget that Beth and I were with her? I called after her.

"Hey! Professor Liu?"

She stopped before swiveling around.

"Oh, oh there you are." Her eyes darted to D'marco. "I was...uh...just looking for you."

Was it me, or was Professor Liu sweating pretty profusely?

Beth must've noticed it as well. "Aye Professor, are you feeling okay there?"

"Hunh?" Professor Liu's erratic breathing grew heavier and heavier as D'marco and his associate slowly approached her sides.

D'marco was the closest to her.

"Mei-Ying, you really look like you could use some rest."

What? They know each other?

"Actually D'marco, I'm fine." Professor Liu spoke calmly. "It's just that, I have to take these two students somewhere they can get some rest, and then I can meet up with you later. Okay?" She turned to me and Beth, tightly gripping my wrist. "Let's go ladies." Professor Liu tried to make another swift turn, but Zuri cut us off—his pectoral muscles suddenly becoming visible through his thin, easily seen through shirt.

"Mei-Ying," Zuri began, "where are you going in such a hurry?"

"My thoughts exactly," added D'marco. "I thought we could *all* go somewhere and have a little chat." I froze as D'marco walked around the professor. I didn't like the way they were closing in on her, and I didn't like the tone of their voices either.

D'marco must've noticed how uncomfortable Beth and I were getting so he backed off.

"My apologies ladies. Mei-Ying—I mean—your professor and I did have some very important business to discuss, but clearly it can wait. You know what—how about I take you lovely ladies on a tour of Cape Town? Would you like that?"

I was hesitant. Beth was not. "Yes! We would absolutely love that!" It seemed as if Professor Liu were about to say something, but D'marco cut her off.

"Follow me," announced the man in the brand name suit. D'marco put his arm around my shoulders and led us back to the tarmac. Zuri walked arm-in-arm with Beth and Professor Liu.

I nervously looked out onto the runway that we'd just landed on. Apparently the tour he was taking us on was going to be above ground—*way* above ground. And I didn't know whether to be worried or excited.

D'marco asked Beth and I to wait by the entrance while he, Zuri and for some reason Professor Liu went ahead to take care of some paperwork for the private tour. I had to admit that I was somewhat wary of

D'marco. Of course, my fears weren't exactly quelled by the abnormally large stack of bills he pulled out from the shiny, silver clip in his pants pocket.

As I waited next to the glass doors that connected the airport to the runway, I noticed a couple of trucks parked out on the tarmac, and I couldn't believe what I saw on one of the truck's backs.

"Hey Beth, look!"

There on the cargo bed of the pickup was an actual real life lion! Granted, he was caged and asleep, but nonetheless awe-inspiring. I wondered what he had been brought here for.

I tried to remember if I had packed my camera in my canvas messenger bag. I unhooked the front latch and saw that my camera was right there—well, technically it wasn't *my* camera. The student newspaper department had loaned it to me for this trip.

Still, after a couple of other cargo trucks passed, I looked around to see if anyone was watching, then swung my bag around my back, and casually walked onto the runway.

Beth freaked.

"Kay!" She yelled at me in a loud whisper. "What are you *doing?*"

I ignored her and ran out ahead. "This could be great for the story," I shouted back behind me. I told Beth before I left that I was going to write a feature for the student paper about my experience here. Maybe this would be part of it.

Beth sounded annoyed. "Kay, will you *please* be careful?"

I chuckled. Beth wasn't usually the worry wart. That

was primarily my department. But for a chance to see a real-life lion up-close, I didn't care about the risk.

"It'll just take a minute Beth. I want to get a quick photo before they come back."

I checked again to make sure no one was watching, then ran the last few steps to the back of the pick-up. If there had been enough room in there I probably wouldn't have thought twice about climbing in, but I immediately saw that I wouldn't be able to fit.

The jungle king was sound asleep, yet I was still thankful that his massive paws were busy resting on top of each other—because he could easily fit his deathly, claw-filled swatters through the wide bars of the cage should he wake up.

My adrenaline peaked a little. Excited, I snapped a few photos as I watched the steady rise and fall of his beautiful golden body. Then I slowly inched the camera forward through the bars. There was still plenty of daylight, and I knew I could get a few good close-ups without having to use the flash—and risk waking this gorgeous creature up.

He just looked so peaceful.

I turned around and peered over my shoulder at Beth. She really had to see this up close.

It was incredible.

I whistled to get Beth's attention. But as I waved, a horrified expression came over her face, and she seemed to be nearly paralyzed. That's when everything went very silent, and then…

Boom!

A green and black cargo truck had just crashed head on into a stack of empty crates—barely missing my body.

I looked back at Beth and realized I had better get out of here before security comes over to check out the scene—and find *me* trespassing instead. I quickly stuffed the loaner camera into the padded case in my canvas carry-on, then zipped it closed and turned around to rejoin my party.

But I would never make it.

And because it was so fast—the fire—the screams—the scorching heat of it all, I almost didn't believe it was really happening. But it was.

KA BOOM! BOOM! BOOM!

It wasn't just a crash this time. It was an actual explosion. I could tell because of the way I went flying through the air, and because I heard the sound of my head crack as it hit the ground when I landed on it.

I could feel the blood pouring down the side of my ears, and I wondered if it were from the impact of the fall, or from the blood clogging my ears that was the reason why I couldn't hear Beth screaming my name anymore.

I could only see her mouth moving, and even that was becoming blurry.

I lie still where I landed and slowly rolled my head to the side to see the airport security units speeding in. I wondered if I would still be conscious by the time they reached me.

I blinked through my tearing eyes at the hazy scene that was rapidly swirling. Everything I saw was turning sideways—the planes—the trucks—the people. I thought the explosion had rocked everything on its side, but it was just me.

And as I lie there motionless, I saw a pair of grey slacks walking towards me. I painfully managed to tilt my head centered, just in time to see who was now towering over me.

It was D'marco.

He smiled at me—in a way that sent a chill throughout my body, and the tears in my eyes down the sides of my cheeks.

That was the last thing I remembered before everything went black.

That was the last thing I remembered before I realized I'd never see Beth, my mom, my dad or even Callum, ever…ever again.

PART 2

7. Taken

Side to side. Side to side. Side to side. It was the methodic rocking of my body that made me aware I'd been stuffed into someone's trunk. And, it was the searing pain in the side of my head that let me know I wasn't dreaming—I wasn't going to wake up from this.

I'd really been in an explosion, and at some point, I'd actually been taken. My heart was in my throat and I'd never been so genuinely scared in my entire life.

I tried to scream for help, but there was something around my mouth that had been tied into a knot in the back of my head.

My heart was pounding so fast I thought I was going to throw up on myself. But I was afraid to think what my captors might do if I made a mess. So I took in several deep breaths through my nose to try to ease the nausea the fear was causing.

I could barely see anything in the darkness as I lay on my side in the small cramped space. The only thing I could make out was that the trunk top above me wasn't solid—it fell in at certain parts as if it were made of cloth. I thought for a moment. My headache was splitting my concentration, but I knew I had to focus.

I was desperate to know how long we'd been travelling, where I was being taken, and how long I'd been unconscious. My hands were tied so I couldn't reach the cellphone in the messenger bag that was still around my shoulder. I tried to think. There had to be some way I could alert someone to where I was.

I thought about the TV shows Beth used to watch in the dorm room. There was always some type of crime show where someone had been kidnapped, and that person was smart enough to kick out the taillights—to alert other cars on the highway that something was wrong. Yes! That's it Kay. Kick out the taillights and someone will call the police.

Though my hands were tied, my legs were free. I tried to figure out which way I was facing—towards the taillights, or towards the wall behind the seats of the vehicle. I definitely didn't want to start kicking in the wrong direction.

But the constant rocking was confusing me, so I tried to feel around with my foot for something that felt as if it could be knocked out. Finally, I felt something hollow and kicked as hard as I could.

I screamed.

The jolt sent a sharp shot of pain through my foot and up my leg, and I was pretty sure that one or both extremities were now fractured.

I reached out towards the intense throbbing, but as soon as I did the vehicle stopped. Whoever had taken me must've heard me kick towards the back of their seats and was probably *furious*.

I thought about the hundreds of fates that could await me, but I stopped running through them when I heard the engine shut off. The next thing I heard was footsteps—which abruptly stopped.

It wasn't long before someone threw back the dark, cloth cover as light poured over my fetal body, causing me to squint to protect my eyes, which had been sequestered in the dark for hours.

Despite being too afraid to move, my deep, penetrating urge to know where I was gave me just enough strength to painfully prop myself up—gradually lifting my head in the hopes that I could identify my new location. But when I finally looked out, I had a hard time believing my eyes.

Because for miles and miles on end, all I could see were orange stretches of sand—sand dunes and sandy plateaus. I wasn't in Cape Town anymore. I wasn't anywhere near a populated city.

I was in the desert.

The sun was low on the horizon, but I couldn't tell whether it was sunrise or sunset. Still, the orange sand matched the pink, purple and tangerine sky; and under any other circumstances I may have been able to appreciate its beauty.

The fog in my head started to clear, and I began to remember the sick, twisted look on D'marco's face before I had passed out. It left no doubt in my mind that he was the one who had taken me, but what I still didn't know was *why*.

As I continued to look in the only direction my sore body would allow me to turn, I saw a dark green, medium-sized pickup truck with a thick, black, cloth cover on its back approaching us. Correction—*two* medium-sized pickup trucks with cloth covers on their backs were heading directly toward us.

My heart double pumped with excitement. Could it be some sort of desert police? Did Beth and Professor Liu call the authorities and send someone to search for me?

I hadn't allowed myself too much false hope, when the very blue eyed captor I suspected walked around to where I was, turned his back, and lit a cigarette. I slouched back down and gave up hope that it was a rescue convoy, for D'marco was too at ease to be about to face the police.

Tears rolled down my face as I grappled with the reality of my current situation. I had nowhere to run, and even if I did, there was absolutely no way I could survive on my own in the middle of the desert.

The sweltering, arid air parched my suffering throat. And I coughed before slowly raising my hand to my still pulsating head, only to feel the dried blood that was now matted in my hair.

The two vehicles we awaited arrived at the same time, causing D'marco to put out his cigarette to prepare to meet them.

No one said anything, but I still held my breath as I watched the driver of the first vehicle carefully step out and slowly walk around to the back of his truck. He smiled as he pulled back the familiar cloth cover from his open trunk, and hauled out a six-foot long, faded black duffle bag. Aside from appearing incredibly heavy, I noted that it had something ivory-colored and pointed sticking out of its ends.

The driver handed the package to D'marco who almost fell over from the weight of it.

Still, D'marco lifted up the eerie looking body bag and shoved it into the back with me. More of the six-foot package was hanging out than was actually in the trunk, so he pushed it in further—not bothering to look at me even once.

Part of me wanted to demand answers. The other part was too afraid to speak—not that I *could* through the tight rag fitted around my mouth.

After the first driver had climbed back inside his vehicle, the second driver pulled up closer; stopped, and went around per procedure to the back. *Please* let them be finished soon, I thought to myself. Please let *this* be over soon, I added in my head.

Not knowing what was going on—what these criminals were up to, was worse than actually knowing what my final fate would be. I waited for someone to acknowledge me, to realize that I was still here. Maybe they'd just forgotten—didn't even know, and would just cut me loose somewhere.

Instead, the second driver spit in my direction—tobacco colored saliva that had built up in his mouth that he couldn't swallow. Then, without even looking, he threw back the second truck's cloth covering, and what I saw underneath it caused a startled sound to escape me.

It was Professor Liu.

She was unconscious and tied up just as I was. Thankfully, she didn't appear injured, but she also didn't seem like she would be conscious any time soon. The second driver pushed her aside, and pulled out yet another of the same type of duffle bag that the first driver had surrendered.

Nothing was making sense. I thought that one of D'marco's associates had caused the explosion to give him an opportunity to kidnap me—that he had some sick plan for me that I should have seen coming from all of the warnings my parents had given me about the dangers of letting my guard down with strangers. But now Professor Liu was a part of it, and I had a feeling that whatever I was wrapped up in was bigger than anything I could have possibly imagined.

D'marco spoke to both drivers in a language I didn't understand and then got back into the truck we had arrived in.

I felt the engine turn on as the two other vehicles pulled out ahead of us. We all seemed to be heading in the same direction, and although I desperately wished someone would just *talk* to me, I knew there was nothing I could do but wait to find out where they were taking us.

As the trucks continued to drive along the sun-drenched desert, I could feel my eyes getting heavy as my vision began to blur. Shortly after, my body slumped over again.

Splash! I actually heard it before I felt the piercingly cold bucket-shower crash onto my face. I shot up, wiping my eyes—adrenaline running through me.

"Where am I??"

I swiveled around. The pounding of my heart increased as I took in the frighteningly large field of dirt I'd awoken in with the dying patches of dry, yellowing grass.

"Sumuka!"

I finished wiping my eyes to find a man with a very long rifle slung around his shoulder by the strap. He was raising his hand toward the handle and yelling at me.

Instinctively, I backed up on the now muddied terrain, flinching from the pain in my foot. But it didn't stop me from noticing that I was encircled by a cluster of about a dozen, crooked, Y shaped trees.

Outside the cluster were a few hole-ridden tents.

The man with the rifle came closer. He shouted again in a language that was identifiably African—but he wasn't using the same accent D'marco used when he'd spoken in isiZulu. This was something different.

"Sumuka! Zvino!"

My body jumped—though still on the ground—at the sound of his voice, scaring me so badly I stuttered. "I d...don't...understand. I don't...speak..." My teeth were clattering together, and I wasn't sure I was comprehensible.

Comprehensible or not, the man with the rifle lifted it shoulder level and took aim at me. "Sumuka! Zvino!"

"Get up!" My head whipped around. The voice had come from a young woman about my age. She had skin the color of dark satin—smooth and radiant, and her hair was cropped into low twisting curls. She was almost my size, but somewhat more petite.

I noticed that she was holding a pile of branches in her arms, but she wasn't paying attention to the burden she held on to. Instead, she was pleading with me in a different though still unfamiliar African accent. "Get up! Please—he's telling you to get up!"

"Oh!" I put my weight on my hands and pushed myself up. "Owww!" I'd accidentally put some of the weight on the fractured foot and immediately felt it. "Ow! Ow! Ow!"

"Dzikma! Dzikma!"

"I don't understand!" I couldn't understand why he kept yelling at me.

The young woman translated for me again. She

126

whispered, "He's telling you to be quiet." And I saw in the man's eyes that it wasn't an optional directive, so I didn't ask any follow-ups.

I guessed that my much needed interpreter had been here for a while because she didn't seem nearly as frightened as I did. Actually, the only fear she showed was the apparent fear for my own safety—I obviously didn't know how things worked around here. I thought about it. Around here, *where?*

I looked out beyond the crooked, Y shaped trees, and the tents with the holes in them. About a hundred yards away was a river. But closer to us was a large dirt clearing with…I gasped. I didn't want to see it, but I couldn't pull my eyes away.

It was a graveyard—a complete and total graveyard. Animal bones and carcasses littered the ground. The bodies were so decayed that I couldn't even tell what some of them once were. But when I saw the largest of the skeletons—it all came together.

Lines and lines of elephant tusks covered the ground, and wooden sticks stuck out of the dirt like graveyard markers. I didn't have to guess about it—this was a poacher's camp. I'd heard about them, but I didn't think that I'd ever see one. It certainly wasn't something I ever *wanted* to see. Yet here I was—in a field full of ivory—in a field full of death.

And I knew why I was here. We'd been taken to help these criminals in their illegal trade. Families had been torn apart by poachers—by their wars—the ones they both knowingly and unknowingly helped finance. Men, women and children had been taken away from their homes to fight—to kill—for what? For someone's leather purse? For someone's furry coat? For a statue made of ivory?

I could feel the man with the rifle breathing down my back. I turned around in a fury.

"I won't help you! You can't make me! I'd rather die than be a part of *this*!" The poacher must've understood me because he promptly raised his gun and took aim.

Of course, I immediately regretted my words and just desperately wanted to run, but I realized there was no place I could run *to*—no place I could hide. I hung my head. I couldn't believe that this was it—that this was how my life was going to end.

Emotionless tears fell down my cheeks as I saw my parents' faces in my head. I'd never get to tell them how sorry I was for the way I acted back in New York. I'd never get to do a lot of things now. I heard the poacher cock his weapon, and I waited for the last sound that I would ever hear.

"Mira!" It was my intercessor. She'd run in between me and the gun; hands raised in the air. "Mira! Anoda Kubatsira!"

I had no idea what she was saying, but it sounded like she was saving my life. The armed man looked at me with suspicion in his eyes. "Ona—ari kuenda," she said. My short haired friend put her hands on my back, and pushed me towards the muddy patch she'd found me in.

The weapon wielding poacher followed us with his eyes—and with the barrel of his rifled gun, until he was satisfied I assumed, that we'd done whatever my rescuer had said.

Once back at our original location, the young woman picked up the pile of tree branches she'd obviously dropped to come to my rescue, and I helped.

But as soon as the rifle owner turned his back, I threw the branches to the ground and took note of what I was dealing with. I counted eight armed men, three exhausted looking women, and several children with dirt on their faces and tears in their eyes.

The children were plucking feathers from birds that were still alive. Poachers were behind them—striking each child that tried to resist harming the poor little creatures.

Two of the exhausted looking women were beating out animal skins for dust. The third woman was sweeping strewn about animal remains. The smell was so rancid that I had to breathe through my mouth to keep from passing out. I shook my head. There was absolutely no way this was going to be my life.

I took another look around. No one was watching. Maybe now I could make a run for it after all. "Come on." I grabbed the hand of the one who just saved my life, and sprinted. I made it exactly one step before I fell face down on the ground.

The young woman hadn't moved an inch—which is why I guess I stumbled while trying to run for two. Instead of moving, she just watched me in bewilderment.

"What are you doing?" She asked me as she curiously turned her head to the side.

"What do you *mean* what am I doing??" I suddenly remembered that we were surrounded by weapons, so I lowered my voice. "We have to get out of here. *Now*— while no one is looking!"

The young woman huffed as she shifted the weight of the branches she was holding. "Clearly I have been here quite a bit longer than you. Do you truly think it has never occurred to me to run?"

I didn't answer. That made her frown.

"Tell me, have you even surveyed the area? There's open space everywhere. How far do you believe you will get before someone sees you? You *do* know what they will do to you when they catch you—yes?"

Yes. I knew. But I was desperate. "Well then, what are we going to do?"

"*We*," she emphasized we as if I were an integral part of the plan, "are going to wait."

"Wait for what?" I asked, genuinely confused.

The young woman looked up. "The sign."

Oh *great*. Either this girl had some incredible master plan up her sleeve, or she was a complete nut job. But she'd kept me alive so far, so I figured the least I could do was to give her the benefit of the doubt.

One of the poachers was approaching us, so I didn't ask any more questions about it. I decided to change the subject.

"What's your name?"

The beautifully dark-skinned girl with the short, curly hair bowed as she answered, "I am Tuki."

"Oh." I'd never heard the name before, but somehow I thought it fit her.

"And yours?"

"Kay."

"I see." Tuki looked back at the patrolling riflemen. "Do you know how to make a fire Kay?"

"No."

Tuki handed me some of her branches. "Well then Kay, you are going to learn, and you are going to learn *quickly."*

Tuki spent the rest of the day showing me what had to be done around the illegal poaching camp, and I spent the rest of the day screwing up—and getting yelled at by men with deadly weapons.

By the time sundown finally came around, I could barely move my arms or legs anymore—from all of the beating of animal skins and carrying of elephant tusks from one side of the camp to the other. The only reason I was able to get anything done at all was because Tuki had untied the ivory bow in my hair to wrap my foot and ankle in. She also made a makeshift crutch for me to use, but suggested I only use it when eyes weren't on me—she feared my displaying too much weakness.

Still, my skinny muscles were involuntarily shaking during the transport of the last load, and I accidentally dropped one of the ivory tusks on the ground. That resulted in my being hit on the side of the head with the butt of one of the poacher's rifles. It hurt—of course— but that's not really why I suddenly began to cry. It was just that, aside from the sheer shock of it all, I'd never actually witnessed a human being intentionally causing pain to another being.

The ability to do so bewildered me.

Then again, as I looked around at the decomposing elephant flesh, and at the torture the poachers were making the young children perform, I became less and less naïve about the evil some people were capable of. I remembered the horrible killings I'd read about in the airplane article, and suddenly I began to shake.

Tuki saw me, and showed me a place on the dirt in the center of the camp where I could sleep—a place where the poachers would keep a close watch on us in case anyone thought about running during the night.

But I wasn't thinking about running tonight. I was thinking about Mom and Dad, and Beth and Callum. I looked over at the little spot in the dirt, which would soon be the same place where my usually frightening dreams would be unexpectedly welcomed—if only for the familiar faces I knew they would contain. So I closed my eyes and hoped that I would wake up somewhere else, if only for the night—and I did.

There, in my subconscious, I lie motionless—that is until the haze finally began to clear. And when it did, I could clearly see the incredible majestic lion walking towards me. His mane was blowing around him, and I wanted nothing more than to reach out and touch it.

Completely mesmerized, I stretched my hand as far as I could—though my sore body restrained me.

It must've known what I wanted because it came closer, and just when the beautiful lion was inches away from my face, it bared its ferocious teeth, and let out a roar that vibrated throughout my entire body.

Suddenly, the lion burst into flames—strangely controlled flames that seemed to be taking shape. I wasn't the least bit surprised when the shape that it formed fit perfectly around me.

It was then that I knew what this was all for—what this all meant.

Two familiar faces waved at me through the flames that surrounded me, and I waved back at the two people who had raised me. I told them not to be sad, and that I would try to return soon. But the heartbeat of their sorrow let me know that soon...or ever, wasn't meant to be.

8. Three, Two, One

"Please! You must get up!" Tuki was shaking me—frantic. The poacher with the evil grin looked more than ready to shoot as he aimed the barrel of his gun where I slept.

I jerked up. "What?? What did I do??" The rifleman frowned. He seemed to contemplate something for a moment, but finally he just groaned and walked away.

Tuki let out the long breath she'd been holding before she scowled at me.

"He almost killed you."

"Why?" I asked, perplexed—still too dazed and still too half-asleep to grasp the severity of what had just occurred.

"You are not allowed to sleep longer than they," Tuki informed me.

"Oh."

I sat up taller as I wiped the muck off the back of my blouse. I was practically covered in it from having slept in the dirt. But when I'd gotten as much of it off as possible, I quickly shook the rest of it out my hair as Tuki helped me to my feet.

Hmm. I noticed that the pain in my foot wasn't as bad as it was yesterday. Either Tuki cut off all my circulation with her makeshift bandage, or the injury wasn't as serious as I thought. I wiggled my toes to make sure all lower systems were a go. Tuki huffed.

"Come Kay. There is much work that must begin if we are to remain useful."

By useful I gathered she meant alive. But that's not all I wanted for today—to just stay alive. Yesterday I did whatever I had to, to get by. Today, I had to get out of here—no matter the cost. I wanted to see my family again. I wanted to see my friends.

And I was just about to ask Tuki about the escape plan she had—the one that involved waiting for "the sign," when I heard two voices arguing. One voice I recognized immediately. It was Professor Liu. The terror in her voice made me want to get a closer listen, so I picked up a nearby animal skin and pretended to beat it out behind one of the trees large enough to be concealed by.

"Please...please D'marco...it's not my fault." Professor Liu was practically cowering while she spoke. "I was on the phone with the buyer in New York. I called him again when we landed. He was *supposed* to be at the airport—*with* the money for the ivory. Please believe me D'marco, I wouldn't try to pull something like this with students in my care." She paused. "I wouldn't try to pull something like this over *you*." She trembled.

The air grew tense as D'marco sauntered forward.

"I wish I could believe you Mei-Ying, but *unfortunately...*"

D'marco snapped his fingers then.

Right before he cut his eyes abruptly up—at *me*.

I dropped the animal skin I'd been holding and felt the flight reflex activate my muscles. I thought I'd been well hidden, but obviously not well hidden enough.

I turned to run. One yard. Two yards. Crash! I smacked face forward into something hard. It was the muscle-filled chest of Zuri—D'marco's right hand associate. He grabbed me by the hair and dragged me to the clearing where D'marco and Professor Liu had been standing.

There, Zuri threw me to the ground, and I scrambled to my feet as I stood in front of the mad man who had kidnapped me.

"Ah, there she is. My collegiate sleeping beauty. You know, it really isn't nice to eavesdrop, but manners aside, your professor here tells me *so* much about you. I hear you're quite the student. Your parents must be incredibly proud."

I ignored his remarks—refusing to engage the psycho criminal. "I hope you'll forgive me, my beautiful Kay, but I had to bring you with us—for motivational purposes of course; nothing personal. You see, your professor here made a very specific request of me. A request above and beyond her usual fine and exotic imports. She wanted to get involved in something she didn't seem to understand. And now we've made a deal that *I* came through on, but that she…well, let's say fell somewhat short of financially. Tell me," D'marco began thoughtlessly scratching the bottom of his chin. "What do you think should happen to someone who doesn't keep their promises Kay?"

Professor Liu's eyes widened as if she were afraid of what I might suggest. I remained silent.

D'marco persisted, "You see, I *always* come through on my promises because I *always* find what I am looking for. But it appears that *some* people need more motivation than others.

For instance, if I told your professor that she only had fifteen seconds to contact the buyer she promised me, before she was *single-handedly* responsible for the end of your very life, well, I think that might be somewhat motivating."

At that moment, D'marco reached for Zuri's rifle while excruciatingly gripping me by my arm—I yelped.

Professor Liu dropped to her knees—pleading. "Don't hurt her D'marco *please*. I don't know how to contact him."

"Fourteen seconds..."

"I...I'm sorry Kay. I didn't mean for this to happen."

"Twelve seconds..."

Professor Liu didn't even bother to reach for her cellphone to try calling the buyer again. She knew that it was pointless, so she just sobbed.

Between being blasted into the air by the jeep collision, being threatened in front of that girl Tuki last night, and now *this*, I'd had more brushes with death in the last 48 hours than I'd ever had in my entire lifetime. Still, a familiar heartbeat sounded in the hollow cave of my chest as the wretched man continued to count down.

"Five seconds..."

I closed my eyes.

"Three...two...one."

D'marco lifted the rifle at the same time that the deafening sound came from the trees. It was coming from every single direction, and you could even feel it vibrating through your insides. It was as if a hundred horns were sounding at once—so intense I thought my ears might bleed. I covered them.

I don't know when she arrived by my side, but Tuki was standing next to me when the horns sounded for the second time. "What *is* that?" I yelled over the blaring noise.

"*That*...is the sign," Tuki replied.

"The sign for *what*??" I actually didn't know that I really cared, seeing as how it had caused a sudden reprieve in my still standing death sentence. Tuki ignored both me and my question, and became intensely focused on something of her own.

"Get ready."

Tuki turned back to one of the weary women who had been captive with us. She nodded once.

All of the sudden, the frail older woman sprung to life—dropping the carcasses she'd been holding so that she could reach inside of her light blue tattered dress. I watched the woman pull out what looked to be a brown glass soda bottle. She held it firmly in her grip.

D'marco was still distracted by the cacophony—as was everyone else—when Tuki ducked and ran behind the very tree I was hiding behind earlier. My mouth dropped as Tuki lowered to the ground and began to dig.

What she pulled up were several dusty glass bottles—like the one the woman with the tattered dress was clinging to. When Tuki returned, she handed me one of the bottles with a piece of cloth, and smiled at me as she rested her hand on my shoulder. "Are you ready?"

"Ready for *what*??" I had no idea what was going on.

Tuki looked back at the two other women on the left

side of the camp. They too began to approach us with liquid-filled bottles in their hands.

As soon as we were all gathered, the horns sounded for a third time, and when they did, several flocks of green and yellow birds ascended to the air. That's when the horns ceased, and when the greedy, evil twinkle in all of the poachers' eyes sparked at the sight of the defenseless creatures.

In unison, each of the poachers pointed their rifles toward the sky. In unison, all of the kidnapped women—except me—removed the caps from their glass bottles and dipped their cloths into the colorless liquid inside.

The poachers began to shoot, and I finally realized what was about to happen—I also realized that it was hopeless. The number of men with weapons outnumbered us two to one. There was no way we could survive what Tuki had planned.

But as I looked around the gruesome camp, I realized I was outnumbered by something other than weapons. I was outnumbered by the much braver women who actually thought we could get through this. I thought about the high school students I read about on the plane—the ones who had fought off dozens of gun wielders with just sticks and stones. I thought about the courage that that took—and the courage that I was apparently lacking.

The women got ready, and without thinking I mimicked their every move, trying desperately to keep from fumbling. Tuki locked eyes with each one of us before silently counting down from three.

When Tuki reached the last number, we all raised our liquid soaked cloths into the air, and planted them square around the noses and mouths of the armed men in front of us.

Just like that, five of the goons fell to the floor. They were completely knocked out by the chloroform fumes—but I knew that they wouldn't be out for long. We had to make our next move quickly.

By some miracle, the other poachers were still so busy shooting into the sky that they hadn't noticed their fallen associates. This time Tuki didn't have to count. We all repeated our actions to the remaining goons who fell to the ground. Success—I thought.

My nerves reached a peak when I realized that I only counted ten unconscious. There were two armed men missing.

This was dangerous.

I turned around to alert our leader, but it was too late. The final two armed men were already running towards us; closing in—only 20 feet away.

I panicked.

I froze like a deer caught in headlights. But Tuki didn't. She spun around like a professional ice skater, and stuck out her leg as she lowered herself to the ground. Thud! The first guy's legs flew straight into the air—tripping over Tuki's leg. I had to restrain myself from clapping when the thug landed flat on his back. He groaned, but didn't get up.

Thankfully, the second poacher wasn't carrying his rifle. He took a close swing at Tuki but missed. Within moments they were engaged in the type of hand-to-hand combat that you only saw in movies.

Tuki was swift, like a gazelle, and was doing a type of martial arts I'd never seen before.

Right kick! Backflip! Duck!

Where did she learn how to move like that?

The large goon took his final swing—and miss—as Tuki bent her knees and let him roll over her shoulder as she tossed him to the ground. She stood up. He was down for the count. Tuki turned back towards the three other women who were involved in the escape.

"We must get the children." It was the fragile matron I'd seen earlier—the one with the tattered dress.

"Yes, and someone must disable the trucks. They cannot be able to follow us too soon." The second woman who spoke, I'd never had a conversation with, but in this moment, there was no denying our camaraderie.

I jumped in. "I'll go with you."

Everyone dispersed. Tuki helped locate the children. The two others headed for the vehicles. And I was just about to join the truck group when I felt something harsh grasp my right ankle. I was suddenly being yanked to the ground.

It was D'marco. Whoever had him as their target, hadn't knocked him completely out with the fume emitting cloths. He looked groggy—and *angry*.

D'marco climbed up my waist as I struggled on the ground to break free. I searched around for a rock, a branch, or anything I could've used to strike back, but D'marco had already made his way up to my throat.

I coughed as he pressed down on the rifle he was holding horizontally across my neck. My eyes searched wildly for help, and that's when I saw Professor Liu standing over me. I couldn't speak, but I begged for assistance with the expression written across my face. I expected her to step in. She didn't. Instead, Professor Liu

it quite a risk to be running in such open terrain.

Though I had jogged every morning back in New York—and had even run track in high school, I was in no way prepared for the dash we were now making for our lives. That's probably why I was the first to tire when we finally reached the thin cluster of crookedly shaped trees in the middle of the safari-like plain.

Tuki noticed everyone lagging behind, so she signaled that we could stop. I used the opportunity to direct my breathless frustrations at this girl who never seemed to tire.

"Hey—*Tuki* are we just...running, or do you have any idea where we're going? Is there an embassy or something, or are we just going to the first town we see?"

Tuki tilted her head to the side—in a way that I'd grown accustomed to. Apparently everything I said was an enigma to her. Tuki once again spoke slowly— something I noticed she only seemed to do—or only felt she *had* to do with me.

"We cannot go to any town Kay. They have seen your face now. Their network is a large one, and they will hunt you down. They will search the area around the camp first, and then they will travel to every city until they find the ones who disabled them—until they find the ones who could expose too much."

Great. I knew that stupid truck sinking plan was a bad idea. "So what are we going to do then? Just hide out in the jungle for the rest of our lives?" I sarcastically nodded towards an extreme stretch of green mountains off in the distance.

Tuki smiled. She seemed to do that no matter what the situation.

"I know a place," Tuki replied. She then casually stretched out her arms as if she'd just finished her usual workout, and proceeded to lie down on the yellowish-green grass that we all exhaustedly stood upon. "We will rest here tonight. Our journey is still quite long, so we will take turns sleeping. Kay, take the first watch. Wake me when the sun is fully to the West."

I didn't say anything and Tuki knew why. She sighed. "To the left Kay."

I mumbled under my breath—why couldn't she have just said that to begin with?

I don't know why, but I got the feeling that she'd sometimes been difficult with me these past few days on purpose; as if Tuki were trying to teach me some valuable lesson she thought I had to learn.

Still, I couldn't stop thinking that if I'd grown up with a sister our relationship probably would've been something like mine and Tuki's. Perhaps it was because of the way she genuinely seemed to care about everyone here.

That's partly why I was so grateful that she had been at the camp when I arrived. So I kept watch as Tuki had asked, and set out to make a fire—again as Tuki had taught me—while the rest of the group got some shut eye. But the sun had fully disappeared into the West, and reappeared in the East while I was still awake.

I guess I'd just been way too wired to go to sleep.

Actually, come to think of it, the last perfectly peaceful night's sleep I had was the night I received the letter. It was the one from the *Sunday Times* informing me that I'd been chosen for the apprenticeship in South Africa.

If only I'd known then what I would truly end up

being chosen *for*!

When Tuki awoke, she thanked me for taking everyone's shifts, and then led us in a direction that she said was northwest. We walked through golden covered wheat fields with beautiful blue skies and fluffy, cotton clouds that kept us company.

I watched as the land color continually changed around us, and wasn't surprised when the earth turned into a rose-colored clay whose matching pink skies rippled into lavender. The pastel colors in the air perfectly framed the setting sun, while the land below was soft beneath our feet. I could even smell the clay-filled water that had been soaked up by the unused road we now travelled on.

Our journey, though long, soon welcomed us to citrine yellow plains—with small growing bushes and tall reaching trees. This was where Tuki said we had to be extra careful—because we were in lion territory now.

We'd each made walking sticks out of long branches before we left our first and only resting place. I was sure that it wouldn't be enough to fight off any wild beasts—but we felt better holding on to them.

"They are more afraid of you than you are of them," Tuki assured us. "But keep watch," she added—*un*reassuring us.

As we walked out the tall grass, our surroundings turned desert-like—but not quite like the beautiful sandy orange desert I was taken through on my way to the poacher's camp.

This desert was bare and scary looking—malnourished trees and dried grey dirt cracked with every step. Vultures circled the air, spying some poor creature below. And even though I didn't see anything or anyone else around,

145

I couldn't shake the feeling that we were being followed.

Tuki finally slowed down, and it was a good thing too. My palms had become sweaty, and my temperature was on the rise. Was it normal to come down with something in perfectly warm weather? Maybe it was just exhaustion. I probably should've closed my eyes for at least an hour when I had the chance.

As we approached what seemed to be jungle region ahead, Tuki yelled out something in one of the languages that I didn't understand.

She signaled for everyone to stop, but for some reason—despite how tired I was—I couldn't make my legs cease moving.

"Kay—you must stop!"

I tried, but my brain signals must've been tripping up its wiring because instead of stopping, I sped up. "Kay! I said you must stop *here*!"

I wanted to. I desperately wanted to stop, but now I was running.

As I picked up speed, I could tell that Tuki wasn't the only one calling my name. It was the entire group; even the children. They screamed.

"Kay! Kay! Watch out!"

9. Paradise

They say that if you're still alive, and you see a bright white light, you probably shouldn't walk into it. But when I saw the shinning beacon in the midst of the thick, luring jungle ahead, I instantly lost control of my body and was suddenly sprinting forward on auto-pilot.

One yard, two yards, ten, twenty, a hundred. I ran so hard my lungs began to hurt—but that wasn't what finally stopped me.

What halted my course was the incredibly majestic lion that guarded its entrance. I didn't fear it, and I didn't doubt whether it would let me enter.

It had to.

I had seen what was ahead in my dreams. I had even had glimpses of it while wide awake. And now, here and fully conscious, it was time to see it with my own present eyes.

Tuki and the others finally reached me, and I turned around and smiled.

"It's okay Tuki. It won't hurt me."

"What won't hurt you, you crazy American?"

I gestured behind me. Tuki investigated with raised eyebrows only to see that the lion was gone.

It had disappeared—possibly back into my imagination. But regardless of whether the beautiful creature had really been there or not, I'd been led here for a reason.

I knew now that it was time.

"Did you not hear me calling you? I demanded you stop for a reason. This area is protected. You could have been killed."

I ignored her. I stood where I'd been beckoned to come, and looked at the deeply covered, narrow entryway I now faced. Thousands and thousands of branches sprawled out their apple green leaves, climbing so high into the sky that only through the smallest opening above did the sun create a spotlight before me. It echoed outwards onto the mile-long, leaf-littered path ahead. Its densely filled green garden closing off the outside world, gave only one direction to follow—forward.

I took one step.

I took another step.

I had no awareness of Tuki and the others behind me. I just listened to the crackling of leaves underneath my boots as I breathed in the warm, water dense air. I felt the hairs on my arms rise the closer inward I pushed, and smelled the wood and tree sap that awaited us at the end of the natural vine tunnel. It was intoxicating.

When we reached the clearing on the other end, there was nothing but the wide circle of chestnut brown ground before us. The round enclosure was encompassed by a dozen hundred-foot tall trees—mammoth layered leaves creating its canopy.

The ambience was set by the dimly lit surroundings. Soft intermittent sunrays peered through the trees like a rotating asterisk. And if it weren't for the diagonally reaching beams, I would have never even noticed the rising human figures fully covered in flora—who were steadily closing in on us.

They hardly made a sound—just the faintest rustle in the wind. And like guardians of the land, they descended upon us, drawing lines in the dirt, daring us to pass.

Tuki came to the front and bowed her head before speaking. The clicking sound she made startled me when she spoke.

"Uxolo, Ngilahlekile."

One of the guardians stepped forward. For some reason, he spoke directly to me. "Uphumaphi?"

I looked to Tuki who spoke for me.

"Ipharadisi."

The camouflaged plant covered warriors studied me carefully, never deflecting to anyone else in the group, until the leader finally returned his attention to Tuki. He spoke with the same clicking sound Tuki made earlier— his on the second and third words of his response.

"Isibusiso, qonda ngqo."

Though I didn't understand anything they were saying, something about their exchange had been so familiar that it made my head throb trying to figure out why. I rubbed my aching temples as Tuki led us past the guarded way, and began guiding us through the approaching thicket ahead.

"Mommy, Daddy, I had a bad dream!" I was eight-years-old, and I knocked feverishly on my parents' bedroom door.

"It's open honey." My father's baritone voice flowed from the other side of the door.

I reached for the oval shaped doorknob and nudged the chiseled wooden door ajar.

"Wait!" My mother folded her arms in the queen size bed and narrowed her eyes. "What's the secret word Nanya?"

I bit my lip and tapped my little foot as I tried to remember—sounding it out slowly. "It's ooh...ooh..." I knew Mom was listening to see if I could make the click sound as she had taught me. "Uxolo! The secret word is uxolo Mommy!"

Mom clapped at my pronunciation and Dad joined in. "Good job Nanya. You may enter."

"Yay!"

Tuki guided the small children among us to the front of the group. Leaf by leaf, vine by vine, Tuki pulled back any obstacle in our weary group's way. We were near. I could feel it. There was something in the air that let me know that soon, all of my questions would be answered.

"Describe the dreams to Dr. Saunders Nanya."

My mother sat with me in the small office, in downtown Brooklyn. It was our third session with Dr. Saunders who had spent our previous two sessions talking with me about school, and asking me to describe my watercolor paintings to her.

"Mommy, do I have to?" I was missing third-grade assembly to sit on the therapist's couch that my mother had found. I didn't understand why I was there. I thought I was being punished for constantly waking my parents up with my nightmare-induced screaming.

"This is very important honey. I need you to see that

150

there is nothing to be afraid of. You're not going to wake up in some jungle fighting for your life. No lion is ever going to follow you home and lead you to your death. They're just nightmares honey. They're not real."

Dr. Saunders wrote down some notes and then turned her attention back to me. "Is this true sweetie? Have you really been dreaming about lions and jungles and…"

"Look!" Several of the children who had followed Tuki yelled out in delight. They were too far ahead for me to know what they beheld, but that would soon be resolved.

I pulled back the last gigantic jungle leaf and nearly lost my breath at the sight before me. It was just as in my dreams—but *real*.

I gawked at the entirely hidden, yet fully bustling village with towering African sculptures and life size lion statues. Men and women of all shapes and sizes moved up and down the open space—laughing and greeting each other, conversing and working away.

Huts, houses and jungle trees were adorned with gold, purple, red and green ornaments. Children danced in front of gem-stoned houses, and women were dressed in the most festive attire I'd ever seen. It was a colorfully vibrant getaway in full Christmas celebration mode.

"Tuki, what *is* all of this?"

Tuki's face brightened as she gestured for the children to go join the fun. The three women who'd travelled with us followed them—their maternal instincts kicking in I suppose after our arduous journey; probably not wanting to let the children out of their sight.

As for Tuki and I, we took our time making our way past several olive-colored grass huts. They were cylinder on the bottom but had tops fashioned like smooth Christmas trees—and were actually decorated as such. Their animal shaped glass ornaments shimmered in the setting sun.

It was all so wondrous to behold. It made me think about all the times Callum and I used to talk about travelling—where he'd been, where he wanted to go, where I wanted to go *with* him.

But that all seemed like a distant memory now.

As I looked around the secret village, I noticed a number of villagers who weren't dressed in festive attire at all. They had what looked to be handcrafted daggers hooked into leather belts around their waists, and it seemed as if they were doing rounds around the village— like some sort of security detail. I watched as they walked in perfectly straight lines—twenty yards that way, twenty yards back. It was on their second patrol that I couldn't hold the questions any longer.

"Tuki, where are we?"

The playfulness left her face as she looked up towards the clouds.

"We are in the garden that was created; the paradise that was forgotten. You will not find us on any map, and you cannot see us from any sky."

"Were you born here?" I asked—mesmerized.

"I was born of here, but I came the way most others were brought."

Intriguing. "In which way was that?"

I waited for her to speak as she made eye contact with the villagers around us. "Some were brought from war— some from persecution. Some from where there was no medicine, and some from where there were no schools.

Some are those who were forced to marry, and some are those who were raped. Some were brought from wide spread terror, and many were saved from death. We bring them all here so they will have peace."

"Like a refugee camp?"

"Like a place of refuge," Tuki clarified.

A light went off in my head. "The poacher's camp. You were so calm… You were there on purpose weren't you?"

Tuki nodded once, and it all started to come together.

"You're like a search and rescue crew."

"I suppose you could say that."

We continued to move towards a massive version of the cylinder huts that we were now in front of. It looked as if the entire village was heading into that structure— everyone holding candles and singing carols in languages I didn't understand.

"So then, you can help me get back home. You can help me get back to my family!"

It was then that she looked at me with her deeply apologetic eyes.

"I am sorry my Kay. But for the dozen who search for you—*hundreds* search for me, even as we speak. I cannot risk leading that kind of evil back to our village."

That sent me into a frenzy.

"So just tell me the way. Just point me in the right direction. I'll find a way to make it on my own."

She didn't respond. We both knew I could never make it out there on my own.

"So this is it. I'm never going home am I?"

The slow shake of Tuki's head caused tears to well in my eyes, and I suddenly became angry with myself for ever having hope.

"Listen Kay, we are about to have our Christmas Eve dinner. Everyone will get to meet their new family now. I wish for you to join us. Besides, you must be terribly hungry. None of us have had much to eat these past few days."

Before Tuki started towards the large candlelit hut, she paused. "Kay, I know you did not ask for this. And I am truly sorry. But I do hope you will find peace here."

I was ignoring her.

My mind was somewhere else. My family had only one rule back home, and that was to never walk out the door without saying I love you to one another. I'd broken that rule only once, when I slammed the door behind me, and look what it had cost me. Now I would really never get to crumble before my mother and tell her how sorry I was. I would never get to hug my father and ask him to forgive me. I would never get that moment back—ever.

Suddenly I was overwhelmed, and the tears poured down my face. I cried over everything that had happened over the past few days. I cried for my family. I cried for my friends. I cried for the handsome co-ed whom I barely had the chance to love.

Mostly, I cried like the sun would never rise tomorrow, and also because I didn't have any hope for what would happen if it did.

But apparently my lack of hope didn't control things like the rising of the sun.

That's probably why a horrible grumbling sound woke me from my sleep the next morning.

I sat up and yawned before realizing I was no longer outdoors, but inside on a large, round pillow that lay low to the ground. Yet I couldn't recall how I had gotten here. I surmised that someone must've carried me to this place last night.

It was too dark inside to see much else, but I could make out two streaks of daylight edging in from my left. I carefully stood up and pushed my hands out in front of me—taking just a few steps, feeling for the door. Only, what I felt didn't correspond with where the streaks of light were coming in from. And I quickly realized that the light that was coming in was coming in from *below* me.

I bent down and could only feel cloth where I thought a small solid door would be. Aside from wondering if I were somehow taking up residence in someone's oversized playhouse, it was just suddenly occurring to me that the low hanging material I was feeling were curtains. Odd. There were no windows, but curtains that started at my chest and lowered down to my feet.

I bent down again and parted the anomaly by the slit in the middle. And after debating the merits of venturing outside, I sucked it up and made my way through the swaying silk exit.

As I looked around at the wide outdoors, the first thing that I noticed was a carefully painted, white, four-foot tall circular wall—which encompassed the entire compound I was in. It was painted with solid green and black triangles, and was designed to appear almost as wallpaper, which gave me the feeling that serious interior decorating had gone on here—the kind that felt whimsical, but that I knew had been carefully strategized.

Inside the enclosed wall were four spectacular structures—one of which I'd just come out of, and was something of the likes I'd never seen before.

It was an acorn.

At least, that's what it looked like—a gigantic, upside down, painted acorn. And the four of them acted as mini residences, together forming a perfect square.

Each acorn shaped structure had a horseshoe shaped doorway, outlined with a different color—pink, purple, baby blue. The doorways were filled with matching colorful curtains; shading the inside from the otherwise penetrating sun on the outside.

An enormous black cooking pot was the focal point of the gated, painted acorn community, and was placed in the middle of surrounding grey rocks—a cooking pit I assumed.

I wondered why anyone would have cooking materials set up outdoors—not that there was any threat of rain from what I could tell.

Actually, there was not a cloud in the sky, which was good because I still had on the same sheer, beige blouse that I'd left New York in—which was completely dirty now, but was still the perfect attire for the not too warm, not too cool climate I currently found myself in.

I folded my body in half, dropping my head and touching my fingertips to the ankles of my boots. My calves and quadriceps were starting to feel the two days' worth of walking we'd done, so I made sure to stretch them out thoroughly.

After I was finally able to stand up straight, I moved past the large cooking pot, and soon found an opening in the surrounding decorated wall. I walked through it to the dirt road it bordered, and noticed that there were two more sets of the acorn shaped houses to my left—two sets more to my right.

This place definitely didn't lack for space, but it was quiet—empty.

Where were all the occupants?

I timidly looked out onto the long, narrow path that I had stepped out on, and wondered if I had the courage to find out what was even further beyond this stone-lined road. But just as I was about to start forward again, a little girl with bright round eyes and maple colored skin ran out of one of the acorn shaped houses, and came right up to me—excitedly pulling on my upper pant leg.

"Ukhisimusi Omuhle! Ukhisimusi Omuhle!"

I was a little taken aback. "I'm so sorry," I said, "I don't know what that means."

The little girl looked at me quizzically. "You don't speak isiZulu?"

"Uh, no, actually…" The bright-eyed youngster shrugged.

"Oh well. I just wanted to say Merry Christmas."

"Oh." I'd forgotten we'd arrived here on Christmas Eve. That *would* make today Christmas morning wouldn't it? It was a little hard to believe. Christmas for me was usually ice skating at Rockefeller Center, and gift shopping at Macy's, not wandering dirt paths on an empty stomach.

The little girl tugged on my pant leg again. "Are you walking to the market?"

I wasn't sure how to answer. "Should I be?"

She thought about it. "Well, are you hungry?"

I put my hand over my stomach to suppress an answering growl. The little girl giggled then jumped into the air.

"Follow me!"

She was off down the dirt road as I tried to keep up. But about halfway there I no longer needed to follow her. My nose had picked up on something indescribably delicious, and I quickly followed my otherwise usually meager sense of smell to an unbelievably amazing scene.

The freshest most exotic looking fruits I'd ever seen were all laid out on tables, calling my name. I leaned towards them, but was distracted by the rhythmic drum music that filled the air.

Women with matching pink and yellow dresses swayed to the beat. They also had on matching head wraps that were tied in intricate towering designs. I was amazed that they didn't fall off the women's heads as they whirled about.

Men were also dancing to the drummer's music, wearing wide pants with long, ocean blue tops that were embroidered with beautiful gold and purple geometric patterns.

My father had once worn an outfit like that to a wedding. He said the colorful top part was called a dashiki.

Dad.

I could feel myself beginning to lose it emotionally again, until something unusual caught my eye. One of the dancing men with a long, dreadlocked ponytail was bobbing up and down with an eighteen-foot wooden pole in his hand.

People were clapping and cheering him on as he continued to dance to the music. And I watched as the talented individual put both of his hands on the pole, stood it upright and climbed the entire eighteen feet to the top.

Amazingly, neither he nor the pole ever fell to the ground.

The agile dancer stretched out his legs and let go with one hand, forming an upside down L with the thin wooden pole. People continued to cheer his gravity defying feats, and I soon found myself clapping along as well.

I finally saw the little girl who had led me here, and she waved at me from the other side of the market. I smiled and waved back. The exchange made me remember why I followed her here in the first place, causing me to promptly turn my attention back to the fruit table. I simultaneously bent over the varied assortment before me.

There were mangoes and pineapples and coconuts, but some of the fruits were items I had never seen before. A group of berries glistened in the sun, and were the color of a wondrous metallic blue. They almost didn't look real.

"Marble berries."

I looked up. It was Tuki and she was nodding towards the bushel in front of me.

"Oh. Hmm." They didn't sound particularly appetizing, and didn't really look like they were meant to be eaten, but as hungry as I was—due largely to my having skipped out on dinner last night, I really didn't care how appetizing things did or didn't appear.

I picked up a handful of the hard, iridescent berries, but before they reached my open mouth, I got a whiff of something mouthwatering.

My nose hit the air and I started sniffing. It was the aroma I smelled all the way back on the path by the acorn huts. Finally, my eyes located the source of the aroma, and I was once again no longer in control of my body.

I ran straight towards the delectable table and licked my lips at the sight of the beef and lamb skewers, fragrant pies, cheeses, sweet smelling breads and stews. Without thinking, I began shoving piping hot food into my mouth—licking my hands clean of the sauces. It wasn't until Tuki cleared her throat that I saw the horrified look on the table owner's face.

I wiped the sides of my mouth with the back of my hand, and swallowed so that I could apologize, but I let out an extremely obnoxious belch instead. Both of my hands flew up to cover my mouth as I felt my cheeks turning red with embarrassment.

Tuki didn't laugh, but I could tell that she thought it was funny. The poor woman however, who had probably labored all night cooking the delicious food wasn't amused. I thought she was going to yell at me, but instead she just sighed and handed me a cloth napkin. "Ukhisimusi Omuhle," she said.

I remembered that meant Merry Christmas, and I sighed in relief. I wanted to show her that I appreciated her hospitality, so I tried to say it return—though I'm pretty sure two turtles could've passed me in the time that it took me to finally sound it out. "Ooh-key-see-moo-see Oh-moo-lay." I couldn't make the whistle type sound at the end that the little girl and the woman here had made, but I did my best.

The table owner smiled extremely politely, but the painful look in her eyes made me gather that my isiZulu was probably less music to her ears, and more like nails on a chalk board.

Oh well, I guess I had some practicing to do.

Tuki patted me on the back. "I am glad to see you are making friends."

I tried to force a smile, but couldn't. Talking to Tuki now made me face the reality of my situation.

"If you are up for it, some of us are gathering at the palace hut—the large candlelit one. Will you join us?"

I didn't want to sound curt, but I figured I'd save her the trouble of continuously inviting me on these group outings.

"Listen Tuki, I really appreciate you being so nice and all. I mean, I don't even know if I've thanked you for saving my life with the others, but I'm just not really in the celebrating mood." I fought impending emotions. "I'm still trying to process this whole idea of never seeing my family or my friends again. So I'd appreciate it if you just gave me some time to *deal*."

I hoped I didn't hurt her feelings. After all, I didn't want to seem ungrateful.

"I know you must be very sad today," she said in an unoffended rebuttal. "I will not lie to you. It will be very sad for many of these days. But you will find comfort when you least expect it, and then you *will* find your place in the world, once again."

I hoped she was right, but for now, I just couldn't imagine it.

"Please," Tuki persisted. "Come join us. There is a time for mourning, but also a time for celebration. Today let us celebrate being alive. Queen Zaina wants to welcome you."

Well that got my attention. "Queen…" I got ready to fumble it out, "Zah-ee-na?"

"Yes. She knows that you are here, and she wants to

greet you."

That threw me for a loop. "You mean you have an actual queen here? Really? I've never met a queen before." For some reason I started to get nervous.

"I think you will like her. She can be a little...oh, what is the phrase? Rough around the edges. Yes. But she cares deeply about her people. And you are now one of the people."

I thought about it for a moment, and concluded that Tuki was right. I definitely felt like mourning, but I did need to go to the celebration if just to make me think about something—*anything* else besides home for a while.

We exited the marketplace on the same dirt path that I'd arrived on. But instead of going straight, we veered off the natural pathway and walked through a grouping of fruit-bearing trees.

I remembered seeing the enormous grass covered cylinder hut that we were approaching from when we first arrived last night, but what I hadn't been able to see from afar were the dozens of beige-brown poles that surrounded the front of the structure—helping to hold the palace hut up towards the sky. I also hadn't noticed that each pole was carved with a different face inside of it. The faces were more artistic than life-like, and reminded me of some of the artwork that my mom had collected back home.

Tuki noticed my fixation and pointed to one of the faces at the top of the third pole.

"That one is me." She said it as if she were pointing herself out in a class photo. "Each of us—everyone here—we are part of this structure, as we are part of this village—this life."

I realized that each of the faces carved into the pole, represented someone who now lived here. I supposed my face would be up there one day—though I desperately wished there was some way to avoid it.

Tuki took my hand. "Come. Let us enter."

She led the way through the rectangular opening, and I was amazed by all that was inside. The inner walls were solid and were covered with beautifully woven tapestry. One in particular was a complicated piece with a lion at its center; a jungle in the background, and an ivory colored dagger woven diagonally to the side.

Colorful oversized throw pillows and silver tealight candles lined the gold, tiled floor of this palace hut.

Men who were dressed like warriors stood next to torches around the room. And even though there were no windows, it was bright as daylight inside the beautiful African architecture.

A woman walked up to us offering us food and drink. She had painted white dots down her nose and as lining underneath both eyes. Several other women had decorated faces and wore pink, orange and white sarongs with matching sandals.

As I admired their elegance, I was simultaneously led along the trail of strategically placed seating, all the way to the back of the palace. And there, seated on a stone, ruby-adorned throne, was a woman just several years older than I—whose beauty I knew I'd seen before.

Her skin was flawless, the color of mahogany, and her eyes were the color of the starry night sky. The queen's finely braided hair rested on her hips, while the pearl-colored cowry shells and pure gold beads that hung from her hair shimmered upon her face as a reflection. The young lady's posture demanded respect from everyone in the room, and I tried to recall the reason for this feeling of familiarity.

I searched my memory while listening to the drums— the chanting—the flames from the fire of the torches that surrounded the room.

I looked into the hypnotizing blaze, and suddenly I was back in my chair at NYU.

Beth sat next to me as the students settled in. We were one minute early for our 10:00 A.M. class, and I watched the statuesque new professor create an intricate piece of art on the blackboard.

The drawing was complete after only a few minutes, and the professor looked over the entire classroom before settling her eyes squarely on me.

"It's a symbol," she firmly announced. Her distinct African accent had momentarily caught me off-guard. Still, I raised my hand.

"What is it a symbol of?"

The regal looking professor smiled and responded. "Death."

I remember waking up screaming, startling the class— Beth unconvinced when I told her I was okay. I also remember feeling that the regal looking woman was someone I was supposed to be able to trust—and somehow, someone I knew I couldn't.

Now, here in this palace, I looked at the woman I'd dreamed about many times before. I wanted to say something—to tell her that I knew her, but the memory faded just as quickly as it came. Within seconds, my head was filled with nothing but haze—and I was once again simply left with that common annoying feeling that I'd forgotten something important.

I shook my head from the daze as I walked slowly towards the queen; Tuki by my side, telling me not to worry.

"Welcome. My name is Queen Zaina. You must be Kay."

I nodded—a bit too intimated to speak.

"I understand this must all be very shocking. I am told you did not come to us through the usual circumstances."

I looked at Tuki—something I'd developed a tendency to do, especially when I was unsure about something. And, just as usual, Tuki clarified what I didn't understand.

"Most who come here do not have anywhere else to go. They have already lost their family, or they have fled with those that they hold dear. You my Kay, were in neither category."

Queen Zaina slowly stood from the throne and approached me. "When Tuki told me of your situation— and naturally, of your desperate desire to go back from whence you came, I was concerned. You see...Kay, this is home—for all of us. It is the one place we don't have to worry about any outside wars—any outside evil; nor anyone who would wish to do another harm. I care very deeply about my village. And there is *nothing* I wouldn't do to protect its secret—which is of course its safety."

I wasn't sure what she was getting at. Surely she didn't think I was going to try to run off in the middle of the jungle—by myself, not having any idea how to get here *or* home, just to try to find someone so I could give them directions to where I'd been.

I couldn't help but to get the feeling that this queen either didn't like me, or just didn't trust me very much; and was starting to feel like the awkward freshman being told where I could and couldn't sit in the cafeteria by one of the not-so-nice seniors in school. Only, in this situation, Queen Zaina pulled a bit more rank.

The queen walked over to my other side. "So, Kay, you are from America, yes?"

"I am."

"And there, what did you do?" The queen began to circle me like a detective during an interrogation. I tried not to let it over intimidate me.

"I was studying to be a journalist."

"I see." Queen Zaina switched directions, still circling. "And would you leave here if you had the chance?"

"Yes." I didn't hesitate.

"You are honest. That is good."

The queen glanced back to Tuki. She seemed to be asking questions to verify whatever Tuki had told her about me—unsatisfied in not finding any discrepancies.

"And your family? Friends?"

I wasn't sure I wanted to talk about them—not in terms of never seeing them again anyway. I knew now the hope that I'd had the two days journey from the poacher's camp to here had been in vain. Still, I just couldn't bring myself to accept it.

I held my head up to the queen. "With all due respect Queen Zaina, I don't feel like discussing that right now."

The queen shrugged. "Very well, we will change the subject."

"Thank you."

In the corner of the palace hut, I noticed a collection of long wooden sticks. They were lined against the wall in pairs, and each pair differed in style. Some were plain, and others had pastel-colored horizontal lines on them.

Queen Zaina—several inches taller than I, stood over me and nodded towards the collection.

"Dlala 'nduku."

I failed to respond.

"Playing sticks," the queen translated.

"Oh." I walked closer to get a better look. "What do you play with them?" I reached out for one, but quickly withdrew my hand, unsure if I had permission to touch them.

The queen picked up a pair and slowly began to twirl them in her hands. "It is not so much a game you play, so much as a way to get to know each other."

Tuki seemed to grow tense, keeping a wary eye on the two of us. I had a feeling I missed something in the interpretation of *getting to know* each other.

"Here." Queen Zaina handed me the pair she'd been holding, and thumbed through the collection for a pair of her own.

I saw a light go off in Tuki's head, and I realized something had suddenly occurred to her. "Zaina, I think Kay is still most tired. Why don't I bring her back tomorrow? Fresh, and well rested."

Queen Zaina didn't pay any attention to Tuki. Instead, she continued to peruse the stick collection, finally finding a pair it seemed she preferred.

"Ah." The queen lifted them up and took each one in a separate hand.

The ones I held were plain and slightly chipped. The ones Queen Zaina held were decorated and clearly superior. "Tuki, will you be induna for us?" The queen passed me as she motioned for me to follow her to the middle of the room.

I wanted to make sure I understood what she had just said. "Induna?" I hoped I repeated it correctly.

"Yes. You would probably say…referee."

I grew nervous. I didn't see any soft balls or anything to hit with the sticks, so what were we about to do that would require a referee?

Tuki didn't look too thrilled but walked over anyway. She put a hand on both of our shoulders. Her gaze, however, stayed fixed on Queen Zaina.

"Now remember, we are not *actually* going to fight okay?"

I laughed because I didn't know why that even needed to be said, but I replied, "sure."

Queen Zaina smiled, but never actually responded. That worried me.

Some of the people in the palace hut started to gather around. The queen widened her stance and Tuki nodded her head, signaling I gathered that Queen Zaina could begin showing me what to do with the playing sticks.

"Ready?"

"Sure. What do I…"

Whack! Swoosh! Whack! Before I could even finish my sentence, the queen was coming at me with the lighting speed of an angry leopard. My glasses flew off my face while her sticks clacked against mine so hard that the vibration skipped the wooden rods and went directly into my bones.

"Zaina! Kancane! She does not know how to donga!"

The queen stopped, but I was already shaking like one of those panicked little lab mice who had just been experimented on.

The queen rested one of the sticks over her shoulder and twirled the other in her open hand.

"What did I say that these are called?" She began to circle me again, this time as if I were prey.

"*Playing* sticks—your majesty." I didn't try to control the sarcastic tone of my voice.

"Yes. They are playing sticks. They are also called *fighting* sticks. I forgot to mention that."

"No kidding." I muttered it under my breath as I bent down to pick up my glasses.

"What was that?"

"Nothing." I decided not to help escalate things. I didn't know what I did to tick her off, but she obviously didn't like me. I wondered if I'd be alive long enough to figure out why.

"Perhaps we should take it a bit slower." The queen spoke condescendingly.

I looked around at the growing group of spectators— the anticipation in their faces igniting my pride. I looked down at the sticks in my hand, and then back up at Queen Zaina.

She waited for me to reposition myself.

"Another time," I replied.

I walked back over to the wall I'd found the playing sticks at, and put my pair back into their iron holding slots.

I felt the disappointment on the onlookers faces before I even turned around, but saw a reassuring validation from Tuki. That made me feel better.

The group of spectators eventually dispersed, and then it was just Tuki, Queen Zaina and I at the back of the palace hut—again by the throne.

"Well—Kay," the queen kept her eyes squarely on me as she reached behind her to put back her donga sticks—not even needing to look to know where the slots were. "I had fun getting to know you." She smiled somewhat less than genuinely.

"And I you." I tried to force a smile, but the corners of my mouth wouldn't turn up for this little white lie.

The queen brought her waist long braids from around her back all to the same side of one shoulder. Then she smoothed out the two-piece dress she was wearing before retaking the seat on her throne.

"Now, if you will excuse me, many matters require my attention before eve's end, and I must borrow my most trusted of my amakhosi."

I looked around for something I thought might be an amakhosi, but Tuki cleared her throat and pointed to herself.

"I am second inkosi here; the youngest of the amakhosi—the chiefs."

"Right." I said it as if it were something I'd simply forgotten. "So that would make Queen Zaina first inkosi."

The queen barked out a laugh. "*I* am the queen—sole ruler of Ipharadisi. All amakhosi report to me. The first inkosi is an old man who lives on an old hill. I do not bother with him."

There was a tense silence before Tuki spoke up again.

"Among other things Kay, I report directly to our queen."

"Oh."

"Will you be alright on your own Kay? Perhaps you will stop at the iQhugwane? You are bleeding."

"I am?" I patted myself down to check for blood, but didn't find any cuts. Queen Zaina pointed to the side of my head, and I placed my hand where she directed. I sucked in air through my teeth. It stung where I touched.

I did feel something whizz by my head while we were *playing*, but it wasn't incredibly painful, so I didn't think much about it. She had probably just flicked off a scab from my earlier injury in the airport explosion, with her so-called donga stick.

I replayed what Tuki just said in my head. "I'm sorry, where did you say I should go?"

The queen jumped in before Tuki could speak. "Nowhere. You do not even look that hurt."

Tuki frowned at Queen Zaina. Was there a reason the queen didn't want me to go wherever Tuki was telling me to?

Her seemingly second in command took me by the arm then and practically used charades to show me how to get to the iQhugwane on an imaginary map. She said the iQhugwanes were the beehive styled huts that the doctor and some of the others at the village lived in.

Before I left, Tuki asked me once again if I would be alright to go on my own. It had gotten pretty dark outside, and she thought that maybe someone should walk with me—not for safety reasons as she assured me safety is what this village was all about, but she was just concerned about me getting lost and having to sleep outside on the ground somewhere.

I told Tuki I would be fine, and in return she whispered something about having a stern talking with Zaina. The queen and her inkosi seemed pretty close, especially being that Tuki didn't even refer to Queen Zaina by her title. So I hoped whatever Tuki would say, would help squash whatever had just happened between myself and the queen.

Thankfully, though it had indeed gotten quite dark outside, most of the houses and huts had torches positioned in front of them. So I was able to walk by their light down the dusty pathway through most of the village on the way to the doctor.

But when I arrived to the beehive huts that Tuki had described, I was a little stuck on which iQhugwane the doctor would be in. There were a total of ten clustered together.

There was also what I could only estimate to be an eleven-foot wide and just as long, eggshell colored tent in the middle of the cluster of beehive residences. My instincts told me to check the tent first because the huts seemed a tad bit small to be practicing medicine in.

But as I approached the tent's opening, I thought perhaps my instincts might have been wrong. I didn't hear any noise coming from the structure and thought that maybe nobody was in. Still, I continued forward and walked inside.

"Oh my!"

I'd walked in on a patient who wasn't even close to finished being dressed. The rather tall, shirt-free gentleman was still guiding his leather belt through the loops in his olive-colored khakis when I walked in.

I told myself to cover my eyes or to face the other way—but before I could, the flickering lantern on the long, metal side table caused his wonderfully infused, dark coffee skin to glow—defining every single muscle on his finely tuned physique.

Little droplets of water were falling off the sides of his shoulder and trickling down his chest. But he used a dark blue hand towel to wipe them off.

"May I help you?"

I whipped around, mortified. I realized I'd been gawking at him like some kind of peeping Tom. I covered my eyes—a little late I suppose—and turned even further to face the metal table.

"I…uh…sorry…" I was having trouble remembering why I'd come here in the first place. Annoyed with myself, I began running my fingers through my hair to help collect myself. But a strand got stuck on the open cut on the side of my head. That re-jogged my memory.

I spoke to the well chiseled patient with my back still turned to him. I shouted over my shoulder.

"I'm sorry, I was looking for the doctor."

"Well then, you came to the right place." I heard what sounded like a shirt being put on.

"Oh. Good. Do you by chance happen to know where he is? Or, if this is a bad time—I could come back later. Would you just mind telling him that someone new to the village stopped by?"

The stranger laughed. I didn't know why it was funny.

"Sure. I could tell him, but it would be kind of pointless."

I folded my arms. "Why?"

The strikingly good-looking gentleman walked around in front of me, fastening the last couple of pearl-colored buttons on his white, short-sleeved shirt, and smiled. "Because I am the doctor."

"Hunh? *You're* the doctor?"

"Yep."

I frowned. "Do all doctors practice medicine half-naked around here?"

"Only the really good ones." He winked at me.

I rolled my eyes.

As he began tucking in his fully buttoned shirt into his loose, olive khakis, I noticed that tiny, crystal water droplets still shone through the opening of his shirt; resting atop his perfectly masculine chest. It was sort of distracting—in an annoying kind of way of course.

"I'm sorry, did I miss the freak rain storm? Why is that you're all wet in here?"

The doctor brushed by me to pick up a taupe, canvas strap watch, then fastened it around his wrist. "Actually, the weather was so pleasant that I decided to take a nice, relaxing bath under the moonlight. Maybe you should try it sometime—*relaxing* that is."

Did he really just take a jab at me? "Excuse me? What is that supposed to mean?"

The tall doctor sighed. "You just seem a little tense Kay. You know—you were a lot less hostile when you were asleep."

I did a mental double-take. "When have you ever seen me...*asleep*?" I'd only been here one night, and that was in Tuki's acorn hut—at least, that's where I gathered I'd woken up this morning. And wait a second, how did he know my name already?

The irritating physician reached around my waist for a nearby cloth, but didn't back up from my personal space after he found it. He shook his head at me before beginning to clean his watch.

"How exactly did you think you ended up in bed this morning—as opposed to the well-fertilized soil I suppose you would've preferred to wake up on instead?"

I remembered that after Tuki had asked me to join everyone at dinner last night, I remained outside, and had sat down near one of the giant mango trees. I must've fallen asleep, and he must've found me and carried me to the place I woke up in this morning.

It was a nice gesture, so I really couldn't figure out why it bothered me.

"So you just go around picking up random strangers and putting them into beds? That's not at all creepy."

The doctor lowered his face to my level. Now that he was even closer to me, I could smell his vanilla and sandalwood cologne. It calmed me as I breathed him in.

"You're welcome," he replied, finally backing up, giving me some space.

I inhaled and exhaled...slowly—and realized why I'd acted so crazy when I saw him—though I refused to admit it to myself.

"Yes, thank you. And I apologize," I said in return. "I didn't mean to come off so...I don't know. I think I'm still in shock with everything that's happened. I didn't mean to take it out on you."

The understanding gentleman put his hands in his pockets and leaned against one of the metal tables.

He gave me a pitying look and adjusted his tone.

"Yeah, I heard—small village and all. I'm sorry you know. Really, I am. But you're a tough one—I can tell. You're gonna get through this."

I closed my eyes and leaned against the opposite table. "I wish I had the same confidence. I had my entire future mapped out back home. But now, I just don't know how I'm gonna make it. My friends; my family. It hurts too much to even think about it."

We both drew in deep breaths at the same time. It was almost as if he could feel my pain.

"I know it doesn't seem like it, but one day you'll come to terms with all that's happened. I know, because in three words I can sum up everything I've learned about life.

It goes on."

I looked up. "That's Robert Frost."

He smiled. "One of my favorite poets."

"Really?"

"Yep. Here's another one of my favorites. The greatest discovery of all time, is that a person can change his future by merely changing his attitude."

"Mark Twain?"

"No. Oprah."

"Oh." We laughed, and I realized it was the first time I had laughed since the start of this whole ordeal. It felt good.

"I'm so sorry. Where are my manners?" The good doctor stretched out his hand.

"I'm Doctor Louron, but you can call me Erec."

"Hi Erec. I'm Kay."

"I know. Small village." Doctor Erec grinned. "So what can I do for you this evening?" He offered me his hand and helped me up onto the patient table.

"Oh it's nothing—really. I was just stick fighting with Queen Zaina and…"

Erec's eyes almost came out his sockets. "You entered into donga with the queen?"

"Well, it was kind of the other way around really. She said it was a way for us to get to know each other."

The doctor burst out into an abrupt laughter. "Well, she wasn't lying. Though I have a feeling she left out a few details."

I rubbed the side of my head. "Yeah, just a few."

Erec pulled out a pair of latex gloves from a disposable cardboard carton, and stretched them out as he put them on.

"Don't mind Zaina. She's a little rough around the edges, but she really does care about everyone's well-being."

"Yeah, that's what Tuki said."

"Ah. Yes, she would know."

"They're close hunh?"

"Like sisters."

I looked down. "I used to have someone who was like a sister to me."

Erec stopped whatever he was about to do, and lifted my chin with his fingers. "You will have someone like a sister again. You will have an entire village like a family. The people here—they care for each other. It's unlike anything you've ever seen."

I tried to manage a smile then—just for him, and couldn't help but notice that he really was distractingly handsome. I felt guilty for being so brash with him earlier, especially after he was so nice to me in return.

"Now, let's take a look at that cut. We don't want it to get infected."

That night, thinking about Erec's suggestion, I asked Tuki if she thought it would be alright for me to sleep outside under the moonlight. Tuki brought out a white and black quilt and set me up outside of the acorn hut. I lay down, and looked up at the stars in the midnight sky, wondering if Mom, Dad, Beth, or…Callum, were looking up at them too.

10. Misfit

I was the last one among the colorful acorn huts to wake up again. This struck me as odd because I thought the one place you could sleep in if you wanted to would be in the middle of a hidden jungle. But Tuki and everyone else in the mini community I was staying in were already long gone. People seemed to start their day pretty early around here.

I got up to fold the beautifully sewn quilt that Tuki had given me last night to keep me warm. I hadn't really gotten a good look at it in the dark, but this morning, with the sun high in the sky, I could see all of the different designs that had been patched in to create one beautiful piece of art.

One patch was orange, with short sets of sea green and baby blue stripes on it. Another patch was purple, with what looked to be a black outlined sketch of a tortoise at its center. The third patch I looked at, I was shocked to have recognized.

It was the same white canvas material with the same black butterfly symbol that my baby blanket had on it— the one Mom kept over the foot of my bed while I was away at college.

I patted myself down for my glasses, but then remembered that I'd put them away last night in my canvas messenger bag so that I wouldn't roll over on them. I found the bag, took out the glasses and put them on to see if the patch was truly the same—and it was.

What an odd coincidence.

I wondered where Tuki had gotten this quilt from, and who had patched in this particular piece. I also wondered where my mother had gotten my baby blanket from. She'd never mentioned any specifics, except that she acquired it on a trip.

I continued to fold, and after I had put it away—back into Tuki's hut, I headed down the same path as yesterday to the village market; observing even more of the colorful houses along the pathway than I had even noticed yesterday.

In between upside down acorn shapes and cylinder huts with roofs the shape of Christmas trees, were shack styled houses painted blue on one side, peach on the other, and mint green on the top.

These led directly to the market, which wasn't nearly as full as it was during yesterday's celebrations. Today the market had more of a business as usual type of feel—although the bright colors on the stand walls still gave the market a bit of festivity.

I walked past the fruits and cooked food vendors to a part of the market where there were about a dozen different stands—some displaying aromatic soaps and fragrant oils.

Others displayed various pottery and other woven crafts.

Outside one particular stand, sat a plump, older

woman, who was using a silk, red cloth to wipe down a beautifully carved wooden comb. There were several on her table, each with the intertwined, patterned swirls of tree rings on them.

But these weren't the only kind on her table. There were others that looked as if they had been made from seashells—shiny, beige, brown and grey mixtures. Some of the combs were even shaped like animals—others, triangular and square.

I studied each one carefully. I hadn't seen a mirror in a week. I had run my fingers through my hair a few times over the past couple of days, but now that I was somewhat coming to terms with my situation, I had a feeling it was possibly time for slightly more maintenance. I took in the aesthetics around me. There were so many beautiful hairstyles I could only dream of emulating.

One woman had thinly coiled, bright red dreadlocks. They were decorated with tiny, silver beads throughout her beautifully styled hair. Another woman had short, cropped, yellow hair that matched the stack of gold necklaces around her long, slender neck. A third woman by the oil and soap table had thick shades of brown hair that flowed into an afro—making my thin limp hair look well, thin and limp.

I started to feel out of place. I drew my attention back to the handmade combs and wondered if I could learn to be as creative as these women with my own hair.

"Cow's horn."

"Hunh?" I looked up. It was the bright-eyed girl from yesterday. Her voice was that of a small child, but her matter-of-fact tone made her seem older.

"They're made from cow's horn—not the wooden

ones of course. The multi-colored ones."

"Oh?"

"Yes. That's why they're all a different color. They're made from different cows' different horns."

"Well," I said, "I suppose the cows made a worthwhile sacrifice then." I smiled.

The little girl huffed. She'd only been around me for less than a minute, and she was already exasperated by me.

"Please tell me you are joking. Do you think that we are poachers? Their horns were taken *after* the end of their lives of course. They weren't killed for us to make combs of course."

"Oh of course." I laughed to myself. I couldn't help but be slightly amused that I was being scolded by a kid who could barely even see over the display table. But I had to say, she was quite an impressive little child.

She picked up one of the combs and pointed it toward the older couple behind the table. "Umama and Ubaba make them." Because the man and the woman she pointed to looked so much like the bright-eyed little girl, I assumed that Umama and Ubaba meant Mom and Dad. That's right. I forgot she spoke isiZulu.

The little girl began wrapping the cow horn comb she was pointing with in a little black cloth. I bent down to her level. "Hey, what's your name?"

"Kayla."

"Kayla? Really? My name's one syllable less than yours. My name is Kay."

The little girl nodded, but methodically continued to wrap the comb; her little tongue sticking out the side of her mouth as she furrowed her brow, trying to figure out how to make a bow. I was just about to offer her some help, when she huffed again and abruptly stopped wrapping.

Kayla thrust out her hand. "Here."

I tilted my head, as it took me a moment to realize that the person she'd been wrapping the comb for was me.

I stood up. "Oh. I'm sorry, I don't have any money."

Kayla shrugged. "It's okay. We don't use money much around here." She plopped the comb into my hand, then walked around to the other side of the table that both of her parents had just stepped away from.

I bit my lip a little. "Um, are you sure your parents won't mind?" I really could use it I thought, but I didn't want to get her into any unnecessary trouble.

Kayla seemed perplexed. "Why would they mind that I have given you a gift?"

I was humbled. What an incredible little girl.

"Well, when you put it that way—thank you."

Kayla shrugged. I had a feeling being generous was something Kayla was accustomed to—something her parents had taught her as a duty to others.

"Tuki!" The little girl had spotted Tuki before I did. She ran around the table to jump into Tuki's arms.

Tuki scooped up the little girl and swung her around. "How are you today my little inkosazana?"

Kayla frowned. "I don't want to be a little princess. I want to be part of the amakhosi, like you."

"Is that so my little inkosazana?" Tuki commenced to tickle Kayla until she squealed with laughter. Finally, Tuki put her down. Kayla went back to stand with her parents, and Tuki nodded for me to walk through the market with her.

Before I left, I thanked the little girl again for my gift, and only then did I follow Tuki down the middle of the market way. I waited until we were around as few people as possible because I knew we had a sensitive subject to discuss.

I started.

"So yesterday, with the queen, what was *that* all about?"

A woman carrying a wicker basket on her head passed by us as we walked. Tuki and the woman acknowledged each other with a slight nod of the head.

"Well my Kay, where do I begin in this? First, I must say with a fervent apology, I did not know Zaina would react most…unexpectedly."

I was silent.

"You see, when I told Zaina of your group's arrival, as usual, she wanted a full report of each individual. She is particularly interested in each person's story who comes to Ipharadisi."

I stopped. I wanted to make sure I heard her correctly. "Did you say, ee-par-ah-dee-see?"

Tuki tried not to laugh as I tried to roll the r the way she did. "Yes. Very good. It is what we call this place. Ipharadisi. It is the isiZulu word for paradise. Peace and paradise are what we have worked most hard to create."

I indicated that I understood, and so we resumed walking.

"When I told Zaina of you and your American associate…"

"Professor." I didn't mean to interrupt again, but after everything that Professor Liu had caused me to get wrapped up in, I didn't want to be known as some lying black market dealer's *associate*.

My blood suddenly began to boil, and I wondered if I would ever be able to forgive Professor Liu for being the reason I would never see my family or my friends again.

Tuki saw my reaction and quickly rephrased. "Yes. The woman who was your professor." My anger softened. Something about hearing Tuki speak about Professor Liu in the past tense made me remember what Tuki had said the other day—about those who would continue to search for us.

Professor Liu had run off during our escape. I didn't have any idea where she had run off to, or who she had run *into* trying to get there. And though I'd still have to work on forgiving her, I certainly didn't wish any harm upon her.

Tuki studied my face to determine whether or not it was safe to continue. She obviously deemed that it was. "Well, you see, Zaina was concerned about your desire to get back to your family."

"Why?"

"Because my Kay, something very terrible happened to our queen many seasons ago—something that came back to her memory when she heard of you."

My curiosity peaked. What could have happened that would make Queen Zaina seem to dislike me so? Tuki led us towards two tree stumps that we then sat down on and rested.

Tuki took a moment to gather her thoughts. Whatever it was, it obviously wasn't easy for Tuki to talk about. Still, she opened up.

"One day, when Zaina was just a little girl, and her mother Queen Ayanna was still queen, one of our rescuers safely brought back a small group from a poacher's camp—much similar to the one from which you were found.

They were a family—these rescues, kidnapped from their village by a warlord who ran several hostile camps of illegal trades. There was only one in the group who was not of blood relation to the others. She was an American, like you."

Tuki waited for a couple of children to pass by before speaking again.

"Queen Ayanna bonded with the American—as they were similar in many ways, but the queen knew that her new friend missed home most terribly.

The American asked the queen many times to help her return home, but the queen refused. For you see, legend was very much wide spread about our village. Many close to the lands know that there is a tribe who seeks out evil—who seeks it out and destroys it—who rescues the lost and safely bring them home. Because of this, there are many out there who wish to destroy us. Then…and now."

Tuki repositioned herself on the tree stump, and then continued the rest of the story.

"Well my Kay, the American eventually grew bitter and set out on her own journey one night. Of course, Queen Ayanna was much saddened, for she feared what may happen to her friend. Days passed, then weeks. Eventually, the queen lost hope and believed that her friend was no more. Queen Ayanna mourned for her friend immensely.

But one day, late in the sun rest hour, Ipharadisi was attacked. Someone had found a way to the queen's

American friend who—possibly out of fear—told these evil ones all of the secrets Queen Ayanna had ever shared.

Much blood was shed. The queen lost many of her trusted advisors. And in the end, the queen's life was also taken.

Zaina was just eight-years-old when she lost her mother and only eight-years-old when she had to take her mother's place as queen."

Wow. I closed my eyes and tried to imagine it. I may not have been able to relate, but knowing her story helped me to understand her better. I felt a single teardrop escaping down my cheek as I thought about Zaina's childhood.

"Zaina remains concerned that you may bring the same fate as was once brought to her mother."

I shook my head. "I would never…"

Tuki rose as she already knew what I would say. "I believe you. And I advised her of as much."

"So, is that what you are—the queen's advisor?"

Tuki seemed to mull it over for a moment. I wondered if she ever got tired of explaining things to me.

"Actually, I am many things to the queen. Ipharadisi is not like most villages as you can see. But yes, I am advisor, peacekeeper and protector. I am one of the amakhosi—the youngest of the leaders, of which there are few. For that, my responsibilities are many."

It sounded complicated, but fortunately—and unfortunately—I would have a lifetime to learn their ways.

As we continued to walk through the marketplace, I caught on to the warm scents of sandalwood and vanilla. I recognized the subtle cologne from yesterday.

"Good afternoon Kay. Tuki—how are we this morning?" I smiled at the way Erec slightly bowed while greeting us.

"We're great!" I didn't mean to speak for the both of us—or so enthusiastically either, but Tuki didn't seem to mind, so I continued. "And yourself Erec? How's your morning so far?"

Erec slowly walked towards me—his hands in his pockets—his eyes locked on mine. "Beautiful," he said confidently. "The morning so far is beautiful."

Tuki mentioned something about the shape of one of the clouds in the sky, but Erec didn't look up.

Neither did I.

There were several moments of silence before Tuki gave us both a strange look, then mentioned that she wanted to check in on Ipharadisi's other newcomers. She said she would check back on me later, so I waved without looking, unable to recall if I had even said goodbye.

Erec waited until Tuki had disappeared into the crowd before extending his hand and gesturing in the opposite direction.

I walked.

He followed.

"So, how does your head feel today?"

I touched the cut that he had bandaged last night, and didn't notice any stinging.

"It's actually pretty good. Thank you."

"Anytime."

I fiddled with the cuff of my blouse a bit before building up the nerve to ask him something I'd been wondering since yesterday. Finally, I spit it out.

"So, are you really a doctor? Or is that just what people call you around here?"

"Well," Erec confessed, "I do mainly study the herbs and plants here, along with their various medicinal properties—which would actually make me a bit of an izinyanga—an herbalist."

"I see…"

Erec smirked.

"But I also have a PhD and medical degree—if that's what you were wondering."

"Oh."

Erec waited for me to say something else, as if I hadn't really asked what I was thinking. And honestly, I hadn't.

"Why?" Erec prodded. "What were you expecting? An isangoma or something?"

"A what?"

"A *witchdoctor*," Erec quickly returned.

I couldn't believe he knew what I was thinking, and I probably should've been embarrassed by my assumption, but instead I laughed.

Erec didn't.

"That's what I thought." He seemed disappointed. "You may want to keep in mind that there are those who are more comfortable with more traditional styles of living, and there are also those who prefer more modern ways. This place is like any other village, or city, or country that way." Erec nodded to a young boy on crutches who had someone burning incense over him. I hoped the individual hadn't heard me laughing.

"People's lives aren't something to be amused by Kay."

I nodded, and felt as if I'd been scolded by my favorite

teacher. Thankfully, Erec didn't seem to linger on it.

"Hey, make a right." He lightly touched the back of my shoulder, gently directing us towards a slender old man's snack shop.

The store front was a mere open cove in the back of the market—different from the causal, open spaced tables in the bustling section up front. This owner's displays boasted spices, hard candies and cashews in round, wooden containers. There were also dried fruits and what looked like chocolate covered insects—caterpillars mostly.

There were plenty of other items that I of course didn't recognize—one of which I picked up. The old man who owned the stand gave me a wide, toothless grin and pointed to what I was holding. It was beige and pink, and about the size of a chestnut. I wondered what it was.

"Kola nut," said the grey-haired man.

I had a sudden thought as I rolled it between my fingers. But the thought seemed rather unlikely so I dismissed it without bringing it up. Still—as I noticed he'd had a knack to do—Erec already knew what I was thinking.

"Sound familiar?" Erec asked this as he wrapped his arms around my waist—only so he could squeeze by me into the small cove area that I was blocking.

I shook my head in disbelief. "Are you serious? *This?*"

Erec gave me an affirming look.

"This is what the first cola soft drink was made from." Erec picked up the tiny little nut and held it to the sunlight. "We still make our own *Coca-Cola* sometimes by fermenting the kola nuts and mixing them with water. You can add sugar of course to taste. Go ahead, try one."

I was surprised but took the little kola in my hand. When I first bit into it, my mouth puckered up like I was chewing on sour candy—but the longer I chewed, the sweeter it became. It was kind of neat.

I picked up a few more from the bowl, but Erec placed his hand over mine before I could lift them up.

"Careful, you don't want to have too many of these."

"Why?"

"Because, these things are chuck full of caffeine." Erec took one from my hand and popped it into his mouth. "They're actually quite the pick me up—provided you don't get addicted of course."

"Then…" I spoke as I thoughtlessly leaned into him—closer than I'd meant to. "It's a good thing I know a good doctor."

Erec smiled—a beautiful smile—and I was suddenly thankful for his company. Erec still had his hand over mine when the queen loudly cleared her throat behind us.

I spun around.

"Queen Zaina, hi." I straightened my posture as I spoke.

"Kay. Dr. Louron."

Erec let go of my hand and gave a slight bow to the queen. I wondered if I was supposed to do the same thing.

"My, my. I see you two are becoming *quite* familiar."

Maybe it was just me, but she didn't seem too happy about it.

I glanced back at Erec—who avoided eye contact with the queen. It made me remember her desire yesterday for me not to go see him. I wondered if the two had a falling out, and thought maybe I should say something to ease the tension if so.

"So, Queen Zaina, out to enjoy the fresh air?" Not exactly the thoughtful icebreaker I had hoped for, but it was all my nerves would allow me to come up with.

The queen kept her eyes focused on Erec—who continued to keep his eyes *away* from hers. "Actually, I am on my way to the assegai competition," said the queen. She must've caught a glimpse of the blank look on my face because she added on, "*spear* throwing."

"Oh."

Queen Zaina turned her attention back to Erec who still had his head bowed. "Dr. Louron, do you care to join me?"

Erec thought about it way too long to give an answer of yes. And, when he answered no, I was surprised to see how disappointed the queen became. Wow. It didn't take me long to figure it out. Queen Zaina had a crush on the village doctor.

But the feelings didn't appear to be mutual.

"Actually, I don't know that Kay's eaten today, and I'm pretty hungry myself. Kay? Did you want me to take you somewhere to get lunch?"

I started to fidget. I immediately realized that whatever this was between the queen and the doctor *wasn't* something I wanted to get caught up in, so I tried to think of an excuse to decline.

"Um...I...I've never been to a...spear throwing event before. Queen Zaina, would you mind if *I* went with you instead?"

The queen was speechless, and so was Dr. Louron. This probably had bad idea written all over it, but I thought about what Tuki had explained to me earlier—

about Queen Zaina having concerns about me. Maybe this would give us some valuable bonding time—valuable bonding time near deadly, sharpened, readily available, metal-tipped spears. I gulped.

The queen cut her eyes to Erec, and then down at me. I was hardly the tall, dark, handsome, herbalist slash medical professional that she had hoped to spend the day with, but I had a feeling she'd rather me spend the afternoon with her—than with Erec. The contemplative expression on her face gave me the feeling that she was thinking the same thing.

The queen decided. "Yes. That will be fine."

She abruptly turned to show me the way, simultaneously giving Erec the cold shoulder. Her parting acknowledgement to him was a simple, "*Doctor*"—saying it as off-handedly as she could. I didn't even bother waving, for fear that the queen would see.

I followed Queen Zaina as she walked to the end of the market and made a left. We headed in that direction for quite a while—Zaina walking slightly faster than I could keep up—until finally, we approached a tightknit group of medium-sized trees with contrastingly massive jungle vines entangled between them. The only space between the middle of the trees was a tall, oval opening like that of the eye of a needle—which we walked through—finally making our way to the other side.

I couldn't believe it as I looked out at the well-manicured field before us. Here I was, thousands of miles away from my New York City home, and I had just practically stepped out into Central Park.

A couple dozen Ipharadisians—that's what I had been told the villagers here were called—were sitting on the three-foot-wide tree stumps that were lined up as bleachers, intently focused on who I assumed were the competing teams warming up.

A group of teenage girls took up the tree stumps to the front right, and were whispering into each other's ears, pointing at several of the teenage boys who were flexing their muscles with their assegais. As much as I didn't miss high school, it was kind of comforting to know that no matter where in the world you travelled, some things would always be the same. The girls giggled as one of the male competitors blew the first girl a kiss.

Queen Zaina exchanged genuinely warm pleasantries with each person in the seating area as we made our way to the wooden throne at the front of the field. This throne was much more casual than the ruby decorated one at the palace hut, but still had an engraving of a crown carved into the back of it.

As we got closer, I noticed that there were actually two thrones. I wondered why that was.

Queen Zaina took her seat just as the assegai competition began, and I stood next to the wooden throne—not even daring to think about asking to sit in it.

We watched the enthusiastic participants line up for the first throws. There were three different teams from what I could tell—the blue team, the orange team, and the red team. Each team's spears—their assegais I mean—matched each athlete's corresponding colors.

One athlete from each team came to the front of the invisible line and looked at the distant target hanging from the average height tree at the end of the field.

The first three young men swung their arms as far back as they could, then simultaneously propelled their assegais forward with all of their might. Two spears hit their targets—one belonging to the representative from the blue team, and one belonging to the representative from the red team.

Everyone clapped.

The successful two athletes rejoined their groups as the other members of their teams stepped forward—to the same invisible line as the first athletes. The strapping young boy with the tan freckled face from the orange team, however, disappointedly walked over to the tree stump seating as several of the assegai fans patted him on the back as encouragement.

Apparently, while all this was going on, I hadn't realized that I'd been absent-mindedly pacing back and forth, trying to think of something to say to initiate a positive conversation with the queen.

"Kay?"

I stopped. She must've been thinking the same thing I'd been thinking. We were totally on the same wave length. "Your pacing's making me dizzy. Why don't you just sit down already?" Okay, slightly different wave lengths.

I looked over at the second throne that she gestured to. "Are you sure—I mean, that it's okay for me to sit here?"

The queen lifted both hands with a shrug. "What do I care?"

Well, I guess it hadn't been reserved for anyone special after all—especially since she was letting me sit in it. I settled in the tree bark throne and was actually surprised by how comfortable it was. It curved perfectly against my back, and had arm rests that were long enough so that my wrists didn't have to hang over them, like with the shortened arm rests in some of the cheap movie theatres back home. There was even a foot stool the perfect distance out, and I didn't waste any time propping up my feet on it.

The weather was so perfect that it actually reminded me of the leisurely vacation Beth and I were supposed to have had in Cape Town. I sighed, and decided not to think about it. Instead, I convinced myself to pretend that I was on a beach somewhere—with a possible new friend—who just happened to be a queen of a secret village.

"You know, all we're really missing is someone to bring us a couple of glasses of lemonade—maybe a couple of grapes. I could actually really get used to this— lying around all day—not doing anything." I yawned. "The perks of being queen."

Queen Zaina swiftly slid to the edge of her throne, a look of pure irritation on her face.

"Is that what you think it means to be queen here? To lie around all day—and do nothing—as you say?"

"Oh, no Queen Zaina." I quickly scrambled to get my annoyingly reappearing foot out of my mouth. "I just meant that…"

The queen abruptly raised her hand to cut me off. She was standing now, towering over me—causing me to slink back into my seat.

"I suppose *anyone* could be queen of Ipharadisi—since all it would mean would be to lie around all day and not do…*anything*—did you say?" I resisted the urge to answer the obviously rhetorical question. The queen waited to see if I would indeed be stupid enough to answer. Thankfully,

I wasn't.

"You know, you are not the first to come to my village, and to look down on our way of life. But let me remind you why your life was saved, and let *me* explain to you what it means to be queen here—so that maybe you will understand the *privilege* it is to live in Ipharadisi."

I wanted to object, but decided against it—especially with Tuki not being around.

"Where you sit Kay—on *this* land—it means sacrifice so that others may have a better life. It means doing whatever is necessary to ensure that *others* are safe." The queen walked around the two thrones, only one having an owner. She lightly touched the empty seat. "It means having to carry a burden that no one else can share."

"You have Tuki," I blurted out—dumbfounded that I'd assumed I had any understanding of what she was talking about. I expected the queen to retort with a quip. Instead, Queen Zaina sat back down on her throne—her voice softening, her eyes remembering. She then cleared her throat—and I wasn't sure she would be able to speak.

"Yes," the queen finally replied. "I have Tuki. But no king. No father. No mother to watch me grow."

I remembered what Tuki had told me about her mother—Queen Ayanna, and found myself wanting to know more.

"What was she like—your mother I mean?"

The queen smiled fondly, unaware of how far down she'd let her guard.

"My mother was the strongest woman I've ever known—yet also the most caring. She was the very first queen of Ipharadisi, and she balanced her responsibilities in such a way that she would wake up *every* day while the night was still, and the moon was bright, just to take me to the nearest school many, many villages away.

And if ever I was too tired to walk as a child, she would carry me the rest of the way—until there were blisters on her feet and blood on her heels. Every day she walked distances you couldn't imagine—to be both queen to a village—and a mother to a child."

The softness in the queen's eyes slowly faded as she stopped staring into the distance. She looked back over her shoulder. "Because *that* is what it means to be queen here. And *that* is what it means to be an Ipharadisian. So, the next time you attempt to confuse *your* desire to do nothing all day—as you say, with mine—or any other Ipharadisian, please, do us all a favor…and *don't*."

The queen turned away, but not nearly quickly enough. Because before she was no longer facing me, I saw the tears that were in her eyes.

"She was killed you know. Before she ever saw me become queen."

"I'm sorry," I said, and hoped she knew that I was being genuine. Because as much of a mean girl that I thought Zaina was, it occurred to me that I never had to trade blisters on my feet just for the opportunity to get an education. And although we'd of course had a falling out before I left, I had a mother and a father back home who had gotten to see every birthday, every play date and every graduation so far.

I'd had it super easy, which is partly why I wanted to get back home so badly. And partly why I realized that I may have misjudged the queen. Because as Erec had helped me to realize earlier, it was hard to think you knew something about someone once you realized how little you knew about—well, anything.

By the time we both focused back on the competition, it was practically almost over. The orange team had gained an incredible amount of ground and was now in first place.

We watched as the last athlete threw his long, sharpened spear into the air. I could tell he was going to miss the target because he had thrown it off his starting mark, and I could see the looming shadow increasing in size.

Wait a second, this guy was way off his mark.

A little *too* off his mark.

Was that thing supposed to be coming in our direction like that?

It got closer. I realized what was about to happen, and I screamed to the crowd.

"Run!"

Everybody jumped out of their seats, but I knew I only had time to get one person out of the way. I threw the queen to the opposite side of the ground—out of the trajectory of the missile like spear. And that left exactly one person still in its target range…me.

I screamed bloody murder when the spear pierced through my midsection. I also heard Queen Zaina screaming my name. "Kay!" She ran to my side, and I turned my head—barely breathing. I looked down.

Nothing.

The queen was furious. "You! What is *wrong* with you?" I stood in front of the crowd full of Ipharadisians, speechless. I looked over at the remaining athletes—all with their spears securely in their hands.

I looked over to the target bag. The spear had perfectly

connected with its mark—which was nowhere near me.

So why did it feel like it had gone straight through my body?

I began to shake when I realized it was happening to me again; first in the park, then at the airport—now this.

"You! Answer me! Why have you thrown me to the ground?? Have you lost your mind?!"

"Yes."

The queen stared at me in disbelief.

Something had been happening to me long before I arrived here. I remembered forewarning myself that it would travel with me—these *things* that I'd been seeing.

I needed help. I needed to talk to someone about this. But who here would understand? *Why* did this keep happening to me?

I tried to think on the positive side—at least there were no mental institutions here—that I knew of—so at least they couldn't have me committed if I told someone how I'd been losing it.

I buried my face in my hands so that the queen wouldn't see the tears that I knew were coming. "I'm sorry," I tried not to cry. And although my face was hidden, my voice didn't suppress the emotion. "Please," I choked out, "please excuse me."

Callum wasn't here this time to comfort me; to tell me I wasn't going insane. So with everyone looking on, I did exactly what my instincts told me to do, which was to run as far away as my scrawny, humiliated legs would take me. happening to me?

I tried to think on the positive side—at least there were no mental institutions here—that I knew of—so at least they couldn't have me committed if I told someone how

I'd been losing it.

I buried my face in my hands so that the queen wouldn't see the tears that I knew were coming. "I'm sorry," I tried not to cry. And although my face was hidden, my voice didn't suppress the emotion. "Please," I choked out, "please excuse me."

Callum wasn't here this time to comfort me; to tell me I wasn't going insane. So with everyone looking on, I did exactly what my instincts told me to do, which was to run as far away as my scrawny, humiliated legs would take me.

11. The Secret Corner

I was thankfully able to find my way back through the thicket shortcut we had taken to the field. But instead of walking through the market, I stayed in the outskirts, and walked in the shadows of the jungle trees where no one could see me.

I kept pushing forward until I came out into an area that I recognized from my second night here. This was Erec's community. I thought about it a while. I didn't know that I honestly felt like divulging my deep, dark secret right now, but I walked ahead anyway.

I remembered how quiet the doctor had been the first time that I'd visited his tent—so quiet in fact, that I had thought no one was in. So I figured I'd probably be sneaking up on him again this time, but when I walked into the open tent, it was empty. I had to admit, I felt a little disappointed.

I thought about checking the surrounding beehive huts to see if he were home. Instead, I decided to walk away. But before I got too far out the gate, I heard the sound of children, laughter and singing. And I found myself drifting towards the joyful tunes.

I walked past the medical tent and through the

mazelike beehive community. There, I came upon a small, wooden school house with a slanted, green-leafed roof and a white, painted exterior with animal paintings on the side of it. The paintings looked as if they'd been drawn by the children inside. So this is where the melodious sound of children singing had been coming from.

I pushed open the wooden door to find about twenty small boys and girls with their hands folded, sitting at their little wooden desks, and singing to the timing of Erec's conductor hand. I couldn't understand the words, but I let the melody seep through me. I found it to be quite soothing—therapeutic even, and I was saddened when the song came to an end. Still, I applauded loudly, unapologetic for having listened in.

Erec smiled, then he sat on the edge of the teacher's table and motioned for me to come forward. I walked up to his side.

"Everyone, this is Kay. Say hello to Kay."

"Hello Kay."

I laughed. I felt like I was eight again, and it was my first day in class.

I gave a shy wave. "Sanibonani." The plural isiZulu greeting was one of the only phrases I had successfully retained since arriving here.

The class responded. "Sawubona Kay."

Erec stood up again, and patted the edge of the table where he sat. We traded places as he began to walk around the classroom.

"Alright class, let's show Miss Kay what we have learned today. How would we say hello to Kay in Xhosa?"

The class answered him. "Molo Kay."

"And what would she say in return to all of you?" A little boy with glasses shouted out, "Molweni!"

"Right!" Erec had made his way to the back of the classroom and was now taking his time on the walk back around.

"How would you say hello to Kay if she spoke Swahili?"

"Jambo Kay!"

"Hmm." Erec was tapping his chin with his finger. I could tell that he was looking for a way to challenge them. He seemed to come up with something.

"How could you say hello to Kay if you were in Ghana *or* Nigeria?" Several kids raised their hands. Erec pointed to a beautiful little girl with a shaved head and a burgundy summer dress.

"Yes, Yemi?"

"You could say it in Hausa." Erec nodded. "And what would you say in Hausa?"

Yemi jumped up, "*Sannu* Kay!"

The class erupted with laughter at her enthusiasm.

Erec gave her a high-five. "Okay, I've got one that if you can all answer correctly, recess will start five minutes early. Who's in?" All hands went up.

"Okay, for the grand prize. What would you say to *me* if I greeted you with Bawo Iara?"

The entire class responded, "Mowa dada ese!"

"And why is that?"

Yemi raised her hand again. Erec gave her the go ahead. "Because you said, 'how are you' in Yoruba. So we each said, 'I'm fine thank you,' in Yoruba."

"And why would I speak to you in Yoruba?"

The whole class shouted.

"Because you're from Nigeria!"

"Thaaaat's right!" Erec blew the whistle around his neck, and all the children ran outside to play. I sprung up.

"Wow, that was amazing. How many languages are they learning?"

"For now, about a dozen or so."

My mouth dropped. "A *dozen* different languages? Isn't that a bit much for...what, second grade?"

Erec began collecting some of the children's leftover school supplies. "Not if you consider the more than fourteen hundred languages spoken throughout the continent."

"The *how many?*" I almost fainted. "Are they going to have to *learn...*"

"Oh no," Erec assured me. "But one day, if any of them want to join the rescuers, they'll need to know how to communicate with those they're trying to help. So they'll need to learn as many languages as possible until then."

"Oh—is that normal? Does everyone here speak so many languages?"

Erec shook his head. "Actually, the primary languages here are English and isiZulu."

"I see. So you're a doctor, a plant specialist, *and* you moonlight as a teacher as well. When do you sleep?"

Erec began putting up chairs over the desks, and I helped him.

"Well, except for rescue season, my medical services thankfully aren't needed that often around here. So I just help out whenever I can."

I watched him as he did the last bit of tidying around the classroom, and thought about how much he does for this village. Erec was kind of amazing. No wonder the queen looks at him the way she does.

When everything was all finished, we leaned against the last two chairs that were stacked. We just stayed there in silence for a while, until Erec looked me over. "Hey, I'm guessing that's your only outfit here hunh?"

I looked down at my dirty blouse. "Oh yeah, well, I just never know what to pack for these kidnapped to Ipharadisi excursions."

Erec grinned. "I have something that I think will probably fit. Follow me."

I followed Erec back to the medical tent. There, he lifted up a thin, gold necklace that he had been wearing under his shirt that had a small gold key hanging around it. Erec removed the key and used it to unlock the small, brown trunk that was hidden underneath a table in the back. Erec then pulled out a neatly folded stack of clothes and handed them to me.

"These should be about your size. Try them on. There's someplace I want to show you."

I took the very neat pile from him and thanked Erec for the clothes—before he left to give me some privacy.

I decided not to dilly dally, and quickly took off the stained, sheer, white blouse I'd had on all week, and looked at the selection before me. There were tank tops and long-sleeve shirts, as well as some beautifully feminine slacks and shorts sets.

But there was exactly one cotton dress in the pile, and I thought perhaps a nice casual frock would be just the thing to brighten up my day—especially after the earlier incident with the queen.

So I pulled the long, purple cotton dress over my head

and tied the drawstrings into a bow around the back of my neck. It had bright green flowers on it and was triangular in shape at the top. The dress flowed out on the bottom and was positively beautiful.

I hurried outside the tent to show Erec. "What do you think?" I spun around a few times for added effect. Erec didn't look like he was going to say anything at first, but eventually he simply said, "They fit."

I don't know why, but I was a little disappointed at his reaction—not because he didn't make a big deal about the way I looked—I didn't care about that. I was disappointed because *he* seemed disappointed. There was something about the tone of his voice that I couldn't figure out. I didn't like it.

I stopped twirling around and moved in closer. "Erec, is something wrong?" I was genuinely concerned. Though I'd only known him a couple of days, I had a feeling it was unusual to see Erec look so down. But just as I was prepared to find out the answer, he shook it off.

"Sorry. Are you ready for a little trip?"

"I guess…" I thought about pressing the question, but I decided not to push it.

Instead, Erec and I walked to an opposite end of Ipharadisi that I hadn't yet ventured to. It was somewhat desolate compared to the rest of the village.

We walked for about half an hour when it started getting darker—not because of the time of day—as it was still early afternoon, but because I could barely see the sunlight through the dense jungle canopy above.

The further under the canopy we walked, the more I began to feel like I was in an exotic pet store. I heard buzzing and bird whistles, and ooh ooh sounds that I'd never heard before. If I were alone, I possibly would've found it a tad bit scary. Luckily, Erec helped me identify some of the sounds I could hear but couldn't see.

"That is a colobus monkey."

"A what? Where?"

Erec took my hand and pointed to something on one of the tree branches that looked as if it were being excessively weighed down.

"The black and white one there—with the white beard and the fluffy white tail."

"Oh." The colobus monkey was chewing on some of the leaves it had taken hostage from the tree branch. From the side, it kind of looked like a skunk, but when I looked into his deep, thoughtful eyes, I detected an irritation at my invasive gawking. So I stopped staring and followed Erec to the next sighting, where he pointed out a creature that vastly differed.

"Wow, that's a splendid sunbird."

I looked up. "You like it hunh?"

"Yes. It's very pretty, but I meant that's what it's called—a splendid sunbird."

"Ohh." I took a step forward. The sunbird's black, purple, aqua-green and burgundy chest shimmered as it caught a ray of sunlight. The beautiful bird almost didn't seem real.

Erec guided me out a little farther as he continued to point out colorful little creatures. I felt as if he were taking me on my own little tour of the world's largest conservatory—and I loved everything that he showed me. Part of me wished we could stay here all day, but eventually the sightseeing ended.

"Okay, stop."

I did as requested, and looked around at the tree enclosed clearing that Erec had led us to. We stood amongst broken tree branches that littered a wide patch of cluttered ground, in an area that looked as if someone had gone over it with a small bulldozer.

Honestly, it was kind of creepy looking, but Erec had gone through all of the trouble to bring me out here, so I tried to think of something nice to say without having to lie. I thought *hard*.

"Wow, this is…um…ecological. *Very* interesting."

Erec didn't respond. He was too busy searching around us, so he couldn't tell that I felt something creeping under my dress. My eyes widened, and I was just about to scream when Erec raised his hand to warn me.

"Don't move."

I froze in place, and felt its rough, dry skin slithering around my ankle. I wasn't sure if I'd be able to hold in my scream as it began slinking up my leg. But it wasn't until its loud alarming blow made the bottom of my dress poof up that I ran at lightning speed, climbing my way halfway up the nearest tree.

"*Kay*, I told you not to move. You scared him."

"Scared *him*??" I looked behind me as I bear hugged the wooden skyscraper that my arms and legs were now wrapped around. How in the world could I scare a slithering, scaly…hunh?

I let go of my vertical security log, and turned to find out why Erec had brought us all the way out here. And, what I saw amazed me.

It was a baby elephant—a tiny, adorable, frightened baby elephant. And it was hiding behind Erec.

"Oh how adorable." I stepped out to sneak a closer

peek, slightly concerned that Erec was standing right in between its long ivory tusks.

Wait a minute.

"Hey, I didn't know baby elephants had tusks at this age."

Erec reached back to stroke its long, ridged, grey trunk. "They don't—baby elephants that is. But he's much older than you think."

"Oh?"

"Yep. He's full grown—a pygmy elephant."

"Pygmy?"

"Yeah, they're quite rare."

Wow. It was a full grown elephant, but the size of a petting zoo pony. I kind of loved it.

"He got lost from the rest of his parade and has been hiding out here ever since. They must've gotten separated during something horrible—poaching I assume—because he won't let anyone near him."

I noted Erec's proximity to the miniature elephant. "He looks pretty alright with you."

Erec patted him on the back. "We have an understanding. Zaina came out here the day I informed her of our newest little arrival. She tried to pet him, but he freaked and ran—trampled most of the vegetation around here. I came back and replanted a few things."

"Aw, well, it's very nice to meet you..."

"Milkshake. His name is Milkshake."

I laughed at first because I thought he was kidding. "You named the elephant *Milkshake?*"

"Yeah. He can't get enough of 'em—probably the only elephant I know that likes dairy."

I shook my head in disbelief. "Do I even want to know

why you know that?" Erec just smirked. "Okay then, it is very nice to meet you...*Milkshake*." The miniature-sized elephant peered at me from behind his protector. Milkshake was timid, yet curious. I liked him.

"He's really something Erec. Thank you for bringing me out here."

"No problem, I figured you'd like him. Plus, you looked like you could've used a pick me up." I was a little surprised. I thought I'd put on a brave face when I entered his classroom after my assumed nervous breakdown earlier. I guess Erec saw through it.

"Was it that obvious?"

"Yes...and no. You came back early, so I guessed that meant things didn't go so well with Queen Zaina."

"They really didn't."

Erec stopped petting Milkshake. "What happened?"

"It's a long story. I don't even know that you'd believe me."

"Try me."

I thought about it for a moment. Aside from Tuki, Erec was really my only friend out here. I guess if I were to tell anyone about my disturbing occurrences; the vision I had today, the dreams I had before I came here—it would be him. After all, he is a doctor—although I wondered if the whole patient confidentiality thing applied in the middle of the jungle.

"Well, there's something that I've never told anyone." Erec was intrigued.

"What?"

"It's kind of hard to explain."

"I'm a good listener," Erec countered.

That didn't stop me from nervously fidgeting. "I don't

even know where to begin."

Erec reached over and wrapped his hands around mine, causing my nervous fidgeting to cease.

"Then that's where you should start—at the beginning."

I paused. "Okay. Well, I guess it all started when I was adopted."

Erec's head turned to the side. I don't think that was the direction he was expecting this to go in. I tried to read the expression on his face but couldn't, so I went on.

"It turns out I was actually born in Africa."

"Really??" Erec was shocked. I suppose I would've been surprised as well. I didn't exactly fit right in.

"It's a long story; but my mother—the one who raised me—sort of rescued me from a burning shack that my mother—my biological mother—was in."

"Wow Kay, I had no idea."

"Yeah well neither did I. My parents didn't tell me until the day before I left America."

"Really? How did you react?"

I thought back to my last moments with my parents and I hung my head. "Not so good. I was so angry I couldn't think straight."

Erec seemed confused. "Angry? For being adopted?"

"No, for lying mostly—but yeah, maybe a little for that too."

"I see. You know Kay, perhaps there's much that you may find unfair, but remember you were chosen. I didn't get to choose my parents, and they never had a choice in me. But someone *chose* you out of love, and it sounds as if they tried to show it to you, despite the fact that they may have faltered in places. I do hope you're okay with all of that now. "

I was. I really was.

"So, was that the beginning, or was that the part you said I wouldn't believe?"

"Oh, well I…" I was just about to explain why I thought my dreams were connected to something happening before I was adopted, when Milkshake started to make the oddest sound. Erec turned around and focused in on the elephant. This time Milkshake made the sound even louder, and that's when Erec realized what was about to happen.

Erec promptly stepped to the side and suggested I do the same.

I hesitated. "Why?" Exactly one and a half seconds later I found out. Milkshake opened his mouth and shot his trunk up into the air—directly pointed at my face I might add—and blew out what looked and felt like everything he had eaten since the beginning of time. I was covered. I was head-to-toe dripping wet and covered in elephant vomit—cute, rare, pygmy, elephant vomit. I flicked my hand free of some of the goo.

"Milkshake hates me doesn't he?"

I waited for confirmation from Erec. "Oh no. He probably just had a little too much to eat today." Erec tried to control his bubbling, hysterical laughter.

"Sure he did." I looked down. "Well, so much for the dress." Erec abruptly stopped laughing—his light mood then disappeared and was replaced by that sad face from earlier.

"Come on. I know a place we can get you cleaned up." He didn't speak another word as he led me towards a loud rushing sound. I thought I felt a light spray, but I wasn't sure.

"Where are we going?"

"You'll see." A shiver ran through me as the words left his mouth. I was having déjà vu—and not the kind you couldn't place either. I knew *exactly* where I was when I'd heard those words before, and I knew exactly *who* had said them—but I couldn't think about him now.

We hiked up the staggered rocks as Erec parted the branches between the last two trees. What he showed me at the top of the cliff—it quite literally took my breath away.

There were waterfalls upon waterfalls in the wide open space, and the entire jungle sung around us. It was larger than life—fairytale even—and I was beginning to feel as if I were in a magical land.

"Come on. Let's get you cleaned up." Erec led us down the cliffs where we carefully climbed into a cave that was cattycorner to the falls.

Part of one of the waterfalls trickled into the cave with just enough force for me to wash off in—but not too much force for me to be blown away by. I practically ran to the little fall to get the rest of Milkshake's lunch off of me.

I untied the string around the back of my neck, but not before I looked over my shoulder.

"A little privacy please?"

Erec tried not to grin. "You know I *am* a doctor. Patients get undressed in front of me all the time."

"That may be, but unless *you* want to end up the patient, I suggest you turn around—*now*."

"Hmm, touché." Doctor Louron made an about face and exited the private little cave as I undressed. When I was finished washing off—myself *and* the dress—I went back outside to join Erec. I secretly wished that I had the cow's horn comb little Kayla had given me so that I could style my hair while it was wet—but I'd just have to let it air dry for now.

I found Erec sitting on one of the lower level cliffs. He was looking out over the vast falls, totally lost in thought. I cleared my throat a few times before I reached him—hoping I wouldn't startle him.

Erec looked over his shoulder.

"You got it clean!" He jumped up with excitement, but then collected himself. "I mean, you—you got clean. That's great."

I let what he said sink in, slowly putting two and two together.

"So, who did it belong to?"

"Hunh?"

I wasn't going to let him throw me off the trail this time. "The lock and key—how you remembered what size the clothes were—the look on your face when you thought her dress was ruined...who was she?"

Erec seemed to have lost his breath, slowly putting out his hand to hold the nearby tree. No—he put his hand out so that the tree could hold *him*. Erec then covered his face with the bottom of his palms, and I wasn't sure that he would ever reveal his beautiful smile again. But finally, he looked up, possibly ready to talk.

"Her name was Nasara. She was my wife."

I was stunned. Though older than I, Erec was still so young to have had a wife. And my heart dropped a little, at the way he spoke of someone he loved in the past tense. I was almost afraid to ask, but I needed to know.

"Erec, what happened to her?"

Erec looked off into the horizon, not able to meet my eyes. "I am not from here—I am sure you know." That I did—at least, I'd had a feeling.

"Where I grew up, life was highly traditional. Children modeled after their parents, and there were often arranged marriages." Erec paused before continuing. "So, when I became of age, my father arranged for me to marry a young girl from a wealthy neighboring tribe. Yet despite how much he wanted this, I knew that it was not possible."

I tried not to seem too eager, but I was desperate to know, "why?" Erec's tortured expression quickly made me regret bringing it up.

"Because Kay, I had already fallen in love—hiding from our parents, and playing on the beach until our laughter left us voiceless—or until our parents called us home. We did not know of arranged marriages then, or understand cruel things of adult ways—of separation—of pain. I only knew then of a love whose eyes were the color of obsidian, and whose laughter was music to the world. So it was clear to me, even as a boy, that I could never love anyone else. That I would die before marrying anyone but my love."

The way Erec spoke of her, it made my heart stop before he spoke up again.

"When it came time for the wedding that my father had arranged I protested profusely, but he still would not listen, so Nasara and I, we fled. We didn't have much at all, so we took refuge in a nearby village, and got married there—hoping that my father and everyone else in our village would be forced to accept us now. And nervously, the day after we were married we returned to our land."

Erec sat down for this last part.

"When we were very close to our home, I had the idea to bring back something to eat—as a peace offering, and also to celebrate. So I sent Nasara ahead to wait for me while I secured an appropriate catch from the hunt. It took me almost the entire day, but when I succeeded, I was so filled with joy that I ran as fast as I could to begin the celebrations. But when I arrived, there was nothing— no one there to celebrate.

In the hours that I was gone, our village had come under attack. Warlords had pillaged our small homes for resources and for workers. By the time I returned, my entire village was burning to the ground.

There were bodies everywhere, and I recognized every…single…face. My friends, my uncle, my aunt, my mother, my father, and Nasara—my bride of just one day.

I was helpless—with not a thing I could do to save them. So I lay down, and I waited for the burning to stop; and it when it became bearable, I lifted each one of their bodies, and I buried them—all of them; the entire village—until I couldn't carry anymore.

For years I wandered, until I found a village that took me in and gave me a new home. I went to school there, and the teacher helped me to go to college. That's where I learned to become a doctor—learned how to always be able to help those who need it. I studied day and night, and hardly ever slept. I received several degrees sooner than my classmates received their first.

One day I decided to go on safari—the way my father and I used to do. Only this time I went alone. But during my travel, I saw a small group running for their lives.

Many of them appeared badly injured. Still, one of them—the most clearly hurt—seemed to be trying to help everyone else. It was Tuki. So I ran to her and helped her carry the injured parties to Ipharadisi.

When we arrived here, I set up the tent I'd been travelling with and began to care for all those who were hurting. And I was incredibly happy to do so.

Queen Zaina came by that day. She said Tuki told her of how I helped care for the people. The queen called me brave, and asked me to stay here with her as her king. I told her I would stay, but not in the way she wanted.

It had been more than ten years since I'd lost my Nasara. But it had felt like just ten days. Zaina wanted something that I could not give her—a heart that had died long ago."

Erec and I stood there together watching the clouds pass by. He knew so much about lost love that I wondered how he tolerated it. He knew more about its joys and its heartaches than I would ever know.

I was thankful for the brief relationship I'd had before my new life here, but I wondered now—knowing all that Erec had endured, if I even had the right to miss the one I left behind.

"I'm so sorry Erec."

"Yes. And I you."

"Me?" I asked, confused.

"Yes. I've seen the sadness in your eyes as well—a different kind of sadness, but sadness all the same. Tell me, who was he?"

I sighed and pictured Callum's deep brown almond eyes. "Someone I'm never going to see again."

We sat there in the passing sprays of the waterfalls

before us. I thought about Callum, and I know Erec thought of Nasara.

It was later that I realized we'd been leaning on each other—as I rested my head against his shoulder, and as Erec wrapped himself around my back; his cheek pressed against mine under the setting sun. We remained that way—for hours—on the edge of the cave's cliff, as we looked out over the vast abyss, towards a rescuing village called Ipharadisi.

12. Saying Goodbye

Over the next several months, Erec and I began to develop a rhythm together. After seeing a patient or teaching a class, Erec would come find me, and I would just be wrapping up at the Gurmu farm, where I'd been getting cooking lessons from one of the village chefs.

And in turn, whenever I got bored or wished I had someone to talk to, I'd just stop by the medical tent, and Erec would be almost finished patching up someone's donga injuries and be ready to eat.

We always came straight to the waterfall cave after packing our lunches, and sure enough, Milkshake would tag along. He'd gotten used to me being around, and I think he'd actually grown to like me—though it could've had something to do with the custard milk tarts I always brought him. I think Milkshake liked the fact that I sprinkled blueberries on top for added effect.

I enjoyed my lunches with Erec because I found that when we were together, I didn't miss my family or home as much. And, it seemed as if when I came around—at times that he would be sitting somewhere and staring off into the distance—that his mood would perk up when he saw me as well.

I think maybe Erec didn't mourn the loss of Nasara as much when we were together.

One person, however, who *didn't* appreciate our lunches together was Queen Zaina. She always managed to find us somewhere around the village—if we weren't by the waterfalls or hiding out at the cave.

In a weird way, I think she saw me as competition. I remembered how Erec told me a few months back that when he first came to Ipharadisi, the queen asked him to be her king.

I guess that's why she always wanted to join in on our little excursions—which I honestly didn't even mind because I wasn't interested in the good doctor that way.

I mean, I wasn't blind. Erec had the face and body of an international supermodel. But I still had unexplainable dreams, and no matter how hard I wished for them not to, most of them still featured Callum. And even if they didn't, the way Erec still spoke about his bride of only one day, I don't think myself, the queen, or anyone else could ever fill the hole that was permanently carved into his unfairly broken heart.

But the days were turning and it was almost spring now, though that didn't mean much in terms of a change of weather in Ipharadisi. Paradise was pretty much always that—paradise.

Back in America, I would have been reveling at the fact that it was almost spring. In New York, the trees would be sprouting leaves again, and the flowers would be blossoming—although they didn't have the kind of flowers back home that I got to see in Ipharadisi.

Here, there were purple flowers that looked like bicycle wheels, with blue pollen centers and polka dots around the middle. There were also pinkish-red flowers that looked like witches' fingers, with startling yellow tips as fingernails.

But my favorites were the spiked white and powdered pink ones that looked almost like electricity—or something that you would only find at the bottom of the sea.

It was undeniable, there wasn't anything in Ipharadisi that wasn't one hundred percent breathtaking.

That's why Erec and I were making our usual lunch trip through the jungle to the waterfall cave when we bumped into Mr. Gurmu the vegetable grower and his wife Larah—the village's head chef.

I got to know Mr. and Mrs. Gurmu back in January— about a month after I arrived here. Erec had persuaded me to get to know my fellow Ipharadisians one day before he and I started making our lunches together a daily event.

Actually, there was a brief period when I didn't think Erec and I would ever hang out at all again, let alone on a daily basis.

For some reason, we managed to get into quite a few silly spats here and there, but one in particular changed everything about the way I looked at my new circumstances in life.

It was three weeks after Erec first took me to the waterfalls to meet Milkshake, and it was becoming increasingly difficult to romanticize my situation. This notion that even though I was trapped, at least I was trapped inside of paradise.

The novelty of Ipharadisi had completely worn off for me and I'd begun complaining about something new every day.

One morning in particular, I'd woken up crankier than usual—missing my down pillows and feather bed, steaming hot showers and cable TV; and had become a bit stir-crazy with boredom. But with Tuki busy with her duties to the queen, I'd chosen the only other person I knew in Ipharadisi to let out my frustrations on. And, rightfully so, he was sick of it.

"Well, maybe if you spent *less* time complaining and *more* time getting to know people, you'd feel *more* like you belong here and *less* in need of a babysitter."

I turned unnecessarily red and stood up from the stool by the surgery table. "Is that what you think? That I need a...*babysitter*?"

Erec was clearly exasperated and barely looked at me when he spoke. It was clear that we were starting to wear out our welcome with each other.

"That's not what I meant Kay. Stop being so cranky."

For whatever the reason, that pushed me over the edge. "I am *not* a cranky person. I'll have you know I won the most joyful and humorous award at camp when I was younger. So there!"

"Are you sure the humor wasn't in giving you that award in the first place?"

I gasped. "And what is *that* supposed to mean?"

Erec slammed closed his doctor's kit. "It *means* if you're so joyful and chuck full of laughter, then wouldn't you be able to entertain and oh, I don't know—take care of…*yourself?*"

I couldn't believe he said that. Aside from the couple of times I pretended to be the new doctor in town, and the one time I accidentally set his flu patient on fire, I had clearly been a complete asset to him—in my mind. But I saw that my presence obviously wasn't appreciated here. I folded my arms.

"Fine! I'll leave then! But don't ask me to come keep you company again." I suddenly remembered that he had never asked me to keep him company.

Erec laughed, and I became even more irritated that he thought it was funny.

I stormed out the medical tent and decided to prove to him that I could be completely independent in this strange new world. And, I would do that as soon as I could find someone to show me how.

I sighed. Erec was right. I had become a cranky, childlike, homesick mess.

Back in New York I was fearless. I was queen of the student newsroom and was on the fast track to becoming a world renowned news reporter.

But here, in the middle of the non-concrete jungle, I had lost all sense of self and direction, and was utterly falling to pieces. I thought about it and decided to take Dr. Louron's advice—though I still wasn't ready to forgive him for being so mean about it.

I figured I could calm myself down with a nice long walk to the market. But when I got to the three-prong fork in the road—where I usually went straight, this time I went left. It was the opposite facing direction of the left the queen had taken us that day on the way to the assegai competition.

I walked down the narrow path, wondering why I'd never ventured this way before. It was quite tranquil—like that of a peaceful countryside.

As I walked further, I noticed rows and rows of fruit trees and planted vegetables to the right side of the pathway. It was a mini farm. And there was a fence to the left of the path where there were animals and livestock.

I stepped off the dirt road and walked in between the lined rows of ripe produce—some of which I recognized from the market, but still couldn't put a name to.

I walked up to the grass-roofed, wooden shack and knocked on the door.

"Hello?"

No one answered. I waited a bit and then found myself wandering around to the back of the grassy shack where I spotted a short, stout, older man, and a petite looking woman of about the same age as he—both sitting around a gigantic, iron cooking pot.

The round, bald gentleman was peeling corn, and the woman was using a wooden spoon almost twice her size to stir the contents of the gigantic steaming pot. The wind blew the steam my way and with it the aromas of coconut, corn, and milk.

My mouth watered. I hurried up to introduce myself to the two residents and had to swallow the saliva that I suddenly began to overproduce on the way there. I cleared my throat when I approached them.

"Um, hello. My name is Kay."

The stoutly man looked up and offered me a gigantic smile. "Jambo Kay! I am Abiodun Gurmu. This is my wife Larah Gurmu." The wife grinned as she continued to stir. "Jambo dear."

Gurmu patted the seat next to him. "Kalia kiti tafadhali." He smiled.

I confessed.

"I'm sorry. I'm sort of new around here. I don't really know that many phrases in isiZulu yet." Mr. Gurmu had a perplexed expression on his face and his wife let out a muffled laugh.

Mr. Gurmu was able to contain his laughter but folded his hands. "I did not speak to you in isiZulu my dear—but in kiSwahili. My wife and I, we are from Kenya. The official languages there are English and Swahili. That is why I say jambo, or habari. Though you may prefer hello."

I turned red. "I'm sorry." I knew from Erec's class that most of the people here were from different places, but for some reason I kept trying to clump everyone together. I felt slightly awkward now.

I began nervously fidgeting with my hair, hoping I hadn't offended the lovely couple with my ignorance. I think Mrs. Gurmu could feel my uneasiness.

Larah stopped stirring and came to sit down beside me.

"Don't worry dear. There are many, many nations here. Yet, we are all one nation at the same time. My husband and I have been in Ipharadisi for more than thirty years now, and I have found that most of its residents are understanding of…" I knew she was looking for the word that described me. "Ignorance." I flinched.

Mrs. Gurmu put her hand over mine. "I do not say that to insult you. I mean it in the purest form of its definition dear. There is just so much that to probably no fault of your own, you do not know yet. If you did not take the time to learn, that would be one thing, but something tells me you are beginning that process." I nodded.

"Of course, there will be some who may be greatly offended if you make incorrect assumptions about them. Ignorance is not *always* so well tolerated. Questions before assumptions are generally best. But you'll continue to learn as you travel throughout Ipharadisi."

I appreciated Mrs. Gurmu being so candid yet polite with me. She was right. Actually, she *and* Erec were both right. I'd have to start making more of an effort. There was so much I could learn here if I just gave myself the chance.

After a few minutes, Mrs. Gurmu got up to check on the coconut stew she had been stirring when I arrived. It wasn't quite done yet, so she left it alone and sat back down.

I wanted to keep the conversation going, so I tried to think of a follow-up. "Um, do you mind me asking, how did you come to be in Ipharadisi?"

Abiodun and his wife exchanged loving looks and smiled at an unspoken memory. There was joy in the exchange, but also sadness.

Mrs. Gurmu was the first to begin.

"Well dear, we were raised in a life where we spent entire days and entire nights working the land for a harvest. As children, we were not even allowed to go to school because it would take away from our duty to the land. Yet no matter how hard we toiled, we still saw not the fruit of our labor."

Mr. Gurmu took over. "You see, a terrible famine was spreading, and with no thriving crops for the livestock to feed on, and no clean water for either of us to drink; we watched as one by one our entire wealth—which was our cattle, starved to death.

We had heard rumors that our government would send help, but no help ever came."

"So we were forced to leave," said Mrs. Gurmu. She got up to head into the house to get some plates, and returned with three of them. Apparently I was being invited to stay for lunch. I was grateful.

Mrs. Gurmu began filling the plates with the coconut chicken stew, as well as something that looked like cornmeal cakes and a side of fragrant greens. Everything smelled delicious. It tasted even better.

Mrs. Gurmu continued. "We were heading west in search of a place that would yield a better harvest, when we unexpectedly travelled into a poacher's camp. We were terrified."

I shivered as I recalled the memory of which she spoke. I remembered that horrible place Tuki had found me in, and while there, the cruelty that I saw.

"We were too exhausted and weak from hunger to even try to turn around and run back. So when they spotted us, we just knew that it was going to be the end. They took all that we had—which were two cows and an empty coffee pot."

Mr. Gurmu lovingly reached over and dried his wife's eyes with his handkerchief. A sole tear lingered where it had been missed.

"But they weren't even satisfied with that," he explained. "They were also going to take our lives in *addition* to our possessions. But just as we thought we were about to see the end, someone appeared in a beautiful, long hooded cloak."

"It was Queen Ayanna," Mrs. Gurmu informed me. "The first queen of Ipharadisi. She was unlike anyone we'd ever seen. And we would have feared her, for she fought like the rolling thunder—quick and unseen. But then we realized she was *blocking* the attacks against us as if she possessed the powerful force of the winds. She was a master of movements we had never seen."

"Yes," Mr. Gurmu confirmed. "She was brave and skillful, and she spared those evil men's lives where they surely would not have spared hers or our own."

"She helped us," Mrs. Gurmu recalled with a smile, "even though she didn't know us. I will never forget that."

Mr. Gurmu stood up and collected the emptied plates.

"She told us she knew a place where we could start a new life—and be safe from harm. So we followed her here, and we have been in Ipharadisi ever since."

The two nuzzled their heads together.

They were sweet.

"We truly miss Queen Ayanna," added his wife. "She was not only a mighty queen and warrior, but she was also compassionate and kind. She did so much for many of the people here."

Mrs. Gurmu studied my face for a moment and smiled. "You know, there's something about you that actually reminds me of her."

I laughed, unable to imagine what she could possibly see in me that would remind her of a warrior queen. Still, I thanked her for the compliment.

As the day went on, Mr. and Mrs. Gurmu told me of many others' stories—how different people had arrived in

Ipharadisi. What I found most interesting, was that although each story was a rescue story, each Ipharadisian who had been saved contributed to making Ipharadisi an even better place.

It was cooling down outside as it was getting late. So, Mr. Gurmu suggested we go inside for dessert. His wife had made plantains in coconut milk and had prepared some coffee. It was quite wonderful the way each course was even better than the last.

When everyone was finished, Mr. and Mrs. Gurmu walked me outside, wrapping up the answer to one of the last questions I'd just asked.

"That's why we volunteered to care for the land here—and to prepare most of the large meals. We didn't want anyone else to ever feel the kind of endless hunger we once had to endure."

"Do you still have to wake up at sunrise, and go to bed after sunset?"

Mrs. Gurmu smiled. "Yes, but here we see the fruit of our labor. And that my dear, makes all of the difference."

I looked up. There were just a few more hours of daylight left. I hadn't anticipated spending so much time in conversation today, but I was really glad we had.

I thanked Mr. and Mrs. Gurmu for their incredible hospitality, and asked if I could visit again sometime. They both assured me that I was always welcomed, and packed me a little something extra to eat for when I got back to the acorn community.

The next day I woke up the earliest I'd ever awoken my entire time in Ipharadisi. But I still hadn't managed to get up before Tuki. And as usual, she'd left out some breakfast for me while I was still getting the hang of things.

Tuki had truly been making sure that I was comfortable here, so I decided that today would be the last day she left out breakfast for me. Tomorrow I would have breakfast waiting for Tuki.

I didn't waste any time this morning getting out and about. Normally, my first stop would be to Erec's makeshift office, but today I was going straight to the palace hut to speak with Queen Zaina about an epiphany I had last night.

I made my way down the short hill, hoping to catch the queen before her day got too busy. But as I got closer to the palace, I noticed that about a dozen or so Ipharadisians were wearing those handcrafted daggers that were hooked into the leather belts around their waists.

They were making the rounds around the palace hut in a way I hadn't seen them do since that first night I arrived here. Of course, I recognized the one who was giving out instructions.

"Tuki!"

Tuki looked back and waved. I speed walked towards her. "Good morning my Kay. You are up early."

"Yeah, I have a question for Queen Zaina. But hey, why is everyone dressed like they're ready for battle?"

Someone passed by us, twirling a couple of donga sticks. "It is ingqondo season—time for the intelligence. We will be heading back out into the lands soon, to search out those in need of help. Ibutho—warriors protect Ipharadisi while we are away—encase a rescuer is captured or is followed back."

Wow. The seriousness of what goes on in this village

231

was starting to sink in.

"So how long will you all be gone?"

"Ah, it is never known. It could be weeks. It could be months. If one thinks a rescue is possible, it may be attempted, but much is involved."

I was extremely interested. "Like what?"

"Well, as in the case of where we met. I scouted that poacher's camp for weeks—hiding in the grass, sleeping in the trees. It took me much time to decide how they operate.

Then, when the time came for an opportunity, I followed the poachers as they headed out to overtake a village for its resources. In the chaos, I pretended to be one of the villagers, and allowed myself to be captured there. I also allowed myself to be taken back to their camp where the worker children already were. That way, I was able to get all of you out at the same time."

I couldn't believe everything that Tuki had done. I had no *idea* how much went into what they did here.

All the more reason to speak to the queen about my epiphany. But first I thought back to Tuki.

"I think I'm gonna miss you while you're away."

"You are with *certainty* going to miss me Kay. I am sure of it. I will try to find time to miss you as well." We hugged, then I went inside the palace hut to find the queen.

As I searched, I heard someone calling my name. It was Erec, but I really didn't feel like stopping to talk to him right now.

He jogged over anyway.

"Kay! Hey Kay! How are you? Where have you been? You didn't come by yesterday."

I ignored him. I suppose we both had some apologizing to do for our soap opera like meltdowns, but first I wanted to find Queen Zaina.

Erec apparently didn't want to wait.

"Look, I'm sorry for what I said yesterday. I think we were both a bit cranky. I know you're still trying to get adjusted, and I think I just had a lot on my mind."

He waited for me to respond. Instead, I watched several Ipharadisians who were sparring with donga sticks—trying to see if one of them was Queen Zaina.

Erec exhaled—flustered. He gently pulled me by the arm and turned me around to face him—both of his hands around both of my arms, making me give him my undivided attention. "Listen Kay, I really, really am sorry about yesterday. I do enjoy your company. And I shouldn't have made it seem like I didn't."

I sighed. I guess we were going to have to talk about it now. But I'd just opened my mouth to respond, when I noticed the queen out the corner of my eye. She was sparring with some poor guy who looked like he'd had more than enough already.

The queen must've had eyes in the back of her head because she turned around and looked right at me. Queen Zaina swung her donga stick, striking her opponent in the back—keeping her eyes on me the whole time. I cringed.

Erec leaned in closer. "Okay *fine*, you're gonna make me say it. Kay, I don't just enjoy your company, I look *forward* to it. There. I said it."

I suppose I'd been so preoccupied with trying to find the queen that he must've thought I wanted him to beg my forgiveness or something—but I just honestly hadn't been paying attention.

I looked up at Erec now as he made the most ridiculous puppy eyes I'd ever seen. Suddenly he seemed a lot less like the poetry reciting doctor I knew, and more like an awkward, teenage schoolboy. It made me laugh. He smiled. We hugged.

Queen Zaina struck her opponent again and this time he yelped.

"So, what are you doing tomorrow?"

"Well, that's actually what I'm here to talk to Queen Zaina about."

He seemed surprised. "Oh. Okay—well, if you have any free time tomorrow, I thought maybe I could make us some lunch, and we could go see Milkshake again. Hang out at the cave."

"Sure. That would be fun."

"Maybe we could even make a regular thing out of it. You know, get away and clear our heads once in a while."

We chatted for a bit longer because I didn't want to interrupt the queen during her match. But the more Erec and I got carried away with our own conversation, the more Queen Zaina seemed to speak to *me*—through her donga sticks.

She seemed...jealous.

Perhaps this wasn't a good time to patch things up with Erec after all.

"Hey Erec, can I catch up with you later? I want to catch the queen before she gets away."

"Sure." Erec kissed my hand as if he were some sort of character from a Shakespeare play. He said that he would come find me later so that we could make plans for tomorrow. Finally, he bid me "adieu."

Someone was helping the queen's opponent limp away

as the match had finally ended. I walked over and noted that I had really poor timing in trying to make friends with the queen. Still, I figured I'd give it one more try.

I put on my best Girl Scout face and hoped for the best. "Queen Zaina, hi!" The queen gave me her usual unenthused smile. I didn't let it deter me.

"So, I was at the Gurmu farm yesterday, and I had an idea about what I could do to fit in around here."

The queen scoffed as she began walking—glancing back at Erec. "It looks to me like you're fitting in just fine." I heard her mumble something unintelligible under her breath.

I huffed. Was this a place of refuge, or a socially competitive high school?

I thought about telling the queen that I wasn't interested in Dr. Louron that way—but that still wouldn't change my Americans can't be trusted status. So she'd probably continue to hate me for no reason—after all, to her, we were all alike.

"Listen, remember how I told you I was studying journalism before I got caught up in all of this?" I paused. I probably could've phrased that part better. "Well, the Gurmus were telling me some of the stories about how everyone got to be here. They even told me stories about your mother."

Queen Zaina stopped in her tracks. I now had her undivided attention—along with a look that told me I better tread carefully.

I nervously cleared my throat. "So...I was thinking, what if someone interviewed all of the Ipharadisians, and wrote down the histories of everyone who has entered Ipharadisi? You know; what brought them here; the names of all those who helped them start over?" I couldn't tell whether or not the queen was considering it.

"It's just that, the Gurmus told me such extraordinary things about Queen Ayanna. And I thought that if someone…well I…gathered everyone's stories—and collected information from anyone who experienced it first hand, we could write down Ipharadisi's history for future generations to learn from."

I waited for Queen Zaina to answer.

But after a few moments, I started to wonder if maybe I should have practiced the speech before I got here.

"Actually Kay, that is not a bad idea."

"Really?" I couldn't believe we agreed on something. "All the information would stay here of course. But I was thinking we could make it like an encyclopedia or something. I could even get started on it now."

"That is fine. Tell me when it is done."

I tried to keep up with her as she walked. "Well it will probably take some time of course to put it all together. And, I would need someone to start with to really get it going. So…how about it?"

The queen seemed confused. "How about what?"

"How about I start with you? You're the daughter of Ipharadisi's first queen. Do you know how all this came about?"

The queen rolled her eyes. "Of course I do. Who would know better than I?"

"Oh no one Queen Zaina." I was buttering her up— something I learned to do during my days as a student journalist. This would be the closest I'd ever get to my now long past dreams of being a hard hitting news reporter. So I wanted to make sure I got the best interview possible—especially if this was going to be my only major contribution to life.

I cleared my head and made room for everything that I was about to learn. I asked Queen Zaina to take a seat—on her throne if she felt more comfortable—and then I began to fire away with the questions.

The queen spoke about the past—the wars and evils as she called them that made refuge necessary. She also spoke about the grandfather who started Ipharadisi—having only one living child when he arrived here. Thus, making her, Queen Ayanna, the only heir to her father's throne.

I was surprised how openly the queen spoke with me. But I found that most of the Ipharadisians were just as willing to share their stories. So I started writing all of them down in the journal Erec had provided me from his classroom.

He came with me to interview anyone whose language I didn't speak. But over the course of time, I slowly began picking up a number of different languages with different dialects to boot.

Over the next couple of months, I had interviewed over three dozen Ipharadisians and had diligently recorded each one of their stories in my journal.

Each story combined with the others to reflect the spirit of Ipharadisi—its successes, its failures, its hopes, its dreams, its legacies—its visions for the future.

I had started this partly just to have something to keep me busy—to prove to Erec that I could do something on my own here. But also, to feel like I contributed something to this place—to all of these incredible people whose lives deserved to be remembered.

But regardless of my original intentions, what it turned out to be, was a way for the entire village to learn things they never knew about one another—bringing each of them—rather, bringing each one of *us* closer together than ever before.

I was proud of myself. I'd finally found some sort of purpose here. Maybe I wouldn't have the life that I had always dreamed of, but I could still do something that mattered.

That realization, however, was bittersweet.

Part of me was happy to be a part of something so incredibly special, but another part of me felt like I was saying goodbye to everything that I used to know— everyone I used to love.

I slept outside again under the stars, to reflect on everything that had happened since I arrived in Ipharadisi. But before I laid down, I pulled out my canvas messenger bag from the wooden trunk I kept it stored in—inside of Tuki's hut.

Even though there were available huts in different parts of the village, Tuki and I had become close, and had decided to stay hut-mates.

I opened the messenger bag and took out the slightly beaten up digital camera that the student newspaper back home had lent me for the trip I never got to take.

I wondered what they would think if they knew what journey I actually ended up going on. The camera was given to me about a week before I had left, and I'd taken some pictures with my parents and Beth that were now stored on the memory card inside—the same memory card that still had the pictures of Callum and I from the summer we spent together.

I had looked at the photos a few times over the past few months—though I always stopped before I got to the ones with Callum in them. Those I wasn't sure I could handle seeing. Still, I'd gone through the images so many times that the battery was now dying, and it blinked red when I turned it on tonight. The scary warning signal let me know that this would be the last time I'd ever get to look upon my loved ones' faces.

I hesitated before placing my thumb on the silver play button and before pressing down—taking in every single photo as I clicked next through the gallery. This time, when I got to Callum's pictures, I took in a deep breath and lingered on each warm memory.

I gazed at his beautiful smile, and could even feel his arms around me—just as tightly as he was holding me in the photos. These were the ones at the beach, just a few hours before he told me he loved me. Just a few hours more before I had that horrible dream.

I pressed the button down again for the next and final photo, and forced myself to breathe as the battery symbol finally stopped blinking.

And, just like that, Callum's face was gone—forever.

That was three months ago.

Now it was spring, and it was raining by the time Erec and I wrapped up our conversation with Mr. and Mrs. Gurmu. But the rain wasn't a problem as we were going to have lunch inside the cave anyway.

Erec and I continued on to the spot that we'd had lunch at every day for the past three months, and made sure to stop and spend some time with Milkshake on the way there.

Erec had of course made a shelter for Milkshake a long

time ago to protect him from the rain. No wonder Milkshake never tried to leave. Erec took incredibly good care of him—as he did everyone in the village.

When we finally got inside the nice, dry cave, Erec made a fire to keep us warm. I rubbed my hands over the dancing flames as the sound of raindrops echoed inside.

I'd made a wild blueberry pie, Erec's favorite, and he had made a smoked fish with a spicy tomato sauce. They were both delicious. We kept a small, iron pot inside our secret hideout, and brought it out now to make some hot tea seeped with vanilla and dried hibiscus flowers.

After we'd eaten, we laid against the cave walls—away from its trickling corner, watching the waterfall before us. I could only see part of the rushing cascade from where we were, but at least we were warm and toasty inside.

I turned my body towards Erec.

"Hey, Erec..."

"Hunh? What's up?"

"I just wanted to say thank you for everything you've done for me these past few months. I really don't know how I would've made it through all of this without your help."

Erec rolled his head to face mine. "It's no problem Kay. Really. You've sort of helped me through a lot as well."

I laughed. "Me?"

"Yes. I think I was dead inside for a long time—and didn't even know it. Being with you, it's brought me back to life again."

"Oh."

I didn't say anything else as we laid inside the cave just listening to the rain. I looked ahead, enjoying the sounds of nature around us. Erec leaned forward to scoop up another cup of hibiscus tea, and I noticed a long scar on the back of his neck.

"Hey what's that?"

"What's what?" Erec looked around as if he expected to see a fly or something.

I lowered the back of his collar on his blue, short sleeved shirt to get a better look at it. It was an old scar, I could tell.

"How did this happen?" Erec felt the back of his neck where my fingers pressed. He realized what I was talking about.

"Oh that. I got it a long time ago, before I learned to defend myself."

"Defend yourself?"

"Yes. Remember when I told you how my village was attacked, all those years ago?" I remembered. I remembered how sad he looked when he made himself re-live it so that he could share it with me. I nodded.

"Well Kay, unfortunately, that happened a lot in that part of the land. Young men are trained early to learn to defend themselves—to protect their village. I, however, didn't learn until much later. I got that scar during the attack. Afterwards, I quickly learned to defend myself."

"Defend yourself how?" Erec smiled. He stood up and extended his hand. "I'll show you."

I thought about it for a moment then shrugged. "Okay, I'll bite." I stood up and put my hands on my hips. He was a doctor not a fighter, so I was curious to see what he knew about self-defense.

"Okay, attack me."

I raised my eyebrows. "What do you mean?"

"I mean attack me. You know, unless you're scared I might hurt you."

I laughed.

"Hardly. I'm from New York."

Erec lowered his hands to his sides. "Then attack me."

"But I thought *you* were supposed to be the one giving *me* a demonstration."

Erec huffed. "Kay, stop being difficult just..."

I tried to surprise him by taking a swing at him mid-sentence. It didn't work. Before I even finished extending my arm, he pulled me in, and twisted my arm behind my head—bending me backwards—his hand on the small of my back so I wouldn't fall over. He smiled. I frowned.

Erec let me back up, and I straightened out my clothes. "Well that was...interesting."

Erec walked around to my other side. "I thought you would think so. I realize you've only seen one side of me all this time. But there's a lot more to me Kay. Would you like to try again?"

I shook out my arm. "Not particularly."

Erec watched as I rubbed my shoulder. He grew concerned.

"I'm sorry. I thought I was being gentle. Are you okay?"

I felt my face turn into a pout. I shook my head.

"Kay..." Erec dropped his hands to his side again, this time in remorse and...

"Psych!" I made another surprise swing at him—my loose fist and arm going the complete opposite direction of his body—just to make it all the way back around, of course, like I was trying to throw a curve ball or something. I was just sure I would catch him off guard this time. And perhaps I did, because he over compensated when deflecting me from making contact—knocking me aside so hard I had to grab hold of his wrist just to keep from falling over. Instead, we *both* fell over.

Anticipating the fall, Erec threw himself to the ground so that I would have something soft to land on. It worked, but we had come down with such a force that we rolled over each other—Erec finally landing on top of me.

We were both extremely serious for a moment, but then we cracked up laughing so hard that our laughter bounced off the cave walls and made us chuckle even harder.

Our hilarity finally calmed down about the same time that a drop of water splashed from the waterfall nearest us—landing directly on Erec's already moist lips.

Light reflected off the tiny little droplet and created a shimmer on the roof of the dimly lit cave. I watched as the water trickled down from the top of his mouth, very slowly down to the lips of mine. Erec's eyes rested on the droplet just briefly before our eyes met again.

Our gaze was softly interrupted by the lightest hibiscus petal that floated in the air, softly landing on the blush of my cheek. Erec didn't have to move much to lift it away from my skin. He also didn't have to move much to cause his lips to lower within an inch of meeting mine, and I could hear our excited breathing as it intensified. But what I heard next instantly startled me.

Thunder exploded in the sky above, vibrating the walls around us. Hurricane season had come early. Erec and I had meant to leave much earlier, but we'd gotten carried away with the time.

"Oh no—that doesn't sound good." I looked up as if I could see through the roof of the cave.

"It's *not* good," Erec said. "I better get you back—now." The urgency in his voice made me nervous. I'd never experienced a tropical storm before. And the way that Erec packed up all of our belongings so quickly, made me assume that he *had* been in one—and that the experience hadn't been a pleasant one.

Erec took my hand and helped me up the large stone that we used to step into and out of the cave on. It was slippery because of the rain, and I was glad to have Erec to walk through the forest with.

Thunder sounded again as we were halfway back to the main huts of Ipharadisi. Then—lighting struck. It was quick and shockingly bright despite the thick canopy above.

The blinding light made everything else seem to fall into silence. It wasn't until I heard the loud cracking thud, and the simultaneous blood curdling scream, that everything came rushing back.

Erec and I took one look at each other, then started to run. Trees flew by us at blurring speeds, and I felt one of the branches tear into my skin as I continued to push my way through them.

We got to the scene before any of the other villagers, but we could see from all the blood that we were still too late. It was the vegetable grower Mr. Gurmu and his wife Larah.

Mr. Gurmu was trapped under a fallen tree. It must've been hit by the lighting strike we saw on our way here. His wife was in hysterics—her screams drowned in and out by the deafening thunder.

Erec got on his knees next to Abiodun. "Mr. Gurmu, can you hear me?" We waited for a response, but the pain on Mr. Gurmu's face didn't relay any information—other than we had to get him out of here.

I was just about to bend down with Erec when another blast of bright light almost blinded me; and along with it, came the frightening experience of body shaking thunder.

These strikes were way too close.

Suddenly we heard the rapidly creaking sound of a tree being split in half, then slowly falling over.

And that was exactly the trouble. We could hear it, but we couldn't see it—and no one knew which way to run.

I panicked, and I was just about to run towards Mrs. Gurmu when Erec jumped up and grabbed me, hugging me closely to him. Another tree had been struck by the lighting—barely missing me, but Mrs. Gurmu wasn't as fortunate.

When I lifted my face from being buried in Erec's chest, I looked down and saw her. She was crushed underneath the split tree. Mrs. Gurmu appeared barely conscious, but was thankfully still breathing—though not without much effort.

Erec went immediately into doctor mode. He looked at Larah, and then back at Abiodun. I could tell he was surveying the damage—the injuries. That's when a horrid realization came to his eyes.

"I can't save them both. There's not enough time."

No.

"We have to try!" I yelled it over the increasing thunder. Erec apologized with his eyes.

"Even with the two of us Kay, we're not strong enough to lift both trees and transport them in just one trip. I need to stop this bleeding to save even one of them—*now.*"

I looked at the pool of blood they both lay in, and I thought about the first day that I had met them; how kind they had been to me. I thought about Mrs. Gurmu, how she had said her only regret in life was that she didn't have any children—and that if she'd had children, she would've hoped that they'd grown up to be like me.

I then thought about Mr. Gurmu, and about how much he reminded me of my father.

My knees buckled a little. I was losing my family all over again.

But a sudden defiance came over me. "Wait here." I didn't even look back at Erec as I ran out into the main square of Ipharadisi. There were half a dozen villagers covering up belongings before seeking shelter. I stopped them.

"You! You! You!" I pointed to each person I saw. "Follow me! Now!" They didn't question me. We ran back to where the Gurmus lay bleeding under the splintered trees.

"We have to get them out," I announced. Erec looked around at the gathered assistance. I took off my jacket. "What do you want us to do?"

He didn't hesitate.

"We need to drag them out, but we have to keep their bodies stable or we could do further damage."

"Okay. You, you and you. Come with me. You, you and you help Dr. Louron." We split into teams and pulled each Gurmu out. We used our clothes to tie them to the stiff parts of the broken off tree—dragging the Gurmus back through the pouring rain and into the medical tent.

"Alright, give him some space."

I held everyone outside…and waited.

My breath seemed to remain in suspense as I tried not to panic—tried to remain hopeful.

Several hours later, Erec stepped outside the tent, and solemnly shook his head. He handed me the handkerchief that Mr. Gurmu had been wearing, and I knew then that he was gone.

I looked once more into Erec's disbelieving eyes, hoping for a better prognosis for Mrs. Gurmu.

But what I saw in them told me—there was just enough time left…to say goodbye.

13. Destiny Calls

I'd never seen someone die before. I'd heard about it—gotten a call from Mom about an uncle, or found out from a friend at school that *their* friend had been in some terrible accident, and didn't make it through.

But seeing someone up close…and holding their hand while their life slipped away, suddenly had me thinking about things that I never really thought were important enough to think about before.

But now, nothing else seemed *more* important, and it got me thinking—and not just casually thinking, but up all night, truly searching for the answers thinking.

The funeral that was held for Mr. and Mrs. Gurmu was unlike anything I'd ever seen before.

Everyone in the entire village came out. They all lined up to give their memories of the elderly couple who had acted as grandparents to so many of the children here.

The Gurmus had been two of the last remaining elders in Ipharadisi—the last to have lived during and really remembered the reign of Queen Ayanna.

Queen Zaina displayed no emotion during the burial, but the tears that dropped down the sides of her cheeks betrayed her.

I felt for the queen, especially as the dirt was thrown over the couple who were being buried next to the home that they had built. I felt for Queen Zaina because any memory she would want to hear of her mother from now on, could only be read in the written pages of the history I had collected before they died.

One of the village leaders said a few words before people began to return to their homes. They were nice words, nice thoughts. Things about being wrapped in someone's arms now, and being in a better place.

But I wondered how much of it was true.

As Erec and I walked back from the funeral, I asked him something that had been weighing heavily on my mind. "Erec, what do you think happens when we die?"

I thought the question might've caught him off guard, but Erec just pursed his lips—as he tended to do when he was teaching, and presented the question to me instead.

"What do you think happens when we die?"

I stopped walking for a moment.

"I don't," I admitted. "Try to think about it that is."

"I see."

Erec continued walking.

"So?" I pressed the question, waiting for an answer.

"So what?"

"So what do you *think*?" I was desperate for something concrete.

"Well, as a doctor," Erec finally began, "I've studied *lots* of evidence, and do you know what I've found?"

"What?" I asked—breath held.

"I found that the best evidence is experience. And Kay, I don't know if you'd believe me if I told you some of the things I've experienced here."

I almost dared Erec to try me. After all, I'd had one or two weird experiences in my lifetime. But instead, I decided to end the discussion there. Because the whole thought of having to answer to some big guy in the sky when I died scared me—which is why I usually tried to put it out of my mind. But after last night, I couldn't—discussions of death or not.

The day after the funeral I made some breakfast for Tuki—who had returned from the rescue search several days early, and who had also, unfortunately, returned slightly injured. She had been caught in the same freak lighting storm that had taken the life of the Gurmus.

Tuki said she was returning to Ipharadisi when lightning struck without warning. It frightened a nearby herd of springboks that nearly trampled her to death. Thankfully, aside from what Dr. Erec said was probably just a hairline fracture in her leg, Tuki was mostly just sore and would recover in due time.

The next few days however were slow—and lonely. It rained a lot, which seemed appropriate for the mood that had fallen over everyone that was missing the Gurmus. But eventually Erec decided that I'd been sulking in the acorn hut too long, and so he told me about an old widower who lived in the Southeast end of Ipharadisi.

Erec said he thought it would do me some good to visit the widower because of where he lived. I soon found out that the limping, older gentleman with the thick, black-rimmed glasses used to own a popular and impressive bookstore in his old home, but had lost almost everything when terrorists burned down the family owned store that his wife so often cashiered for him. Erec told me things like this were often done where the bookstore owner grew up, to discourage women from gaining too much access to knowledge.

When Mr. Ibhuku lost his wife in that terrible tragedy, he graciously accepted help from the Ipharadisian rescuer who came for him—and who came for everyone else there in trouble.

So Mr. Ibhuku had left all of his material possessions behind to come to Ipharadisi. He did, however, manage to collect and carry a few treasured books with him and was now the village librarian.

Mr. Ibhuku had lovingly turned his new home in Ipharadisi into a makeshift public library, openly sharing his now modest collection; some books having been donated by villagers who had various texts on them at the time of their rescues.

Per Erec's suggestion, I visited the widower and spent the entire day reading through the short book stacks in his incredibly elegant residence. I skimmed the pages of some of the books Mr. Ibhuku had recommended—spending more time in the ones that didn't say things that scared me. But, Mr. Ibhuku caught on to what I was doing, and suggested that I stop skipping past the stuff that I usually found too overwhelming to think about.

That's why I spent the entire next few weeks by the fireplace in Mr. Ibhuku's beautifully decorated home. But finally, as the village librarian was closing up one evening while the sun was beginning to set, I picked up a book to take back to the acorn huts as reading material for the rest of the night.

Mr. Ibhuku made a note of the borrower as I thanked him for his help, and soon, I was back on the narrow path that led the way home.

Home.

I smiled as I realized it was the first time I had called Ipharadisi what it had become to me.

As I walked by the light of the torch lined road, I looked down at the book I had randomly picked up before leaving. The book had a thick, black, material cover to it, with gold cursive writing on the front. It read: "Destiny Calls."

The title looked familiar, but I couldn't quite recall why. I opened up the aging hardcover to one of its first yellowing pages.

There, inside, was the most beautiful illustration of a rising phoenix. And though the book was barely held together by its loosening bound, gently as I could, I turned the page and read the fading printed ink inside.

"Destiny is that which is inevitable. It is something that *must* and will occur, regardless of an individual's will or desire for it to happen."

I slammed the book shut between my hands. I knew why the title had looked so familiar. I'd read this book before…in the library back in my old home.

I remembered how oddly frightened I was when I read the inside of that old, dusty, loosely bound book. I thought about those school stacks, and remembered the reason it frightened me so, because it made me remember the dreams I had when I was eight—the ones that I somehow knew deep down inside, were more than just dreams.

I began to massage my temples. I was starting to get that aching feeling in my head again—the one I'd get sometimes when I tried to force myself not to think about something that was nagging at me.

Hoping it would go away, I ignored it, but then my heart started pumping in overtime. I noticed the quick, uncomfortable movements of my chest, and was actually breathing quite heavily when I abruptly bumped into someone, causing me to let out a startled cry.

"Oh! I'm so sorry sir." I apologized to the old man who I'd just walked into.

The old man leaned against a beautiful, wooden rod—a walking stick, and had flowing, silver dreadlocks that rested against his rich, chestnut infused skin—skin that glowed even in the fading dim light. I also noticed that he smelled of lovely fragrant oils.

The old man gave me a genuinely warm smile. "No apologies are needed, I was hoping I would see you here."

"Really?" I was surprised—he didn't look familiar. "Are you sure?" I asked with uncertainty.

The old man seemed to think it over. "Actually my dear, will you please take me to where everyone is gathered?"

"Oh. Of course." The old man must be new here. That must be why I'd never seen him before. "This time of day sir, most of us usually get together at the palace hut. I'd be happy to take you there."

"That would make me most happy," replied the silver-haired gentleman.

I wrapped my arm around his as we walked together to the palace hut. I also asked him a lot of questions on the way there, but he wasn't exactly overly talkative.

Once we arrived, we entered through the open doors, and I waited with the old man to let me know what his next move would be. I patiently stood by his side as he took his time searching the room, finally speaking up.

"What is your name my dear?"

"Oh I'm sorry sir, it's Kay." I wondered why I didn't introduce myself earlier. The old man nodded to himself as he continued to look around the room, eventually turning his attention back to me.

"Pardon me for saying so, but you do not look like a Kay."

I laughed just a little.

"Actually sir, it's a nickname. My real name is Nanyamka." I didn't generally offer that information to complete strangers, but he seemed like he would appreciate it.

The old man rubbed his right ear and asked me to repeat it. "Nanyamka," I said, slightly louder.

"Ah," said the old man. "What is your full name?"

Oh boy, I thought to myself. "It's Nanyamka Apiyo Morowa. I know, I know. It's kind of a mouth full."

The old man rubbed his left ear this time. "I'm sorry young one. Will you repeat that louder please?" I hesitated, but still repeated it.

"Again please?"

Okay, either this guy was seriously hard of hearing, or, he was totally making me do this on purpose. I stopped speculating and decided to do as he asked anyway. I cleared my throat.

"My name is *Nanyamka Apiyo Morowa!*" I chuckled to myself. If he didn't hear *that*, I would have to take him to visit Dr. Erec.

I started to focus my attention back on the elderly man, but noticed that the room had suddenly gone silent—completely silent. I took a cautious look around. Everyone in the room was staring at me. Actually, not only were they staring at me, they were starting to *gather* around me.

Tuki was among one of the first faces to step out in front, and she was serious—*very* serious.

"Uxolo? *What* did you just say?"

"I...I'm sorry. I didn't mean to yell so loudly. It's just, this guy ..."

Tuki leaned behind me. "What guy?"

I turned around. There was no one there. I huffed. "Great. Thanks for leaving me hanging," I mumbled to myself.

I spoke louder for Tuki. "This old man kept asking me to repeat my name."

Everyone in the palace hut gasped. Tuki lurched forward.

"*Your* name?"

I stepped back a little. I know I had been a bit interruptive, but I didn't think it should have caused *this* much of a deal. Still, I nodded. "Yeah. It's the really, really, long version of Kay." I rolled my eyes as I said it. "Nanyamka Apiyo Morowa."

This time there wasn't enough space between us for Tuki to lurch forward, so she grabbed the collar of my shirt instead. "Kay!...Nanyamka—where were you born?"

I realized I had never told her the story I had shared with Erec—about everything that my parents had revealed to me the night before I left. I tried to figure out where to begin. "Well, it's sort of a long story, but it turns out I was born somewhere in South Africa—in a place called Langa."

"No." Suddenly the queen parted through the crowd that had gathered and stepped in between Tuki and I—

her pupils widened.

People were whispering my name to each other at feverish speeds. *"Morowa?* Nanyamka Apiyo *Morowa?"* The emphasis seemed to be on my last name, and the queen looked as if she might faint.

"No—no! I don't believe it!" Tears welled up in her eyes as she ran out of the palace hut. Tuki called after the queen but didn't follow.

What the heck was going on?

"Do you understand what your name means?"

I sighed. "Yeah, that which is long and difficult to pronounce."

Tuki quietly shook her head. "Kay...Nanyamka...I do not even know where to begin. How is it that you do not know? That you were not told—all this time?"

I was confused. "Told what exactly?"

Before Tuki could answer, the queen's screaming voice was heard all the way from outside the palace. "No! I will not allow it! She will *never* take my place!"

My mouth dropped. "Tuki, what is going on?"

"Nanyamka. Apiyo. Morowa. You are God's gift. First born of twins. And...Queen."

People began to murmur again. I began to tremble. "I...I don't understand."

"Your name," Tuki explained, "that is what it means. It is the same name you share with your sister... Queen."

No. She must be mistaken. "Tuki. It's just a coincidence. My birthmother died in Langa, in a fire. Queen Zaina's mother died protecting this village. You see, it's a mistake."

Tuki smiled, but it was a sad smile. "Queen Ayanna also died in Langa...in a fire."

I didn't believe her. "But you said she died during an attack on the village—the one caused by the American. You said that's when Queen Ayanna's life was taken."

"No, I said in the *end* Queen Ayanna's life was taken—and it was. After the horrible attack, Queen Ayanna soon received word of a desperate rescue mission. The rescue was for that very friend—the American, who Queen Ayanna had long forgiven. This is why Queen Ayanna went in search of her friend herself."

I looked around for a cushion. I thought perhaps I should sit down, if this was going where I thought it was going.

Tuki continued.

"The place in which the queen travelled to, to rescue her friend, was in Langa. The mission was extraordinarily long, and exceptionally difficult—especially for a newly pregnant queen. But during the queen's time there, she gave birth to a little girl, who Queen Ayanna had told her father before she left would have your name. And that one day the little girl would return as a woman—as queen, to Ipharadisi." Tuki repeated what she said earlier. "God's gift. First born of twins…Queen."

Something stuck out to me. "First born of twins?" That was wrong. I pointed it out to Tuki. "Queen Zaina is older than me. We are not twins."

She smirked. "You are when it comes to rights."

"Hunh?" Tuki took my hands in hers. "Your mother gave you that name Nanyamka so that everyone would know your right to the throne of Ipharadisi. Yes, Zaina was born several years before you. That makes her first in line.

But one night, just a season before you were to be

257

born, Queen Ayanna had a dream. In it, the one given your name reigned as queen of Ipharadisi. This was because you were to return at a time when her first born could no longer be trusted. This is why she named you with the birthrights to the throne. Kay, I never used to think it was true—that it could be possible. But here you are in front of us."

Tuki planted her face in the palms of her hands. It looked like I wasn't the only one having a hard time taking this all in. I remembered the quilt Tuki had loaned me to keep me warm during one of my first nights in Ipharadisi. There was a patch of cloth on it that perfectly matched the baby blanket that laid on the bed in my old home. And I knew now, they were one in the same.

I was truly from Ipharadisi—at least, my birthmother was.

And wait—what was that about her having a dream about me before I was ever even born? Could that explain the weird dreams I'd always had—the things I saw even during the day? Had it been hereditary? Maybe I wasn't such a freak after all.

I closed my eyes and thought about the jungle, the fire, the lion. Had they been leading me here all along? Perhaps this wasn't the random accident that I thought it was. Perhaps I was truly being prepared for something…bigger.

"Morowa." I said it out loud for the first time knowing what it truly meant.

Tuki looked up. "Yes. Your family name. The name you share with your sister. Zaina. Acacia. Morowa."

Wow. I have a sister.

Beth was the closest thing I had to one back in

America. Although, if I'd had a choice in the matter, I would've much preferred to have Tuki as a sister than Zaina. But I didn't have a choice. Actually, I felt like I didn't have a choice about a lot of things lately.

Still, I was just beginning to fit in around here; to make sense of everything that had happened to me—and now this. A total curve ball had been thrown to me—yet again—and I didn't know what to do with it.

Going over everything in my head, I thought about Zaina's middle name which struck me as odd.

"Acacia?"

Tuki hung her head. "It means thorny."

"Oh."

I could see the conflict in Tuki's face. I put my hand on her shoulder and gave her a light squeeze. "She's your best friend." Tuki nodded.

Poor Tuki had been caught in the middle from the very beginning. Zaina had instinctively harbored bitter feelings towards me ever since I arrived here.

And Tuki had tried her hardest to neutralize the then unknown sibling rivalry, but my close relationship with Erec—the man Zaina wanted to be her king, didn't make Zaina like me any more than she already didn't.

Now it seemed as if Tuki would have to play mediator once again, only this time, the potential stakes were much higher.

I tried to think of something that would give Tuki some comfort. "Listen Tuki, I know Zaina and I haven't exactly been best friends since I've been here, but this whole thing about Zaina becoming someone that can't be trusted—and me taking her place—that couldn't possibly be true."

Tuki sighed. "It's all been true so far." And regardless of how much we didn't want to, we both knew that *that* was one fact we couldn't deny.

With everything going on, I knew Callum was probably the last person in the world I should've be thinking of, but for some reason, I kept seeing that horrible dream in my head—the one where he laid dying in my arms as the church bells rang. But I would never see Callum again, so I knew that would never happen. This excited me.

Because this meant that everything my mother had dreamed about, wouldn't necessarily happen—which was a relief, because I certainly wasn't ready, willing or capable of being anybody's queen.

I asked Tuki to wait inside while I stepped out for a minute. I wanted to find Zaina. We needed to talk.

There was no more pretending I didn't exist. No more acting like we didn't matter to each other. No more non-verbal bickering over the village's most eligible doctor. We were sisters—and we were going to start acting like it.

I was surprised at the resolve that had suddenly come over me, and I went outside expecting to find Zaina in hysterics, but when I found her, she was sitting on a rock in tears.

"Zaina?" It was the first time I ever addressed her without the title of queen. I thought about leaving it at that, but I figured the first olive branch could be to continue to show my respect for her. I addressed her again. "Queen Zaina?"

Zaina slowly rose to her feet and just as slowly lifted her face.

I smiled. She spoke.

"You…"

The tone of her voice alarmed me. It was aggressive. The queen looked as if she were going to pounce on me.

I quickly discarded all ideas I had about having a heart to heart right now.

"You are the reason my mother is dead," she screamed. "I had to watch her go back into that fire…for *you!*"

How in the world could Zaina have watched it? She wasn't there when it happened.

Was she?

I thought back to the night that Mom had told me how she found me. She had sat down on the couch and revisited her memories.

"I was on my way to Paarl Tokai—to Pollsmoor Victor Verster with the other journalists—when a young girl ran out in front of our van.

The poor little girl was frantic Nanya. 'Please! Please! Help! Please!' The moment I got out of the van she began tugging on my pant leg and pointing in the opposite direction. I asked her why she needed help, but she was so small, I don't think she knew any other words. No—there were two others. 'Langa! Fire!'"

My goodness. The little girl who had run out in front of the van was Zaina. She had run all that way to get help for our mother—for *me*.

But instead of saving us both, she was forced to watch the only mother she ever knew die saving the sister she never wanted.

"Zaina, I'm so sorry." I reached out for her hand, but she knocked mine away.

"Sorry doesn't bring her back."

"Listen Zaina, I know how you feel, but…"

Zaina exploded. "You have *no* idea how I feel—what I lost. She was my mother!" Zaina sobbed.

"She was my mother also."

"Don't remind me," Zaina sneered. Then she left.

"Zaina..." I called after her just as Tuki arrived by my side.

"Kusasa Nanyamka."

I huffed. "Kusasa?"

"That means tomorrow Kay. Much has been learned tonight, and Zaina will need some time to process it. Rest tonight. What is left can be talked about in the morning. Kusasa."

I thought about it and ultimately agreed.

"Kusasa."

14. Lesson 1, Lesson 2

I didn't sleep that night. I just stared up at the stars, trying to see past them. I watched as morning came; the sun just beginning to rise, and the sky slowly changing from its midnight blue to the softest lavender.

But I could no longer wait for the powder blue sky to arrive, so I rose from the woven mat I'd been sleeping on, and went for a jog.

I couldn't remember the last time I'd gone jogging. I'd forgotten how incredibly peaceful it was. And, for the first time in a long time, I was completely alone with my thoughts, even as I jogged through the usually crowded market—which was now uncharacteristically empty.

And I was just beginning to feel like the only person in the world again when I saw him.

About thirty yards west of the marketplace was the old man with the long silver dreadlocks—the one who had changed everything.

I yelled out to him.

"Hey!" The old man didn't turn around. He just kept walking down the stone-lined road. I followed as I jogged still far behind him.

"Hey!" I yelled again.

I knew that he'd heard me because there wasn't any noise outside to block the sound—so what was he trying to pull here?

I picked up the pace as I jogged after him, and unsurprisingly, the old man picked up the pace as well—but the longer I followed, the shorter the gap became between us.

Still, he continued to ignore me, turning down the narrow path into a dark cluster of trees—escaping into an area of Ipharadisi that was entirely hidden.

Great, I thought to myself. He's going to make me search for him. I made the same turn as the seemingly elusive elder—but nothing.

Where did he go?

I parted my way through the dark cluster of woods and hiked a few minutes through Ipharadisi's inner forest. At last! I exited onto an enormous, moss-covered, hilly clearing.

I carefully took in the sprawling green earth that surrounded me. Butterflies and brightly hued birds floated amongst the flood of light that burst throughout the air—each winged creature sung its very own melody. Even the butterflies' wings fluttered a most soothing tune.

I stepped out further, bending my head as far back as it would go, and still, I only *glimpsed* the top of the surrounding hills' largest peak. But there—right in the center of a mountain deeply green and eternal sat a magnificent house of the likes I'd never seen.

I made my way closer, and as I did I saw that the beautiful dwelling was made of hundreds of colorful stones and delicately placed about gems.

Rainbows danced around the jewel lined edges as the sun shone brilliantly upon it—its reflection so immense that it caused me to shield my eyes. And though I could barely look directly at the magnetic work of perfection—neither could I pull my eyes away.

For the only force strong enough to draw my attention from the wondrous sight was the incredible blazing fire that burned carefully on a wooden pyre, several feet from the entrance of the no doubt powerful owner's home.

No sooner did I have that thought did I spot there by its side, the old man with the silver dreadlocks who had led me here. And, I had the sneaking feeling that he'd led me here for a reason.

I made my way up the steep hill to where the old man sat by his fire.

He didn't look up, so I sat down on the log that was just big enough for exactly two people, and gazed with him into the fire before us. I didn't quite know what we were doing, but still I waited for him to speak.

When he did, I wasn't the least bit surprised by what he had to say.

"I've been waiting for you."

"I know," I replied.

"Do you remember me?" He asked hopefully.

I thought very seriously as I continued to stare with him into the crackling fire.

"I'm not sure," I finally answered.

The old man was.

"I have always been with you Nanyamka. Even when you could not see me. I was there in your heart, and in your mind."

I closed my eyes, and finally saw him. He seemed so

much bigger then—but then again, I was so much smaller.

I saw his face. He looked exactly the same as he did now. I could see my tiny little hand reaching up to touch his cheek, and I could see him smiling back at me. Then, without warning, my mother's words came to life in my head.

"I hadn't even had time to take it all in when the man your birthmother sent me to find came out to where I was waiting. And when the silver-haired gentleman came out and stood over you, you started to giggle. And oh Nanya, it was the prettiest little sound I ever heard.

The old man smiled at you, and placed his hand on the top of your head. He started to chant something I couldn't understand. I think it was a prayer."

The memory stopped, and I opened my eyes. Tears welled in them. "Grandpa?"

"Yes my dear. It has been a long time."

Before yesterday, I would have thought the old man was crazy. I would have thought that *I* was crazy. But after hearing the prophecy that Tuki believed, and after having vision after vision myself, I think I was finally ready to stop trying to fight it—to stop trying to deny whatever was happening here.

So I sat there with the grandfather who had so patiently awaited my return. He explained many things to me—about helping the mother who raised me escape to a safer place. And the instructions he had given her that she decided not to follow.

"I told her she must tell you of from whom you were born. I told her she must return you one day to those who were waiting. But the woman who took you in loved you so intensely that she was afraid to let you go, and by following her own desires a conflict has arisen—one that need not have occurred."

I thought about the struggle between Zaina and I, and wondered what our relationship would have been like if we had grown up together. Grandfather put his hand on my shoulder and smiled. "But all is well now, for still you have found your way back home."

I was able to pull my eyes away from the fire, and look out onto the hills of Ipharadisi.

"I had dreams about this place."

"I know."

"My birthmother, she had dreams as well?"

The old man reached behind the log and pulled out something wrapped in a white cloth. "Yes Nanyamka. You come from a very gifted line."

With that, my grandfather unwrapped the thin, white cloth he was holding to reveal an ivory-white dagger that he held to the sun.

He lowered it to my eyes and showed me its carvings.

"I made this for your mother when she became queen, as a symbol to be passed down through generations. Long ago, I carved the handle from wood, and painted it to resemble ivory; to create remembrance for why Ipharadisi exists—for refuge, for peace, and to seek out all those who want it. This is why you are here—and why you dream about it so. You have been called Nanyamka, to care for its vision."

Grandfather handed me the ivory dagger so that I could feel the weight of it. It wasn't easy to hold.

I turned to confess. "I don't understand them—these visions…these dreams."

267

Grandfather understood. "That is because they are given to you in pieces—in parts. If you received the entire puzzle at once, you would never learn—you would never grow. So they are simply meant to guide you—to prepare you—for what is to come."

I stood up from the log, still with many questions, but grateful at least that I now knew there was a reason for the things I'd been seeing all my life.

"All this time I've felt like such a freak."

Grandfather furrowed his brow. "There is no reason to feel that way Nanyamka. It is not only you who has these gifts. Everyone in Ipharadisi possesses such a gift."

I was shocked. "*Everyone* here has visions?"

The old man put some kindling into the fire as he spoke. The flames jumped up a bit, but then settled back down into their previous low-key sway. "Not each person possesses the same gift, but *a* gift just the same."

I sat back down on the log, completely intrigued. "What type of gifts does everyone here have?" I wondered what Tuki and Zaina hadn't told me yet. I wondered what special gift Dr. Erec might possibly have.

"Many are the gifts of the rescued," said Grandfather. "I am proud because they have each learned how to use them wisely. Some possess the gift of leadership. Others, the gift of service. Some have the gift of teaching while others share the gift of compassion."

Wait, I had to stop him there. "Those aren't gifts Grandfather. Compassion isn't a…*gift*."

He smiled. "It is to the person who receives it. Much like to the person who receives from the one who possesses the gift of generosity."

I thought about the little girl who had given me the

beautiful comb only my second day here. It was a small thing, but I didn't have much of my own when I arrived here, so her small, kind gesture that day had meant a lot to me.

And though I certainly appreciated the kindness and generosity Tuki and Kayla and everyone else here had shown me, those weren't the kind of gifts I thought we were talking about.

"But Grandfather, I was talking about abilities *beyond* those." I guess I must've said something wrong because the old spry man swiftly stood up.

"What abilities does one need if one has not even mastered what has already been given? Both gifts and abilities are useless if their purpose is ignored." Grandfather walked over to the fire and smothered it with dirt. "Do not be fooled Nanyamka. Many have been called, and many are those who have missed their destiny because they have so ignored their purpose."

Grandfather sat back down on the log with me, and there we remained for the rest of the morning as I thought about all the dreams I'd had back home—all the visions—all the blindness I had—until now.

The hours pushed on, but it was still early afternoon when I found myself walking back towards the palace hut. And, as I got closer, I noticed quite the commotion outside of its doors. Many people were gossiping. Others ran inside.

Eventually I spotted Tuki.

She was standing in the entry way, putting most of her weight on her brand new walking stick, pointing to several Ipharadisian warriors, and gesturing for them to hurry inside.

Something wasn't right.

I ran the rest of the way to the palace hut and pushed my way inside. It was packed. "Excuse me. Sorry. Pardon me." I made my way through the room full of Ipharadisians to where Tuki and Zaina now stood.

I struggled to their sides. "What's going on?"

Tuki put up a hand, letting me know she would answer me in a moment. Zaina totally ignored me. Instead, she pointed to a young man who was dressed as an Ipharadisian warrior, and spoke.

"Unathi, report."

The young man stepped forward, hands behind his back. "Six were injured on the northern and western scouts. Four of the injuries are critical."

Queen Zaina nodded. "Have we confirmed all who have not yet returned?"

"Yes your queen. Adanech, Essien, Xola and Fynn are all still missing."

"Fine. Make sure Dr. Louron gets the others back on their feet immediately. We will need a search party as soon as possible."

"Yes Queen Zaina." Unathi bowed and ran out of the palace hut.

I turned back to Tuki. "Tuki—talk to me. What happened?"

Tuki finished doing a headcount of the children in the room. "We just received reports that poacher camps have been stepping up security. Several camps have bonded together and are learning our ways. As such, every one of this season's rescue attempts has been intercepted. And worse—the recent storm has played out in the favor of these camps. A number of our best rescuers have not yet returned home. We are greatly concerned."

I was horrified. "What are we going to do?"

"*We?*" Zaina looked at Tuki so that I would know who was included—and who was not. "*We* are going to handle this. *You*, are going to go back to the acorn compound and be silent." The queen was clearly on edge right now.

I knew I'd probably regret speaking up again but I did it anyway.

"With all due respect Queen Zaina, it looks to me as if you can use all the extra help you can get right now. You for one won't be able to do much because you need to stay here while reports come in. Tuki can still barely walk, and the only other rescuers you have left I assume are all being treated in the medical tent. But if you let me, I can help. Tell me, have you ever even tried to talk peace with these poacher camps?"

The queen scowled at me so intensely that I saw several shades of red build up underneath her mahogany colored skin.

She blew.

"How *dare* you come in here and try to interfere! This does *not* concern you."

I flinched from the force of her voice but spoke as calmly as possible in return. "I'm just trying to help Zaina."

Zaina grabbed someone's donga stick and threw it across the room. "*Queen* Zaina! You will *always* address me as *Queen* Zaina! Do you understand??"

I breathed in slowly through my nose—maintaining as much composure as possible.

"Yes, Queen Zaina. I understand." I paused. "But do you understand that I'm a part of this now—whether you like it or not? If anyone should be involved right now, it's me."

Zaina looked like she was about to explode again. Tuki stepped in between us and faced my furious sister.

"Nanyamka is correct Zaina. I cannot perform a rescue or even a search in my condition. But Nanyamka has learned much over the last months. She is diligent, capable, and I can train her to move as we do."

"No!"

Tuki persisted. "I will teach her everything I know."

"Absolutely not." Zaina spoke through grinding teeth, but Tuki wouldn't give up.

"We still need time to gather more intelligence about these new occurrences. We will also need time to organize and re-group. By then, Nanyamka will be ready to take my place."

"NEVER!!!" Zaina's yell was like the roar of a lion. It scared me, but not Tuki.

"Just on the next rescue. Too much is at stake for me to attempt it myself while injured."

Zaina scoffed. "Too much is at stake to rely on some American *outsider*."

That made Tuki put her foot down—literally. She stomped. "No—too much is at stake to let your pride get in the way. Listen to me. We will send out the two who are not badly injured to begin the search for those who are still unaccounted for. We will send Zere who returned with me last week to begin collecting intelligence. With three on the field, that will take at least a month to two months' time. In that time, Nanyamka will be ready to perform any necessary rescue in my place." She looked back at me. "I assure you."

Zaina didn't seem so convinced. "You really think you can teach her to be one of us?"

"She already is." Tuki gently reminded her.

The queen's nostrils flared, and I knew that Tuki had won. Zaina stormed out, leaving Tuki to turn her attention fully back to me.

"Do you know how to defend yourself?" She asked it the same way she had once asked me if I knew how to make a fire, back when we were at the poacher's camp. I responded the same.

"No."

Zaina's most trusted advisor grabbed me by the arm. "Then you are going to learn—and you are going to learn quickly."

That began day one of my training.

Tuki taught me how to find my bearings while travelling through the jungle, and also in open terrain. We didn't know if those poachers from my kidnapping were part of any of these banded camps, so she instructed me to always stay low to the ground during rescues.

"You must learn to blend in with your surroundings Nanyamka." I still wasn't used to being called by my real name. "You will have to learn to become invisible, but also to sustain and nourish yourself with only that which the land provides. And, it is imperative Nanyamka that you remain alert as there are many dangers you will encounter on a rescue. Dangers you will hear, but never see—see, but never catch."

Tuki looked out past the walls of the palace hut as if she were trying to remember something she could hazily see in her mind.

"Nanyamka, we are not the only village of our kind.

There are villages that are good, peaceful. Others are violent and destructive. Those are the ones you will need to prepare for the most.

We try to avoid them, but if I understand these reports correctly, you may have no choice but to walk through such valleys of darkness." I hoped that last part was a metaphor, but I had a feeling as I gulped that these dangers Tuki was warning me about, were as real as the flesh that covered me.

By the third day, Tuki had convinced Zaina—and not without an entire night's protest—to assist in training me in the donga sticks. Tuki had overdone it yesterday with all the hours spent on her injured leg. She needed time to rest.

The queen finally gave in.

"Here, hold your stick like this. Ugh. No. Like *this.*" Zaina roughly plucked my fingers off the donga stick and practically crushed them back down—re-positioning my hands closer to the middle ends where they were supposed to be.

I tried to keep my sweaty hands steady. We'd only been at it for a few hours today, but Zaina was already fed up with me. My hand slid down again, and Zaina huffed. I slid them back up to where she had put them.

"Now," continued Zaina, "when you strike your opponent, you are looking for any open access point. It is not like when you are doing it for sport—where the allowed strikes are restricted to certain parts of the body."

I had no idea there were restrictions when playing it for sport. The last time Zaina and I *played* donga, she practically knocked my head off. Then again, maybe to her that *was* a sport.

"Are you paying attention?" Zaina caught me unpleasantly reminiscing.

"Yes," I replied.

"Do you have any questions so far?"

Only about a hundred. "No."

Zaina knew I was lying. I tried to build up my confidence. This wasn't the time to be intimidated.

Zaina warned me how brutal donga fighting could get, and let me know that not many women were well trained in this discipline. But she said I could use that to my advantage because if I had to fight my way out of any situation, the attacker wouldn't expect me to know this type of martial arts.

As the days went on, I became more and more comfortable with both my offense donga stick and my defense donga stick. Though I used my defense stick much, much more than the offense one. I wondered if that would be in general, or just with Zaina.

It'd only been a week, but the training had been non-stop. I didn't know how she did it. I barely got any sleep—and when I did, it was often interrupted from rolling over on the bruises Zaina had given me, and waking up to Tuki's self-amusing battle calls—though I was quickly getting used to the erratic sleeping pattern.

One night, it occurred to me that I hadn't seen Erec in over a week, but I knew he was busy with the injured rescuers. Still, I couldn't believe how much had happened since the last time we saw each other. I wondered what he would think about all of this.

"Focus Nanyamka!" Clack, clack, swoosh, clack. By day ten, Zaina and I had gotten into a pretty good partnering rhythm. I could anticipate the way her body would move and avoid getting struck—blocking her offense stick with my defense—which made me very happy—less bruises.

However, Zaina warned me not to get too used to her particular style of movement because it could prove disadvantageous with another opponent.

Clack! Squish! She flicked my fingers with her donga stick, and the quick blow made my sensitive fingers throb. "Oww!" I shook them out, trying to shake away the intense pulsating. Several people in the sparsely populated palace hut looked as if they could feel my pain.

I recovered my ground and fought back.

"You know Zaina, eventually we're going to have to talk about it."

"Talk about what?" Swipe! Hit. Miss.

I tried to stop breathing through my mouth so that I'd have enough breath left to talk. "You know, Mom's dream."

Clack. Break! Zaina hit my donga stick so hard that it broke in two. I tossed it to the side and picked up another one. We began sparring again.

"I do not believe in such a prophecy," Zaina retorted.

"I didn't say prophecy. I said dream," I pointed out.

Zaina paused for a moment, then picked back up. "Either way, I suggest you do not give it much thought."

I struck Zaina in the back of the knee and then on her shoulder. They were both rare strikes and Zaina didn't look too pleased. "Well, I do think about it," I admitted. "Grandfather said…"

"*Grandfather?* You have spoken to him? He is an old fool. Do not listen to him. That is why he is so far away."

I didn't like the fact that she'd referred to our

grandfather as a fool. I struck her in the side—twice. Zaina grunted. "Do not do that again Nanyamka."

I challenged her. "What? Strike you? Or talk to our grandfather?"

"Both," she sneered. I had a feeling to her, they were probably one in the same. Zaina had lost the mild amicability she had at the start of the session, and had become extremely irritated by my mere mention of the dream prophecy she already knew. She also obviously had some deep set resentment towards Grandfather, and I wondered why.

I quickly figured it out.

"He's the one who told everyone the prophecy. Isn't he?" Zaina widened her stance.

"Careful Nanyamka."

I pushed on. "You're angry because he believes you're capable of doing exactly what it says."

"Careful…"

I ignored her threats. She had to see what she was doing. "Don't you get it Zaina? By being angry, and pushing Grandfather away, you are just ensuring the vision comes true.

But you forget—it was just a dream Zaina. Mom had a special gift, but she wasn't a prophet. Your actions are turning it into a self-fulfilling prophecy. But that's not what Mom wanted."

Zaina screamed. "Stop it! You stop talking about her right now! Don't you talk about *my* mother *ever*!"

"Or *what*?" I folded my arms in defiance.

"Or this!" It was her rhetorical warning. I saw her offense stick rise into the air, and I looked up. That was the last thing I remember before she knocked me unconscious.

By the time I woke up, everyone had left, and I groaned from the splitting headache that her attack had caused. I then became seriously concerned.

Between the airport explosion, the poacher's camp and Zaina's uncontrollable temper, I'd been knocked unconscious three times in the past few months. I wouldn't be surprised if I had a concussion by now.

As I thought that, I heard someone laugh.

"I really hope you negotiate rescues better than you fight." I rolled my head to the side. It was Erec. Someone must've ran and gotten him for me.

Erec poked me in the rib. I squirmed. "So, this is the prodigal daughter. You know, I expected you to be taller."

I forgot we hadn't seen each other since the revelation. I tried to roll my eyes at him, but the splitting headache made it difficult for me to display sarcasm. I'd have to happily wait for that feature to return—along with the feeling in my legs. They must've fallen asleep when I passed out.

I struggled to prop myself up. "A little help?"

Erec scooped me up in one swift movement and held me close to his chest. Our faces were just inches apart, and I could feel his chest expanding against mine as he breathed.

Erec looked me over in deep contemplation, then carried me to the iQhugwane community where his medical tent would be.

Neither of us said a word the entire way over.

As he carried me through the gate, we made a right past the medical tent. I didn't understand why we hadn't gone inside.

"Hey," I put my hand on his chest. "Where are we going?"

"I'm taking you to my place."

I realized I'd never seen his place before. Maybe it was just because I'd been overworking myself, but suddenly my heart began to pound, and my palms began to sweat. I realized—I was nervous.

"Um Erec, why are you taking me to your place?"

Though I'd never been inside, I knew immediately which hut was his. I could see the tealight candles and the medicinal flowers in the windowsill.

Erec smiled. "Relax Kay. The medical tent's overcrowded. You can rest here so I can keep an eye on you—make sure you don't have a concussion. That's all."

"Oh."

Erec tilted his head. "Why, what did you think I was bringing you here for?"

"Nothing. I didn't think anything."

Erec carried me through the door and laid me down on his bed.

"Now try not to get too irritated with me, but I'm going to have to wake you up every couple of hours to check for a concussion. We don't exactly have state of the art equipment here—or any equipment really, but you didn't wake up as easily as I would have liked back at the palace hut. So I'd rather be safe than sorry."

I scratched my head. "If you're asleep, how are you going to wake me up every few hours without an alarm?"

Erec took off the light jacket he was wearing and hung it over the foot of the bed. "I'll just have to stay awake all night."

I sat up. "You would do that for me?"

"Of course." Erec took off his watch and laid it on the wooden table by the bed. He signaled for me to lie back down.

"But then, when are you going to sleep?" I asked him genuinely concerned. Erec yawned as he pulled his blanket over me.

"Kusasa Nanyamka. I can sleep kusasa." With that, Erec bent down and kissed me on the forehead. But I fell asleep deeply wishing that he had kissed me on the lips.

15. The Darkness

Over the next few weeks, my training would be threefold. Tuki would push through her leg injury to take over my fighting lessons, and, under her training I would watch myself become stronger, faster and more agile.

Erec would begin to teach me about healing—about when to use herbs and medicines, and also when to pray. He taught me so that I would learn to not only care for my own injuries, but to care for others—and their needs.

The third part of my training was offered by Grandfather. He would help me to see clearer when it came to the things I saw during the day and in my dreams at night. He would also help me to hear better when I needed to listen to someone other than myself—especially if the one I needed to listen to couldn't be seen.

This last part was the hardest.

"Tell me Nanyamka," Grandfather said as he saw my despair, "why are you so disheartened?"

I thought about it. Much time had passed, and I had been feeling the heat of the days getting stronger. It was already late in the sixth month—belonging to the third season, and I was becoming increasingly worried about the rescue mission ahead.

I didn't feel brave enough to face the dangers that I knew I would be forced to face in Tuki's place. I didn't feel smart enough to navigate the terrain outside on my own. And even though these were the exact things Grandfather was trying to teach me, I still couldn't help but to feel skeptical.

I just felt like everything I'd been doing here was pointless.

I finally confided in him. "Grandfather," I slowly began, "I've enjoyed these lessons very much, but it's been saddening me—the reason that what I am doing will be needed at all. I don't understand it—these people who would harm another."

My grandfather sat down beside me, on what had become our log, and placed his still powerful hands over mine.

"You must know Nanyamka, that there are many things in this world that were not originally intended to be.

Such are the evils of greed—of hate. Some people are so full of hate Nanyamka that they cannot even see the evil in their own hearts.

These people are lost and are easily misled. They have listened to dark, dark things with tempting promises. The promise of material things. The promise of power. This is enough for some to want to inflict pain on others, for their own satisfaction and gain."

I suddenly felt an entire world of doubt come down upon me. I asked Zaina that day in the palace hut if she ever tried to negotiate peace with the poachers in the harming camps. Maybe she never tried because it wasn't possible.

"Grandfather," I asked, "how can I possibly fight against such evil? Perhaps I'm not equipped to go on such a rescue after all."

Grandfather tossed the rest of the kindling he was holding into the fire. He let the rising flames settle back down before looking deeply into my eyes.

"Do not think of such nonsense. All you ever have to do Nanyamka is simply speak the truth. You will be surprised how deeply truth penetrates."

I hoped it would be that simple. But some of the things I saw when I was in that poacher's camp so many months ago, made me think that not everyone could be so easily reached. Still, I would try. Lives were at stake.

The next morning I rose early. Zere had finally returned with the intelligence report that all of Ipharadisi had been anxiously waiting for.

"Queen Zaina! Queen Zaina!" Zere ran at full speed into the palace hut where everyone was gathered. It was unusually packed for this particular time of a day, but one of the village guardians had sent word the moment he saw Zere returning from off in the distance.

Word had spread like wild fire, and almost all of Ipharadisi was now crowded into the medium-sized palace, waiting to find out what Zere had discovered.

"Report Zere." Zaina directed him loudly, letting him know he had permission to divulge his findings in public.

"I have searched through all of the West Queen Zaina, as well as through all of the East. But as it was not permitted to me, I did not cross into the North or South lands."

Zaina nodded as Zere continued. "My queen, I fear

283

Atsu and Themba may have been taken there while trying to gather intelligence on those ends.

We were supposed to meet on the fifth day at the middle point, but neither party arrived. So I waited as usual my queen for two sun downs, and only then did I continue east. But alone, I could not trace the other rescuers. I did, however, discover a banded camp of unusually large proportions in the eastern region. And from what I was able to see, rescues are most desperately needed there."

"I see." Queen Zaina took in Zere's report, but hesitated in responding with orders. Zere began looking around, fidgeting as if there were something more he wanted to say.

Zaina never missed a thing.

"Is there more Zere? If so you must tell me now."

Zere looked down again. For some reason he was afraid to meet her gaze. Finally, he came clean.

"There is one more problem my queen."

"Tell me Zere, what is it?"

There was a short silence, and then he whispered.

"The Ubumnyama."

"What???" Everyone in the palace hut gasped—everyone except me that is. Clearly, I still had a lot to learn about this place, and even more about what lied outside the tree-lined walls of Ipharadisi.

I moved in closer to Tuki, and asked what it seemed everyone else already knew.

"What is the... Ubumnyama?"

My question invoked another loud set of gasps.

Tuki slowly turned around, and I suddenly felt like I'd been thrown into some creepy 80's horror movie, because right at that moment, the eeriest bone-chilling wind blew throughout the hut, just as I spoke the Ubumnyama's name.

The fierce gust of air blew out one of the intensely lit torches, setting the mood for what Tuki was about to tell me.

"The Ubumnyama is the darkness. It hides deep inside the jungle, waiting for any unsuspecting victim it can destroy."

I shuddered before asking for clarification. "It's a...thing?"

"No." Tuki motioned for Zere to re-light the smoke blowing torch before continuing. "It is a people so full of evil that they are stripped of all humanity; a people who have taken all that is holy, and twisted it into nothing but death and destruction. They are violent like no creation was ever meant to be.

For them, peace is not a thought, nor a desire, but something to be crushed and sought vengeance upon. The Ubumnyama is simply, evil in its purest, darkest, most destructive form."

Now I really shuddered. Who would live to terrorize others that way? I tried to put it out my mind, but then I had another thought. "Um, will they...I mean...are they coming...*here*?"

Queen Zaina spoke quickly as I could see by the fearful realization in the crowd's eyes that I had asked yet another startling question.

Zaina held up a hand to the low frightened murmurs echoing throughout the palace hut. She spoke loudly for everyone to hear. "The Ubumnyama rarely ever leave their hiding places. There is little risk of them coming here."

I let out a sigh of relief, as did several others who were put to ease by Zaina's announcement. Still, I couldn't help but notice the number of Ipharadisians who seemed to be relatively unconvinced. Tuki as well appeared to be straddling the fence.

"I have to admit, it is surprising that they would make themselves seen in the open. It is almost as if they *want* us to find them—as if they are daring us to attempt a rescue where it appears they are now patrolling," Tuki openly inferred.

Zere returned to the center of our group with his head bowed. He turned to Zaina who was stroking her temples, clearly lost in thought. "My queen, may I please have your permission to speak?"

Zaina nodded as if she already knew what he was going to say.

"I know what we do is of the utmost importance my queen, and I am not suggesting that we leave anyone in trouble to their own suffering, but as I am sure you have already estimated, it would be incredibly difficult to attempt a rescue in the eastern lands. The Ubumnyama will undoubtedly spot a rescue group many miles away. And as you know my queen, the Ubumnyama are very, very easily provoked."

Tuki had been nodding to herself the entire while that Zere was speaking, almost as if she were using each of his sentences to devise a plan. "Yes," she exclaimed. "If we are to have any chance of success, a rescue attempt in that area will have to be attempted alone."

"But Advisor," Zere addressed Tuki by one of her multiple titles. "They may recognize any one of us from our encounter with them just seasons ago."

"Yes," Zaina said as she walked straight to me. And for someone who usually avoided me at all costs, a direct, unplanned approach made me nervous.

"Then," Zaina continued, "It will have to be someone they will not recognize."

I knew what she was thinking, and although this pure evil that they spoke of did send chills down my spine, I was still prepared to do whatever I had to, to save those who were facing the same fates I once faced.

Besides, this *is* what I'd been training for.

Zaina skipped the formalities and went straight to logistics. "You will avoid confrontation. You will not stray from the rescue at hand. You will locate those that require assistance and get them out of the assessed danger—quickly."

I wanted to comply, but I thought about my talks earlier with Grandfather—about those who were misled—about the penetrating ability of truth to those who were lost. I cleared my throat.

"What if I have a chance to talk peace with those that are holding them hostage?"

Zaina dismissed the idea. "This is not the time to talk peace."

I dared not ask when *was* the time? Instead, I just continued to pay attention to her directions. The next bit of information however, came from Tuki.

"The Ubumnyama know the terrain you will travel better than our best rescuers. They will attempt to deceive you with all kinds of tricks, and will use their ancestral blades against you if given the chance. You are to avoid them at all costs. Do you understand?"

I did. That wasn't something I would have to be told twice. And, even though I tried not to let it, I couldn't help but to feel the fear that was beginning to settle in. I was starting to doubt myself again, along with all the skills and lessons that I was supposed to be so prepared by.

"Tuki?" I whispered, speaking timidly now. "What if when I get there, no one listens to me? The rescues I mean. It's just that, you and I are so different. You're so strong, and you're a natural leader. People listen to you. What if no one listens to *me*?"

Tuki shook her head, then reached out and put her hand on my shoulder—something Tuki hadn't done since the day she let me know that we were going to escape that poacher's camp together. It was immediately reassuring, the way a familiar caress of the hand is from one's mother.

"Have faith Nanyamka. Yes, they may be scared after all the horror I am sure they will have seen. There will be much tragedy there—much lost. And it is easy to feel powerless when one has lost so much, so you must be patient and understanding.

But it takes just one person to inspire another; for that person will inspire yet another and it will continue until the courage has spread. You can be such a leader—the one to ignite that inspiration—if you will just have faith."

I took in what she said and hoped that I was up to the task. The thing was, my faith was shaky, but I wanted it to be strong.

Queen Zaina asked the rest of the onlookers in the palace hut to clear out so we could focus. Because while I was worried about whether or not I could inspire an entire poacher's camp full of people, Zaina was concerned with whether or not I could make it there at all.

"The Ubumnyama will undoubtedly be expecting us—though it will only be you Nanyamka. We will wait as long as we can—until we think the Ubumnyama believe we are no longer coming their way. I do not wish to make the needed rescues wait any longer than they already have, but the only advantage we have right now is the element of surprise."

I agreed, and knew now that I would have to take my training more seriously than ever before. There was little time left to prepare, but I would make the most of every second of it.

So that night—alone, I took out a pair of donga sticks, and trained harder than I ever trained before. I trained in the cold of the pouring rain. I trained in the scorching heat of the blistering, morning sun.

I tested my own strength; pushed my own limits—like neither Tuki, nor Zaina, nor Grandfather had pushed me before.

Night and day—day and night, I swirled my donga sticks and practiced no matter *how* sore my muscles ached. I got up no matter how many times I fell face down in the mud. And I continued to train, until one day, when the sky was still dark, and the sun just beginning to rise, I put down my training sticks, and I was ready.

"Here, drink this." Grandfather handed me a split open coconut with a greenish, muddy colored liquid inside. He'd been making me drink these ever since I arrived in Ipharadisi.

The raw brew of roots and herbs was supposed to help improve my eyesight—and it had. So much so, that I no longer needed my glasses. I was grateful, especially considering the journey ahead.

"It is time," Tuki informed me.

We were all standing on the edge of Ipharadisi by the Assegai field. The sky was in its early lavender, and the sun was still orange. The smell of wet grass filled the air.

Tuki stopped looking at the sunrise and unwrapped two of the most beautiful wooden donga sticks I'd ever seen. She rolled them out the dark brown cloths they were wrapped in, allowing me to see the tiny carvings one-inch below the top of each stick. The carvings almost looked like carefully placed claw marks.

A thin piece of black leather hung from the top of the right stick, and white dots circled the top of the left. "I want you to take these with you. They have provided me with great protection over the years—a gift from my own grandfather." Tuki told this to me as she put the pair of the sticks into the holding slots in the back of my brown leather vest. She secured them tightly, using the copper clasps sewn into the back of the vest for extra security.

Kayla's family had given me this top and matching skirt set with gold embroidery around the waist as a gift—for no particular reason at all—aside from their natural gift of generosity. It turned out that not only did they make beautiful handcrafted combs, but they also used the cow skins—taken only from the cow after a natural passing of course—and made garments from them.

I had taken to wearing the outfit especially while training as it provided incredible flexibility for my movements. I wore the garb now for the arduous journey ahead.

Tuki looked me over in the fighting gear that I hoped I

wouldn't need to use. Zaina stood to her left. Erec, who hadn't left my side these past few days—even though I didn't speak much during my intensified training sessions—walked towards me with his shoulders hunched over.

We had grown close enough to each other that I had learned to know exactly what he was thinking—without him having to tell me, and vice versa. Still, his eyes contained an unfamiliar sadness behind them, and I didn't know what the reason could be.

But before I could figure it out, Erec gave me a light, playful punch in the arm—with an accompanying forced smirk. "You be safe out there." He tried to laugh, but he was having a hard enough time trying to manage the pretend smile.

I suppose I would have eventually guessed the reason for the sudden façade, but without much warning at all, Erec grabbed me and hugged me close. He hugged me for so long that I wasn't sure he was ever going to let me go. And though he wouldn't meet my eyes, I could tell the ruse was over.

"*Please* be safe out there Kay." Erec was the only one who still called me by my nickname. He liked being the only one who had a different name for me.

Our relationship had been pretty much the same as it had been since I first arrived here—which was comforting I suppose.

But I still vividly remember the night he carried me back to his iQhugwane; the same night he kissed me on the forehead. The night I deeply wished he had kissed me on the lips.

I kept waiting for the right time to bring it up, but with

everything that had happened since then, our quasi-romance had quickly taken a back seat, and we hadn't had another evening like that again—much to Zaina's approval.

"She will be fine Erec," Zaina loudly huffed. Despite everything, Zaina *still* never missed an opportunity to interrupt a potentially romantic moment between Erec and I—which for now, was probably for the best.

Because the only thing that seemed to give me the courage to go on such an insane mission right now was the feeling that I didn't have anything left to lose.

I was already permanently removed from the only home I'd ever known. I had made a new one here, but my relationship with my newly discovered—not so enthused queen sister was still tense.

And even though I cared for the people here—Tuki, Erec, Kayla—I more so volunteered for this mission because of how badly I wanted my life to count for something.

I had been feeling that way ever since I read that article on the airplane—the words Nelson Mandela issued after he was imprisoned.

At the time, I didn't know I could ever be capable of caring for complete strangers so much so that their plight would be something that I would be "prepared to die for."

However, if I learned anything over these past few months, it was that there was more to me than even I ever knew was there.

So I took in a deep breath, and said my temporary good-byes, then set off in the direction that Zere told me to go.

Straight forward into the lion's den.

16. I Come in Peace

Whack. Swish. Whack. The tall blades of wild grass only came up to my hip, but were beginning to wear me out as my hands and lower arms struggled through the dense terrain—not to mention that the whiplash I was receiving due to my feverish swinging was starting to irritate my skin.

Then again, maybe it was just the sun that was bothering me. I seriously should've asked around for a hat or something before I left; anything that would've stopped the unrelenting sun from beating down on my naked skin so unforgivingly.

I took out the one leaf of aloe that was tied at my side. It hung from a piece of string that was looped through one of the rope notches on my leather skirt. Unfortunately, I didn't have a knife, so I dug my nails into the leaf, creating little semi-circles in a vertical line down the middle.

I pulled along the line of anxious fingernail markings, exposing a bit of the cooling gel inside. Quickly, I scraped out some of the goo and thoroughly massaged it into my aching skin. I sighed.

It probably would've taken Tuki half the time it had taken me to reach the first marker on the map Zere had drawn—the one that he made me memorize and then burn so that no one could find it; so that no one could find Ipharadisi in the event I was ever followed.

I would never let that happen of course, but I wasn't as adept in navigating my new surroundings as Zere was. That's why when he asked me to burn the map before I left, I did—technically. I started a fire and held the parchment-like paper over the flames. That is, while Zere was still looking. But the moment he turned to walk away, I quickly blew out the lit part of the map and tucked it away in my skirt's inner pocket.

I wasn't trying to be deceitful, but everyone was counting on me to successfully pull off this rescue, especially with all the other rescuers still M.I.A. And I just really, *really* didn't want to screw this up—especially not by getting lost on my way there.

I figured if worse came to worst, and I was somehow captured by one of the poachers in the eastern territories, I could always just *eat* the map like I used to see people do in the movies.

Wow, it just occurred to me that I had spent all of this time without a television, or even my dearly departed cellphone—a tool for which I once upon a time received every single breaking news story on. And although I was never truly one of those people who were super obsessed with technology, I was still surprised by how quickly I had grown accustomed to my new way of living. It was…peaceful.

As I continued to walk through the mix of faded green

and wheat-colored grass, I saw something up ahead that almost stopped me in my tracks.

I know Tuki told me to always stay low to the ground, but when I realized what I was seeing, I couldn't help but to practically skip forward. Because less than a 100 yards away, was a long-stretching river, and drinking from it were real life *giraffes*!

I crouched down and crept forward. To my delight there was an entire herd of antelopes, wildebeests and flamingos, all drinking side by side. There were even the brown-bodied zebras with the black and white-striped legs that Tuki had described to me. She said they were called okapis.

The okapis stood next to the giraffes, whose beautifully long necks and gentle looking eyes were bending down, thirstily transforming their usually narrow pouts into suction cups inside the cool moving water. And because the legs of these gentle giants were spread almost into a split, it had caused their incredibly tall bodies to descend to the same level as the rest of their thirst-quenching peers.

I'd long been without the digital camera I'd flown to South Africa with, so I stood there in the middle of the plain and took in the memory. It was my own private safari with my own private view. I loved it!

And though I tried to remain in the moment, I couldn't help but to begin to wish that Erec was here with me. I missed him now. I missed the way we could just sit together and look out into any distance, and not feel the need to say a word.

When I had first met Erec, I felt guilty for being so attracted to him—because of all the unresolved issues I'd left back in my old home. And for some reason, part of that guilt was still with me. But there was never any pressure with Erec, so I never felt anything that I felt *forced* to face.

As I looked towards the sky, I realized that it would be dark soon. I would have to leave my four-legged friends and find some place to rest for the night—some place I wouldn't be eaten during my sleep.

I thought about spending the last few minutes of daylight scouting for twigs and leaves that I could use as camouflage—but decided against it. With my luck, I'd immediately find poison ivy or a bunch of leaves that a wild boar had just peed on.

So instead, I rolled out the sheep's wool blanket that Tuki had packed for me, and dug a ditch deep enough to sleep in—far away from the river—just encase something slightly less friendly than a giraffe got thirsty in the middle of the night, and thought I might make a good addition to its late night snack.

After lying down, I pulled up the wool blanket over my face and turned over on my side. Not surprisingly, I was asleep before the night owl could whoo, or the jungle lion could roar.

The evening air blew coolly over me. And I couldn't tell whether I was dreaming, or just remembering a dream from long ago, but something came to me that night in a way I hadn't experienced in quite some time. Actually, in a way I hadn't experienced since I was kidnapped back in that poacher's camp.

I was surrounded by fire, and no matter what I did, it just kept getting larger, brighter, hotter. But despite its increasing intensity, I held back the scream that was gathering in my throat. I should've been afraid, but I felt calmer than ever before. Because at that very moment, I saw him as he walked through the fire to get to me.

"I will find you." His almond shaped eyes stared into me. The handsome man stepped forward and extended his hand. He wanted me to go with him somewhere. But when he did, the other woman I'd been dreading appeared and stood in between us.

I couldn't make out her face, but I recognized her voice. "It's time Nanyamka." She too extended her hand, and I knew I had no choice but to take it—and the moment that I did, I woke up.

I used part of the wool blanket I'd been sleeping under to wipe off some of the sweat from my forehead and chest. It was one of the many recurring dreams that I hadn't had my entire time in Ipharadisi, and I thought it strange that I would suddenly have it now.

More importantly, I thought it strange that *he* was in it. I hadn't thought about him in months. He seemed almost like a stranger now, and it'd been so long since I'd seen his face that I couldn't even be sure that it was truly him—though deep down of course I knew it was.

Still, I shook off the odd montage and looked around. It was just daylight again, and if I wanted to continue to keep out of sight, I would need to crawl my way to the river behind me and see if I could catch something I could put a fire to for breakfast—before anything or *anyone* lurking out there woke up.

I still had a lot of ground left to cover, so whatever I caught, it would have to hold me over until dinner— whatever find that would be. Ready to get started, I rolled up my blanket and headed over to the watering hole—

crossing my fingers for something good.

Over the next two days, I continued to use the stars in the sky as my guide, just as Tuki had taught me. I also made a conscious effort to stay alert in open fields so that I could see any possible attacks—animal or otherwise— coming my way.

I was thankful that nothing had become aggressive. On the contrary, the cutest baby elephant took to keeping me company every now and then, walking with me and letting me rub behind its ears. The adorable little creature reminded me of Milkshake.

I hadn't visited poor Milkshake in over a month. I really hoped he wasn't holding it against me. I'd have to make him some of his favorite blueberry treats when I got back.

When my current companion finally went back to join its mother, I stopped walking for a moment to check my progress. According to the river and tree drawings on Zere's map, I was less than half a day's walk to the double-banded poacher's camp—the one local villagers had given Zere intelligence about. Unfortunately, those same villagers didn't have any leads to where Ipharadisi's missing rescuers may be.

Other villagers. I wondered. Zaina had given me strict orders not to interact with anyone who wasn't part of the mission. Tuki, on the other hand, had just given me a gentle reminder that I was—and always would be—on the lamb from whoever had kidnapped me.

I'd forever be on the lookout for people who abducted, traded and even *killed* other people for money—people who wanted nothing more than to do the latter to me for all the trouble Tuki and I had caused their operation. I shuddered when I thought about what they might do to me if they ever found me again.

Any thought I'd just had of further exploring the world outside of Ipharadisi was slowly beginning to fade. Within seconds, it was completely gone.

As I folded the map to put it away, I noticed something odd about the enormous line of trees I was approaching. The leaves were rustling in the direction *opposite* of the wind that had begun to blow.

I took a step forward to get a closer look at the anomaly, when all of the sudden—*whiz*! Ouch! I grabbed my arm.

I don't know what hurt more—the piercing whistle as it shot past my ears, or the stinging slice of the narrow object that painfully grazed my right shoulder, taking a piece of my flesh with it.

I panicked.

I looked around in the grassy clearing behind me, then again at the jungle trees before me. There was an enormous rustling sound that was getting louder and louder, and I didn't know which direction it was coming from.

To my left! No. The right! Slice! Another bloody cut, this time to my thigh. *Who* was attacking me? Why couldn't I see them??

Then, as quickly as I remembered the danger that Tuki told me would be ahead, was as quickly as they began to appear—one-by-one.

It was the Ubumnyama.

The darkness both Tuki and Zaina had warned me about were now here. These were the ones whose sole purpose in life was to inflict pain, death and destruction on anyone who was not part of their clan. They killed, and they terrorized—and they enjoyed every vile moment of it. My muscles tightened.

All red. All black. All beige. All olive. All blue. These were the singular colors they wore. Dark star tattoos with a sinister eye in the middle covered their hands, and all I could see through their cowardly masks were their malice-filled pupils, which were bleeding with evil.

None of them knew me, but their hatred wanted me dead.

So did the tips of their large curved blades.

Swing! Swipe! Slash! Several of them cut through the air at lighting fast speed. With each swipe, they hoped to take my life—but I wouldn't let them. I kicked one above the ear, causing him to stumble into another.

The beige one stepped in. He swirled two curved blades, one in each hand. My heartbeat picked up speed. Zaina said my objective was to avoid the Ubumnyama at all costs. So we skipped training with the…*blade*! Eleven o'clock. Thank goodness my reflexes were so sharp. I didn't even realize that I'd ducked to the side.

My quick action was only useful for a moment because less than a second later, the one in olive kneed me in the ribcage, and I dropped forward.

Remember why you're here Nanyamka. It's not just your life at stake.

I wrapped my arm around my ribs, and held myself together as if I'd fall apart if I let go. Clunk! The one in red had lifted his blade above his head and had tried to bring it down on me, but I had rolled over, causing his blade to go into the ground with a heavy sound.

Fight Nanyamka! Don't just lie there—fight back! I

scrambled to my feet, flinching from the pain in my side.

I remembered doing cartwheels and backflips when I was eight—as if they were the most natural things in the world. Now, the most natural thing in the world was the need to stay alive.

So for a moment, I let myself fly.

The world seemed to meld itself into slow-motion as I flipped through the air—my body turning upside down, then horizontally, and upright again as I landed on both feet.

No use.

Several of the Ubumnyama had beaten me to my landing position. I tilted my head as five points of five blades were at my throat. I had failed.

I thought about all the people in that horrible camp who may never know peace because I'd been too weak to fight the darkness that stood in my way. I thought about the innocent men, women and children who might spend the rest of their lives suffering under other men's evil ambitions.

No. This couldn't be it. I had to look deep down within me for some last piece of strength—some no holds barred, pull no punches, straight to the mattresses attempt.

I was dripping with sweat and panting like a hyena, but I still had one more round left in me.

So, I took all of the leftover energy; all of the leftover lifesaving desperation and screamed. I yelled it all out at the top of my lungs, energizing myself for the final round of hand-to-hand combat ahead.

And what do you know? It worked—but not in the way I expected it to.

The Ubumnyama were prepared to do unimaginable things to me—to stop me from my mission, but apparently *crazy* was the one thing the Ubumnyama *weren't* prepared to deal with.

Because just as I stood on my toes, waving my arms around and hollering like a mad woman, the Ubumnyama seemed to become very confused, slowly and carefully starting to back away. One-by-one, just the way they came, each of them looked at each other, then *ran!*

It was priceless.

I was so ecstatic that I began jumping around like I was Muhammad Ali, loosening up, just getting *ready* for the fight. I threw my hands back in the air and continued to bounce around. "Yeah, you *better* run!" I laughed. I never felt so truly relieved before.

That is, until I felt it.

The heat of its sweltering breath wasn't unfamiliar to me. I'd felt it many times before in a dream. But now, I froze as the creature's fiercely heavy breathing blew against my backside, raising goose bumps large enough to acknowledge my intense fear of its low warning growl.

Still, I knew I had no choice but to turn around and look. So, there I was, staring into the mouth of the king beast.

This lion was *definitely* no figment of my imagination. Nor was it caged or sleeping like its sedated counterpart in the wooden airport crate.

This animal was wild.

The snarling jungle beast paced back and forth—well within swiping distance of my easily torn face—with a starving look in its eyes as if it had finally found what it was hungering for; as if it had finally just found lunch—

me.

The sight of its razor sharp teeth paralyzed me, causing my shaking legs to buckle beneath me, quickly bringing me to my knees. Saliva dropped from the lion's fiercely muscular jaws, and what didn't fall to the earth, collected into a building foam around its flesh-eating fangs.

Suddenly, the lion lowered its head, and then its shoulders—the way a linebacker does before a tackle. I gulped.

The 500-pound wild animal was about to pounce.

In that moment, I became so terribly afraid that I closed my eyes and did something I had never really done before.

I prayed.

Perhaps it was no use, because shortly after I did, the lion let out a loud, ferocious roar. It was a roar so powerful that it vibrated throughout my entire body, in a way that made me think my heart might stop. And it *did*—briefly, when I realized that the lion that had roared wasn't the one in front of me, but there was another one—behind it!

This one was different. It didn't have a mane, which let me know that this creature was the *queen* of the wild—the majestic lioness. The lioness walked with authority, and now stood in *between* me and my all too energized enemy. The female let out a roar that caused the unrelenting, stalking beast to let out its own deep, threatening growl in return.

I watched with panicked breath as the two squared off with their eyes, circling one another over and over until the hungering lion tired of trying to find a weakness in the lioness's defense. Instead, the beast turned around, once again making me the sole center of its petrifying attention.

My heart pounded as it slowly licked its lips—then jump! It sprung onto its hind legs and started for me.

I gasped.

Just as I thought I'd taken my absolute last breath, the ferocious animal turned around and just walked away—as if it were somehow being controlled—never once glancing back in my direction—its muscles shaking as if it wanted to give me just one last intimidating look—but couldn't.

It was incredible.

No.

It was a miracle.

But I wondered if I was yet in the clear because the lioness that had warned off my would-be death maker continued to keep me in its sights. Yet, for however unexplainable the reason, I didn't fear this one that had rescued me.

Perhaps it was just the post-traumatic stress, but I was getting the strangest feeling that there was something my rescuer wanted me to *do*.

I looked deep into its eyes, something I was sure I *wasn't* supposed to do, but when I did, the majestic creature headed towards the trees that the Ubumnyama had been hiding in—and waited for me to follow.

I took an extremely cautious step forward—my foot landing in one of its paw prints. I stepped forward again, and this time I heard it let out a roar—not a warning to me, but a warning to anything that might try to harm me. That's when I let go of all reservations and let it lead the way.

I noticed my heart rate beginning to slow down as I no

longer worried about what was hiding in the dark part of the jungle. And, all the fears I once had were beginning to subside because even though I didn't know *how* I knew now that I *was* being protected. I had been delivered from the lion's paw, and I knew that everything would be okay—in the end.

At some point, my magnificent rescuer had fallen back to give me room, even though I could still feel its strong presence surrounding me. And only a few hours had passed before I finally reached a parting in the trees at the end of the deep, densely filled jungle.

I climbed up one of the shorter trees and looked out into the large clearing beyond.

There, right exactly where Zere said it would be, was the largest, most heart-wrenching, violently abusive poaching camp anyone could ever imagine possible.

There were dozens and dozens of scarred adults and small, crying children slaving away under the brutal, blistering sun.

Patrols of cowards with rifles struck women with the ends of their barrels, violently beating anyone who wasn't transporting elephant bones, lion skins or even tiger body parts fast enough. No wonder I'd had an escort here, these monsters had to be stopped.

And although I was only in that poacher's camp—the one that I was kidnapped to—for just a few days, the sight of the large, dirty tents here and animal graveyards brought back memories that brought with them floods of tears to my eyes. So I was certain, I would do *everything* in my power to get these people out of here—no matter the cost.

I climbed back down the mahogany tree and dug my

hands into the dirt. I wiped the dark black soil along the sides of my face as well as across my forehead. This way, when I sneak in, I'll look like I've been in the double-banded camp just as long as everyone else. No one should suspect me.

After I was finished camouflaging myself, I surveyed the camp clearing and searched for an opening. But I didn't have to scout long because it turned out that security was actually pretty lax in the front part of the perimeter. This seemed odd.

I wondered. What if whoever's in charge here knew about the willing evil outside? Could someone in this camp have made some sort of deal with the Ubumnyama to act as patrol for the perimeters leading to any outside contact?

It's possible.

And, if that were the case, then I would have trouble coming—a *lot* of it. Think Nanyamka. You're going to have to find a way to get these rescues out of here—and *soon*.

I climbed down the short hill that connected the cluster of trees I was looking out from, to the entry of the camp. There, I found some tattered clothes that had been discarded by the waste area and put them on over my short brown training outfit.

I casually walked in, spotting a group of women who were hauling tiger, rhino and elephant bones across the camp. I immediately joined them and was thankful that no one even looked twice at me. Good, I thought. I blended in.

But to do what I had to do here, I would have to show these women, these men, even the children that they could trust me—and that would take some time—time I wasn't sure I had.

Still, the first day I kept my head down. I didn't want to bring any unnecessary attention to myself. I did exactly as I was told by the poachers here, and avoided the beatings I'd become all too familiar with in the first camp I'd had the unfortunate experience of.

The second day, however, I made contact with one of the kidnapped—a young woman who seemed immensely aged beyond her years. I could tell she hadn't been faring so well—because she had the scars on her back and face to prove it.

My heart fell as she moved as someone who had long given up on life. Her sad humble eyes did most of the talking, and they silently told of how she just wanted to die in peace. She must've been here for a very long time—possibly much longer than anyone else.

I immediately took to protecting her, and intervened several times over the next few days on the young woman's behalf—just as Tuki had once done for me.

That's why Addane softly whispered her name to me—so that I would know whom I was defending. "Ah-dahn-neh," she carefully pronounced it for me. "Nanyamka," I whispered back.

Addane shared with me the unthinkable acts that she had been subjected to in a previous camp. There she had been taken as some depraved individual's sex slave.

Addane was raped and abused on a daily basis and had been suffering through such inhumanity since the tender age of ten.

It was more than a decade before her township's government did anything to shut down the incredibly vile operation. Officers took statements from the women and children, as well as from the men who had been forced into such acts under threats of punishment and death.

Shelters had been set up for the victims—but deathly afraid that she would be separated from the child that she bore while entrapped in that awful camp, Addane decided to flee. She was certain her government would have deemed her an unfit mother after having been denied an education for all of those years.

But Adanne didn't make it far in her escape. Because starving and near death, she soon realized that she could not provide for her young one, and made her way back to poacher's land, hoping to arrive at some arrangement, only to be brought here instead.

Addane was beginning to think that she was being punished just for being born, and would have given up on life completely if it wasn't for the infant she now cradled in her arms.

Her fragile little gift was the only reason Addane made the conscious decision to get out of her mattress missing, hard, wooden bed every morning and keep going. "He didn't ask to be here," Addane had said, "But I am the reason he is here, and now I must protect him."

I admitted that I was surprised the poachers here let her keep her baby at all. But then I realized it was simply so that she could nurse the children of *their* own base indiscretions.

That, unfortunately, explained why I could see the ribcage of Addane's small child sticking out as it expanded and collapsed in steady interims—because by the time Addane was allowed to tend to him, she would often have already run out of milk. This enraged me. No one deserved this.

Addane had endured this kind of suffering for so many years, that with each passing day, she came closer and closer to giving up. She would continue to nurse her little one—but for how long? For Addane, there had been no end in sight—no hope. She didn't want to fight any longer. She simply wanted to—as I surmised when we first met—"die in peace," Addane cried.

I met many others over the next week and a half, and I spent as much time as possible getting to know each individual. There were so many more people in this camp than in the one I once knew—so many more stories.

Yet there was one common theme among them all. They'd each felt so beaten down by life—by their situations, that they'd all begun to feel utterly hopeless. But I was here to tell them that it wasn't hopeless. I was here to tell them to have faith. Yes, I knew that now. My mission wasn't just to get them out, it was to encourage them to have faith that it was possible.

The sun began to set as I pondered the situation at hand, and as I thought back to my own rescue. What did Tuki do that was so pivotal? It wasn't just the things that she had said.

Then I remembered. She encouraged me to look at my circumstances, and to decide whether or not what I wanted was worth taking a leap of faith for. She made me see that the impossible was *indeed* possible and in the end, that knowledge paid off.

And although those here would eventually have to make that same decision on their own, they would first need the courage to do so.

But what could I possibly say? What could I possibly

do that would inspire *anyone?* I wasn't much of a motivational speaker, so I knew that my words probably wouldn't motivate someone who'd been kept down in the dirt for years.

The only thing I could do right now is to tell them what I learned from my own experiences. Perhaps that would be enough to inspire them. Perhaps.

The poachers in the camp here took shifts supervising our sleep that night—not that anyone slept much on the hard, wooden crates passed off as bunk beds.

The poachers apparently didn't want any of the kidnapped slave workers to have even the slightest luxury, as even the singular chair in the large dirty-beige tent had no cushion to it—despite knowing that it would only be used by the rifle holder who would keep watch over the workers' sleeping quarters.

Still, when the wicked man finally ran out of off-key tunes to sing, he unintentionally began to doze off in the too-small wooden chair.

I waited until I heard his practically chainsaw like snore before creeping out of the bunk I lay in, and before crawling on my hands and knees past the dozen rows of wooden beds to Addane's section of the tent.

While everyone else drifted in and out of a not-so-peaceful sleep, Addane lay still on her back, cradling her little boy; her eyes wide open as if she could see through the dismal looking tent and into the freedom bearing sky above. I kneeled down beside her—though she didn't stir, and prepared to share my story.

"Addane," I began, "I know you've been through much, and this may be hard to hear, but you should know there's a reason why I am here."

It was day seven that we'd been friends, and I thought it was time she knew. "This is not my first time in a place like this."

Addane was worn down by the nearly 20 hour work day, but something that I'd said brought an alertness to her eyes I hadn't seen before. It also caused the others who were awake to turn a curious ear to me.

"I was taken somewhere—like here before. I was on an airplane, on my way to an opportunity to make all my dreams come true." I paused. "But then I was in an explosion…and the next thing I knew, I was in the back of someone's trunk—unconscious. It was then that I soon realized my old life was over."

Addane tilted her head, even more curious than when I first began. "I was petrified," I explained. "The violence. The cruelty. I still remember the first thought I had when I arrived there."

"What was it?" Addane needed to know.

"That I didn't have it in me to survive. That my life was over." I smiled. "But I didn't think that way long because someone interceded for me. This person gave me the courage to fight—the courage to live. She helped me to find a better life."

"You escaped?" Someone in a nearby bunk asked in a thrown whisper.

"I did."

"But you are here—somewhere—like here again." Addane pointed out.

"I am."

"You were captured again," questioned the voice from the nearby bunk.

"No," I replied.

Addane seemed to think of an improbable alternative. She asked anyway. "You came here on your own?"

"Yes."

"But...*why*?" Addane's reaction was mixed with both confusion and anger.

"For you Addane." I looked around. "For everyone."

I cleared my throat and spoke loud enough for everyone who had gathered to hear.

"Listen, I know it looks hopeless—that it's been unbearable. You've been dealt this unfair hand through no fault of your own. And I don't know how anyone could stay in this condition as long as you have, and not feel the hopelessness that so many of you have told me you feel.

But it's not the end of the road. I *know*, because I've been through it. I got out, and you can too. But only if you believe you can. Only if you have the courage to have the faith that you'll need for what's ahead."

I told them everything I'd experienced since I'd been to Ipharadisi. I told them about the life that was possible—a life without fear—a life full of peace.

When I was finished speaking, someone from an even further away bunk made her way to me. It was the first time in a long time that I'd seen someone of her complexion.

Her straw colored hair was mixed with grey, and I couldn't help but to notice the blue veins under her thin, pale skin.

"If they catch you, they will kill you," she said.

"I know," I responded.

The frail, weak woman nervously shook her head. "You would risk this...for strangers?"

I nodded without hesitation.

"*Why?*" It was the same question that Addane had asked earlier.

I thought about the day I was rescued, and the purpose I'd found in life ever since I had been. I turned around and looked into the eyes of the one who had asked the reason.

"I would risk it," I replied, "because someone once risked the same for me, and I couldn't live with myself if I didn't do the same for you. But I know that no matter how much I want it for you—no matter how hard I fight for you—there's nothing I can do, unless you're willing to do it for yourself. And if you are, I will stand right there with you—but I need to know, is there anyone who is willing to stand…with me?"

Tears welled over in the frail woman's eyes—not the sad kind, and not the overjoyed kind, but the kind you let go when a heavy burden's finally been released. She stood there a moment as she dried her eyes, and after she could see again, she said it.

"I will stand with you."

"So will I," said the small boy who had been helping to hold her up.

"Me too," said someone else—someone I couldn't even see.

Almost everyone had found a renewed strength—the faith that they had been searching for—everyone it seemed except Addane.

Addane bit her lip as she looked around at the multitude of people who were now standing together. And it was with considerable difficultly that Addane sat herself up—careful not to brush her bloody and beaten back against the wood of her confined sleeping corners.

Her baby began to cry and she gently rocked him back and forth, wishing him back to sleep.

"No one's ever fought for me before," Addane confessed. "No one's ever cared."

I dropped back down to my knees and held her free hand in mine.

"I care for you." I spoke louder. "I *care* for you." I rubbed her hand in mine. Adanne slowly nodded, finally knowing that it would be okay.

So when they asked me what the plan was, I told them the same thing that a crazy, funny, nut job once told me. "We're going to wait."

"Wait for what," they asked.

"The *sign*," I replied. I laughed a little to myself, then crawled back to my bunk and closed my eyes.

The next daylight, we lined up in the meal tent for our breakfast rations. We'd been receiving two servings daily of whatever animal part stew was leftover from the day before. It wasn't exactly appetizing, but it was always sharply on time.

This camp was much more organized than the one I had been in—a little *too* well organized.

And unlike Tuki, who knew there were other rescuers waiting with horns in the trees, I had no such help here. Here, it would be exceptionally more difficult to execute a successful escape.

But the increasingly unbearable and extremely dry heat was taking its toll on the rifle bearing poachers—so much so, that even though they were supposed to be on patrol, one-by-one they began to enter the meal tent for the minimal relief that the tent's thin cover provided.

First one poacher came in. Then two poachers came in.

That's when I had the idea.

I nodded to Serah—the frail one with the greying straw colored hair. I darted my eyes to the younger woman next to her, hoping Serah would get her attention, and she did. They both knew what I was signaling them to do. So slowly, Serah and the young woman rose from their eating benches, and carefully crept outside of the tent.

Quietly, they made their way to the large mahogany tree I originally hid in when I first scouted the area. It was a path they were only able to take because of its now patrol-free zone—thanks to the oblivious three poachers who had left their posts to come inside the tent.

Not long after, two more, then three more poachers came under the tent's inviting shade, chatting with the other poachers as they walked in.

So, I signaled to two more, then to three more of the kidnapped individuals who quietly and without attracting any attention to themselves, crept past the even newer patrol-free zone—without anyone ever noticing.

And between the dizzying heat and the tent remaining at the exact same occupancy—thanks to my impromptu one in, one out, two in, two out strategy, no one suspected a thing.

The tent was still full—almost entirely with heat relief seeking poachers. But I realized that if the rest of us didn't make our move soon, one of the rifle wielding mad men might realize what was going on.

"Follow me," I said to the two remaining rescues.

The three of us casually exited the tent. "Stay close to

me," I whispered.

We walked softly—as to not even step on a twig that could make a betraying sound. Just a few more yards, I thought to myself.

Dau, one of the adorable little boys, squeezed my hand as if he were having the same anxious thought I was having. He looked up at Addane who walked with us, holding her small child to her breast.

We quickly picked up the pace.

Forty more yards to safety.

Thirty yards.

Twenty.

And that's when I felt it—the burning clutch of someone's forceful grip. It was so violently tight that the pain seared through my arm.

But worse than that was the voice—the voice I hoped I would never...ever hear again.

It was the voice that filled me with the fiery anger of having been taken away from everyone I ever loved. It was the voice that had the audacity to speak to me after not only threatening to take my life, but after attempting to follow *through* with it.

"Sawubona beautiful."

I turned around.

His piercing blue eyes twinkled at the sight of me, and it was as if I were looking straight into the eyes of evil.

The evil spoke to me.

"Well look at you. I thought you would be long dead by now." Furious, I shook my arm free.

"Sorry to disappoint you *D'marco*." I said his name with a vile disgust.

D'marco ignored it.

"You know, you and your friends cost me a *lot* of money in that old camp, and I was really, *really* hoping I would see your pretty little face again." D'marco flashed his deceptively charming smile.

This devil in sheep's clothing was the main reason Tuki was afraid for me to ever leave Ipharadisi—in case I was ever recognized or found by this deviant again.

And she was right in her concerns—although I should've known that she would be. Because according to Tuki, who'd met plenty of scum like him before, D'marco was the kind of low-life criminal who never ever forgot a face—and who never ever gave up searching for his victims. "I *always* find what I'm looking for." That's what he had said to me the day he told me I had fifteen seconds left to live.

The chance that we would ever meet again was so slim to me that I had truly never worried about it. What *were* the chances that I would cross paths with someone like D'marco more than once on such a large continent?

Apparently the chances were good, especially with this organized network of black market poachers.

But to accomplish this type of organized crime, it would not only take serious resources, but serious *funding*—more than just the kind they could get from trading and selling their illegal goods—forced free labor or not. It was almost as if they were getting extra backing from somewhere, but *where*?

Before I could give it anymore thought, an all-black SUV slowly pulled up beside us—one of those government looking ones that I used to see all the time back in New York. The windows were tinted, but they slowly rolled down as the SUV parked and turned off its engine. Still, I could barely make out the individuals inside.

The two front doors opened and the same number of men quickly exited. The first, the driver, was Serah's complexion, and wore a black, fitted driver's hat and a matching uniform. The second—whose nose was peeling from apparently having been in the sun for an extended period of time held a rifle, and stood towards the middle of the vehicle; very still, very security like.

The driver then opened the back door, practically throwing himself to the side—clearing the way for whoever was about to step out. Finally, a shoe—cream in color; ivory slacks; beige shirt and a tipped down, cream-colored fedora made of straw exited the heavily guarded SUV. The man in white spit out tobacco as he stood directly in front of me. "Well, what do we have here?" He asked in a drawling, husky voice that was deceptively friendly. I ignored him and looked away.

The stranger looked to D'marco. "Aren't you going to introduce me to our little guest?"

D'marco tightened his grip around my arm, causing me to bend in the knees from the pressure. I gritted my teeth.

"Just a troublemaker sir. She was one of the ones who got away in the old establishment. One of the ones who disabled our jeeps—and stole the lot of our inventory." D'marco grabbed a handful of my hair as he recalled the memory, yanking me back as he pictured all of the money that Tuki and the rest of us had caused him to lose—the money in the form of ivory that he didn't know was in the bottom of the river by the old camp, right where we had left it.

The man in white seemed intrigued. "Really? And she's

been out *there* all this time?" He gestured towards the dark cluster of trees in the distance. His glance to the differing terrain turned into a focused stare—a searching stare. But he quickly snapped out of it and spoke directly to me. "One would think the jungle would have eaten you up by now."

Dau and Addane had been standing still this entire time—nervous sweat dripping down their temples.

It pained me that they had to witness anything that would cause them even more fear than they were already experiencing.

But it wasn't over.

The man with the beige shirt and reddening skin ripped open the buttoned seam of my tattered blouse—the one I had put on so that I would blend in here. I still had on the handmade leather vest underneath—which he had just exposed.

Tuki's donga sticks remained snugly strapped to my back.

"Interesting choice of dress," D'Marco's devious associate mused. "Tell me, where have you been all this time?"

I didn't answer. Instead we stared into each other's eyes.

And although I couldn't put my finger on it, something was giving me the uneasy feeling that he knew more than he was letting on. This man wasn't just generally curious about me. He was looking for answers to something.

Something—or *somewhere*.

17. Trouble in Paradise

"I *said*," my interrogator screamed louder, "*where* have you been all this time?"

Silence.

"*Where??*"

His yell was meant to be intimidating. Instead, it was motivating. I remembered why I was here, and everyone who was waiting for me to return to Ipharadisi. That's when I twisted my arm free from D'marco, and head-butted him in the same swift movement.

"Run!" I shouted at Dau and Addane who were still glued to my side.

The entire tent full of riflemen whipped their heads around the second my desperate plea reached their overly alert ears. Sadly, when they saw Addane and the young boy about to make a run for it, the more than dozen blood lusting criminals took out their rifles—and that's when the horror began.

It was a complete barrage—the most heart-stopping sound of shots being fired. The disgusting noise startled even D'marco and his cohort who both ducked for cover—not having any idea where the shots were being fired from.

Little did the two know, cowardly weapons weren't being used in their direction at all. The cacophony was simply the welcome sound of dried pig bladders being popped in the distance.

I knew this because the first thing I did when I arrived here was to survey the area—just as Tuki had taught me. And, my short but thorough scout turned up a multitude of discarded carcasses lying around the perimeter—bladders still intact.

Before I had even taken one step into this awfully forsaken, double-banded camp, I had painstakingly carved out each pig bladder—while blowing into the hollow organs with all of my might—wiping my lips quite often I might add. I then tied each one into a balloon before hiding them behind the tallest trees in the mahogany filled forest.

So those items were there now, and although I never had the time to tell anyone, I had faith that at least one of the rescues would be able to figure it out—and someone had.

Serah? Joseph? Lilah? Whoever it was, they were using whatever slice of rock they had found, and were methodically popping the makeshift balloons in such a way that it sounded as if a full-fledged war had been waged upon this illegal, ivory network.

So now, when all we needed was a distraction to make it out of here—a sign if you will—that it was safe to make a run for it, the rescues who I inspired last night were there—just as they said they would be. They were standing with us now when we needed each other most.

"Runnn!" I yelled again, desperately urging Dau and Addane to move faster—Addane pressing her baby against her heaving chest.

D'marco and his falsely macho boss were still on the ground, covering their heads as the popping sounds continued. Thankfully, they were still ducking for cover by the time the three of us reached the tree-lined perimeter.

"We've got to keep moving," I yelled out to everyone. Hopefully, the riflemen wouldn't dare run into the forest thinking there was an entire battalion waiting in the trees for them. That should give us enough time—and enough space to safely make our escape.

The rescues and I were in such a rush that I completely forgot about the Ubumnyama, and never even thought about the wild lions—the hostile one, or the one that had saved me.

Regardless, we didn't encounter either on our way back. I didn't know what type of luck to attribute that to because there were almost two dozen of us to be too easily seen—and just as easily picked off by any wild and hungry beast.

Still, our large group kept running. We ran even past nightfall. But we finally had to stop when Serah began limping through the wheat-colored grass with just half a day's journey behind us.

I broke off from the group once I led them to the watering hole that I had once found rest at just a week ago in these very plains.

I then set off to see what I could find.

When I returned, I held in my hands several flowers

that were shaped like claws—the fruit of which Erec had taught me could be used for healing and to alleviate various pains. I quickly began dressing the injuries of anyone who admitted they were hurt. By the second night however, physical relief wasn't enough, and many of the rescues were beginning to ask the big question.

"What now?"

I tried to remember what the Gurmus had said about my birthmother—what Queen Ayanna had told them at the time of their rescue. She'd told them about a place where they could start over—a place where they would be safe from harm. "Peace," she had explained to them. I turned to the group before me and offered them the same hope.

"But how long?" Someone shouted as the anxiousness started to spread.

"It's not much farther," I announced. "Please everyone, just hang in there."

Dau, who only looked to be about seven years of age, tried to comfort a small boy even younger than he—Atikem, Dau's cousin I believe.

Atikem sniffled as I wiped the tiny teardrops that were leaving salt stains on his five-year-old, beautifully courageous face. "You're doing great." I reassured him. "Both of you," I added.

When we finally reached Ipharadisi, we returned via the same naturally created, vine covered tunnel that Tuki had originally brought me through upon my first arrival here. The ritual was the same. The guardians asked where I was from, then offered me a blessing as I repeated the sacred words that ultimately granted re-entry.

The walk into the main square was a triumphant one.

Ipharadisian warriors met us and escorted each rescue to a place where he or she could get some rest, as well as food into their undoubtedly hungering stomachs.

I looked around at the incredibly relieved expressions of this wonderful group who would soon become family. Mr. and Mrs. Gurmu would have been so proud, which made my successful return this afternoon somewhat bittersweet.

What was far from bittersweet however, was the overwhelming emotion I felt the second I saw Erec's handsome face.

I don't know why, but the sight of him brought tears to my eyes, and the cry that I let out shocked me. It all happened so fast that I didn't even realize I had run into his arms until he was swinging me around in circles—half a dozen swirls before he finally placed me back down on my feet.

Erec let out a sigh of relief.

"Kay, I've been so worried! I've just been counting the days." Erec frantically patted me head-to-toe, checking for any unseen injuries.

I laughed through my tears. "I'm fine Erec. Really."

Erec took a moment to catch his breath. He'd obviously run from wherever he was to meet me the second he heard I was back.

"I missed you Kay. I mean I really, *really* missed you." The tears that continued to fall down my cheeks let him know that I felt the same.

We couldn't stop embracing so we held each other as if the earth would crack if one of us let go. It was as if we hadn't seen each other in years, rather than the mere week and a half it had actually been.

"Nanyamka!" It was Kayla. She was enthusiastically waving to me from on top of Tuki's shoulders. I waved back.

"Hey kid!" Tuki let her down, and Kayla ran straight into my arms. I rustled her curly, barrette decorated hair before setting Kayla down on the ground. Kayla skipped her way back to Tuki.

I threw my hands into the air.

"Tuki! Your leg is healed!" I said it as I looked down at her bandage free leg—crutches nowhere in sight.

"Yes," Tuki replied. "It remains a bit sore, but I have regained full function of it. You will not have to go on another journey like that again." She smiled as we hugged.

I thought about the rescue I'd just accomplished, and shook my head in bewilderment. "I can't believe I actually did it Tuki. There were a few times out there when I didn't know if I was going to make it back."

Tuki nearly laughed. "I did not have any doubt that you would accomplish what you set out to do Nanyamka. I have seen your heart, and it is capable of many, many good things."

I thanked her for her confidence and high-fived Kayla as Zaina approached. "Queen," I said in acknowledgement.

"Nanyamka, you have returned."

I couldn't tell whether she was pleased or disappointed.

"Yes, I am back." And I was mostly glad to be so. The welcome from Erec and Tuki had been extremely warm. This welcome from Zaina—not so much.

"So do you care to report on what you found during your mission? Or, perhaps the journey was too much for

325

you. Should we wait for you to rest?" She gave me the once-over. "A little beauty sleep perhaps?"

I sighed.

I suppose two weeks wasn't exactly enough time to "make the heart grow fonder" because it appeared her primary focus was still to belittle me in front of Erec.

I decided to ignore it.

"I am ready to report Zaina." Her eye twitched just a little. Yeesh, I thought to myself. "*Queen* Zaina." Some battles just weren't worth fighting over.

My addressing her by title seemed to temporarily quell her need to continuously remind me that even though we were sisters—and even though our mom once had a dream that I would ascend to the throne—that the throne was now and would forever be *Queen* Zaina's.

She circled me now—as she had developed a habit to do, and ordered me to report what I had seen while I was in the double-banded camp.

"It is as Zere has said," I began. "It is remarkably well organized...*twice* the size of the camp I was kidnapped to. There was a man there who seemed to be in charge—even more so than..."

I glanced at Tuki. I didn't want to alarm her because I knew how much she worried about him finding me again, but I had to tell them everything. "D'marco, Tuki. D'marco was there."

"*What??*" Tuki exclaimed this in anger, not in surprise.

The probability that I'd run into him again—if I ever left Ipharadisi—as I just had, wasn't as slim to her as it had been to me. But she still dreaded the thought of it. Tuki knew—just as much as I knew now—that if he ever got his hands on me again, it might be the last time...*ever.*

I subconsciously rubbed my throat as if I could already feel someone choking the life out of it.

Erec raised a curious eyebrow. Zaina didn't seem to recognize the name either, but those details weren't important right now.

"It's not him I'm worried about," I quickly added. "It's the other man. He wanted to know where I've been all this time. He was *extremely* adamant about it."

Zaina's head whipped around. "And what did you tell this man?"

I was insulted at what Zaina was insinuating.

"I didn't tell him anything."

Zere, who had been standing off to the side, suddenly stepped forward. "And you are sure you weren't followed back?"

"Of course not," I said as I rolled my eyes. "I mean, it's not like I gave him the map I…"

At that moment, I patted the breast pocket of my tight brown vest. It was empty.

"Oh no."

I patted the other pocket, and continued patting myself down until I had checked every location on my person. The further down I patted, the more out loud I panicked.

"Oh no, oh no, oh no, oh…*no!*"

Zaina stalked forward. She was practically snarling at me now. "The map you…*what* Nanyamka?"

I stood with an open mouth.

"The map you *burned* you mean." Zaina meant it rhetorically. Ashamed, I looked towards the ground, and closed my eyes so that I wouldn't have to meet anyone else's.

"I didn't burn it," I admitted—reluctantly.

This time even Tuki couldn't defend me. "Nanyamka! What do you mean you did not burn it? We watched you as you held it to the flames before you left."

"I did…I mean…I was going to. It's just…I was so scared I would get lost, I blew out the flame and took it with me." I showed them my empty pockets. "But now it's gone."

The horrified sounds that escaped everyone around me spread throughout the main square of Ipharadisi. First Zere, then Tuki. Erec was the only one who didn't seem utterly disappointed with me—but I wasn't going to ask him to defend me now.

I tried to explain myself. "It must've dropped during the scuffle…it was all so chaotic."

Zaina laughed sarcastically, and I knew she would take pleasure in what she would now be able to say.

"I knew you would be a reckless disappointment." Zaina swiveled around. "Do you see Tuki? This American you have brought here—they are all the same. First my mother was fooled by one, and now you have brought ruin to our village by bringing *her*.

I warned you of the danger she would cause."

I was shocked by what my sister had said. I thought Tuki would speak up for me, but she was too disappointed to even look at me.

Zaina didn't care. "You realize that evil cannot be allowed to come here."

I emphatically shook my head. "They won't Zaina. There's nothing here that they want. I will go back if you think they would come all this way just to get revenge on me. I will go back and…"

Zaina scoffed. "No one wants *you* Nanyamka. It is *our*

328

resources they are after." She looked at Zere. "Our resources...and our rescuers."

I didn't understand, and she could tell.

"There is so much history here you could not even begin to comprehend...*sister*." I wanted to protest, but I knew she was telling the truth.

Tuki finally spoke to me again. "Our village has been the reason of much disruption in many poaching camps for many decades," she began. "It is not always so convenient to sink ivory that has been slaughtered for, in the river. And there are not always rescues of the *live* kind that are needed.

Sometimes the best thing we can do to disable these cruel camps, are to take hold of their resources and bring them here—where they cannot sell them for profits of war or weapons or people." Tuki looked up towards Grandfather's jeweled-stone house on the mountain. "And they know we have been protecting much precious material and gold."

"I had no idea," I conceded.

Zere stepped forward from the small crowd. "That is because we do not care about those things, so what is it to speak of them?"

"But there are those who would *kill* for such materials," Zaina pointed out. "And you have led them here. *You* have led them straight here."

I tried to speak—but could only stutter. "No...I...I don't think we were followed."

Zaina ignored my frantic explanation. She turned to Zere and to the other half a dozen warriors who were now healed along with Tuki. "We will need to take care of them permanently now," Zaina announced.

Erec was shocked. So was Tuki. I would have been as well if I'd realized what she meant by *permanently.*

"I will not allow what happened to my mother to happen here again. We will head out at first daybreak, and make sure these *animals* can never harm us, or others again."

"*No* Zaina!" Tuki couldn't believe what she was hearing. "You can't be saying what I think you are saying."

"I am. My mind is set. There is nothing you can do to change it now."

Something told me that Zaina had been looking for a reason to take revenge on these camps for a long time now, even though they weren't the reasons—or the ones responsible for our mother's death—as far as I knew, but they were indeed those who our mother had fought against her entire life.

And now, my sister had finally found a reason to take them out once and for all. Perhaps she thought by doing so, she would also be able to take out her own pain with it.

But she'd only cause herself more grief.

Erec slowly walked to Zaina's side and took her hand in his. He gazed into her eyes—earnestly—lovingly.

"Zaina," he whispered, "It is not for you, or I, or anyone else to take another's life." He gently touched the naked skin along her shoulders. "My queen, we have not been threatened. We do not know that the map is in anyone's hands. It could have fallen anywhere. Please, take some time to think about this. No blood has to be shed."

Suddenly, the fierceness in Zaina's eyes began to

subside. It seemed that Erec was the only person she would listen to—the only person whose opinion she cared about.

My sister took in a deep breath as her harsh expression softened. "For you Erec. I will hold off on this for you." She wanted him to know that she valued his opinion. She wanted him to know that she valued his heart—and everyone who was there could see—she still desperately wanted him to be her king.

I felt sorry for her.

Zaina adjusted her crown before walking away—looking back only once, hoping Erec would follow.

He didn't.

Tuki finally exhaled. "I know her Erec. She will not hold off on this for long."

"I know," Erec returned. "What are we going to do?"

"Not us. *Nanyamka*," Tuki replied.

"Hunh?" I was totally lost.

Tuki sighed as if I were missing something that was common knowledge. "You must challenge her as queen of course. Many will die if you do not."

I backed up, almost tripping over myself. "*Please* tell me you're joking."

"I do not joke Nanyamka. Taking life goes against all that Ipharadisi stands for. By doing so—even claiming to protect it—she will be destroying it—the very heart of Ipharadisi."

"Tuki is right," Erec agreed. "You have the birthright given to you by your mother. You have the right to challenge Zaina. You must!"

Had they both gone completely insane? I couldn't be a *prom* queen, let alone a real queen. I wasn't challenging

Zaina for that. I thought maybe we were all just being a little too hasty here, so I put my hands up as if they were a couple of stop signs.

"Listen guys, I think we're all getting a bit ahead of ourselves. Zaina said she would hold off. There's not going to be any war today so let's just take a breather and get some rest."

Thankfully, we all agreed. I still felt horrible about losing the map, but there was nothing I could do about it now. So we each went back to our respective huts to lie down.

I was still staying in Tuki's acorn community, but she had decorated my own personal hut for me while I was away—right next door to hers.

It was even fully furnished with a beautifully woven mat soft enough to sleep on, a bed shaped like a perfectly round pillow, a carved wooden table—the legs of which were shaped like animals, and even clay pots that stood in the corner next to a wicker stool.

The clay pots were already pre-filled with water for me to drink, and there was some fruit and salted fish on a wooden plate on top of the stool.

I couldn't believe how much Tuki and everyone else had thought about me while I was away. I had such an amazing family here, and was truly thankful for everything I had.

I slowly undressed. The leather of my skirt and vest had been sticking to my thigh and chest thanks to the brutal sun, and I didn't want to pull off any flesh my first time taking it off during the entire journey.

Once I carefully peeled everything off, I put on a powder blue nightgown—one that had been in the pile of clothes Erec had given me when I first arrived here. Once dressed for bed, I stretched out and lay down. It was good to be home.

And though the sun was rising by the time I'd fallen asleep, I was still oddly energetic when I awoke. So I got up and rinsed my mouth with some of the water from one of the clay pots, but I didn't see the wooden toothbrush Tuki had left out for me until later. Oh well. I did a quick breath check. Not bad. I could wait to brush my teeth until later—I was anxious to go for a walk instead.

Somehow my walk led me to the palace hut, and I was surprised to see that the door was already open.

I peered into the large, regal room only to see Zaina mid-training session. There were several others in the palace hut with her, but apparently she had opted to train alone. Zaina was practicing with daggers today instead of the usual donga sticks we regularly sparred with.

She saw me as I entered the room, and Zaina did *not* look happy. But for the first time, I genuinely didn't care. Things were going on here that were bigger than some petty, sibling rivalry. This was bigger than our feelings for Erec and bigger than being the owner of some title I didn't even want. So I decided to be diplomatic.

I boldly approached Zaina as she thrust at an imaginary opponent with the daggers that she held. "We need to talk," I said calmly. Zaina stayed focused on her invisible foe.

"I have nothing to say to you," Zaina grunted. Sweat dripped down the sides of her temples as she sliced through the air with the edges of her sharp blades.

"Then *think* of something," I pressed.

Zaina flung one of the daggers past my face and into the center of the lion's eye on the tapestry that hung on the back wall.

"There are a *lot* of things I can think of," Zaina retorted. She walked over to the mural and pulled out the dagger. "But none I think you truly want to hear."

"Try me," I dared.

Zaina let the dagger shimmer in the light of one of the torches.

"Okay. I shall. Do you want to know what I truly think of you?"

"You mean, besides that I'm a careless, dangerous, worthless disappointment?"

"No," she laughed. "You are more than that. You are a *plague* on Ipharadisi. You have disrespected me—and you have disrespected Zere—who put his life on the line for you and for everyone else here.

You think that just because you were also born of *my* mother that you know what it's like to have Ipharadisi run through your veins.

But you do not.

You do not know what it is like to have the blood of all the lives you have lost in a rescue on your hands. You do not know what it is like to have to choose which villages, which kidnapped souls, which small children will receive our help, and which will have to be left to die.

No one knows the responsibilities of the decisions I make, but I. Yet, you think you can come in here after only *six* months, and know *all* of the right choices to make. Tell me, are you so proud of your *one* accomplishment that you do not even know what it takes to accomplish something to truly be proud of?"

"Fine!" I yelled, sucked into her game. "Then *teach* me how to become someone I can be proud of."

Zaina eyed me doubtfully.

She looked at the dagger in her hand.

"It is not something that can be taught so easily. It takes practice," Zaina said as she again thrust the dagger into the nearby wall—leaving it there for later I assumed. She then bent down and picked up a donga stick, tossing me one to spar with.

"It takes dedication," Zaina grunted as she tested me with several of the moves she had taught me before my mission.

I countered each one easily.

"It takes perseverance—a willingness to go on when you feel you no longer can!" Zaina did a side sweep with her donga stick to my ankles. I jumped into the air, letting the wooden weapon glide underneath my feet until I came back down. I turned and tried to kick it out of her hands, but missed—right about the same time that I noticed our sparring was growing increasingly intense.

Zaina remained extremely focused while I tried to figure out what she was getting at.

"I can learn perseverance Zaina. If this is what you mean, I will go back to that camp—back through the Ubumnyama—and disable the double-banded operation so that even if they found the map, Ipharadisi will never be bothered." I stood confident. "I got those people out. I can take that operation down. I've done it before."

Zaina snorted. "Simple luck, sister. You do not have it in you to do it again."

I wanted to show her that she was wrong, but when I charged at her, her side sweep knocked me to my feet this time. And when I scrambled back up, she just knocked me back down again.

It continued that way until I grew exhausted.

"Okay. That's enough," I said of our intense sparring session.

Zaina didn't listen.

She continued to come at me. "You must be strong!" She yelled at me—determined to teach me a lesson. Zaina struck me in the shoulder—with all of her might—part of her donga stick cracking off as it met my shoulder blade below. The pain there was searing—very possibly dislocated.

"I said, that's enough Zaina!"

She continued to strike me.

Hit! Strike! Hit!

This time I felt it in my back. It vibrated down my spine. I tried to signal for her to stop—to beg for her to stop. But she struck me again—in the face.

I fell over.

Finally, Zaina went in for the final score as I forced myself up to my knees and reached for her donga stick that was coming down on me—directly onto my head. I knocked it away and clinched Zaina by the wrist. I shouted.

"*Enouuuuugh!*"

Silence.

Everyone in the room froze still.

Several mouths hung open in disbelief. I quickly got the impression that no one had ever spoken to her majesty the queen that way—certainly had never yelled at her that way.

I expected her fury to come down on me any second

336

now.

Instead, Zaina looked around the room—furious—but quiet. Blood trickled down her nose—her blood pressure spiking no doubt. I'd pushed her too far.

I tried to think of something to say, but before I could, she stormed out of the palace hut—blood dripping behind her.

This wasn't good, I thought to myself.

Not good at all.

18. Choices

For the rest of the day, Grandfather and I practiced simple breathing and relaxation techniques. I'd gone to his hut, hoping to get rid of the uneasy feeling I was having about my last encounter with Zaina.

Because although it had been fuzzy the majority of my time here, for some reason, our recent confrontation had brought back the flood of visions I'd had about Zaina in my old home—the ones where she'd cut through me like butter with an ivory-colored dagger.

And now the visions were haunting me.

It seemed that no matter how hard I tried, the images sat there in the back of my mind, rearing to the front every time I thought I'd finally pushed the awful occurrences away.

"Grandfather...?" I stopped walking in circles to address him.

Grandfather casually leaned in from the log—without looking up—the way he often did, somehow already knowing whatever question I would ask.

"How accurate are my dreams Grandfather? Not the usual ones, but the visions? The ones I see during the day sometimes. You told me once that they were given to me to guide me—but then, why is it that sometimes they leave me *more* confused than I was before I had them?"

My grandfather smiled at me. It was the smile he reserved for questions he'd been waiting for me to ask.

"My young one," Grandfather began, "such visions are not meant for you to trust in them alone. Some come from a good place. Others, from a dark place. But as you seek truth, you will find it. But only if it truly is the *truth* that you seek—and not merely the fulfillment of your own desires."

I nodded, and meditated on what he had said.

We both looked out onto the orange sky, and I listened to Grandfather hum the time away as the moon began to appear though the sun still remained. And there was just the smallest amount of daylight left when two butterflies glided in from behind Grandfather's jewel-stoned house, searching for the perfect flower from which they would find nectar.

One was as red as an Ipharadisian's heart, the other, as black as a rich, onyx gemstone. They floated along the breeze as I waited for them to decide where they would land.

"Giant Emperors," Grandfather said.

"Emperors of what?" I joked.

"Ah," Grandfather delightfully responded. "Now *that* is the question."

I took the long road back to the acorn huts that night, not stopping to see Erec as I had originally intended to do.

Instead, I decided to spend some time alone in my private hut, and think things over.

It wasn't long before I drifted off into the type of sleep that allowed me to dream a dream unlike any one I'd had since I'd come to Ipharadisi.

My breathing intensified, and I could feel the pupils behind my eyelids darting back and forth along the surface.

It was an odd feeling, knowing I was dreaming, but not being able to force myself awake. It would have become most uncomfortable if it hadn't ended so very quickly.

But it did.

The fog in my head took its own sweet time clearing out, leaving me with just the few memories I would need to know what I would have to do today—something I long hoped I would never have to do. But it was also something I knew I could make no other choice against either.

Tuki returned to the acorn compound after having gone for an early jog. She hadn't mentioned it to me, but I knew her schedule by now.

And though I would join her on a brisk run most days, I had declined to join Tuki this morning in lieu of spending some time alone before going to confront Zaina. Still, as I made my way outside, I noticed that Tuki had returned to the huts unusually winded.

"I cannot seem to find Zaina anywhere," she said—pacing, confused. "I do not understand where she could be. I needed to speak with her before your lesson today."

Someone must've told Tuki that Zaina and I had been training at the palace hut yesterday. She was probably under the impression that we had picked up where Zaina and I had left off before my rescue mission.

And, I really wish I could've told her that that was the

case.

"There will be no lesson today," I was forced to inform her instead—with more matter-of-factness than the somberness that I felt inside.

Tuki was utterly caught off guard.

"But Zaina did not inform me of this. *Why* did she not inform me of this? Do you know where she will be instead?" Tuki walked around the unlit cooking pot, stopping only when she was face-to-face with me. She sternly placed her hands on hips; tapping her foot, burning off extra energy.

I remained in contrast entirely still, that is until I began tightening the thick straw belt around my brown leather skirt. I hadn't planned on wearing it again today, but that was before my dream last night.

That was before I knew that I'd need battle gear in the morning.

I adjusted the straps that crisscrossed on the matching handmade top that I carried my donga sticks in, and after everything was secure, I finally replied to Tuki. "Zaina is in the Assegai field. That is where we will meet today."

We hadn't made plans to meet there, but I could see her there in my head. Zaina was holding an assegai in one hand and an ivory-white dagger in the other—just as she had in my dream.

I breathed in.

"Please gather everyone." I requested it without turning around. "I will need more than one witness."

Tuki's voice sounded a concern that I'd never heard before. "Witness…to…what Nanyamka?"

I kept my gaze facing forward, in the direction of the field—but only for a moment. I then lowered my head, dreading what I was about to say. No. Not just dreading it, fully not *believing* what I was about to say.

"It is time to fulfill the prophecy. For today, Zaina can no longer be trusted."

I thought about the dreams—the ones I had in the past; the one I had last night and the one Mom had before I was ever even born. I thought about the incredible series of events that had led me here—out of all places. I thought about the things I didn't believe in— and yet, the things I had now experienced. I thought on all these things as Tuki stood silent behind me.

After a few moments, I heard her turn around and head north. Without saying anything, Tuki had left and was preparing to do as I had asked.

Several hours passed, and I was the last person to arrive at the Assegai field. I didn't want this to happen. But destiny had called me here, and I was finally ready to answer the call.

All of Ipharadisi stood on the sidelines of the field. Zaina stood in the middle—the assegai spear in one hand—Grandfather's ivory-white dagger in the other.

I walked cautiously towards her, stopping with several yards between us.

Zaina expressed no emotion among the crowd that had gathered. She seemed merely curious, and not at all deterred by the plans I knew she had made.

"So…" Zaina twirled the ivory dagger in her hand. "How did you know I would be here?"

"We're sisters," I reminded her—for more reasons than one. "We share a gift."

It was the same gift our mother had. And, it was the gift that allowed both of us to share the same dream last night. It was the same gift that allowed me to see the murders, the pre-emptive war, and the destruction Zaina had planned.

"Ah," my sister whispered. "Then you know what has to be done. The mess you made must be cleaned up." The look in her eyes beckoned me to come closer.

I shouted from where I stood.

"I know there is a choice Zaina. I know there is *always* a choice, and you don't have to make the wrong one."

Zaina laughed. It was a callous type of laugh—even for her.

"The *right* choice…*sister*…would have been *not* to leave a map to our village in the hands of our enemies. *That* would have been the right choice."

"It was an accident Zaina. And no mess has been made. You do not even know that the map was or will ever be found."

"I don't *need* to know. I know everything I need to know about *you*," she sneered. "I wouldn't be surprised if you left it there on purpose." Zaina spit on the ground—hurting me more than any physical blow she could strike with. I would never do anything to hurt my sister, but I knew at that moment that she could no longer be reached.

I knew because in the dream, Zaina had become the most powerful queen on the continent—conquering and destroying every single poaching camp in the nearby lands. She also freed all of the kidnapped, the beaten, and all of the unaccounted for rescuers in the process.

In this dream, without any peace talks at all, Zaina had permanently taken down some of the largest human evils that we knew of. And I would have applauded her, except for the fact that there was one, tiny, little problem—Zaina would have to *kill* every single enemy to do so.

She didn't seem the least bit bothered by that.

I moved in closer.

"You will not harm those people Zaina."

This time Zaina's laughter echoed throughout the field. "*People?* They are terrorizing animals. They deserve to be put down, once and for all."

"That is not for you to decide Zaina."

She was unconvinced. "Then who?"

"Someone greater."

"And that someone greater is *you* I suppose?" I shook my head, disappointed that she would think that way.

"I am not the judge here Zaina. Only one can judge that way." I looked up, towards the top of the highest mountain.

Tuki stepped forward, and looked out amongst the rest of the villagers who were silent on the edge of the field.

She spoke loud enough for all to hear. "This particular matter is for the queen only to decide."

Zaina nodded, and raised a smirk in my direction as if that would be the end of it.

"That is why Nanyamka will challenge Zaina as queen!"

Zaina gasped. "Tuki!" My muscles tensed. I was ready to spring in between them if Zaina tried to make any move against Tuki. She didn't. Instead, Zaina seemed to become extremely calm—too calm.

Zaina walked around Tuki in a slow, methodic circle.

"So, this is what it has come down to. After everything we have been through, you would just offer up my throne…to *her.*"

Tuki didn't allow herself to become intimidated.

"Zaina, if you kill to win this—this battle between us and all those who do evil, we will become that evil. Yes, we have been forced to witness death, but we have never caused it. We have never killed—we have *never* taken a life. And if ever you cross that line, you will be destroying the very heart of what Ipharadisi stands for. I am sorry. We cannot allow it. Nanyamka will use her birthright given to her by Queen Ayanna, to challenge you for the throne."

This was all really happening.

I started to wonder if I'd gotten in way over my head.

Erec must've sensed my trepidation because he stepped forward from the crowd, and took my face in his warm, reassuring hands.

It was the first time he had looked at me this way since that night in his iQhugwane—the night I had so desperately wished that he had kissed me on the lips.

"Kay, I know we joke around a lot, but I want you to know that I believe in you. And what I need you to do now is to find the courage for *you* to believe in you. Because we all know that you will make an amazing queen." Erec paused. "And anyone would be lucky to be your king."

I heard the weight of what he was implying—what he was offering me—something my sister so desperately wanted from him; something he had never found any reason to give…to her.

Erec kissed me on the cheek, but from where Zaina stood, I knew it looked as if he had kissed me on the lips. At least I assume so because I could see the burning jealousy in her eyes.

I touched the tips of Erec's fingers with the tips of mine, then walked to the edge of the field where Tuki had gone. I gave her a hug before attempting to walk back to the middle of the field with confidence. Zaina and I were still only a few yards apart.

"Zaina, I am willing to discuss this. We can sit down and figure something out, but I do not wish to fight you."

I meant it, but when I saw the years of resentment build up in her eyes, that's when I realized—that the enemy Zaina had unknowingly been training me to fight all those months…was her.

She responded to my offer with nine simple words. "If you do not wish to fight," she said, "then *die!*"

Zaina lifted the metal spear in her hand, and threw it as hard as she could towards the center of my body. I dropped to the ground, allowing the spear to fly right over me—entering the ground behind me. Zaina charged.

I didn't hesitate. I put my hands behind my head where I lie—elbows facing up, palms facing down—and with a momentum I didn't even know I had, I kicked my legs up and out, launching myself back into a standing position. There was no time to reach for my donga sticks.

Swipe! Zaina lunged towards my face with the ivory dagger, but I bent backwards as she missed.

I dropped to the ground again and kicked in the back of her knees, causing her to fall on the front of them.

I swung my legs over my head, somersaulting upright. Zaina beat me into getting back on her feet.

I wasn't vertical for more than a second when her leg extended sideways and kicked me in the stomach. I hunched over, grabbing my mid-section. Zaina kicked towards me again, but I moved—quickly.

The next thing I knew, she was swiping at me again with the dagger. This time I grabbed it from her and threw it *far* away from us. But we were still too close. I needed more space.

I spread my arms out into a T figure, and bent my knees to propel myself off the ground. I back flipped through the air without ever using my hands to the touch the ground. I then did several accompanying cartwheels to cover more ground.

I landed in runner's position near the ivory dagger.

I picked it up without Zaina seeing, and waited for her to catch up.

She came towards me at full speed. I widened my stance, centering my weight in my hips, and waited for her to approach. When she did, I grabbed her arms in front of me and threw myself on my back—flinging her over my shoulders—with a force that knocked her flat on the ground. I pulled out the ivory dagger from the belt I'd hid it in, and pointed it at her as I kneeled by her side.

Zaina raised her hands in defeat.

It was over.

"Zaina Acacia Morowa, in attempting to kill your own sister, you have proven you are not trustworthy, and are no longer fit to be queen." I removed the head jewels she wore and unclasped our mother's necklace from around her neck. I laid them across my shoulder.

There I stood—as the regal, jewel-adorned woman I once saw in a vision many, many months ago. And though I had seen it—envisioned it, I still couldn't believe that it had actually come to life.

When I gathered the courage to face everyone who had gathered on the sidelines, I walked slowly back to the edge of the field and stood still. At that moment, all of Ipharadisi bowed before me—even Erec, even Tuki.

I felt a maturity I'd never felt before. Everything my parents had taught me—all of the lessons that I learned here—had all been preparing me...for *this*.

Zaina sat up defeated yet still defiant. "Sobohla Manyosi!" She screamed it at me, knowing I wouldn't understand, repeating it in a way that I could.

"The honey will end." She smiled.

I wasn't sure I wanted to know, but I asked Tuki anyway. "What does that mean?"

Tuki looked disappointedly at the former queen. "It is a Zulu proverb. It means, what you have will end one day."

I considered that for a moment, then nodded to Zaina. "Perhaps...but not today." I motioned to several of the guardians who were represented on the field. "Take her away."

Zaina glared at them as if she were daring them to touch her—daring them to remove her from what was *her* field, in her mind. The guardians looked to Zaina, then to me.

Tuki had been holding her breath at the possibility that things would turn very quickly. I had asked her to gather witnesses so that every Ipharadisian could see the truth.

And that truth was that I didn't want to be their queen. I didn't want to be responsible for the lives and safety of an entire varied nation of peoples. I didn't want to be part of some prophecy that I still didn't fully believe in. But here I was, exactly where it was foretold that I would one day be.

"Destiny is that which is inevitable. It is something

that *must* and will occur, regardless of an individual's will or desire for it to happen."

The words of a book I once read replayed in my head.

Tuki finally exhaled when Zere stepped forward. Zere wasn't a warrior or a guardian. He was part of the intelligence—the ingqondo, but his allegiance to the peace of Ipharadisi was pledged not to a particular person, but to an ideal.

"You heard her," Zere yelled out. "The birthright is clear. Do as Nanyamka says." Zaina's expression was incredulous, but Zere looked past her and motioned to me to let me know that my authority would be respected.

I ordered for Zaina to be placed on house arrest until further notice. Dumaka and Bour, two of our best Ipharadisian warriors guarded Zaina day and night. And they did so for three full suns and three full moons. But on the fourth day, when I arrived at her confinement quarters—a small hut on the isolated end of Ipharadisi—to see if my sister would consider speaking to me again, I found no sister—no friend. Dumaka and Bour lay bloody on the ground—barely breathing.

Zaina had escaped.

19. "I do."

The past week felt like a dream—though I knew it wasn't. I had barely gotten any sleep since my epic showdown with Zaina, and I certainly hadn't been getting enough sleep to allow my subconscious to take over.

But now, as I lie on Erec's chest inside our hideaway in the cave overlooking the waterfall, I could feel my eyelids getting heavy. They finally lost the battle when Erec began stroking the side of my face, stopping from time to time to massage my neck.

I awoke to the sound of Milkshake whining. He was so spoiled now. Erec had kept him constant company every day that I was away on the rescue mission.

Erec had also been bringing him baskets full of blueberries to make up for the lack of blueberry tarts while I was gone. Still, Erec really could've made them himself. After all, he was more than a capable chef. But he said it just made him too sad to think about me, to try to make my famous blueberry tarts without me.

"Ipharadisi just didn't feel like home while you were away," he said one day when I started baking again.

I smiled as he continued to massage my head. It was nice to know that he had missed me as much as I had missed him.

"The sun will be going down soon. We can start heading back now if you'd like. Or..." He whispered into my ear, "we can spend the night here...if you'd like."

Erec and I had spent every waking second together since the...partnership he had alluded to back on the Assegai field. It still surprised me, because it seemed so unlikely that he'd be offering to spend his life with *anyone*—especially me—considering the fact that he was once as emotionally unavailable as I had been when I first arrived here.

It was as much the time and the place then as the traumatizing experiences we had both suffered through before meeting one another. But here, finally having reconciled once lost loves with new found beginnings; the prospect that he—a young widower—and I, a lost dreamer—could build a perfectly happy life together was evident.

"So, what it'll be?" He asked. "Darling." He added.

I bit my lip as I debated the pros and cons of spending the entire evening here with Erec, listening to the sound of the waterfall, and not going back to face my duties until tomorrow, when I heard the laughter of what sounded like a romantically giddy couple.

Though it was a pleasant sound, it wasn't the soundtrack to nature that Erec and I had possibly hoped to spend the evening with. Oh well, I thought to myself as Erec shrugged. We then packed up our belongings before climbing out the side of the Ipharadisian cave to investigate our joyful visitors.

The young woman with the healthy looking baby in her arms was almost unrecognizable. It was Addane, smiling and laughing—and as completely care free as a tropical bird.

The young man who was bellowing laughter with his strong tanned arm around her wasn't familiar to me, but Erec seemed to know him. The young man recognized Erec as well.

"Dr. Louron! Hi!" The young man dropped his arm from around Addane's shoulders as if he'd just been caught by his father making out with a girl.

"Hello Rudo," Erec chuckled as he politely waited for Rudo to introduce him to his new friend.

I did it for him.

"Erec this is Addane. Addane, Erec. She came back with me on the last rescue."

"That's great news. Welcome." Erec extended his hand and gave hers a gentle shake. Addane shook his in return, but without taking her eyes off of Rudo.

I looked Addane over. She was grinning ear to ear and joyfully rocking back and forth on her heels. I'd never seen her so happy before. She was practically glowing.

I suddenly realized that the pair had probably come all the way out here to spend some time getting to know each other—*without* the growing number of eyes in the main square of Ipharadisi. I nudged Erec and coyly cleared my throat.

"Well Addane, Rudo, we'll just be getting out of your way now."

"Oh no," said Addane. She was vibrant, confident, but still spoke in her notably soft voice. "Please, you two stay. It's nearly time for Francis's feeding. I should go back to the iQhugwane if you don't mind." She spoke to Rudo who was lost in the melody of her voice, but he came to in time to give her an affirming smile.

"Of course my love. But sweetheart, would you mind if I caught up with you in a few minutes? Or, I can walk back with you if you think it's getting too dark. There's just something I wanted to get some advice from Nanyamka on."

People were coming to me left and right for advice now—ever since I unofficially became queen. It was…weird.

Addane kissed Rudo on the cheek. "Okay, don't be too long. I'll miss you."

"I'll miss you more," Rudo replied before kissing both Adanne and little Francis on the forehead. The couple looked at each other lovingly, then parted ways.

I laughed.

"So, what can I help you with?"

"Well…" The young man began to fidget a bit. "You know Addane and I have been spending a lot of time together."

"*Yeah*," I said—tauntingly, "I noticed."

"Well…I can't see ever being with anyone else. So…I guess what I'm wondering is…if you were a girl—which of course you are, what would—I mean *how* would you want someone to propose to you?"

"Hunh? Uh…I'm not quite sure I understand."

"Addane," Rudo explained, "I want to ask her to marry me."

My mouth dropped. "You want to get *married*? Already??" I slightly stuttered. "But…you two just met."

"Yes, but we've both lived a lifetime," Rudo pointed

out. "When I saw her here, I knew that we were kindred spirits. Two of a kind. And we think as one."

I was still in shock.

How could he think about marrying someone he just met? My mind was blown thinking about marrying someone I already *knew*.

"I don't know what to say Rudo. I mean, that's great—really. Addane, she deserves some happiness in her life. And you'd be taking on a huge responsibility with the baby and all, but…" I looked back to Erec and thought about all the decisions we still had left to make. "I just don't really think I'm the one to give out that kind of advice," I finally admitted.

Rudo seemed saddened by my response. Still, he pressed on. "Well I don't need specifics," he said as he drew a squiggle in the dirt with his sandal. "Just a suggestion maybe? What would *you* want one day?"

I blanked on the answer, so I just told him the truth. "I've never really thought about it Rudo."

Rudo became discouraged. I felt awful that I couldn't advise him on this matter, but if there was one thing I knew less about than being queen, it was anything about how to properly be in love.

Erec wrapped his hands around my waist and gently pulled me to his side. I knew he could tell that I was grabbing at straws here. Thankfully, he stepped in for me.

"Rudo, listen, there's a thousand different ways you could go about it. Flowers, candles, stars and moonlight. You can be creative, or traditional…but I think it's all in what you say—you know, she'll be paying attention to whether or not you *mean* what you say." Erec gave him a stern look. "So I hope you mean it. And I hope you're ready."

Rudo nodded.

Erec went on. "If I were going to ask a woman to marry me, I would start by telling her how much she means to me." Rudo began patting himself down for something to take notes on, but Erec didn't pay any attention to Rudo's movements.

He was focused on me now.

"I would tell her how empty I was inside before the day we met. I would tell her how unfair life seemed to be before I knew she cared. I would tell her that it's not just me who's in love with her, it's all the stars in the sky that light up at night just to see her face.

Her beautiful face.

I would tell her that I would go to hell and back to protect her, to keep her safe. And I would tell her that there's nothing I wouldn't do to make sure that she knows she's loved. Because she is—and I do, love her."

I drew in a breath, and was embarrassed when I felt a tear roll down my face.

Rudo thanked him for his honest response before leaving.

As for Erec and I, we stood in silence, for nothing else needed to be said. We just held hands and walked back to the iQhugwane huts to prepare for the long-awaited coronation.

Tuki hadn't given me a moment's rest about it. She'd been pestering me about this event ever since my showdown with Zaina.

According to Tuki, I would have to go through the ordaining ceremony before I would officially be named queen. The problem was, I didn't *want* to be named queen—officially or not.

I tried to remind her that the only reason I confronted my sister in the first place was because she was plotting the destruction and murder of the very human beings we *weren't* supposed to be like.

I would have never been able to forgive myself if I would've just stood by while there was something I could've done about it. And to be honest, I had absolutely no idea whether or not I was even going to be successful when I made my decision to face her. The only thing I knew for sure was that I had to try.

But I had won.

By some inexplicable miracle I wasn't killed—and as a result, I'd somehow brought on the second right of queen. *And*, for some reason that I still couldn't explain, everyone here was okay with that.

I had begged Tuki to accept the crown for me—to take my place, but she had refused. "Only the one with the birthright given, may sit on the throne—may rule Ipharadisi."

So here we were. Tuki, Erec and I waited in the medical tent while Zere, his Godmother Ndeye and some of the other villagers were putting the finishing touches on the ceremony decorations in the palace hut.

I was hoping by asking Erec and Tuki to wait with me that I could do a last minute convincing of Tuki to be queen, but it was of no use.

"This is an incredible honor Nanyamka. No. It is more than an honor. It is a *duty*. It is one that you share with your mother, Queen Ayanna. You should be proud to accept your birthright Nanyamka. I know she would be proud of you." Tuki smiled. "If only she could see you now."

"*I* can't see me now," I complained. Tuki was draping some silk material around me as I simultaneously tried to unravel myself from the various pieces of fabric she had already tightly wound me in.

"So what exactly is going to happen tonight?" Tuki rubbed some oil on my arms before starting on my hair.

"In order to make the ceremony official, you will have to accept the blessing of the queen. After which, you will be responsible for the peace and safety of *everyone* in Ipharadisi. It will all be on your shoulders from now on—as queen."

I took in several deep breaths to try to stop my body from shaking—but it didn't work.

I turned to Erec.

"I don't know if I can do this."

Erec walked over to a covered table, and picked up the gold, emerald and ruby necklace that Zaina so often wore as queen—the one that once belonged to our mother. He held it in his hands before speaking over my shoulder. "Tuki, may we have a moment alone please?" Tuki hesitated, but didn't ask any questions before exiting the tent.

"Kay, there's something you should know. When I first met you, I thought you were self-involved and pompous." I frowned.

"Gee thanks."

"Let me finish," he said. "You spoke arrogantly, and seemed so close-minded about our way of life—about our traditions, that I would've bet an entire fortune that you would've *never* learned what it would take to become Queen of Ipharadisi."

"Yeesh. You know, if you're thinking of going into the motivational speaking field, you may want to rethink your options."

Erec sighed. "The point is, I was wrong. I learned that very quickly. You're not narrow-minded *or* self-centered, you've just always known where you stand—and you're always willing to stand firm on that ground. You're not easily swayed by the wind, and you know where your moral compass lies." Erec put a hand to my cheek.

"But that doesn't stop you from listening, and caring, and being willing to lay your life on the line, even if it's for the same people who wouldn't have thought twice about taking your own. Because you have a heart that never stops you from doing what's right, even when you're frightened. You've overcome a lot during these past months, not because of anything any of us have taught you, but because of what *you* were willing to let into your heart."

He pointed to what was beating behind my chest.

"What I'm trying to say is, I went from thinking you would never fit in, in Ipharadisi, to knowing that no one would make a *better* queen for Ipharadisi—than you. This *is* your destiny. It has been all along."

I stood silent, reduced to a whisper.

"What if I screw this up?"

Erec held up the necklace that he'd been holding since Tuki had left. It shone from the warm light emanating from the tent's lantern. And I stood calmly as Erec walked towards me, not stopping until there was nothing but air between us.

He unclasped the necklace, and facing me, fastened it gently around my neck. His hands lingered there, only until he lowered them to lift my own hand—for a kiss.

First Erec kissed the inside of my palm, and didn't stop moving his lips along the bare skin of my body until he made his way up my shivering arms.

Then slowly—very, very slowly—our lips moved in closer. They inched further and further forward until just one more breath's distance in my direction—his direction—it didn't matter; our lips would finally meet.

Erec made the final last moves. One inch, half an inch, a quarter of an inch—I held my breath, but not before tilting my head as far as it would go. Was I hallucinating? Was this some sort of manifested guilt from my past?

No. It was really him.

"Callum?"

Callum stumbled back. *"Callum?"* It was definitely him, clear as day, but I couldn't believe his face—it was sunburned red; chafed and scaling. He looked as if he were coming apart—unraveling—as if he'd travelled thousands of miles in the desert—in the tortuous blistering sun.

Suddenly, realizing the disconcerting situation he'd caught me in, I immediately pulled back from Erec—but it was too late.

Callum was already backing out the tent, trying to get away from me—and the handsome doctor who had been holding me in his arms.

"Callum!" I ran outside the tent and called after him. He didn't turn around. He continued to stumble away. His feet crossed over one another as he forced himself in the opposite direction—walking sideways, barely able to hold himself up. My gosh. I looked down at his feet. They were calloused; dirty and trickling with blood.

"Callum!" It was half yell, half sob. I was shocked...glad...confused...and thankful to see him. I called his name one more time, but he wouldn't stop.

Instead, Callum collapsed on the ground, and I screeched to a stop as I watched his eyes shut closed. And, I almost fainted when I realized that they may be shut closed forever.

20. Death's Door

"Erec!" I screamed for him at the top of my lungs. "Erec! Help!"

Erec ran at full speed out the medical tent.

"Kay—what happened? Are you alright?"

"Help him. Help him please!" I was sobbing through hysterics.

Erec looked at me in a way that let me know he was more concerned about my extreme frantic reaction than about any other emergency at hand. But thankfully, his medical instincts quickly took over, and he began to focus on Callum.

"Hey. Hey you." Erec was lightly slapping Callum on the face. "Hey—can you hear me?"

No response.

"Okay, we should get him inside." I was still in so much shock that I couldn't move. I stood there, trembling. For a moment, Erec didn't know who to tend to first—the unconscious stranger, or the frozen paralyzed soon to be queen. "Kay!" His stern call snapped me out of my daze. "I need you to help me get this guy into the tent."

I silently nodded.

Erec and I bent down, each putting one of Callum's arms around our shoulders. We then stood up and dragged Callum the several yards back into the medical tent.

We got him in front of the steel patient table in the middle of the room. Erec counted off. "One, two, three!" We bent our knees and lifted his body onto the cold metal slab.

We exhaled.

Erec spoke first—reaching under the table for his medical kit. It was somewhere slightly out of his reach. "So, do you know this guy?"

I nodded—again. It was the only thing I'd been able to do besides scream for help. Still, I hadn't considered the fact that Erec's back was turned to me, and couldn't see my silent gestures.

I dreaded making a verbal attempt.

"Yes," I was finally able to manage as I swallowed the extra saliva that my nerves had produced.

Erec found what he was looking for and rose back up to his feet. "Geez, this guy is in pretty bad shape Kay." I watched as Erec propped Callum against some towels he had stacked on the steel table, and as he dipped some cotton into a wooden bowl of water. Erec squeezed it between Callum's chapped, chalk white, deathly looking lips.

"He's going to need as many fluids as possible. Our best bet out here is going to be coconut water." Erec took off his long-sleeve shirt and tied it around his waist. "I'm going to run to the old Gurmu farm and see what I can find. I'm also going to try to locate some aloe for those sunburns of his."

Erec told me to wait here with "the guy," as if Callum were some kind of stranger. I guess he was to Erec—but not to me.

It was…geez…almost a year ago today when Callum laughed as he held my hand on the boardwalk. I remember it now. I remembered all of it.

"It's no comparison Kay. Here is definitely the only place that feels like home to me." I'd just asked Callum where his favorite place to live had been. He had travelled all over America as an army brat, but today, Callum was taking me to see the fireworks at Brooklyn's Coney Island Boardwalk.

"Well, I've lived here all my life," I informed him, "and can attest, New York does have a certain way of capturing the heart."

Callum shook his head—smiling at some inside secret.

"It's not New York that has my heart Kay."

I blushed. "Well…it'll still keep you good company while I'm away."

"You know, I could just go to South Africa *with* you." Callum looked at me very seriously. I stopped—shocked.

"You mean, you would travel all that way—for *me?*"

Callum sighed as he picked a stray piece of pink cotton candy out my hair. "Kay, I would follow you anywhere. You should know that by now."

I did know that now. And because of his word, here Callum was, lying on a cold steel table in the middle of an unmapped jungle—nearly lifeless.

I gently touched the side of his red-patched, sunburned face. If I didn't know any better, I would've sworn I saw it sizzle. His blistering skin was so fiercely hot that I could feel the heat from within his body absorbing through the tips of my own cool fingers, and I hung my head—because I couldn't stand the painful sight of him.

Just then, Callum's eyes slowly began to open, and I'd never been so relieved to hear the whispering of his deep—though now somewhat raspy voice. "...Kay?"

"Callum!" I nearly jumped out of my seat. "Callum! You're awake! How do you feel? Are you okay? Erec went to get you some fluids."

Callum painfully raised himself up as he squinted his eyes from the bright light of the tent's lanterns.

Callum didn't understand. "...Who?"

I'd forgotten that he knew as little about Erec as Erec knew about him, so I quickly changed the subject.

"It doesn't matter. I just can't believe you're really here." Not only couldn't I believe it, I almost wished he *wasn't*. Because this incredible once upon a time love had just risked his life to find the desperate, injured girl he'd probably been praying he'd at least find in one piece—only to find instead a completely unharmed, adorned with jewels and shimmering oils, finely dressed, soon to be queen of a peace-forging nation—in the arms of another man. I couldn't imagine what was going through his head right now.

I lifted the small wooden bowl that still had some water in it, and held it to Callum's lips. I made him drink. He finished it—down to the very last drop, and made an "ah" sound that let me know how truly thirsty he'd been. I took solace in his momentary relief.

"Callum, how on earth did you find me?"

Callum looked away. "It's a long story."

"But...you could've been *killed*."

"I know."

"Then that was stupid!" I furiously yelled at him. "Why would you have risked something so innately *stupid*?!"

I don't think he meant to, but Callum suddenly snapped at me amidst my thankless interrogation. "Well I'm sorry! I *thought* you were being held against your will. I *thought* you were waiting to be found. So I *risked* it because I didn't know if there were some horrifying reason you couldn't get *away* from whoever was holding you hostage—and *that's* why you never made it back home—because you couldn't." Callum assessed me from the bottom of my gold laced sandals to the top of the glimmering jewels that decorated my hair. "But I see now that we were wrong."

"We?"

Callum shook his head in disbelief.

"Beth, Kay. She stayed in Cape Town for weeks—showing your photo to every local, tourist and television station that would listen. And your parents—my goodness. They must've gone to every embassy in the continent...just trying to find you."

"My parents?" I hadn't allowed myself to think about them in so long. With the way I'd left things, I wouldn't have been surprised if they'd just decided that they were better off without me. It never occurred to me that they might have any regrets of their own—let alone that they would travel halfway across the globe to try to find me.

Callum was finally able to straighten all the way up—though he still rested some of his upper body weight on his hands. His knuckles wrapped around the table. "You were all over the news for weeks. But after a few months, the police just eventually gave up. But your parents didn't. Beth didn't." Callum looked painfully into my eyes.

"I didn't."

At that moment, Erec came jogging back to the tent. Sweat was dripping down his chiseled chest. After he put down the wool sack he was carrying, he unwrapped the white blouse around his waist and wiped the accumulating moisture from his brow.

He saw that Callum was awake.

"Hey there. I'm surprised to see you up. A while ago you really looked like you were at death's door. And I'll be honest, I didn't know if you were going to make it." Erec laughed, trying to keep the mood light—something I'd seen him do with most of his patients.

For some reason, Callum was unusually irritated by it. "Well as you can see, I'm fine."

Callum was about to get down from the table, but Erec walked in front of him. He ripped open one of the two-foot long Aloe Vera leaves and held it up. "Well, I don't know about *that*, but at least you're breathing. Either way, we're glad to see that you're awake." Erec used his hands to scoop out some of the meat and gel from the Aloe Vera leaf that he brought back from the Gurmu farm, and was about to lather it on Callum when I stopped him.

"Here, let me."

Erec hesitated. He seemed to sense some ulterior motive as to why I didn't want him to do it—or why Callum *really* wouldn't want him to do it, but I didn't think now was the time for ex-boyfriend history lessons.

Still, Erec passed me each leaf as he ripped it open, and

I applied the cool gel inside of it as gently as I could to Callum's sun tortured body.

I spread it evenly over his face, and lifted his shirt to apply it over every cut and bruise that was to be found. Goodness only knows what he'd gone through to get to me in this condition. I didn't know what could possibly survive this kind of beating.

"Love."

"Hunh?"

Grandfather was standing in the tent opening, watching everything that was going on.

"Oh," I said—startled. "I didn't see you there. Wait. I'm sorry, what did you say?"

"Love," he repeated. "I was just checking on you my love. Are all things in order for tonight's coronation?"

"Oh…um, something's come up."

"*Really?*" Grandfather acted overly surprised—even though nothing ever surprised him, which is how I knew he was up to something.

But I'd have to get it out of him later.

"Yes actually. Someone's arrived in pretty bad shape. His name is…"

"Callum," Grandfather said—finishing my sentence.

My eyes grew as wide as an owl's. "How do you know his name?"

"No time for chitchat Granddaughter. I am sure there are many things you must focus on before the coronation. I will come find you later."

Grandfather looked to me, and then to Callum. To Erec however, he nodded. "Dr. Louron." Erec bowed. They had a brief unspoken conversation with their eyes, and it only ended when Erec seemed to give in to something.

Erec took in a deep breath. "Okay, here goes."

"Here goes what?" I asked—cautious.

Erec didn't answer me. Instead, he simply took my left hand in his as a sudden intensity overcame him.

"There's something I've been meaning to ask you Kay."

Erec took out a small, cedar, wooden box from his pocket. The box itself was beautiful. The ring that it slowly opened to was even more beautiful.

Erec carefully took the ring out and raised it to my eyes—which I had to close for a moment to collect myself. When I opened them, Erec was down on one knee.

I nearly fainted.

"Erec, what are you doing?"

"Sorry, I dropped it." Erec was reaching under the steel table that the ring had rolled underneath. I guess I hadn't seen it fall while my eyes were closed. But when Erec finally got up from the reason he'd bent down, he dusted the ring off and held it in his hand.

"Erec, what's going on?"

"This was my mother's ring," Erec began. "My father made it for her when they were just teenagers."

I looked at the tiny, gold lion in the shape of a ring.

"She always wore it as a necklace because it was too small to fit on her actual finger." Erec suddenly seemed amused by something he said—probably an earlier childhood memory. Erec then took off the thin, gold chain around his neck and threaded it through his parents' symbol of love.

"I know you'll be wearing the queen's gems tonight."

He spoke of the gold, ruby and emerald necklace that he had fastened around my neck earlier—the one passed down by my own mother—the one my sister used to wear. "But I want you to have this. I don't know, maybe you can just wrap it around your wrist or something." Erec paused. "I think she would've liked that—to have someone to pass it down to."

Erec tried to wipe away the stray tear that was falling before I could see. "I just...I wish more than anything that she could've met you, you know? She would have loved you—just as much as I do."

I didn't know what to say.

"Nasara, I didn't get a chance to give this to her before she passed away—before I made it back to my village that day—before I saw everyone I loved taken away. I just really wanted to make sure I gave this to you—because you know how much you mean to me." Erec unclasped the necklace and wrapped it around my wrist.

I didn't utter a word as he kissed my hand before leaning in for a kiss on the lips. I turned my head slightly, just enough to ensure that his kiss landed on my cheek— just enough to be close to him, but not close enough to upset Callum.

Erec apologized to "our visitor," as Erec referred to him, for the public display of affection. "She's just a really special woman you know?" It was a question he didn't have to ask.

Callum already felt the same way.

I waved good-bye as Erec left to assist Tuki and Grandfather in the palace hut. He also let Callum know that he was welcome to stay here for as long as he wanted.

It turned out that wouldn't be long at all.

"I never should've come here." Callum stood up from the table and grabbed a clean shirt from the top of the towel stack he had been lying on. He painfully removed his sooty, torn white shirt and replaced it with a new blue one. Callum turned towards the tent exit.

I panicked, not wanting him to leave.

"It's not what it looks like," I said hurriedly.

"It looks like I should go home." Callum spoke blankly. I walked up to him—as close as he would let me get, and tried to explain.

"Callum, I found out that I have family here."

I thought about Grandfather—who he'd already apparently met. I also thought about the sister who recently tried to kill me, and who then fled to who knows where. Family might've been a strong word for what I had found here—but still, a sense of belonging. "It's complicated Callum, but I just can't leave now. So much has changed. *I've* changed."

I thought about all the people I helped during my first rescue mission before I unofficially became queen. I thought about all the Ipharadisians who were now looking to me to be a leader, and I held close to my heart all the traditions and family secrets I would soon be sworn to protect.

I didn't know how to explain it to him. "There's just so many things you don't know about me now."

"I don't care," he quickly spit out.

I flinched at his abrupt response.

Callum sighed. "I just mean, I wouldn't have minded spending the rest of my life finding those things out." He then looked down at the gold ring that was steadily sliding from my wrist to my fingers. "But it looks like that role's already taken."

Callum began walking towards the tent flaps again, and I didn't try to stop him. But as he exited through them, I could tell that he was still in pain, and it was a bigger pain than the physical one that he arrived in. He was walking through the agony now just to get away from me.

I ran after him.

"Callum, you can't leave."

"Why? You obviously don't need me. You've made that clear so many times." Callum stopped in front of one of the iQhugwane huts, steps away from where he originally passed out. "I don't know why you pushed me away all those times, but each time you did, I deluded myself into thinking that you just needed more time—but I was wrong.

I thought that one day everything would fall into place—that one day you'd tell me why you just gave up on us. I thought we had this unbreakable bond we both felt—that we were *meant* to be together. But we weren't. We aren't...*meant* for anything. Are we?" His question was rhetorical. He lifted his head to the sky.

"You know, you were right Kay. There is a lot I don't know about you, but that's only because you were never gonna let me get close enough to find out, were you?"

Another rhetorical question.

I'd had almost seven months to think about what I would say to Callum if I ever saw him again. They were all the things I wanted to say the day I intentionally crushed his heart in the student newsroom. It was also the day I forced him to walk out the door, yet the day he never stopped loving me whole-heartedly.

371

And so Callum had come all this way *not* to prove his love to me, but because he truly *did* love me, and would have given his life to get me home. And though I knew that, I also knew that part of him was still holding on to the hope that I would finally tell him what happened all those months ago.

But as I looked at Callum in all of his tragic state, I saw no reason to try to explain it to him—here, where the end of our relationship had fully been realized.

"You can't leave in your condition Callum. I'll send a squadron to escort you in the morning."

"That won't be necessary. I found my way here. I can find my way back."

Callum walked exactly half a step before he nearly collapsed again, and had to hold onto the trunk of the nearby moabi tree for support.

I think he held on longer than he meant to.

Slowly—and softly, I lifted my hand to Callum's shoulder. "Callum, please? Don't leave tonight."

Callum tried to stand on his own, but when I placed myself underneath his arm to help him, Callum took in the longest, deepest breath I think he could've possibly mustered, then finally let it out.

"Fine."

Callum reluctantly allowed me to show him to the medium-sized acorn hut he'd be spending the night in. He didn't seem at all surprised by the living arrangements. Maybe he was just too tired to be amazed by it.

After I got Callum settled in, I sent Kayla—who only lived a few huts down from me, over to the palace hut to find Tuki.

I told Kayla to let everyone know that the coronation

would have to wait until tomorrow. Because getting all dressed up and attending some shindig in my honor just didn't seem appropriate right now. Besides, even though I'd come to know Ipharadisi as a place of refuge, Callum didn't belong here, and he would have to leave soon.

I battled against being honest with the subconscious part of myself. The part that would force me to admit that the real reason I called off the coronation tonight was so that I could spend these last few moments with the only man I've ever truly loved—the only man I've ever truly wanted to be with.

As Callum lie asleep in my bed, I sat on the wicker stool and watched him in his slumber. I only meant to do so for just a few minutes, but that turned into just a few hours—which of course turned into the rest of the entire night.

No matter how hard I tried, I just couldn't take my eyes off of him.

It was as if a thousand different emotions had come rushing back—everything I had felt before I found out the truth about my destiny. It was all of the joy and the wonder we shared before the night that I had my stomach wrenching dream—the one that let me know that if Callum and I ever vowed to spend our lives together—in front of our family, in front of our friends—that *that* day, the love of my life would surely die.

Grandfather had done everything he could to try to teach me when to trust, and when *not* to trust my dreams. Yet I still didn't quite understand—though I didn't have to worry about ever making sense of it now.

Callum would leave soon, and everyone would be safe—primarily Callum. And I, I could start thinking logically again. I could start thinking about settling down and building a safe, meaningful life with Erec again.

I yawned, and only thought of Callum.

When I awoke snugly in my bed the next morning, the disappointment quickly settled in, and my heart slowed down to a putter as I thought about the ridiculous—yet delightful dream I had about Callum actually having come to Ipharadisi.

I laughed to myself and decided to take my time getting out of bed. It had been a long while since I'd last slept in. I stretched, and then wrapped my arm around the t-shirt that was balled underneath my head as a pillow. Hunh?

Who put a t-shirt under my head?

It dawned on me. Callum! Callum was really here!

I lurched up—frantically swiveling around. "Callum? Callum where are you?" I remember now that he slept in my bed last night and that I fell asleep on the wicker stool. But now I was in the bed, and Callum was gone.

My heart began to race as I thought about the possibility. No, please, *please* don't be gone already. I thought I was going to become ill at the thought of not having the chance to say good-bye to him—again.

I grabbed his t-shirt and raced outside the acorn hut. My body was running faster than my feet could keep up, and I nearly tripped over myself running to any place I thought he might be at.

"Callum??" I ran through the side trees along the main pathways, shouting his name every dozen yards. "Callum? Callum?" It was no use. He was nowhere to be found.

I ran to the market. I ran to the farm.

No one.

I ran back through the side forest, all the way to the palace hut. When I found no one there, I ran straight to the waterfalls. And when I exhaustedly reached the edge of the cave that I knew was empty below me, I dropped to my knees and clutched at the pain in my chest.

Opening up the balled t-shirt in my hands, I buried my face in it, trying to be thankful that he'd at least left something of himself behind.

It was of no solace.

Milkshake must've heard me crying because he'd come out from his hiding spot behind the marble berry plants, and moseyed over—putting his tiny little trunk on my shoulder.

"I know," I said to my small comforter. "I should've told him everything when I had the chance. Maybe then he would've actually stayed—even if it were just for a while."

Milkshake nuzzled me the best way he knew how, but then became distracted by something off in the distance.

The small elephant backed up several feet and shot his trunk straight into the air. Then, with a force I didn't even know he had in him, Milkshake blew his cords so loud, even the birds in the trees—which were used to Milkshake's various sounds by now—flew away from fright. But as they simultaneously dispersed, someone else came running towards us.

"Callum!"

"Kay! Are you okay? Kay, stand back." I realized that Callum thought Milkshake might hurt me, so I quickly raised my hands to let Callum know that it was safe.

"It's okay Callum. It's just Milkshake. He won't harm me."

Callum seemed hesitant.

"He's a pygmy," I explained. "Oh he could probably do enough damage on his own, but he's sort of a mascot around here. Milkshake's harmless."

Callum was still unsure about the situation, but ultimately took my word for it.

"Callum, where were you this morning? I thought you'd left without saying good-bye."

Callum glanced towards the ground.

"To be honest, I almost did. Seeing you with that doctor guy, it just threw me a bit, I guess."

Callum shoved his hands into his pockets—something he used to do a lot back home—whenever he was feeling vulnerable. This time, however, the left over sunburn made it somewhat uncomfortable it seemed because he immediately took his hands back out and shook them.

I lightly touched his unhealed palms as if they were delicate feathers. I brought one up to my lips, and gently blew cool air on it—desperately hoping to ease Callum's pain. I did the same with the other hand—and didn't let go of either.

"Callum, you have no idea how much I've missed you—how much it means to me that you risked your life to find me. You must know that I tried to get back to you. I *wanted* to get back to you so badly, but I just didn't know how."

I searched his face, unable to tell whether or not that offered him any solace.

"No one would help me Callum. Everyone said it was too dangerous—and it *was*. I've only been away from here once, and I barely made it back. So I can't tell you how grateful I am that you're safe because I don't know what I would've done if anything would have happened to you."

That seemed to make Callum feel a bit better—not that that's why I said it. It was simply the truth.

"I just don't have any idea how you even found me out here. I mean…I thought it was impossible."

"It was impossible. At least, that's what he said it would be."

"He who?"

Callum averted my eyes before speaking. "You wouldn't believe me if I told you."

"Try me," I challenged.

"Alright then, a guy in my dream."

I tried not to appear too shocked.

"What about this dream?"

Callum hesitated. He had an expression in his eyes that I'm sure I'd had in my *own* eyes more than once before—when I didn't want to confess the answer to something. The only difference was, was that Callum was willing to be honest with me.

"I had a dream that… Well that…" I nervously waited for him to come forth with it. "It was your grandfather Kay. He was in my dream. That's where I met him. I mean, it's not like he was physically there—but it was him, plain as day. He told me that you were waiting. He told me not to lose hope." Callum shook his head as if he couldn't believe what he'd just told me.

"I don't expect you to believe me. I know it sounds crazy."

It didn't.

Because that would explain Grandfather's reaction last night—that miracle of experiencing something that no one would ever believe—but that you have no *other* choice than to hold on to faith to because you know with all your heart that it was real.

And after everything that I'd experienced—after everything that had led me here, I knew that we were part of something special—something that was *destined* to be.

Callum continued to speak. I listened.

"When we all got back to New York—Beth, your mom, your dad—they were starting to wonder if they would ever see you again. Every single lead we received turned out to be a dead end.

But then I started having these dreams. It was as if someone were calling me—as if I were being drawn here—even though I didn't know where here *was*.

But in these dreams, this silver-haired elder man—your grandfather, he was showing me this symbol. It looked like a butterfly—but different, and I kept seeing it every time I closed my eyes. So I finally drew it on a piece of paper and flew back to Cape Town.

I showed that symbol to everyone and anyone I came across. Finally, a small grocery store owner recognized the drawing, and told me where he'd seen it before. He said it was in a garden that was protected and that couldn't be seen from the sky.

This man told me about a woman named Ayanna—a woman who had saved his life once."

My mother. Someone had told Callum about my birthmother.

"The store owner was reluctant to give me any more information, but then I started speaking in a language even I didn't understand. I must've heard it in one of the dreams and had forgotten it. But the store owner understood me. Whatever I said, it was enough for him to trust me, so he pointed me in the right direction. He also said not to worry if I got lost because where I was going, the people there had a habit of meeting you on the way—especially if I got into trouble."

I wondered if any of our rescuers had Callum on their radar then—not even knowing who he was to me.

"I remember thanking the man," Callum continued, "and asking him if I could use his landline to call my uncle. When Uncle Joe picked up, I asked him what he thought I should do. I thought he was going to tell me that I'd lost my mind—that I was crazy."

"Did he?" I asked protectively.

"No. He just wanted to know if I was carrying his army bag. When I said yes, he told me there was a compass inside and wished me luck."

Callum must've noticed me looking around.

"I had to toss it when I got to the third border. I think it was somewhere near Rwanda. I met a lot of friendly people on the way. But Kay, there are so many wars going on. Not just the big ones, but the everyday struggles some of these people are going through. I never thought I'd see some of the things I witnessed there."

It broke my heart that Callum now knew all of the horrors Ipharadisi was trying to fight against. But what broke my heart even more, was that our small little village could only do so much to help.

"Everything I needed was in that army bag Kay—the water bottles—the sunblock...obviously. To be honest, I thought the desert vultures would pick me off before I ever got close—close enough to see you one last time."

"Callum..." I whispered his name.

"I knew you were still alive Kay. Deep down—after everyone else gave up—I knew you were still alive, and I would've done anything—*anything* to get to you."

"Oh Callum!"

I threw my arms around his body as we embraced. But it didn't last as long as I would have liked it to because soon he peeled me off of him, and gently pushed me away.

The ring Erec had given me had been pressing into his chest. It left a tiny little mark in his skin above the place where his heart should be.

"But now that I know you're okay, I guess I can leave now."

Callum looked back towards the trees that led to the main village. I ran around to his other side to block him.

"Please don't leave Callum. Not yet."

Callum stopped mid-stride.

"Kay, from the first day we met, I had this unexplainable feeling that we were going to mean something to each other—something important. I don't know how I knew, but I just had a feeling.

But maybe I just made an assumption about the *type* of relationship we would have. Or, I don't know, maybe I was just wrong about how long it would last if we had a relationship at all.

Perhaps not everything's meant to last forever. And I think after seeing you with that doctor last night, I've finally come to terms with it."

They were thoughts I'd had myself, but I underestimated how painful it would be to hear it come from Callum. I wanted to believe that we were meant to be more than some finite equation, but before I could justify it, we both heard Erec calling from off in the distance.

"Kay? Kay are you there?"

Callum and I were running out of time to be alone.

"Callum, I want to go back with you. Part of me already *is* back there with you. But another part of me is—and always will be—here." I turned in the direction of Erec's voice. "So much has changed Callum. Everything I know about life—about myself—it's changed. And I don't even know if I would have any idea how to begin to explain it."

Erec called out again, but we didn't answer. Instead, Callum took me by the hand with pleading eyes. "Then show it to me."

I wasn't sure I understood.

Callum could tell.

"Listen Kay, I've experienced a lot over the past few months that I don't understand. But I'm here now. And I'm willing to listen. So please, just *show* me what you think I wouldn't understand now. That is…" Callum closed the gap between us. "If you want me to stay… For however long you want me to stay."

I couldn't believe that after everything he'd been through—that everything *I'd* put him through—that Callum was still willing to fight for me.

I knew now why I'd had such a hard time letting him go—why I was never fully able to give my heart to someone else.

I lifted my lips to the side of Callum's beautiful face. I whispered into his ear. "Come with me."

Callum obliged.

I never even noticed when it happened. It felt like such

a natural thing—Callum taking my hand in his, us walking side-by-side, my cheek to his chest as we entered the fully prepared palace hut.

It was as if Callum had been here for years—even longer than I. Because as soon as we walked into the dimly lit room, Callum raised my hand to his lips, then slowly lowered it down with a kiss, somehow knowing that the rest I'd have to face on my own.

I stood amongst the hundreds of candles that had been lit in my honor. Some were purple to symbolize royalty. Others were white for the new queen's pure heart. The reflection of the gold tiles along the floor danced in a soft shimmer on every wall, and I breathed in the rose petals that led the way to the gem-stoned throne that I would inherit by the beckoning night's end.

All of Ipharadisi was gathered at attention, though no one had noticed me yet. I don't even think Tuki had seen me enter, but we had grown so close that I knew she could feel me near.

Tuki walked with incense as she approached the steps at the bottom of the throne.

I held my breath as everyone in the palace hut became silent.

"Nanyamka, where do you stand?" She looked to the back of the magnificent room and signaled for the crowd to part.

"I stand here," I replied, as a direct path had been made between us.

"And where do you vow to stand in the midst of trouble, in the dark hour of despair?"

"I stand with my people," I declared. "I stand with peace. I stand with the light. I stand with hope. I stand with unity."

"Uxolo?"

I echoed Tuki.

"Uxolo."

"Impilo?"

"Impilo," I returned.

"Ipharadisi?"

"Forever," I replied.

After the confirmation, Tuki made her way through the crowd and placed the feathered crown upon my head. The jewels that hung from it were heavy, but I graciously bared the weight of all that it represented to my new family.

I knew it wouldn't be long before she would blow out the incense as the benediction had already been offered—and now it was official.

"I present to you, Nanyamka Apiyo Morowa. *Queen* of Ipharadisi!"

I listened to the roars of the village, and became humbled as each Ipharadisian kneeled on the silk pillows before them, bowing in the name of peace, bowing to accept my authority.

This was the hour the peace seekers became my people. And this was the hour I became their queen.

21. I Do

"Tuki have you seen Erec? I wanted to talk to him." I was surprised that I didn't see him at the coronation.

"I have not seen him since yesterday," my new advisor informed me.

Odd. A few days ago, Erec said he'd be the first person in the front row cheering me on. But today, at the actual ceremony, he was nowhere to be found.

The strappy parts of my gold sandals were cutting into my calf as I danced with the village elders. I had to hold on to Tuki with one hand as I bent down to take them off. When I did, I felt a tingle go up my spine as I finally felt relief.

The coronation itself was shorter than I expected, but the celebration afterwards didn't seem like it was ever going to end—not that I wanted it to. I was enjoying watching Callum stuff his face with the milk tarts and mulva pudding Zere's aunt had made for after the celebratory dinner.

Bonfires burned outside in every major location; the market, the pottery house, the old Gurmu farm. But Callum and I were a couple of the only ones who chose to remain inside the palace hut—to leisurely enjoy the rest of the festivities.

I had asked Callum several times if he were ready to turn in for the evening, but I could hardly pull him away from his new little friend. He and Kayla had really hit it off, in part because Callum had been making clown faces and juggling guavas all night, causing little Kayla to giggle quite incessantly.

I never realized what a natural Callum was with children.

"The rest of us are going down to the main square for dancing. Do you wish to join us?" Tuki had taken it upon herself to make sure everyone was having a good time.

"Oh that's okay. I'm pretty beat," I admitted. I couldn't remember the last time I partied this hard. The candles flickered as if they were the lights in a city club, fighting to stay on past closing. I noticed Kayla's parents relighting a few, helping them to win the battle.

"Your friend—the visitor, he seems to be enjoying himself, no?"

I watched Callum bouncing Kayla around on his knee. Probably sensing us watching, he looked back with a warm smile.

"Yes," I replied. "He seems happy."

"And you?"

I wasn't sure how to answer. After all, it's not like she knew my brief history with Callum. I would have told her of course. Tuki was my best friend. But no one had time to clarify because the rain came down outside, and we all decided to go to our respective homes while it was still a light enough drizzle to avoid being completely poured on.

The next day I awoke with a firm grip on my bearings. I knew that Callum was truly here. I knew that I was now officially queen. And I knew that in this moment, I was mostly, blissfully happy. Mostly, because I'd avoided meeting with the guardians to discuss Callum's departure...for now.

"Ow! Ow! Ow!"

His yelling woke me up, and I'd just stepped out of my hut in time to see Callum hopping up and down on one foot while blowing smoke from the tips of his fingers. I was surprised he didn't drop the fish he was holding in his left hand, or the oil drenched t-shirt in the other.

"Callum, what on earth are you trying to do?"

Callum sucked on his superficially charred finger. "I was trying to get the stupid fire started under that pot." Callum pointed to the two-foot tall cast iron cooker in the middle of our four huts. I realized that he must've tried to set fire to the oil soaked shirt in his hand in place of a match. But in true Callum fashion, he'd set *himself* on fire instead.

"Callum, what on earth were trying to do that for?"

"So I could make you breakfast."

I took that in.

"You got up this early to make me breakfast?"

The sun was hardly up, and the fish mongers usually left the market before full sunrise, as they only supplied enough catch for new rescues who weren't accustomed to our lifestyle yet. Callum must've snuck out in the middle of the night to be the first in line.

"Well, yeah. I figured it was the least I could do. Is there something wrong?"

I tried to resist the urge to throw my arms around his adorable face and cover him in kisses.

"Not at all," I replied. Very calm. Very casual. I

extended my hand for the t-shirt and put the dangerous thing away. I then showed him how to make an actual fire.

After we finished the delicious breakfast Callum had successfully cooked, I showed him a place where he could wash up. It was obviously too early for my usual evening bath, so I took Callum to the falling river—an area downhill of the acorn huts where everyone in the acorn community took turns showering.

While he was gone, I took care of the dishes with some boiling water and antiseptic oils I had in the clay pots in my hut. And when Callum returned, all cleaned up, not a sunburn or a dirt spot on his now freshly shaven face, he looked exactly like the handsome co-ed I first met in the student newsroom back in New York. The only difference was that he'd used the same sandalwood soap and vanilla fragrances that had been left out near the falling river—and now he smelled exactly like Erec.

Erec. Where on earth was he?

Callum distracted me by mentioning something about Milkshake that gave me an idea.

"Hey, are you up for a trip?"

"That depends," Callum replied—apprehensively. "The last trip I went on almost got me killed. Not to mention it left me with a wicked sunburn." I looked over his now beautifully healed body, and contemplated having a sketch artist called over as Callum buttoned closed the green-plaid shirt I had found for him to wear today—something donated to us by one of the recent rescues.

"Well, it may take a little faith on your part," I spoke hopefully.

Callum laughed. "Kay, faith is all I came here on, so

lead the way." He spread out his arms indicating that he would follow me in any direction I chose.

I chose North.

In all the time that I'd been here, Erec and I had never ventured below the cave that we'd spent so many afternoons in together. So I figured now would be as good a time as any to explore more of what Ipharadisi had to offer.

I led Callum back through the forest that led to the waterfalls—the ones that he had found me at yesterday, but instead of going straight, the way Erec and I usually did, I made a turn right; past the sleeping tree frogs and left of the splendid sunbird nests.

Our trek led us downhill for quite some time until we found ourselves walking in wet soil. It was at the same time that I detected the sound of trickling water, so we followed our ears—and squishy, sliding feet to its source.

To my surprise, what we finally discovered was the most serene flowing river, enclosed by naturally arching trees—the leaves of which almost concealed the aging brown, beautifully carved out canoe that rested flatly on the edge of the somewhat hidden bank. On the canoe's side was a drawing—a beautiful black butterfly—of sorts.

"Hey! That's the symbol I saw in my dream!" I didn't even have to look. I knew what it was. It was the symbol on my baby blanket. Grandfather had explained the meaning to me one day during one of our many training sessions.

"That's an Adinkra symbol," I told Callum. "Adinkra have been around for nearly two centuries—messages if you will. This one is special to me. It means, 'that which does not burn.' It is a symbol of imperishability and endurance." Callum brushed his fingers alongside the outlined drawings on the canoe.

"See this one?" I pointed to a free-flowing stalk with leaves on it. "Nyame Nti. Grandfather said it is the staff of life—that which only comes from God, for survival."

"What does this one mean?" Callum pointed to linked circles. I don't know why, but for some reason I blushed. "Me Ware Wo," I softly said, looking into Callum's eyes. "I will marry you."

Callum beamed with hopefulness. "That's what it means," I clarified. "I will marry you."

"Oh," Callum responded—disappointed it seemed that I made such an effort to clarify.

We stood there—awkwardly for a moment—until I put out my hand and nodded to the canoe. "Help a girl inside?" I asked him—demure.

Callum rolled his eyes at my obvious attempt to seem less skilled than I truly was. Still, he chivalrously accepted my hand and helped me into the long wooden vessel. Callum made sure that I was settled in before getting in behind me.

I reached for the paddle, but Callum grabbed it first. "Oh no my queen, you just sit back and relax. The ruler of a nation shouldn't be paddling a commoner down the river. So…just allow me." It sounded like a joke, but I knew him too well. Callum had been bottling something up—and it was starting to spill over.

I let him paddle a while before speaking up.

"Callum, is there something you want to talk about?"

"Not at all your highness."

That was a major yes.

"Look Callum, if there's something you want to say,

389

now would be the time to say it." I put on a brave face because I didn't know what it could be. We had gotten off to such a good start this morning, but then again, playing house wasn't ever the same as facing life in reality.

Callum stopped paddling and rested the wooden handle over the canoe. He folded his arms.

"You know, it was pretty impressive the way they all bowed down to you last night. I bet you could have anything you wanted around here. I bet your every beck and call never goes unanswered." I remembered my perception of queen Zaina when I first arrived. Still, I was insulted.

"Is that why you think I don't want to go back with you? Because I'm enjoying myself too much? Because I'm too busy ordering people around—being spoiled by luxuries? Is that what you think I do all day?"

Callum shrugged.

"Callum, being queen here isn't about power...or servitude. It's about *service* to others. It's about sacrifice for peace. It's about fighting against what's wrong— what's destructive and evil. It's not about me Callum. It's about the people of Ipharadisi. Those here—and those who are to come."

Callum hung his head—ashamed of himself it seemed. He slowly unfolded his arms.

"I believe you Kay. It's just that...well, couldn't someone else do it? I mean, couldn't you have someone else take your place? Just tell them that you'll come back to visit—and then come back to New York with me." Callum leaned in over the wooden separation. "Don't you know how much I miss you Kay?"

Suddenly I felt something tremble inside of me. It was

something that I had to fight every time I heard his voice, every time I saw his face. It was the part of me that wanted to give in—to go back to New York and be with him—to forget everything I'd seen here in Ipharadisi.

But it was in this very place that all of my questions had finally been answered—questions about my dreams—about my visions—everything I've wanted to know since I was eight.

And Tuki was right. I felt honored to have the duty to protect this incredible sanctuary of refuge. To be part of something that provided hope and peace to everyone who wanted it. Nowhere back home could I be a part of something *this* important. Not even with the love of my life. Not even with Callum.

"Just come back with me." Callum wasn't giving up.

"I *can't.*"

"Is it because you don't love me?"

It was the question Callum had always feared the answer to. "Of course not Callum."

"Then why did you run to your aunt's house in L.A. just one day after I told you I loved you?"

I decided to tell him most of the truth. "I ran because I was scared. I had never felt that way before, and I would've give up *everything* to be with you"—including his life because according to my dreams *that's* what the price of our love would've been. "I didn't know who I was without you, and that scared me. I didn't want to lose myself before I even knew who I was yet.

Besides, I figured you would've met someone else over the summer, and would have moved on. I thought you would've met someone else by *now* and would have *moved on.*"

Callum spotted a small stone at the bottom of the canoe, and I was very silent as he picked it up to study it. "I guess that's the difference between us. You see, people aren't replaceable to me. *You're* not replaceable to me." Callum pulled his arm back and let the small stone fly over the water—skipping several times before it sunk. "Not like I am to you."

"That's not true Callum."

"Yeah well, it's getting dark."

I peered through my extremely thick, somewhat unruly, long brown hair up at the soft grey moon and the teetering sun that were peacefully sharing the sky. Just a few more minutes and the moon would soon take over. That's how it was the afternoon Callum took me to the boardwalk—just hours before the fireworks had gone off—mere seconds before our first kiss had made me fall completely and utterly in love with him.

I looked into the water beside our gently swaying canoe and saw my reflection there in the moonlight. The face that stared back at me was both familiar yet unknown. It was the same woman I saw in my vision that day in the park—the wild haired royal with my mother's face—my face. It was just an image then, but now it was so much more—it was my spirit.

"Callum, I had no idea what lay ahead back then, but I do now, and I'm proud to have this incredible responsibility before me. So no matter what you call it, chance...destiny...this is where I've chosen to be. And this *is* what I'm going to do with my life—from now on."

Callum sighed in a way that let me know he understood, finally putting the paddle in the water and steering us back to the embankment.

We were silent the rest of the boat ride back.

When we docked, Callum got out first, before putting his arms around me and lifting me out the canoe. He carefully set me on my feet. But after the conversation we'd just had, I wasn't sure what this kindness meant for how far apart Callum would want to be on the way back. Not that it mattered now. Not that it would ever matter now.

If only I could just make myself forget—about my hopes—about my dreams. If only there was some sort of switch to turn off my emotions. I would be so much better off. But I knew there was no such apparatus. Because even though there were times that I thought I had finally forgotten him, I too often learned that it was simply my head playing tricks on my heart—trying to command it to do something that my heart would never submit to.

Too bad. If only life were fair.

At least Addane and Rudo would get a fair shot at it. And I couldn't get over how beautiful Addane looked in her vibrantly colored wedding gown with her beautifully braided hair. The African irises around her wrist were of a special delight to baby Francis. I could tell by the way he kept putting the fragrant white petals in his tiny little mouth. He giggled.

The moon had fully risen now, and Callum and I had made our silent journey back—just in time to see everyone gathered under the candlelit tree by the Gurmu farm for the ceremony. Tealight candles and protea flowers lined the path to the marriage tree from the actual house that the Gurmus used to live in.

I had suggested that Addane and Rudo take up

residence there so that they would have a place to make a future. Some of the villagers had even volunteered to make an extra room for baby Francis—for when he got older.

I had good faith that Rudo would take special care of the farm, and of all the memories that had been built upon it.

Thankfully, Callum and I arrived at the ceremony just in time to get a good standing position near the front. I wanted to be close because I was expected to give a small speech with my blessings to the couple.

The speech I had prepared was brief. It mostly talked about the frightened woman I'd found in the poaching camp, and the courageous woman I met the day she decided to break free. I then asked Rudo to step forward, and requested him to state his reasons for wanting this sacred union. After hearing him out, I gave my approval and presented the minister who would be presiding over the ceremony.

Mr. Inyosi was one of the brave ones whom I'd met during my one and only rescue mission last month. Mr. Inyosi was also on a mission of his own when he came face to face with the rifle bearing black market traders who took him to that awful, forsaken poaching camp. But Mr. Inyosi had such strong faith that he never questioned his fate, and was the only one in the entire group who was wholly unsurprised when we entered Ipharadisi.

I, however, was largely surprised when Callum took my hand as the couple passionately recited their vows. Rudo said his first, and then Addane lovingly followed.

"In sickness and in health."

"In sickness and in health."

"To love and to cherish."
"To love and to cherish."
"Til death," he said.
"Til death," she said.
"Do us part."

22. First Wave

After we had eaten some of the toasted kola nuts that were left over from the wedding last night, Tuki went back into the acorn hut and brought out the jebena—a traditional Ethiopian coffee pot that had once belonged to her father. She also brought out a roasting pan for the coffee beans she planned to prepare.

It was a little known secret that Tuki made the best cup of coffee in all of Ipharadisi. And today she was preparing a small coffee ceremony for Callum and me.

I know I was *supposed* to have had a small squadron escort Callum across the nearest border yesterday, but I wasn't ready to say goodbye then.

It was almost late in the afternoon, and I still wasn't prepared to say goodbye *today*.

So instead of building up the courage to make either of us part ways right now, I offered to help Tuki grind the coffee beans using the mokecha, but Tuki would have none of it. So as she continued to prep, I explained each of the steps of the coffee ceremony to Callum—who was as wide-eyed—and as wide-nosed from the aroma—as a small child.

I let Callum know that there would be three rounds of coffee—the abol, the tona and the baraka. I assured him that he would enjoy them all, regardless of whether he took it black, with salt or with one of Tuki's spices instead of sugar. And I was right. Callum enjoyed them even more than I imagined he would.

After everyone had finished, Callum thanked Tuki immensely, letting her know how much he enjoyed the experience. I think Tuki enjoyed his company as well—but not nearly as much as I.

Sadly, I couldn't stall the inevitable any longer.

We packed a travelling bag for Callum, and then called on Dumaka and Bour to gather any of the warriors, guardians and rescuers who'd made the trek to the nearest crossing line before, to accompany Callum until the seeing bounds—as I couldn't allow any Ipharadisians to make themselves visible past that point. I hoped this would solidify Callum's chances of making it to the nearest embassy to receive safe transport home.

Callum of course made some protest, saying he didn't want to take anyone away from protecting Ipharadisi—especially now that he knew how important our purpose here truly was—and especially with some of our rescuers still feared being held hostage in one of the poaching camps, or *worse*. But after doing a quick scout, the front line guardians let us know that no threats had been detected and that they likely wouldn't be needed in the area for a quite a while.

After confirming this, I invited all of the protectors who would be travelling with Callum to feast in the palace hut while Callum and I spent our last few minutes together strolling through the market. After all, it was still such a beautiful day outside.

"You know," Callum said as he stopped wistfully—his hands holding mine. "I still can't believe everything that's happened here. I honestly thought our biggest problem back home would be finals and graduation, not continents and sacred duties. But I get it now. I do. I'm just having a hard time not begging you to allow me to stay."

I didn't want to state the obvious.

"I know," Callum answered—rhetorically. "I don't really fit in here."

I laughed.

"Neither did I when I first came here. But still, here I am."

"Yes, here you are."

We thought about the impossible, but didn't torture ourselves for long because we both knew that there were other reasons Callum needed to leave now. There were people who were waiting for word about what he had found.

No one in my old home knew about Ipharadisi. But my parents, Beth, his uncle—they would all want to know where Callum had been—and if I'd be coming home with him.

More importantly, if I didn't come home they'd want to know—why not?

We decided that Callum would tell them the truth.

That there had been an explosion back at the airport. That I had been kidnapped amidst all the distraction. That I had been taken to a poacher's camp somewhere near the desert. And that somehow I had escaped.

But then he would tell them that there weren't any witnesses as to where the kidnapped women went. That it was believed we were in hiding for fear of retaliation from the evil, illegal poaching networks.

That he had heard of a group that was helping others who were being held against their will, and who were working to stop the needless suffering and brutality of every living creature. He would have to tell them that this was somewhere in South Africa, so that no one would come looking for me further in the continent. And that if anyone ever tried, Callum would deter them from the spots that he knew they were getting too close to.

Because no one could ever find this place. *Callum* would never have found this place if wasn't for the messages he had received in his dreams—though I still don't know why or *if* Grandfather called out to him that way.

Callum shook his head. "You truly won't know how much I'm going to miss you Kay." Callum brushed my cheek—slowly, lingering. "Your smile, your voice— your...spirit. Everything that made life so beautiful—for a while." Callum pulled me in close and squeezed me to his chest. He then asked for a kiss—something that he could always hold with him...in his heart.

Callum's tall frame leaned down to softly touch my lips with his. He kissed me, quite literally as if it would be the last time we'd ever kiss again.

I held onto my love for dear life. And even though I had happily let my guard down—just for this brief moment, Callum ironically was the one who was suddenly perfectly in tune with all of our surroundings.

So when he saw the silver-tipped, whistling dart speeding towards us, Callum whipped me up and flung me behind him.

It evaded me, but shot directly into the center of Callum's heaving chest; fatally puncturing him; blood spurting red—the color of a true angel's heart.

I screamed. "Callum!"

Whiz. Whiz. Whiz. Darts continued to fly, hitting people left and right, terrorizing its frantic victims.

"Nanyamka!" Tuki ran head on into the chaos.

"Tuki stay down!" I screeched at her through the hordes of people. Villagers everywhere were fleeing and screaming from the unseen danger, and I didn't know where the attack was coming from next.

I also didn't care.

I saw the blood pouring from Callum's unmoving chest as I dropped down to his side. I cradled him in my arms as everything else went silent around me, holding Callum's still, lifeless body in my hands.

Callum was the one who had been pierced in the heart, but I was the only one now feeling the pain.

I covered my mouth when the ground started spinning. And when I couldn't hold it in any longer, I threw up.

No.

This can't be happening. It wasn't supposed to *be* like this. I was sending him home. We were never going to be together. No church bells. No family and friends. I did what the dream wanted. I did everything I *thought* the dreams had wanted.

"NO!" The rage tasted like fire and sulfur in my mouth.

I wanted someone to pay. Whoever it was, I would find them, and end their life as they just did the love of mine.

"Nanyamka! Ngakwesokudla!"

Tuki was warning me in isiZulu, but before I could realize what she was saying, I slowly began to see the evil that had invaded us.

It was the Ubumnyama. I swiftly rose from my knees, but just as I was about to attack, I was struck unconscious by the back of someone's widely curved blade.

It was lights—out.

The sun had set by the time I'd awoken.

I groaned and tried to suppress the nauseating migraine that the blow to my head had painfully caused. Finally, opening my eyes, I saw both Tuki *and* Erec on the floor—being held hostage in one of the grass hut brigs with me.

Wait.

Erec.

Where had he been all this time?

I tried to replay everything that just happened.

Erec had been nowhere in sight; nowhere to be found. He was completely unseen as were those who had attacked us. But Erec would have no reason to attack me, unless he knew that Callum would save me and that *Callum* was whom his target was all along.

No. That's crazy. This is Erec we're talking about.

Then again, if he did know how I felt about Callum, if I'd somehow carelessly given it away back in the medical tent; if maybe he saw us holding hands somewhere— possibly at Addane's wedding; would that have been enough to send Erec into a jealous rage?

Would it be enough for him to want to get *rid* of Callum if Erec viewed him as a threat in his eyes? What if I didn't know Erec as well as I *thought* I did?

Erec put his hand on my arm to caress me. I shook it

off.

"Hey, what's that about?" Erec feigned confusion.

I wanted to spit.

"Where were you during the attack?"

Erec was genuinely shocked.

"What do you mean where was I during the attack? I was near the palace hut when I heard you screaming. I ran here as fast I could."

I involuntarily laughed—it was sarcastic, borderline psychotic. Erec leaned forward from the wall.

"Wait. You're not implying what I think you're implying?"

Silence.

Erec stood up. "Are you?"

"I don't know!" I yelled in anger—confusion; tears streaming. "Where have you been all this time?"

"I was helping a patient."

"It doesn't take two days to get to any patient in Ipharadisi. It doesn't take two days to get *anywhere* in Ipharadisi!" I was uncontrollable, shaking.

"You're right," Erec casually responded. He moved in closer, the oddest look upon his face. "But are you sure you want to know the truth Kay? I mean, are you absolutely sure?"

I closed the distance between us, daring him to tell me the truth.

"Alright," Erec shrugged. "The truth is, I didn't *want* to come back. To *you*," he clarified. "I didn't even want to see your face today."

I was stunned. I didn't know what would prompt him to say something like that.

"I saw you two together—when I was calling you, the

other day by the waterfalls. You ignored me. You were *completely* ignoring me. Just so you didn't have to be interrupted with…*him*."

Erec took in a short breath.

"It hurt. After everything that we've been through, you just pretended like I didn't even exist." Erec closed his eyes as if he were reliving the moment. "You have no *idea* how much that hurt."

Suddenly I felt awful.

"Are you satisfied? Is that what you wanted to hear? That I hid in a patient's house because I was too hurt to even see your face again?"

I stood with my mouth slightly parted, embarrassed by the conspiracy I'd concocted in my grief.

"Of course not Erec. I had no idea. I'm sorry I didn't tell you everything there was to tell you about him. I just thought we'd talk about it later. And there was so much I needed to talk to…" The more time that passed, the harder it was to say his name, "*Callum* about."

Erec cut me off. "I understand. Priorities. Callum—your one and only priority," he sneered.

That infuriated me, but I couldn't say anything in response. The truth was, if I hadn't been so wrapped up in my own emotions, I may have been more attentive to the danger that was coming. I may have noticed that it was too quiet in the market, that no sound was travelling from the palace hut—where if unharmed, there would've been dozens of warriors and guardians all gathered in one place for lunch; and that we were being surrounded by Ubumnyama who were hiding in plain sight.

If I had been paying attention, I might have been able to stop the attack before…

Before…

Before Callum was killed!

His beautiful life taken right in front of my horrified, helpless eyes.

It was all I could do to keep myself from screaming. Because I didn't even have permission to miss him now. I had responsibilities; responsibilities because I was still queen. I had a village to salvage and family to protect.

"Erec, we don't have time for this. I'm sorry for hurting you—for ignoring you, but we need to focus on the situation at hand."

I spoke with authority, knowing that every fiber in Erec's being would want to continue arguing—and maybe he had the right to, but I wouldn't allow it.

"Yes," Tuki interjected. She rubbed Erec lightly on the shoulder. "We must focus now."

"Yeah…alright," Erec reluctantly gave in.

We all took a moment to let the tension pass. Then Tuki spoke up.

"Odd. They did not kill us—which is highly unusual for the Ubumnyama so there must be something that they want."

I cleared my head using the techniques Grandfather had taught me and began to brainstorm. Then it dawned on me.

"Yes. Either there's *something* that they want, or there's *someone* that they want—someone they're waiting for."

Tuki didn't catch on. Neither did Erec.

"That man at the double-banded camp," I explained. "He seemed to know something—something about where I'd been. It was almost as if he were looking for more information about this place. I don't know if it's the gold or the jewels you once mentioned, but there's definitely something in Ipharadisi that he wants. But what I don't understand is, why he's not here to get it."

"Hmm," Tuki considered it. "Perhaps you are right. It would not be the first time we have been attacked for our resources. But either way, we need to get out of here if we're going to get to your friend in time."

That brought me back down.

I closed my eyes—numb, saying the words as automated and emotionless as they would come.

"He's gone Tuki. Callum's dead."

Tuki gasped.

Erec hung his head—guilt stricken from the things he'd said earlier.

I too thought in regret. All the things I should've told him, all the things we could've done; a future lost—forever.

"Why do you say such a thing?" Tuki asked—horrified. "I saw Kayla drag him behind the acacia tree; wounded—yes, but dead—I find unlikely."

My heart stopped.

Then it started again.

I grabbed Tuki by the collar of her shirt—frantic. "Tuki, you saw him...*alive*??"

She nodded matter-of-factly. "You were unconscious, being carried here by one of the Ubumnyama by the time your friend's chest gave clear movement. But with any luck, Kayla will keep your friend safe."

The hope that welled up in me felt as if it might burst through my chest.

"Of course we will need to get to him before he loses too much blood."

"That I can do," I said determined—blissful—ecstatic.

"That's good news," Erec was genuine. "But any ideas on how to break out?"

I surveyed our surroundings, totally revitalized and once again thought back on all the training Grandfather had prepared me with. When I did, the answer became mind numbingly obvious.

"What if we *don't* break out?" I questioned aloud to confused stares. "What if we make *them* break *in*?"

Erec's eyes narrowed. "I'm not sure I follow."

I didn't know if anyone was listening outside, so I motioned for both of them to lean closer in.

I used mostly hand gestures, but also whispered my plan with as many details as I could before we all spread back out. I held my breath, nervous about the sanity of my idea.

"So, what do you think?"

Tuki practically jumped. "I think you're a genius!"

"Erec?"

"I concur," he said. "Pure genius."

Okay. Everyone was on board. But I needed to be sure my loved ones knew what they were getting themselves into.

"Now, if we're going to do this, we're going to have to make sure we're *perfectly* coordinated because if this doesn't go *exactly* as planned, we won't just be seriously injured, we might possibly kill ourselves. Do you both understand that?"

Tuki nodded.

Erec hesitated—but only for a moment.

"I believe in you," he said. And I knew he did because despite it all, Erec had always been there to support me.

It hadn't quite been an hour before we each ripped apart enough of our clothes—mostly Erec's—and used the long grass from the inside of the roof to create the ropes that we would need to wrap around the several columns that held up the brig hut.

I checked to make sure mine had enough resistance.

"Okay, on my mark," I commanded.

Tuki closed her eyes.

Erec said a prayer.

I counted down.

"On three. Two. One."

The three of us yanked the ropes we had tied around the columns, and I watched as Erec and Tuki executed theirs perfectly.

Mine got stuck on a chip in one of the columns.

Fail.

This is it I thought, and with that, the entire hut imploded down upon us. The roof came right down on our heads, and I heard two loud splitting cracks come from Erec and Tuki's directions. My heart stopped. Dust smoke was everywhere.

I could hear the Ubumnyama yelling what was probably profanity in their language. Aside from that, all I knew was that there was nothing but rubble on top our flattened bodies.

Was Tuki okay? Was Erec alive? Had either one of them survived the compound collapsing down on us? The Ubumnyama continued walking over the rubble—stepping over our grass covered, hidden bodies in the dust.

Ow. One was standing directly on top of me, and I couldn't even yell out to let anyone know that I was beneath the debris.

My breathing slowed down until it could barely be heard anymore. Then it was quiet—perfectly quiet.

Time seemed to freeze as I hoped for a miracle. The plan could still be salvaged if we could all somehow get back in sync.

Suddenly I heard the oddest, faintest sound in my head, like that of a ticking clock. But there weren't any clocks in Ipharadisi that I knew of. Still, the sound grew louder and louder until it was so distinctly clear that I couldn't hear anything *else*.

Six months ago, I would've assumed that the sound I was hearing was my brain misfiring—a delusion. But in this moment, somehow, deep inside, I knew that there was a purpose to it—to everything. I also knew that I wasn't the only one hearing it now. The intensity of the ticking left me with no doubt that Tuki and Erec could hear it as well.

I hoped.

Tick. Tock. Tick. Tock. Tick. Tock.

Boom!

The three of us burst through the rubble and flew into the air; our bodies somersaulting over one another until we landed in a perfect triangle, fleet planted firmly on the ground. It was as if we'd all been perfectly attuned to each other—some internal consciousness with three simultaneous moving parts.

The shock on the Ubumnyama's faces was priceless. But there'd be time later to enjoy it. Right now we needed to take advantage of our surprise.

Wham!

Erec threw a punch to one of the Ubumnyama so fast

that the red masked coward spun around *twice*. Tuki threw herself into a headstand, using her left leg to kick down on the Ubumnyama in beige. She brought herself back upright as I blocked not one, but *two* Ubumnyama trying to corner me in an attack. I raised my arms—wrists lateral. Right block. Left block. Hit! I threw both of my fists to their faces, and watched as they dropped to the ground.

We stood in the middle of our fallen foes, and nodded as all of the Ubumnyama laid flat on their backs—still breathing, but butts thoroughly kicked.

"Tuki, do you think you can tie them up?"

"No problem, get to your friend."

I nodded and ran to Kayla's hut.

Erec wasn't far behind me.

He had made a short detour to run to the medical tent to get some surgery and stitching supplies, and I realized how desperately he would need them when I arrived at Callum's side.

Because during the night that my group of three was being held hostage for a reason still unknown, Kayla had put a small stone over the hole in Callum's chest. She didn't know a metal dart was in there, so she wrapped over it with a cloth to make sure that the stone kept pressure on the wounded area—ensuring no more blood than necessary escaped Callum's weakening body. But the dear girl didn't realize that she may have been causing the dart to move closer to his heart.

"I've been giving him water to drink. But we had to be very quiet...because of the Ubumnyama."

"Thank you my darling," I said to my young friend. "Thank you for taking care of him." I was shaking.

"What happens now?" Kayla asked, knowing there was nothing she or I could do. I looked at his bluing lips and wondered the same.

Even if Callum somehow made it through this, he couldn't stay here. If he didn't make a quick—and I mean *quick* recovery, we would have to move him somewhere with better medical care. But there was no travelling to a hospital or to an embassy right now. It was way too dangerous.

Zaina had been right. Because of me, this once peaceful village had been invaded by evil—because of *my* stupid errors. Because I didn't burn that stupid map before my first rescue when I was told to.

Callum opened his eyes—briefly, then closed them again. Erec returned with the medical kit.

"Is he conscious?"

"He opened his eyes for a moment," I said—wiping the bullets of sweat from Callum's forehead and chest, "but then he was out again."

"Alright, you may want to hold him down. We don't have time for any type of anesthesia so…" Erec pulled out an intense looking scalpel. "This is going to hurt."

Erec sliced the sharp edges across Callum's bare chest. Callum's eyes flung open, and he screamed, right before his eyes rolled to the back of his head and then closed again. I ground my teeth then scowled at Erec.

"Was that absolutely necessary?? Did you have to *rip* him open like that?"

"Well what would you prefer Kay? That I take my time? That I drag this out?"

"Can't you just get the dart out through the hole that's *already* in his chest?" I yelled at him.

"Oh yeah, I'll just stick my hand in there—mess around a bit—start yanking stuff out, see what I can find!"

Kayla backed up into a corner, and I realized that everyone was just a bit too tense. So I shut up and let him work. I knew part of Erec didn't want to be doing this at all—making it so that I could possibly once again be with the undeniable love of my life.

But I also knew Erec. I knew his heart—his love, and I knew he would never make any other choice—than to do what was right—than to help someone in need.

Erec pulled back just enough skin to see the round top of the pointed metal dart sticking out. He used something that looked like small pliers to get it out. Next, he picked up a thin, curved needle type scalpel, and threaded it through one side of Callum's flesh—pulling it out with the string attached through the other side. Callum was foaming at the mouth but didn't scream. I think he went into shock.

"Erec, please hurry."

"Seven more stitches," Erec informed me, "then we can put some gauze over the hole and let him rest."

When Erec finally finished the last stitch, and lightly covered the wound with the gauze so it could breathe, we all exhaled—even Kayla. I'd forgotten to tell her to leave, but she wouldn't have anyway. I think she had a little crush on Callum.

"Is he going to be okay now?" Kayla asked—eyes bright.

"Yes," Erec replied. "He just needs some rest, but someone should probably watch him overnight to be safe."

"I'll watch him!" Kayla raised her hand as if she were a student back in Erec's class. Erec looked to me—wondering if I would say no; offer to stay myself instead.

I didn't.

"Thank you sweetie." I brushed Kayla's hair with my hand. "I'll be back soon," I added.

"Where are you going?" Erec wiped his hands with a beige towel while walking over to me.

"Someone should check on the rest of the villagers," I pointed out.

Erec nodded. "I could imagine everyone's pretty startled by the attack."

"Indeed. But I need to see Grandfather first. I don't think this was just any attack."

"What do you mean?"

"I'm not sure. But they were definitely here with a purpose."

Erec began packing up his supplies. "Then I'll check for injuries in the palace hut and along the market. Let me know if Ubabamkhulu tells you anything."

I ran out Kayla's hut, realizing I hadn't even thanked Erec for everything he'd done.

We'd certainly have a lot of talking to do later.

Much later.

When I arrived to Ubabamkhulu's—Grandfather's jewel-stoned house, it was oddly silent. I didn't see Grandfather, but a voice did startle me.

"My queen."

"Zere?" I was surprised to see him here. "Hey, have you seen my grandfather?"

"Oh yes, he's right inside. Thank goodness the Ubumnyama didn't make it up here. Your grandfather

412

could've been seriously harmed."

"But he's okay?"

"Of course," Zere answered as he put a reassuring hand on my arm. I flinched—I had a gash there from the hut implosion.

I shook it off, instantly relieved that Grandfather was alright.

"He was actually just coming down to celebrate." Zere spoke as he lighted several candles, placing them on round wooden tables outside Grandfather's house.

I urged Zere to clarify as I didn't really see this as a celebrating time.

"We were just attacked Zere. Do you truly think this is the time to party?"

Zere shrugged. "It is your Grandfather's idea. Just a small toast—as far as I know—to celebrate the small victories."

"I see…"

I still didn't think we should be indulging ourselves right now, but if Grandfather had suggested it as Zere had said, then I would comply.

Zere held a yellow pot full of Grandfather's honey wine. He stirred it up a bit to mix up whatever fruits had settled at the bottom.

Zere then poured the aromatic liquid into two small ceramic glasses.

"Your grandfather is a very wise man, but forgive me for saying, he is still in his elder years. So he may yet be a while. We should start," Zere suggested. "As you said, there are other things to be done today, but I would truly be honored to raise the first glass to you—as queen."

Zere handed me one ceramic glass and raised the other. "To Queen Nanyamka, who's cunning and bravery is that of which no one else could have gotten us through

413

this outrageous attack."

I had to interrupt. "It wasn't just me Zere. I had plenty of help."

"Still," Zere continued, "to our queen."

Zere took a sip and then waited for me to join in the toast. I raised the glass to my quite thirsting lips and then stopped. I put the glass down without ever allowing my lips to touch it.

"You know, we really should wait for Grandfather, especially if this *was* his idea."

I didn't know why, but I felt that something was off.

"Why don't I go check on Grandfather to make sure he's okay?"

"No!" Zere put down his cup. "I do not think that will be necessary."

"Still, I will check on him anyway." I turned to walk, but Zere stood in my way.

My muscles tensed.

"It would be wise of you to move Zere."

I was serious. He did not want a fight with me right now—and that's what it would come to if he didn't move out my way.

Zere laughed—quite loudly, and I couldn't imagine what could possibly cause him to be so audacious.

That is, until I realized that I was no longer standing my ground with him—I was watching him—from the *dirt.*

Immobile, I could do nothing as the creeping dizziness wavered over me. I fought against the paralyzation with all my strength, and tried to push myself up from the ground, but collapsed again—lying still.

Zere sucked air behind his teeth.

"Tsk, tsk, tsk. What a *sight* to behold. The all but prophesized Queen of Ipharadisi, falling asleep among the mopane worms."

Zere dipped his hands into a pot of water, rinsing them clean. I could see from the water that splashed over the top that there had been blood on his hands.

I slowly looked down to the pulsating on the side of my arm—where the gash was—the gash that Zere had accidentally touched when he first saw me. The pulsating intensified, and I tried to put everything together.

There had been no accident. Zere must've put poison on the tips of his fingers while he was waiting for me. He knew I would come here after the attack. He knew that if he touched any open wounds with his poison that I would still be too frantic to think his touch had any ulterior motive.

But it did.

"Still just as naive as the day you arrived." Zere said it as he looked at the bubbling cut that was blackening with poison—the poison that had made its way directly into my blood stream.

I waited for the hills to stop spinning—to stop being blurry—to give me enough leeway to barely make out Zere's evil face.

"Sobohla Manyosi."

His words were familiar, and I remembered when Zaina had said them to me after our battle in the Assegai field. And, I knew what it meant now.

My honey had ended.

I looked up at Zere—someone I thought I could trust. That was before he ripped the royal decorations from my head.

"You will never be the *rightful* queen of Ipharadisi. However, she *will* return." Zere stepped on my hand. "Surrender, second-born, or prepare to join your ancestors."

I had no idea Zere had such hate in him. I had no idea he could be so cruel. Then again, under my sister's bidding, I suppose anyone could be capable of such treachery.

I watched the bottom of Zere's feet as he walked away, only now noticing the small tattoo with an eye above his ankle. I then wept for him and for his choices, and wondered how many would become lost like the now hate-filled vengeance seeker I no longer knew.

My body then went into a seizure. And the last thing I saw before the moon faded into darkness was Grandfather running out of the old stone house. He dropped his walking stick as he ran to me, desperately yelling my name.

23. Clarity

"Please! Hold on!"

It was Callum. I'd awoken in Grandfather's house. Callum still had blood on his freshly patched wound, but when Grandfather had sounded the horn for Erec, Kayla knew I was in trouble, and she helped Callum find his way to Grandfather's house.

Now, Callum found himself wrapping his arms around me in Grandfather's wicker bed, troubled about my proximity to the end of this unexpected life.

If my body would have allowed me to, I would have let out a shaken laugh—an ironic one. Because here, where I'd finally found peace and purpose to life, I also found this: I had brought death with me.

My eyelids fluttered, but I could only keep them half open as my body continued its seizure.

Erec's voice became desperate. "I'll go into the city— any city—find a hospital that has something strong enough to counteract this." Erec had been brainstorming since before Callum arrived.

"There is no time doctor. She must sweat it out." Grandfather spoke rapidly.

So did Erec.

"Sweat it out? No. That won't work. We have to keep her temperature down until I can get some sort of anecdote—figure out what this is!" Erec punched the inside of Grandfather's stone wall—so hard that I thought his fist might break. He was wild with fear for my life, and I was sorry if I ever underestimated how much he cared for me.

"I know that is your usual practice Dr. Louron, but this type of poison comes from the darkness. The Ubumnyama are dedicated to death, and I am afraid that keeping her temperature down without actively drawing out the toxins will only help her to part from us quicker."

I could hear Erec pacing, weighing the risks. "Well, she's not going to just sweat it out. She would literally have to be hot enough to *burn* the poison out. We'd have to practically torch her over a fire."

"Then a fire we shall make."

I heard silence. Even Callum dropped my hand for a moment.

Finally, Erec spoke up again. "With all due respect Inkosi Ubaba… that's…crazy."

"With all due respect doctor," Grandfather replied, "your medicine is new. The medicine she needs is of the kind that was used long before you were born."

"The fire could kill her," Erec argued.

"Perhaps, but it is our only chance now."

"Should she be breathing like this?" It was Callum. My eyes had fully opened again—and so had my mouth.

"She's already begun wheezing. The poison is in her lungs now," Erec informed him.

Callum squeezed my hand. I knew what he was thinking. I was weak.

418

Two minutes passed.

I was weaker.

Erec was outside helping Grandfather now. Callum had been conflicted about whether to help build the pyre that might help to save my life, or whether he was to let go of my hand, and not be here if something should happen.

Erec, ever the peacemaker, told Callum to stay with me, and to call him if I went into seizures again.

I was glad Callum stayed inside. If my next gasp for air would be my last, at least I would in his arms when it happened—the end that is.

My eyes finally shut closed as I lost the last bit of strength I'd had to keep them open. The poison would soon carry to my brain. I heard Erec say so. But also, I could feel it.

I was oddly sure I heard other voices as I was being carried out of Grandfather's house into the chilly midnight air, and the voices became louder as I was being set on top of the pyre that was to be lit directly underneath my body.

I wondered if other Ipharadisians had gathered on the hill, or if the voices I heard were those of angels waiting to take me home. Then again, with everything that I'd caused here, I wondered if there were any way to know for sure that I'd go someplace where there were angels.

As I thought that, someone lit the flame that ignited the fire beneath me. It quickly spread out around my body, and I could only hope that it wouldn't catch on the wooden slate I was laying on in the middle of the pyre. The slate was wet, having been thoroughly soaked in water, causing me to be safe—for now.

Grandfather began the singing. I didn't know the song—or the language, but soon other voices joined in, and it was beautiful.

The lullaby helped me drift off to sleep, but peace still evaded me. The heat caused me to wake just shortly after, and this time I almost fell off the pyre, directly into the fire, with my violently wild movements.

"She's convulsing," Erec announced. "I think she's trying to bring up the poison, but her lungs are too weak."

"This is ridiculous!" Callum was getting angry. "She's going to choke to death! Stop this! Stop this now!"

"The flames are too high," Erec yelled back.

"I don't care! It's *frying* her!" I opened my eyes just wide enough to see Callum running towards me. He was preparing to jump through the fire to get to me.

No!

I tried to get my lungs to work so I could scream it out loud because Callum wouldn't rescue me, he'd only end up burning with me in the process.

Grandfather grabbed his arm just in time.

"No, Callum. Trust her. Trust the voice that called you here. She can do it Callum. Have faith."

"No!" Callum yanked away. "I'm not going to allow this!"

"But you *must.*" Grandfather grabbed him by the arms. "Don't you see? It was your love that made her face her destiny in the first place. Your unconditional love, it awoke something inside of her—something that gave her the courage to come home—to come here to Ipharadisi."

Grandfather spoke softly then. "But she wasn't the same without you. And by coming here, you have awoken that fight in her once again—that passion. She is fearless with you. And she will fight this *with* you. All she needs to know is that you are here."

And he was here. He had always been here—in my heart. Callum had been with me even when I was eight. When I began having the dreams. When I remembered my mother in the fire. We had been chosen for each other at the same age that Callum lost his parents as a young boy. The age Callum was when his father died of a broken heart.

We needed each other then—even though we didn't know it yet. We were connected—and would always be connected.

'Til death did us part.

At that moment, two of the logs that had been stacked on top of each other, to hold up my fragile wooden bed, caved in, and in an instant the third log gave out.

Crack.

Smash!

I dropped into the fiery pit that exploded as high as the eye could see.

Everyone screamed.

Everyone screamed, but me that is. Because while onlookers saw me fall to my doom, I saw what was in the magnificent burning flames that engulfed me—protected me. It was that which had followed me—all the days of my life. It was the lion in the forest—the destiny in my visions—the miracle in the desert.

It was the blazing bird of fire that represented all that I now knew I could become. So I exhaled, loud enough to let my loved ones know that I was finally out of danger—and prepared for what was ahead.

Whatever Zere had given me had either sweat itself out or had boiled up in my blood.

Either way, Callum lifted me off of the pyre and carried me back to Grandfather's house. It was then, out of danger, and no longer in fear, that I happily fell asleep in Callum's arms.

The next morning, Callum went to shower under the falling river. He was a terrible patient according to Erec—who was both Callum's doctor *and* recent surgeon. "Your friend's mistaking adrenaline for energy. He should really be resting with you." Erec quickly clarified. "Separately. Resting...as you are...separately."

Grandfather had made everyone breakfast. However, for me, I was only allowed to eat certain herbs, and greenish-brown liquid concoctions that he said would help my blood continue to purify itself.

Yet, I couldn't eat, because I had at least a thousand questions about what had happened yesterday. The majority of the questions could wait of course as there was only one that I truly wanted the answer to.

"How could she have done this to me?"

Grandfather briefly closed his eyes—saddened. "Your sister has much unresolved anger."

"But I don't understand. I've never wanted to hurt her. She knows that I've only done what was right."

Grandfather got up from his round, wicker chair and came to sit on the edge of his bed that I now rested on. He picked up my hand and softly rubbed it while trying to decide how to explain this to me.

"My granddaughter, something happens to those who are already lost. When tragedy strikes—when they face difficulties, their fear, their confusion—turns to anger.

There are those who instead of seeking that which can give them eternal peace, reject that which is free to receive, and seek instead comforts and promises of the worldly kind."

I tried to imagine anything more important than family—than love.

"Even as sisters you handle life so differently. And although I have no doubt that deep down it is not her intention to hurt you, I know she does so because she seeks control and power—mostly over her own life, but it escapes her as she tries to seek power over that which she cannot control. You see, Zaina does not understand what true power is—that true power comes from the strength to ask for help when help is so greatly needed."

"I've tried to talk to her so many times Grandfather."

"I know."

"You told me that all I ever had to do was to speak the truth and that I would be surprised by how deeply it penetrates—but Zaina wouldn't listen, at *all.*"

Grandfather understood. "Sometimes Granddaughter, the hardest thing for someone who is doing wrong to hear—is the truth. But you have planted a seed there, and all you can do now is pray that it will grow." Grandfather kissed my hand as he got up to leave. "I truly believe that one day she will be ready to accept it. But rest my child. You will need your strength—now more than ever." Grandfather then blew out the lantern and left me to regain my strength.

So I slept—for two straight days.

Callum never left my side.

When my system was finally perfectly cleansed, I got out of bed feeling more energetic than I'd ever felt before. I stretched, making sure I was still as limber as the days before the attack.

"Is it daylight out?"

"Not yet," Callum replied. "A few more hours."

"How do you feel? Your chest..." There was a slight bulge under Callum's light grey t-shirt—where the bandage was.

"I feel good actually. It only hurts if I move a certain way, but I've pretty much just been lying on the floor by you." Callum nodded to Grandfather's throw pillow and blanket on the floor by my bed.

"What a pair we make." I said it with a smile as I became too somber to laugh. "Zere? Zaina?" I was asking Callum for information because I remembered Zere's threat that Zaina would return; that when she did, there would be death waiting for me if I did not surrender.

"Zaina..." Callum said her name as if he were trying to place her. "Your sister right? Yeah, your friend Erec said that there was no sign of her, but..." Callum seemed to stop and consider whether or not to tell me the rest.

"But what Callum?"

"Well, there have been rumblings that the Ubumnyama have been regrouping—the ones left I guess that aren't tied up in the palace hut. There's also word that the rest of the intelligence knows where your sister has been holding up."

"Where?" I asked anxiously.

"In some large camp that you'd been to. Apparently, something of hers was found outside of lion territory. Someone named Addane said it's the place where you two met, and if it's true, you're not only going to have your sister and the Ubumnyama to deal with, but possibly an entire—'double-banded camp' coming your way."

I took it in. I never thought I'd be receiving an official report from Callum of all people, but here we were.

Callum stood up, wondering I assumed if his report had been too much for me to process.

It hadn't been.

"I had a dream about you."

Callum was only slightly taken aback. "Oh yeah? When?"

"Before we met. You said you would find me. You said you would always find me, and you did. Thank you Callum."

Callum gently brushed the hair away from my sweaty forehead before Grandfather returned.

"Ah, Granddaughter. You are awake." Grandfather pulled the burgundy curtain back that hung from the doorway of his bedroom. There were a total of three rooms in the beautiful jewel-stoned house, and Grandfather had been letting us stay in one of the spares.

"How do you feel Granddaughter?"

"Much better."

"I am pleased." He turned to Callum. "Do you mind terribly if I have a moment alone with our precious queen?"

"Oh of course not." Callum gathered a few personal items—a comb Kayla had given him—among other things, before excusing himself from the room.

Grandfather had an odd expression on his face upon Callum's departure. "So, how do you *really* feel Granddaughter?"

I was perplexed. "What do you mean?"

"Exactly as I have said. You have been through much

these past days."

"Sure, but I'll recover. My shoulder's a little sore still from the compound implosion, but now that the poison is out of my system, I'm sure I'll be fine by the time Zaina gets here."

Grandfather vigorously shook his head. "I was not asking about your physical condition. You pay much attention to your cuts and scrapes, but what of how you feel?"

I realized what he was getting at, but didn't respond.

"I would imagine there has been much confusion in your heart, yes?"

I sighed and gave in.

"You mean Erec."

Grandfather acknowledged his name. "You may not know this, but Erec is like a son to me. A very good man. You two are a logical fit. You share many goals in common."

I wasn't quite sure why he was bringing this up.

"Grandfather, don't you think we have more important things to discuss right now besides my love life? Honestly, I think this is hardly the time for this." Grandfather smiled the way my father used to do when I wanted him to let go of a matter, but knew he was only just beginning to speak.

"I have witnessed many wondrous sights in my long years on this earth Granddaughter. I have seen a lion make friends with an antelope. I have seen a mother lift an entire tree off of her young one. But never in all my life have I seen a love so strong as the love your Callum has for you. You two share one destiny—and that I find *most* important."

I thought about it for a moment. "You called him here, didn't you? Callum—he said you appeared in one of his dreams. But if you think Erec and I are so logical together, then why bring Callum here?"

"Alas Granddaughter," Grandfather said as he stood up from the king-sized bed. "It is not in my power to call or to bring. I can only ask that which is needed. And my dear, you needed to know your true feelings. You needed to face what was in your heart."

"But for what purpose?" I asked—frustrated. "He cannot stay here, that much I know."

"Indeed," Grandfather softly replied.

"So where does that leave me?"

"It leaves you with knowledge. It leaves you with someone in Ipharadisi who loves you completely, and to whom if you do not feel the same—if you are not wholly in love with—then it may be best to release that love for another—for someone for whom that love will be mutual."

At that moment, Tuki walked in through the burgundy curtains. She stopped at the edge of the room before entering.

"May I come in?"

"Ah yes. I was soon leaving." Grandfather turned to me before exiting. "You will think on what I have said?"

I thought carefully before answering so I wouldn't have to lie.

"Yes, Grandfather. I will consider what you have asked." My response seemed to satisfy him because after he acknowledged Tuki, he left.

"What's up Tuki?"

"I am afraid I have news of a most disturbing nature

my queen."

I stopped her. "Tuki, you don't have to call me that."

"But it is what you are my queen." I would have protested further, but I knew Tuki well enough to know that arguing wouldn't do any good, so I left it alone.

"Okay then," I conceded. "What's this disturbing news?"

"My queen, several herds of springboks have been steadily forging our way. They are acting most erratically, but their numbers this way are drastically increasing."

"Okay..." It was hardly the disturbing news I was expecting. Tuki waited for me to say something—to understand the point.

I didn't.

"My queen, when was the last time a herd of springboks moved this far north?"

I thought back to the day the Gurmus had died; to the day Tuki had returned with an injured leg from her rescue mission stampede.

"During the storm," I replied.

"Yes my queen. And are you aware of any storm on the horizon?"

I tried to remember my walk with Callum through the market before the attack. There were perfectly normal skies above, and unless anything had changed in the past two days then no storms should be on the horizon.

"No, Tuki. But something has to be stirring them up. They wouldn't be moving like this unless they were frightened." I sat up further on the bed. "What do you think is scaring the springboks so?"

Tuki echoed my words from the brig. "Not what my queen...*who.*"

So my assumptions that day were being confirmed. The double-banded poaching camps *had* formed an alliance—and they were heading here with the rest of the Ubumnyama as Callum had said—led I was sure by the woman who was now only my sister in name.

I was afraid to ask. "Do we have any idea how many?"

"We do not."

"Then we need to evacuate. Get everyone as far away from here as possible."

Tuki cut me off. "But what of those who cannot travel? What of the elders? Those who are with child? The still injured? A group of our size cannot move easily. And those who can, will not leave others behind."

I knew she was right.

"So then what?" I knew there was only one alternative, but Tuki still answered my rhetorical question.

"If the attack comes, we must stand our ground and fight back! For our land—for our people—for Ipharadisi!"

I'd never seen Tuki so riled up, but I knew why she spoke up so. Countless Ipharadisians had perished during the last attack on this peace seeking village—when my mother was queen—when she trusted a stranger with her secrets. And I knew Tuki would do everything in her power to see that that never happened here again. And as queen, I was the only one with the power now to decide what we would do about it.

"They will have weapons Tuki."

"I know."

"Rifles."

"I am aware."

"And we have none."

"That does not change things."

I buried my head in my hands—but then looked up.

"You want to literally bring knives to a gun fight."

"Why not? We have done it before."

I thought back to the first time we faced D'marco and his criminal band of poachers. I also remembered an article I read on an airplane so many months ago; the children who fought off a violent assault with just sticks and stones and courage.

I then remembered how many had died, and wondered if the trade was worth the risk.

"We were lucky Tuki. When we went up against those violent men with rifles, it was plain and stupid dumb luck that we weren't killed in the process."

"I do not believe that," Tuki replied. "We were being watched after by the same power that will watch over us now."

I wasn't as convinced.

"I don't know Tuki."

"You don't have to. All you must do now is to give the word. I have faith that all will work out as it is supposed to."

"And the rest of the village? Would they be so okay with their lives in my hands?"

Tuki laughed.

"Their lives aren't in your hands. But the people do trust you. If it wasn't for you, many of them would already be dead. And you have rescued many more already."

"Listen Tuki, maybe Zaina was right. Maybe it was never my place to get involved here in the first place."

"Or, perhaps this is where you were *always* supposed to be. My friend, we do not always get to choose our roles in this life—the role we will play in someone else's life—or even the roles we will play in history.

But of our choices, we can choose to be too scared to stand up for what is right—*or* to do that which we know is good in our heart. And your time has come my queen...to decide."

So I did.

I thought about the richness of this land and the hearts of its people.

I thought about everything there was to fight for. I thought about peace. I thought about love. And then the decision was clear.

We spent the rest of the day going over different strategies, making sure there were no holes in either plan—plans a, b or c.

Yet we also knew that no matter how sound any of our strategies were, they were all equally likely to fail. Yes, we would fight for Ipharadisi. But neither Tuki, nor I, nor the guardians or any of the warriors or rescuers in this village were disillusioned as to what the outcome might be—or how many lives would be lost in the process.

So as the horns finally sounded throughout Ipharadisi, I closed my eyes and asked Tuki one last thing. There was something I needed to know.

Because they were here.

24. Battleground

We were running.

"Can you see how many?" I breathlessly asked one of the guardians.

"Yes my queen!"

"And??"

"It's bad," Erec jumped in. "Really bad."

It was pitch black, but Erec had been keeping watch with the guardians for any sign of the Ubumnyama's second wave, and the horns had been sounded half an hour ago at first sight.

I was quickly picking up speed as I headed towards the middle of the Assegai field. I yelled out. "I'm gonna need something more specific than that."

"There are too many to count," Tuki spoke for Erec as she approached my side. "And their numbers seem to be increasing."

My goodness, I thought to myself. We're gonna be slaughtered.

I looked back to the guardians.

"How far off are they?"

"Less than a kilometer."

"Is she with them?"

"Yes. She leads them to the battleground."

I stopped running and paced myself. My head was pounding so hard I had to massage my temples.

"This doesn't make any sense. Why would Zaina join with them? I thought she was coming here on her own—with Zere—maybe a few others. Why would she join with the poachers? The Ubumnyama? What's in it for her? Can this all really be about the crown?"

"Maybe she's on our side after all," Kayla exclaimed—hopeful. She stood next to her parents in the dark. "Maybe Zaina's just pretending to be on their side because they were coming here anyway."

Kayla always remained optimistic, which is why she would never say it, but I knew what everyone was thinking.

This was my fault.

All hell was breaking loose because I'd lost that stupid map in that double-banded camp. The map that everyone had trusted me to burn before I ever even got there. Instead, I had disobeyed direct orders from both Zaina and Zere and had led every level of evil straight to us.

Tuki chimed in. "Perhaps my little inkosazana, but then Zaina would not have threatened Nanyamka's life if she truly wanted peace. She would not have done such evil when no one was looking if Zaina truly wanted to do what was right." Kayla hung her head—all hope finally lost. I watched her little face slowly lose its innocence; its joy. That's when I made my decision.

"Then I will go."

"Yes," Tuki shouted. "We will all go."

I put up a hand. "No," I said—slow—somber. "*I* will

go. Alone."

"That's insane." Callum had come with Kayla's family and stood with us now in our jagged circle. He had never met Zaina, but from the little he'd heard about her, Callum knew that my own sister if given the chance would take my life in a heartbeat and re-take the throne without a second's regret. Yet, if I thought it was right, I would give up the queendom in an instant. But Zaina had made too many dark choices, and I knew not what she would do with new power.

I walked over to Callum and put my hands on his still healing chest. We stood closer than we'd ever been before—both physically and emotionally. And so I laid my head upon his shoulders, wishing I could freeze this moment.

But I couldn't.

"If there's one thing I've learned here Callum, it's that there's no greater love than the love of one to give his life for another. I learned that from you Callum, and I love you. I love Kayla. I love Tuki. I love Ipharadisi. I'd rather die than let anyone here get hurt. Because I am queen now. Peace is my responsibility—and I will give my life for it—should that be the price."

Callum was frozen without response; torn between saying the selfish thing, and allowing its painful other. But the way he held me now let me know that he'd chosen to respect my decision. So I turned and spoke directly to Tuki.

"Listen, if this doesn't work, if I go out to the front line to meet Zaina, and I walk into a trap, do not negotiate for my release—should that become an option. Do not even think of me from that point forward. Do whatever becomes necessary to ensure peace for Ipharadisi—not for me."

"And if it *does* work?" Tuki refused to think on the negative. "If you are able to speak sense into Zaina?"

"Then we will protect Ipharadisi as a family. Perhaps evil will not be so quick to assume victory without permission."

"And if she's not interested in peace?" Erec had been standing in the back with the guardians, only now coming within ear's reach.

"If she gives any aggressive order from her end, then prepare to fight. But no one lifts a finger unless it is at my command—if I am so able. Understood?"

Erec nodded, as did everyone else.

"Akia, Kirabo," I called out to the lead guardians. "I want you two on the South end. *No* one can get through to the main village. Milandu, lead the other guardians on the Northeast of the field. I don't see those who are coming pursuing the eastern part of the land, but the fight could spill over. Erec, I'm gonna need you there—left side, to remove anyone from the field who gets injured, but *please* be careful.

Kayla sweetie, I want you to find Addane and help her to barricade the palace hut with Rudo." Kayla opened her mouth to object, but I cut her off. "No arguments okay? You know you can't be here when they come." Kayla thought about it then sighed, right before hugging her parents a final good-bye, and then leaving the field.

I turned to see Callum waiting for his orders.

"And me? Where do you want me to be? Do you want me to fight with the rescuers?"

I thought it had been obvious.

"Callum, you can't be here for this. It's too dangerous."

He didn't seem to understand.

"Callum, what these people want, they'll do anything to get. And they're not going to take hostages or give us the choice to leave should we surrender. So you have to go now Callum. It's time."

"No."

"I'm not going to argue with you. You have to leave. *Now.*" The tone of my voice let him know that I was serious.

He shook his head. "No."

I wanted to scream.

So did he.

"How is it that you can push me away—so easily, every single time?"

"I don't. That's not true."

"But it is. The night after the boardwalk. The day I got *here*. That afternoon in the newsroom. It's just so easy for you, isn't it?"

I didn't know what to say. We only had a few seconds left. But I wanted my last words to be honest ones.

"Callum, letting you go was the hardest thing I *ever* had to do. Please, you have to know that. That whenever I wasn't with you I felt as if I didn't exist. And I had to realize Callum that it wasn't normal."

"But who cares about *normal?*"

I did. I cared about the boathouse and the wedding and the church bells and the children that I would never get to have—that the dreams told me I would never get to have with him.

"Callum, the truth is, I never wanted to get wrapped

up in one of those out of control love stories." And I didn't—until I met him. "I just wanted to learn about life. I had to find out what my purpose was. And I finally found it. And you can't be a part of it." I'd finally spoken in full honesty.

Callum looked as if the world were falling down on him, and he tried to hold himself up as the tears came. Mine fell first.

"Callum, I need you to go."

Callum choked back a sob that he wouldn't let out. "No, Kay."

A rumbling came from the ground then, and I knew the Ubumnyama, and the double-banded camps, and my sister, and all of her allies were closing in on us.

"Listen to that! If you stay you could die!"

"I don't care."

Callum stood his ground—resolute.

"Then do you care about me? Because if you stay, you're going to get me killed."

The vibrations underneath our feet intensified, and I knew that I could no longer afford to be distracted.

I had a village to protect.

"Dumaka, Bour take this man to the border of the nearest embassy. I do not care what you see or encounter on the way there, but do not leave his side until he is safe—away from here." Bour and Dumaka each put an arm around Callum, and I trusted them to drag Callum off if they had to.

"Nanyamka, please don't do this." It was the first time Callum had ever called me by my real name. "I'm not going to leave without you. I *need* you."

A single teardrop finally fell from Callum's eyes down

437

to his chin, and I desperately wished to kiss it away.

"Goodbye Callum," I said instead. I turned my back on him and prepared to join the others, but I heard him yell out before I could move forward.

"Promise me." I knew what he was going to ask, but I desperately didn't want him to. "Promise me you'll get through this."

I didn't answer. I wouldn't let the last thing I said to him be a lie. So I listened, because I couldn't watch—as I signaled Bour and Dumaka to take him away. Far away. Somewhere I could no longer follow.

I knew I would regret not giving Callum a passionate last kiss, so I lifted my fingers to my lips and softly blew him one without his knowing. I then held back the last tears I would ever shed for him, and hoped that I'd see him again one day—not in this life, but in the next.

"Are you ready?" Tuki asked me as she stepped to my side.

"Yes." I answered without hesitation.

"Good, because it is time."

I remembered then, that if you're still alive, and you see a bright white light, that you're not supposed to walk into it. However, I saw one now, and the light that I saw was inescapable. But I didn't fear it, because even though I'd put my faith into so many different things until now—luck, people...dreams—there was finally a clarity that illuminated my entire being; a realization that had escaped me even until the late hour of last night. But now, after all these years, I finally understood what I had to do to accomplish my purpose here—in this life.

"Tuki, there's something I need to ask you—something I need to know." Tuki had just come into

Grandfather's house to tell me about the okapis' erratic movements; the ones that had alerted us in time to strategize a defense of our land.

"Yes, Nanyamka?" Tuki didn't have any idea of the mystery that was on my mind. It was in the form of a question I didn't want to ask, but if I was going onto that Assegai field tomorrow, then it was something I *had* to know.

"What is it my queen?"

"Tuki, how do you pray?"

It was something I'd only done once before on my own, and not even on purpose—it had been an involuntary response at the time; something my spirit had known to do without my brain even telling it to.

Which is probably why Tuki seemed so puzzled that I would ask this.

"My queen, haven't you ever prayed before?"

"Once," I confessed. "When I was confronted by a wild beast after a fight with the Ubumnyama."

"And, what did you say?"

I was hesitant to answer. "Please," I finally remarked. "I was so frightened that all I could think to say then was…'please.'"

"And yet you were heard." Tuki wasn't asking, she somehow already knew. And she was right. I had been delivered by a miracle in the wilderness that I didn't then truly believe.

"The thing is, I want to know more," I explained. "What if 'please' doesn't suffice for the type of prayer I'll need for what we're about to face?"

Tuki understood what I was asking, so she sat on the side of Grandfather's bed before thoughtfully responding.

"My queen, you are able to accept into your heart that which has already been offered. All you have to do is ask."

I took in a deep breath, biting my lips. "Can you do it for me?"

Tuki placed her hand on my shoulder then; one last light squeeze for the road. "I am sorry my friend. That requires a choice—and it is not a choice I can make for you."

I thought about all the things I'd experienced here. I thought about the miracles that I'd seen.

I knew that I had been led here, but I still didn't know why. So I prepared to say what was on my heart—while Tuki sprinkled water over me by the river.

That was last night. The sun had set, risen again, and had traded places with the moon by the time we arrived to the Assegai field as the horns increased in frequency.

All of Ipharadisi was gathered in the center of the field now. We were one family, and we would encourage each other as such. This is why Grandfather raised his voice to sing.

There would be no whispering tonight.

We sang as loud as our voices would carry. Because we knew that they were coming, and they knew that we were here. So there was no reason for us to hide—no reason for us to be silent.

I took out my donga sticks, and the guardians took out their staffs. We pounded them into the ground as we chanted because not one among us was any longer afraid.

Suddenly, the ground began to tremble beneath us, and it did not slowly subside as it had done just an hour beforehand. This time it intensified.

The herd came first, running no doubt from the legion of vehicles plowing our way. The Ubumnyama as well as the poachers were coming to take us down; to steal, to kill—to destroy. But I would not accept that as our fate. For this reason the warriors, the rescuers and all of the guardians readied their donga sticks, but I held up a hand. I remembered my promise.

I would go to the danger first.

"There!" Erec shouted.

"Do you see her?" I wanted to be sure.

"I am certain. It is her." She was just a speck from this distance, but we would soon be face to face. I marched ahead as Zaina met each one of my steps with a gain of her own.

"Sister." I greeted her only several arms lengths away.

Zaina glanced over the silent crowd behind me. "Sister? Do sisters greet each other with such an army?"

"No," I offered in acknowledgement. "So please ask yours to turn around."

Zaina smirked.

"Ah, then you know. There are many on their way, and I assure you, you are no match for the forces I have gathered."

"But why Zaina?"

Zaina dragged her sandaled foot along a patch of dirt. "Why not? You have taken my own family from me. You have made a mockery of my home and wrongly wear my crown. But this will not be for much longer. I could not defeat you on my own, but now there are those who will help me regain what I once lost." Zaina gestured to the trees behind her—the trees that rustled with anticipation.

"Sister, you must know that what you're doing is

wrong."

"I know no such thing. I only know that I will win—and that you will lose."

Wrong.

"How can you truly win when you will have such regret when this is finished—whatever the outcome?"

"What makes you think I will have any regrets," Zaina asked as she slowly glided past me. "Or that anything you could say would ever change my mind?" I quickly closed the space between us, standing in between her and Ipharadisi once again.

"Isala kutshelwa sobona ngomopo," I pointed out. "The wrong-headed fool who refuses counsel will come to grief."

Zaina tried to intimidate me with her laughter. I remained focused and unafraid. But most importantly, I remained her sister.

"Look into your heart Zaina, and please, forget about your hate, your disappointment, your perception of life's betrayals.

You and I, we may not get along, but you're taking it out on the wrong people. Who do you think will suffer if you let this go on? Who do you think will be poisoned if you continue to cling so tightly to your anger? Think Zaina. This is not what you truly want for yourself. This is not what *Mom* would have wanted for any of us."

Zaina felt both the guilt of her past and the confidence of her future. I saw it there on her face. I also saw that there was still hope left—if she should so decide to choose it.

"It is too late," Zaina rejected instead. "It has already begun."

This didn't stop Zaina from looking back at the family that hadn't yet given up on her. Tuki. Grandfather. The entire village. Erec. He stepped forward, never straying from Zaina's heartbroken eyes.

"It is not too late," Erec assured my sister.

Zaina drew in a heavy breath—appearing exhausted. Erec was still the only one who could ever get through to her. Several emotions passed over Zaina's face. She then feverishly shook her head. Zaina seemed to be debating herself.

"There is nothing I can do to call off the attack. The Ubumnyama, the men that I have made deals with, they will be here in mere minutes. What could I possibly do that would change anything?"

"You can come back home." It was me this time. Not Erec.

Zaina took a moment before speaking.

"But even if I did, Ipharadisi still wouldn't win. I am sorry, but you do not know what I felt forced to do…the hate I felt towards this place because of you. And now you have no idea how badly we would be outnumbered should I help you try to defend what I already vowed to destroy."

This time I was the one to laugh.

"A thousand ants cannot take down a skillful lion. What we have on our side, no man can beat."

Zaina looked back at Grandfather, whom himself had made a vow—that he wouldn't leave the field until there was peace among us. So when he smiled, confidently heading back to the top of the tallest mountain, I knew then that my sister had made the decision to finally return home.

We hurried back to rejoin the others.

"Where is Zere?" I asked her as we approached the center of the field.

Zaina suddenly became too pained to answer, but I knew that she would tell me the rest one day should we prevail.

The air became very still then—as it often does before the onset of a storm, but it wasn't long before the ground shook again and we soon beheld the reasons why.

Seventeen masked Ubumnyama rode in before us on the same number of swiftly galloping horses—horses that were dressed for war. The Ubumnyama swirled their blades as their steeds leaned back and neighed in the air, just as ready to fight as their destructive, terror dedicated counterparts.

Close on their tails were the green and black jeeps that I hadn't seen since I'd awoken kidnapped in the middle of a sun-drenched desert. They sped towards us now, not appearing to be able to stop.

Thankfully, the vehicles screeched to a halt in front of an invisible drawn line less than a dozen yards away. I counted. One jeep. Two jeeps. Three jeeps. Four. No five. Seven. Ten—all full of heavily armed, ready to kill, ready to take, poachers.

Still, Ipharadisi stood its ground.

So I was surprised when three familiar faces had the guts to get out of the middle vehicle and to face us. They were D'marco Ibo, Zuri Dyakov and the curious man in the white outfit from the double-banded camp.

The latter of the three brazen criminals stood the most surprised of them all—which puzzled me. Because even though he'd come completely surrounded by weaponry, he had stepped out of his armored SUV with an expression of fear, which had quickly turned into an expression of awe.

The man with the white hat made of straw stepped forward as if to get a better look. He scratched his head in disbelief.

"Is this your entire village? The so-called mighty legend of the lands? No, this can't be. Where are the rest of you?"

I wasn't sure I understood.

My former interrogator clarified his inquiry. "The voices that we heard. So many voices…as if there were a thousand men in your army."

He must've heard us singing. And I couldn't tell whether he was genuinely confused or whether he was just disappointed that he wouldn't get to harm even more peace seeking villagers than he had initially planned to destroy.

"We are it." I announced this as I spread out my arms—gesturing to all whom remained and to all whom were able to fight.

The sadistic inquirer burst out into laughter. Several Ipharadisians raised their eyebrows.

"Why, this is quite unbelievable. Do you realize that a number of my caravan did an about face because they actually thought that *we* would be outnumbered? But you're just a puny band of misfits posing as a mighty army. How funny."

The irony was quickly wasted as the joke was now on him. I could see the frantic twitching of his goons' nervous eyes; their legion of pupils darting about the field. They were scared because they too didn't believe that we were alone.

And his caravan was right.

We did have help, but it was the kind that these violent men couldn't see. I took a step forward and even though I already knew the answer, I asked him anyway.

"What do you want here?"

I watched as the greed from within bubbled up to the top of his face, and as he looked up towards the gold-filled mountains that cradled the gemstone house that Grandfather had built. "Well, there are a *thousand* things I could make use of from this unworthy, troublesome place; but mostly, even more so than wanting to watch all of you *suffer* for the losses you've caused my camps, and even *more* so than letting every warlord, slave driver and black market dealer you've ever crossed know exactly where your little hideout is, I just simply want to make sure that *none* of you interfere with any of my operations—*ever*—again." He paused as he looked at Tuki as if she were somehow familiar.

He shook his head then went on.

"Do you have any idea how much money you people have cost me over the years? And might I declare, this place has not been the least bit easy to track. And tracking you I have been—been trying for years; every time one of you encouraged *my* free labor to risk their lives to depart, rendering my operations useless."

So we *had* made a difference out there. This insane man would not have come all this way; gone through all of this trouble unless we had been making a dent in saving people's lives, in taking down the operations that he and the Ubumnyama had been using to terrorize the innocent.

This made me feel good, good enough to negotiate.

Zaina and Tuki knew what I was thinking, so they quickly approached my sides.

"Okay, I understand that is what you want. But now here is what we want. I am sure you know that we will not leave our home—regardless of the number of evil you bring here. And as you also must know by now, there is a power that protects us. So I offer you a truce. Let those whom you have kidnapped go; ensure the Ubumnyama stop terrorizing their fellow man, and we can all pledge ourselves to live in peace."

The fedora wearing miscreant laughed.

"What kind of deal is that? My Zaina, I thought you went ahead to secure their surrender—to regain your power, the riches—the glory. But I see you have turned traitor once again. Ah well, I will just have to dispose of you with the rest of those worthless peace seekers."

Zaina started forward, but I stopped her with my hand.

"I give you one last chance to rethink your destructive ways," I firmly warned him.

He seemed to contemplate my offer as he stared at the hopeful faces behind me.

Finally, he answered.

"No deal."

A dry storm exploded in the sky—thunder and lightning sparked ferociously without a single drop of rain. But the sound didn't scare the opposing forces who readied their weapons as the rifle wielders left their vehicles, and came to the front lines. The Ubumnyama tightened the reins on their horses and yelled out in evil excitement.

This was it.

447

Mr. Ibukhu knew there was no turning back now—nowhere to run, so he took out an old book and began to read from it. He read in the hopes of quelling the fears of those who thought that evil would win here.

"The Lord is my light and my salvation—whom shall I fear? He is the stronghold of my life—of whom shall I be afraid?"

The lively responses echoed throughout the field.

"Though an army besiege me, my heart will not fear; though war break out against me, even then will I be confident."

The man who had once turned Zaina against us nodded to D'marco who turned to ready their legion. Zuri raised a hand to queue the Ubumnyama who needed no agitation to attack.

Mr. Ibukhu stood strong—unphased. He continued to read out loud.

"My heart says of you, 'Seek his face!' Your face, Lord, I will seek. Do not turn me over to the desire of my foes, for false witnesses rise up against me, breathing out violence."

The few who remained in the poachers' vehicles revved up their engines while the sound of their deathly machines vibrated throughout the field. I watched as they anxiously waited to stomp their feet onto the pedals.

The Ubumnyama were positioned next to the trucks—pointing their long, curved blades towards anyone who dared look them in the eyes. D'marco yelled over the truck engines. "Ready..."

Mr. Ibuhku shouted to us even louder.

"I am still confident of this—I will see the goodness of the Lord in the land of the living. Wait for the Lord; be strong and take heart and wait for the Lord."

There was a curiosity in some of the Ubumnyama's eyes as to what Mr. Ibuhku was saying.

But the curiosity dissipated when the lighting once again struck in the cloudless night sky, seconds before D'marco yelled out.

"*Attttack!*"

The trucks sped forward—aiming for Ipharadisians who somersaulted over the hoods of their jeeps. I jerked around and signaled to the village behind me.

"Position one!"

Kirabo and Milandu repeated my commands to each of the sections behind them. Together, each person held up a piece of the broken off boulder that I had earlier instructed the villagers to collect from the cave. Each squadron raised the large rocks past their ears now—arms at a 45 degree angle.

I signaled for them to hold their positions until we were ready.

"Now!"

The massive rocks propelled into the air, with a force that was powerful enough to knock the rifles out of the poachers' unprepared hands. The rifles had landed behind our attackers before even one shot had been fired. The opposing forces looked behind them, but there was no time to go back for reinforcements.

The battle had already begun.

"Sister!" Zaina and I yelled for each—closing the last bit of space between us, standing back to back. Nothing would break our bond now.

We would defend Ipharadisi as one.

We dug our donga sticks into the ground, and used

them to hold our bodies stable as we kicked out horizontally with both legs—taking down several of the weaponless poachers around us.

But we only got a few.

The rest were getting too close.

Several of the jeeps continued speeding forward, but were stopped when Tuki signaled her section to use our rarely used daggers on their thick, rolling tires. Any poachers wanting to take us down now would have to fight us on equal ground.

So they got out their trucks.

Zaina gave me a boost onto one of the stationary hoods, and I pulled her up so that she could stand on another. Three of the Ubumnyama rode in hard to our sides—two on my right, one on Zaina's left. We didn't let them box us in.

Strike! Hit! Zaina used her offense donga to knock one of the Ubumnyama off of his horse. Slice! Swipe! The two on my side made attempts at my neckline, but I used my defense dongas to fend them off.

Zaina twirled one of her sticks in her hand before launching it at the two Ubumnyama—successfully sending them both to the ground.

She lifted me onto her shoulders, allowing me to propel backwards and to land on the back of the horse with another approaching Ubumnyama. He took a good swipe at me, but missed, falling off of his horse after losing his balance. I pulled back on the reins and hopped off.

There were four down, but the Ubumnyama and their horses continued advancing forward.

We would have had the advantage, except that six of

the ten jeeps were still operational. And five of them were being quickly re-occupied by the poachers who realized that they didn't have a chance against us on foot.

Tuki signaled her section for another attack that would disable the remaining trucks, but not before one of the vehicles knocked two Ipharadisians down.

It was Kayla's parents.

Erec ran out from the sidelines and onto the field. And he was just about to kneel down beside Kayla's mom when he violently collapsed. D'marco had cowardly struck him in the back. Naturally, D'marco wasn't worried about the consequences as Zuri stood behind him as a bodyguard.

But they obviously didn't know Erec so well.

Erec was only down for a second when he threw both of his legs around D'marco's ankles, dragging him to the ground. Erec locked his legs around my former kidnapper like a boa constrictor. D'marco gasped for air, but Erec was *not* letting go.

Zuri tried to find some space to jump in, but changed his mind when he saw Rudo and one of the warriors named Okoth heading his way.

Zuri abandoned his associate and ran back towards the jeeps.

Erec finally released D'marco when he fell asleep due to the force of the leg lock. But Erec knew that D'marco wouldn't be out for long.

The quick moving doctor got back onto his feet and lifted Kayla's mother off of the ground, carrying her outside of the field's perimeters. Erec was back within seconds, helping Kayla's dad to safety next. The brave doctor made sure to get both of them into the safety zone before tending to their injuries.

I watched.

Concussions and broken bones it looked like—both parties were largely unresponsive.

I hung my head.

When Zaina had come back to the family, it had given me hope that we might win this, but now, I saw that Kayla's parents weren't the only ones who were injured. Almost *half* of Ipharadisi was limping or holding a wounded body part somewhere on the field.

I didn't understand. Zaina and I had been doing so well.

How did it all go so wrong so quickly?

The answer didn't matter. The trucks were coming straight for us now. But Zaina wouldn't leave my side.

There was a screeching sound as a truck swirled in behind us. Another truck blocked off our exit. We were cornered. The rest of the poachers' engines roared as they pushed full steam ahead—with us as their targets.

So my sister and I held hands as we closed our eyes, and as I said a prayer. But when the poachers stomped their feet on the brakes, throwing some of their accomplices forward, our eyes flew back open.

Because something had frightened the Ubumnyama and all of the evil on the field to the depth of their cores.

For over the roar of the engines was the roar of the lion that had saved me—it had found me even here.

The Ubumnyama's horses went wild with fear, galloping away in an all-out frenzy. Ubumnyama who weren't on their horses dropped to their knees, and the poachers in their topless jeeps didn't move a muscle as everyone else kept perfectly still.

A sudden hush then fell over the Assegai field, and you could've heard a pin drop if weren't for the rippling thunder that burst throughout the sky, causing the frightening winds to whip over the troubled battleground below.

I saw the one who had organized the attack out the corner of my eye reach for one of the fallen rifles. He struggled as the wind blasted against his face.

But no sooner did he slowly bend down to retrieve his weapon did the roar of a *second* lion—the beast that was yet hidden, vibrate in everyone's beings as the wind carried its loud growls into a fierce echo around us. Every person on the field waited with bated breath as it appeared out of the darkness; once again coming face to face not only with me, but with my protector.

This time the wild beast assessed me—as if I had on an armor it knew it couldn't penetrate. So it ignored me and turned to the Ubumnyama who stood next to the poachers who were paralyzed in their fright.

The lions stalked forward—and I knew then that battle would soon be over.

"*Runnnn!*"

A conscious D'marco yelled as one of the 500-pound creatures leapt into the air—landing, if not somewhat ironically, on the ones who had come to attack us below.

Several poachers who still held onto their rifles were so stricken with fear that they dropped their weapons at their feet. Only one thing got them to move—the desperate urge to avoid the gruesome sight of watching their own being entirely consumed by a fully embodied darkness; just as bent on death and destruction as they had been.

There was silence, and then a fleeing moments after

the first scream. Only D'marco, Zuri and the ominous man in white remained on the field. My protector and the beast that it now had under its command had chased nearly every other poacher and Ubumnyama away. Only two goons had actually never gotten out of the middle SUV at all.

And, I realized I was possibly the only one on the entire field that wasn't the least bit surprised by the ever timely help that had arrived—unsurprised...and grateful.

"Looks like the battle's finally over." I spoke directly to the disappointed stranger who had come here to destroy us—but who had been defeated instead.

His blood boiled as his neck turned pink from its own heated flush. Yet, I took no enjoyment in his anger. Instead, I thought on what we would do.

"My second in command will take you to the nearest authorities at the appropriate time. Until then, you will remain here in confinement."

Tuki didn't waste any time stepping up to show the failed conqueror to his quarters.

But I wished that she had.

Because before anyone could warn her, before I or Zaina could scream for our loved one to watch out, the merciless barbarian who had become an unrelenting force of terror here, dived to the ground and grabbed hold of one of the strewn about rifles.

And, when he pulled back on the small, deadly curve that propelled that very rifle's narrow, life-ending projectile straight at her, I yelled out for the best friend who had become like a sister to me. I yelled for her as her body twisted—and as it dropped with a thud face down to the ground.

"Tuki!"

Erec screamed out for his dear companion as well, running as fast as he could towards the fallen body, knowing with eternal agony that it was too late.

The moment that Erec reached her, he was struck viciously in the head by the thick handle of an Ubumnyama's blade. D'marco had obtained one of the Ubumnyama's tools and now used it against the man who had earlier subdued him in an unconscious rendering leg lock.

Blood trickled down the side of Erec's beautiful face.

"No!" Zaina started in a panicked sprint towards him, but stopped when the one with the rifle let off another deadly sound into the air.

The true darkness spoke. "Not another move!"

The monster of a man grabbed a young girl by her arm and flung her in front of his chest. It was Kayla. I ground my teeth and clenched my jaw. Why on earth hadn't she stayed at the palace hut as I told her to?

Zaina desperately looked to me for the green light, but I shook my head. This man was crazy, so I wasn't going to provoke him right now by making any move that might actually end up harming Kayla.

This was it.

Evil had won.

"Is that enough? Do you surrender? Or must I give you *further* reason to quit?" The maniac tightened his grip around Kayla's arm as she screamed from both fear and pain.

"No! Stop!" I was pleading with him. I knew what he would do to Kayla if we let him continue.

"Good." His expression was infuriatingly smug. "I'm

so glad that's settled now. However, there is one other matter that I may require your assistance with. You know, now that you're all surrendered and all." D'marco cracked a satisfied smile next to Erec. Zaina was torn apart inside, knowing the part she had originally played in helping to devise whatever plan this man still had up his sleeve. "So, if you will be so kind, you two will now follow my associate to your awaiting transportation."

Zuri held out his hand—as if I would ever take it—waiting for Zaina and I to make our way to the armored SUV they had all arrived in—so that my sister and I could be transported somewhere else.

I turned from the hired thug and faced his vile boss with resolution, speaking as if each word were its very own sentence. "You—will—not—lay—another hand—on anyone—here."

The man in white confirmed it with a tilt of his hat, and although I had no idea whether or not I could trust him, I had no choice but to turn and get into the vehicle.

I looked back at Kayla, then gave one last loving gaze to Erec—who sat cradling Tuki in a pool of her own unfairly spilled blood.

I then tried not to go into convulsions as I climbed into the all black SUV.

Zaina was dragged in—screaming.

Once the door was finally shut and securely locked behind us, the man with the bloodied shoes spoke solely to D'marco out the slightly cracked window; casually handing D'marco the same weapon he had used on Tuki. He gestured to the injured Ipharadisians—then to Erec and to Kayla.

"Get rid of them will you? I'd hate to leave such an

456

incredible mess behind." The soulless fiend callously pressed the close window button as Zaina and I practically clawed at the walls of the SUV, desperately trying to break free.

We had almost jigged the lock to an opening point when Kayla yelled out.

"Please, no!"

Erec threw his body over Kayla then—but it was to no avail.

I screamed.

The two sounds that I heard go off after that would scar me for life.

25. Tears for Ipharadisi

I tried to console Zaina while simultaneously trying to console myself.

She wasn't interested.

"Shut up! You do *not* speak! *You* are the reason Tuki is dead! My sister!" I didn't even process what she said as Zaina pounded her fist against the thick window of the dark, moving vehicle. Her back heaved with grief as she tried to scream through the bulletproof glass towards Ipharadisi. "My king." I knew she spoke of Erec now. I, however, couldn't speak.

Couldn't think.

Couldn't breathe.

I had no way of knowing how long we'd been driving because when Zaina and I tried to break the locked doors open shortly after leaving Ipharadisi, two of the bodyguards came into the back with us and put black, cloth bags over our heads, in addition to tying our arms to our sides to keep us out of trouble.

Not being able to see along with being swayed by the movement of the SUV we were in had caused both of us

I assumed—at least me anyway—to fall asleep.

And even though I had no idea how much time had passed when I awoke, I managed to put my head between my legs and to use my thighs to pull off the sweltering bag that had forced me into the dark. I saw that Zaina had already figured this trick out and was fully awake by the time I regained my bearings—though I wasn't sure this was a good thing.

Because when I looked out the window, all I saw was chaos—a complete and utter war zone. Smoke and fires billowed from the surrounding shacks, and all we could hear were the sounds of weapons being used in the distance. I didn't know where this man had taken us, but I had a feeling it wasn't too far from hell.

I continued to remain alert as we approached our destination—a concrete building with water stains along the sides, enclosed by a barbed wire fence. I don't know why, but I could feel it in my bones—there was something not right about this place.

The truck rolled through the gate that had been opened for us and finally slowed to a stall.

Zaina's door opened first. She was dragged out by one of the goons who had covered our faces on the way here. Zuri had also exited the SUV and waited for me to come out willingly.

I hesitated before sliding myself out Zaina's side of the vehicle. Having our hands still tied in front of us would make it difficult for either of us to protect ourselves—if we had to, as I had no idea what these monsters had in store for us.

The one who had ordered for us to be brought here remained in the car as he spoke through a crack in the tinted window.

"Yakov, Zuri, will you show our lovely guests to my office? There's something I'd like to show them."

Yakov nodded as he pushed Zaina ahead. Zuri gave me a warning look as he held onto his rifle.

I walked forward.

The two led us into the dilapidated, water-stained office building, where we stopped in front of a two-car elevator bank and waited for one to open. When the elevator door on the right began creaking ajar, Zaina and I were roughly ushered inside—neither party saying a word, neither party making any movements.

There were five floors marked on the rusty, old elevator console. The light abruptly left the button marked lobby and didn't blink on again until two—then again at three. I used the time to glance down to Zuri's waistband where something sharp caught my desperately searching eyes.

It was a dagger.

I wondered if I could snatch it and cut myself free in time to disable Zuri and Yakov before we reached whatever floor they would make us get out on.

The console light moved to the button marked four as Zuri softly whispered into my ear. "Don't even think about it."

I begrudgingly let that plan go.

When the elevator doors opened on five, I became distraught by what I saw—yet wholly unsurprised.

Zaina's mouth hung open as she stepped up behind me, unable to fully comprehend what we were witnessing.

Because before us, on each side of the large, marble floored room, were six-foot-tall elephants—dead—and stuffed. Over a dozen helpless creatures were chained to the walls of the ivory-colored room. Beautiful tigers and large spotted leopards were positioned with their mouths hung open and their eyes wide with fear. It was unsettling that horror had followed them even after their deaths.

Ivory rhino statues also filled the room. Thick, pure gold rings had been placed over the horns of each needlessly displayed death—with rubies and green emeralds in place of the creatures' once gentle eyes.

But none of this was what troubled me.

What struck both my sister and I to the core was there, on a large pool table made of glass. It was a perfectly scaled down model of the green, beautiful mountains and rainbow laden waterfalls of Ipharadisi—our home. A model that could have only been made by someone who had been there before—who knew its true beauty—who had not only planned its recent takeover, but who had played a part in its destruction during the time that our mother was queen.

"You were there," I said, stunned and unsettled, "with the American. Before I was born. During the attack when all of those people were killed."

A sudden realization came to Zaina's face that nearly caused her to stumble. A blood red fury then rose to the surface of her cheeks as her hands balled up into fists. Her fingers curled so tightly into her palms that the veins on her hands protruded through Zaina's fiercely, trembling skin.

She spoke directly to the wretched man before us.

"I do not know who you are.

And I do not care.

But if I find out that you had *anything* to do with my mother's death, I promise you—you *will* you join her."

His eyes widened—then he smiled.

"Could it be? The shy little girl who was so glued to her protective mommy's side? My, my. Look how you've grown."

So I was right—he did know our mother.

"She saved you, didn't she? And you betrayed her." I didn't need him to answer. I looked deep into his eyes and knew it to be true.

Zuri leaned in a little closer then. And so did Zaina.

"Betrayal is such an ugly, ugly word," said the unfathomable villain before us. "However, your…*suggestion* is accurate. I was indeed brought to that land you dwell in when some poor fool in a butterfly cloak thought I needed rescuing from one of my own camps.

But I played along—and I'm glad I did because by *golly*, I knew the moment I laid eyes on that place of yours that I'd make a *fortune* off of it—if I got it into the right hands of course. And oh how I tried.

Matter of fact, I even remember the young woman who helped me with my plan—a journalist of about your age."

His words triggered something in my mind that I didn't have time to think about.

"I remember how I convinced that woman to befriend the one the villagers there called queen—to learn everything there was to know about that place. And when she did, the two of us made a run for it.

I sold that information to the first warlord we came across. Quite frankly, I think the deal I made was quite impressive. But when the warlord and his gang returned with only *half* of his previous assemblage, and *without* paying me my sum, well, you can imagine I was quite upset. But I knew I would find that village again, and that when I did, I would exterminate those dreadful rescuers who keep interfering with my business, as well as anyone who tried to prevent me from collecting the riches—not to mention free labor I knew that place had to offer."

Something inside of me snapped as I unintentionally kicked my foot against the glass pool table with the replica of our home.

I was furious. "Money! That's what this all comes down to! You had innocent people *murdered* to make a profit!"

The deviant only shrugged, but the tears that flowed down Zaina's face poured as if they would never cease.

The sobs that she screamed out were full of anguish and longing.

And for the first time since we had found each other, I could fully feel her pain.

"You know, why couldn't you people just disappear," said the deluded camps owner. "Just fall off the planet somewhere? I could have all of that beautiful land to claim for myself by now. And yes, money. Land, people and money. The good life," he looked at Zuri and Yakov before speaking again. "Rodents I tell you. Every time I think I've gotten rid of them, they just get right back up—which is of course why I brought these two here— to help me whip the rest of them into submission. But I realize now, these girls would just fight me all the way on it. Just like they did when they decided to work together on that battlefield."

I jerked slightly when the fiend slammed his fist on the table. "*Why* won't you people ever give up? No matter what I do, you *people* just keep on persevering!"

I wondered to myself why he thought that would ever change. Still, the increasingly twisted individual took a moment to collect himself as he smoothed out his neatly pleated white, linen suit. "That is, except for your mother of course. That problem I finally took care of— *permanently.*"

And with that, Zaina completely lost control. She screeched as she threw her entire body at Yakov before Zuri could even react.

I ran over, hands still tied in front, and kicked the butt of Zuri's rifle into his stomach, causing Zuri to double over. We moved like lighting as I swiped the rope around my wrists against the jagged edge of the dagger in Zuri's waistband, kicking Zuri's rifle across the room.

"Zaina, here!"

I called for her as I pulled out Zuri's dagger to cut her rope loose, but when I turned around I was in such a state of shock that I dropped the dagger on the floor.

"NO!"

Zaina had Yakov's rifle pointed at the one who had confessed his crimes just seconds ago—her finger around the thin, sensitive trigger.

"Zaina, don't!"

"He killed her," she said, tears falling from her eyes.

"Zaina, you don't want to do this."

"He killed her," she repeated—not listening to anyone but the constant replay of grief and sorrow in her head.

"Zaina, please, let's talk about this."

She didn't hear me. She pointed the rifle closer, touching his ear now.

"Zaina!" I didn't know what to do. There wasn't

anything I *could* do to stop her. All I could do was yell.

"Zaina! It won't bring her back! It won't!"

Zaina finally turned around and lowered the rifle.

"I know," she said—heartbroken, defeated. "You're right." She looked back at him.

"But I don't care."

It all happened so fast then.

Zaina raised the rifle so swiftly that when she pulled back, the sound that was heard shook everyone to the bone.

BANG!

I screamed. And so did Zaina.

Because what I thought would give her pause to rethink her actions after I'd thankfully reached her in time to knock the rifle off the course of its intended victim, instead, gave Zaina more fuel to be angry.

"What is wrong with you?"

"What is wrong with *you*?!" I snapped back at her. "Are you insane? You're not a murderer!"

"This man *killed* our mother! Does that not mean *anything* to you?"

"Of course it does. But his punishment is not for us to decide. There are authorities we can report him to."

"Look around you Nanyamka! Where are we going to find anyone to help us? This world is polluted and corrupt and evil is done every day with no repercussions. Who will rid the world of hate and people like *him* if we do not do it ourselves?"

Zaina lifted the rifle again, and I tried to think of a truthful answer that would cause her to have faith in good and justice—because I knew it was possible. But before I could give her a reason to find peace, Zaina wrapped her fingers around the deadly weapon again.

"Zaina, I won't let you do this."

Zaina tried not to laugh. "And what could you possibly do to stop me?"

I didn't answer.

Zaina's muscles prepared to do the horrible deed.

"Sister, don't."

She ignored me. Zaina smiled sadistically as I watched her index finger twitch just slightly and, "Ahhh!"

Zaina yelled as I threw Zuri's dagger at her hand, knocking the rifle to the ground, slicing her knuckles enough to draw blood. She clutched her hand to stop the bleeding while I made a dash to the still deadly weapon and picked it up. Zaina fumed.

"*You...*"

Boom!

The entire building shook, so I ran to the window to investigate, and when I did, I saw that the war outside the building gates had just spilled over, and the explosion had sent two guards flying into the air.

"Look, we have to go." I turned around to show my sister, but Zuri and Yakov were making a run for the other rifle—the one I had kicked across the room. If they got a hold of it, that would put them back in control, which is most likely why Zaina was running out of the door now, past the elevators and down the stairs.

I looked back out the window. An angry mob was rushing past the guards and into the compound. If they made their way upstairs, neither Zuri, nor Yakov, nor the coward who intentionally caused others pain would survive this endless cycle of violence.

I knew I should stay and help, but it would be my only

way out—my only way back—back to the land that I once called home.

So I took my advantage and hopped onto the windowsill, counting backwards from three before slowly allowing my feet to slip off the concrete ledge.

Three…two…one.

Jump!

I grabbed hold of several small groves on the side of the building on my way down—so that I wouldn't break my legs from the five story fall.

Thankfully, I made it down entirely intact—no broken bones.

And because I was still so bruised and slightly bleeding from my cuts from the battle in Ipharadisi, no one tried to stop me as I pushed my way in the *opposite* direction of the raging crowd before me. I'm sure anyone who saw me assumed I'd had enough of whatever I'd just been through.

But when I finally got past the gate and back out into the fire ridden, war torn area, I realized that I had no idea where I was.

So how in the world would I find my way back?

Think Nanyamka.

I desperately tried to remember my training as I looked around the chaos that surrounded me. Then finally it dawned me. I didn't have to know where I was or how to get to where I needed to be. Because Zaina knew. After everything we just found out, she'd no doubt go back to where it had all started. And all I would have to do is to track my sister's movements.

She would lead me home.

I hoped.

I kneeled down and closed my eyes. Relax Nanyamka. You don't want to miss anything, so take in a deep breath and relax.

I opened my eyes and prayed that I would recognize whatever I was searching for. I just needed one clue to set me in the right direction—one clue to set me on the path home.

I kneeled down.

I could taste the dry earth of the dust that had clouded the air. And as I ran my fingers over the cracking soil that I hoped would contain some form of information in it, I simultaneously let the infertile dirt run through my fingers and disappear into the wind. I did it again, several times, waiting for something to come to me.

Nothing.

Perhaps it was hopeless, but I wouldn't give up. I ran my fingers further out along the dead, brownish-grey soil before I saw it. It was a piece of Zaina's now torn battle skirt.

I crawled forward.

Yes! It was a footprint. Two footprints. More! I checked each of them. They were all the right size, the right imprint of someone her weight, and definitely the right gait for Zaina. Incredible. And with not even that much of a head start, I should be able to follow these—possibly all the way to Ipharadisi—all the way to whatever was left of the peaceful village that I had lovingly learned to call home.

So I carefully tracked every clue that Zaina left behind—for what seemed like an eternity—my nerves biting at me the entire time.

And although my journey had begun early with the sun

positioned high in the sky, it had arched and was setting by the time the clues had stopped just a kilometer short of the apple bearing trees that covered the entrance to the vine created tunnel that I knew was hidden behind it.

This is why I thought it odd that the two footprints facing forward were smudged. Because even though Zaina *should* have gone directly straight, she had instead turned her body away. I could tell because the next set of footprints I saw were headed east—toward Ubumnyama territory.

Why?

Everything and everyone we loved was just beyond the short plain that led home. But then I remembered—past tense Nanyamka. Past tense. Everything...and everyone...we *once* loved *used* to be just beyond the short plain that gave way to the luscious garden my best friend said long ago had been forgotten.

Suddenly a terrible man's voice replayed in my head. "Get rid of them, will you? I'd hate to leave such an incredible mess behind." Then I heard the sound of the rifle—three times, and everything went black. I returned to the present—both solemn and sorrowed.

I took one last look at the narrow footprints that had turned away from Ipharadisi, then dutifully forged my way forward.

There weren't any guardians protecting the entrance. There weren't any secret words that had to be exchanged. No warriors defended the homefront, and the sound of children laughing was nowhere to be heard.

I grieved.

What if the poachers had come back? They had run away without their jeeps the moment they'd heard the

469

lion's roar. What if the evil men had come back for what they left behind?

All of the frightening, stomach-wrenching possibilities began to race through my head as I took step after step, forcing myself through the clearing, past the wide circle of chestnut brown ground, and through the cloud reaching trees that on any other day would let the sunlight through.

I took in a deep breath as I stepped out onto the grass trampled hill that overlooked the main square. I thought back to the first time I had seen this place.

It was a fully bustling village then, with towering African sculptures and life-size lion statues. Men and women of all shapes and sizes moved up and down the open space in a vibrant Christmas celebration mode—laughing and greeting each other, conversing and decorating their huts.

Now, it was a completely ravaged, entirely desolate—and nearly uninhabitable land. Grey skies shed tears for Ipharadisi that landed on my achingly tender skin.

I buried my face in my hands and only lifted up when a singular survivor called out to me. "Queen?" I peered out, wondering which Ipharadisian had made it.

And my mouth involuntarily dropped at the sight before me.

Because there, at the bottom of the hill, alone and weary stood Erec. His shirt was torn, and the dried blood of countless Ipharadisians still covered him. But he was alive. I ran to Erec and threw my arms around his neck as he buried his face in my hair, kissing me on the ear and shoulders—on my arms—on my hands. It took everything in me to finally let him go.

"Zaina thought you were dead. She was certain of it. But I couldn't even think about it. I couldn't... I couldn't..." I was shaking from the aftershock of all that had happened—everything that I finally let sink in. Erec wrapped me in his arms again and helped me to calm down.

But I still wanted to cry—for Kayla, for Tuki, but there was nothing left in me. So I tried to comprehend the damage—the loss, but it eluded me.

"Is this all who survived?" I looked out now as I saw just Addane and Rudo with Milandu and Akia. They were sweeping the wreckage of parts of the market that had rolled into the main square during the battle—during the fierce winds of the dry thunder storm.

Erec shook his head. "We've turned practically every hut into a recovery station, but no one was fatally injured."

Understanding what that meant, I nearly wept—overjoyed. And that along with an abundant exhale would have been enough, had there not still been Ipharadisian rescuers who were never found after their last mission, and who were now possibly lost forever. For after seeing the dark mind of that which had wished to harm us, I absolutely feared the worst for anyone who may have come across him during their rescue missions.

I sighed.

Erec noticed my continued grief as he took my hand. "What's wrong?"

I didn't even bother speaking, knowing I wouldn't need to say what Erec could see in my eyes. A shocking realization then came across his face.

"Oh! She's okay—fine—more than fine really."

I didn't understand. Erec could tell.

"It missed her. Actually, it bounced off the jeep right next to her, and the shrapnel from the bullet scraped Tuki up pretty badly—on all sides—that's why she lost so much blood, but that guy was a terrible shot. He missed all of us by at least a foot."

I was stunned. "And Kayla?"

"Really Kay, did you think I was going to let anything happen to her?"

I smiled then, not even being able to imagine the heroics Erec must've had to perform to save not just himself, but his fellow Ipharadisians as well. I tried to resist the urge to laugh, but finally I gave in. Erec half-laughed as well. Our giddiness was born out of relief, but soon turned into a laugh of victory.

Because at that very moment, a sound was heard across Ipharadisi that practically incapacitated everyone therein. Everybody covered their ears, and no one seemed to know what it was—but I did, and if she were standing with us, so would Tuki.

"It's the sound that comes from a cow's horn when many of them are played at the same time—with a few moderations of course." That's what little Kayla had told me one day when she wanted to know about my rescue from the poacher's camp. That's why she knew what it was as she came running up the hill from one of the acorn huts.

The horns continued to blare as dozens of Ipharadisians poured out of their huts. Many looked curiously at each other before moving in the direction of the intensifying sound.

Then it stopped.

And there, off in the distance, was each and every unaccounted rescuer marching towards us—all those who had been lost after the storm that had once temporarily sidelined Tuki, thereby propelling me to my destiny. The rescuers came back home victoriously with all those they had saved during their missions at their sides.

I was elated. Good had found a way to triumph over evil after all, and no lives had been lost in the process. So, I decided that as soon as all were well, we would celebrate. Because it was finally—at long last—time to celebrate.

The time for the victory dinner came even sooner than I expected, and when it did, everyone in the village pitched in. Some cooked. Some baked. Some decorated and others provided melodious entertainment. We celebrated like this for many, many days, and all of Ipharadisi rejoiced.

On the third day of celebrations, Erec sat next to me at the welcoming banquet for the new rescues, but our intimate conversation was interrupted by a shaken up gentleman in tattered clothing.

"Excuse me," said one of the new additions to Ipharadisi. "Is there anyone who can help me? I *have* to get back home."

The man was desperate.

I looked to Erec who nodded with a smile and then I excused myself from the table.

I faced the inquiring individual and asked him his name.

"Thomas," the frantic man answered. He said it with a very familiar accent.

"Hello Thomas. You are a very far ways from America,

yes?"

"I am," replied the older man. "But I've lived in Tokai now for over a decade. I've been gone from my family for over a week. Please, I'd like to go back home."

I thought about it for a long while with empathy. "I am sorry Thomas, but I must ask you to wait here."

I'd been so busy with the festivities and with sorting all of my new responsibilities that Tuki and I hadn't really had a chance to talk one-on-one since the battle. I visited her, of course, during her convalescence, but we didn't speak much as I wanted her to focus on getting better. But I sought out my dear friend today as I needed her advice.

"And his face was never seen by his captors?" Tuki questioned, "how so?"

Xola recounted the rescue for Tuki and I. I let Xola finish her account before excusing her from the palace hut.

"Tuki, what do you think?"

"I think it is safe for him to leave."

"And you are sure of this?"

"Yes," Tuki replied.

"Then he is free to go." I said it without hesitation. I trusted Tuki's advisement.

I was just about to walk out of the palace hut when Tuki raised her hand to stop me.

"Well?"

"Well what?" I stared at Tuki quizzically.

"Well...do you want to go with him?"

I was stupefied—mouth open. The thought hadn't even occurred to me.

"No," I quickly replied. "*This* is my home. How could

you even ask that?"

Tuki could tell that I was slightly offended, but continued. "I am sorry my friend. It is just that...I know there are many where you are from who would be glad for your return. Perhaps you should sleep on it."

I could tell that she didn't really want me to. Neither did I. No amount of sleep would change the way I felt about Ipharadisi—or about my family here.

I didn't have to think on it any longer because another new rescue had found me while in the middle of my discussion with Tuki. The little girl pulled on the bottom of my flowing purple skirt. She spoke timidly.

"Hello..." She said this with her curious, youthful eyes—the eyes of an eight-year-old I believe. "Are you really a...I mean, someone said that you're really a...you know."

I smiled.

"I am Queen Nanyamka Apiyo Morowa. Daughter of Queen Ayanna, granddaughter of Inkosi Ubaba. Welcome to Ipharadisi. You are safe now."

The little girl beamed with excitement and thanked me before leaving. I turned back to Tuki.

"Tuki, I had a dream last night. We were back with Zaina on the Assegai field, and a man was standing with us. He was our father. Yes?"

Tuki nodded.

I closed my eyes. "Why didn't you say anything—all this time?"

"Because...you needed to focus on bonding with Zaina. You and I, our relationship was strong from the beginning. But you and Zaina—I was concerned for that. I thought perhaps if you assumed you had only one sister, it would help to motivate you to work on the tensions the two of you shared. But I would have told you sister...eventually."

I rolled my eyes. "When? After you borrowed my favorite dress without asking?" Tuki laughed. I cried. And she knew why.

"You miss them."

I did. She saw right through me. Though it would be difficult to readjust to my old life, if I were honest about it, I never really let it go—I never really let *him* go.

Tuki turned her face then—wiping her cheek, and it occurred to me that I had never seen Tuki cry before. She embraced me as we hugged for what seemed like the entire brief lifetime that we'd known each other.

Finally, we let one another go.

So I slept under the stars that night for as long as I could, then I rose, and went to find the American who would drive me to Tokai.

Epilogue: Honey

The American remembered exactly where he had left his car—the one he had abandoned to get a closer view of the lion he'd been trying to capture on film. Thomas had followed it so far that he'd gotten lost, and was picked up on one of the most recent Ipharadisian rescues.

And although I didn't mean to, I laughed when he told me his story. I too had gotten "lost" once while trying to get a closer look at a lion.

The American was kind enough to drive me to the embassy in Tokai, where I hurried to find the man there Grandpa once told me I could trust. My grandfather had told me about this individual one day not long after I arrived in Ipharadisi.

Something told me now that deep down, Grandfather had always known how this was going to end.

So, I found this old acquaintance and explained to him my story—well, the part about being kidnapped by poachers and getting lost in the jungle anyway. I sort of left out the whole Queen of Ipharadisi part. I did, however, mention Grandpa's name to him—whose name even after all these years still carried immense weight.

Within hours, I was being driven to the nearest airport, and the soft rocking of the vehicle helped cradle me to sleep.

Once we arrived at the airport, the nice embassy agent purchased my plane ticket and made sure everything was taken care of for my flight.

I thanked him before entering the terminal.

As I waited for the boarding call, I looked through what was left of my old, canvas messenger bag. All that was inside was my passport, an old beat up camera and a cow's horn comb.

A little girl with excited eyes watched me as I lifted the last item, and asked her mother to offer me money in exchange for the extraordinarily beautiful comb. I smiled and politely told her that the comb wasn't for sale. The little girl shrugged, but I think she understood.

When the PA system finally announced the arrival of my flight, my heart skipped a beat because there was still one last thing I had to do before I boarded any plane.

I rose and timidly made my way to the back of the terminal. Every muscle in my body was shaking. Still, I stuffed my boarding pass in my back pocket before picking up the yellow handset that belonged to one of the payphones that was attached to the freshly painted wall near the bathrooms. I dialed, and then waited for it to connect.

It seemed like it took me forever to speak as I could barely say the one word that I'd been wanting to say for over seven months now. The line connected, and I spoke through choked back tears. "...Mom?"

Everything went silent for a long time. That is, until the PA system turned back on, and announced the five little words I absolutely thought I would never hear again.

"Now boarding—New York City. Now Boarding— New York City."

I sat on the airplane, trying to control all of the overwhelming emotions that attempted to bombard me. I gazed out the window and thought back to my last few hours in Ipharadisi.

"Grandfather?" No one answered.

Though I wasn't much for goodbyes, I still went back to the hilltop hoping to see his usual burning fire. It wasn't there—and I didn't see him in any of the usual places, but it didn't matter, I felt him. And I knew that everything would be okay. However, that didn't stop me from crying at the coronation.

"I present to you all my confidant, my loyal friend, and my sister—*Queen* Tuki Adaeze Morowa." I placed the crown upon her head as everyone cheered.

"All hail Queen Tuki! All hail Queen Tuki!"

Erec stood in the back, but I knew eventually he would stand by her side.

They were sort of perfectly matched that way.

And although I would miss him, so would I miss everyone that I'd met on my incredible journey home.

That's why I held onto that memory through the rest of the flight, through the landing, through the hordes of photojournalists and through the dozens of news crews that were waiting for me at the landing gate. I held onto the memories even tighter as I stood next to the podium in the NYU auditorium.

What would Tuki do? That's what I wondered when I received the call from a local news station asking if I were going to make a statement about my disappearance last year. I was still far from used to being back, and things were happening much quicker than I could keep up with; but there was so much that I had learned, and so many stories I wanted to share—stories of hope, and of bravery and of faith.

So I told the calling reporters that I would ask the Dean if I could hold an assembly before my university on Friday.

I checked the calendar and realized the somehow turned press conference would fall on Nelson Mandela's birthday, which brought a smile to my face as I recalled an article I once read on an airplane. I also then realized that it would give me an extra day to decide *how* to speak about what I had learned in Ipharadisi—without actually telling the world that it existed.

I looked out into the sea of news cameras and students who were waiting for me to speak.

My parents still weren't here yet. Traffic downtown was bumper to bumper. Apparently, I had become a pretty huge news story while I was away. I just hoped that the attention didn't last long.

My parents and I hadn't really had a chance to discuss everything that had happened. And I still had so many questions that I alone couldn't answer. But with all of the media attention and camera crews outside our apartment, I didn't quite feel that it was a good time to get into an in-depth discussion just yet.

I quickly moved to the side as someone adjusted the microphone in front of me, smiling awkwardly at Beth who had come here with me.

Beth had stayed in the same dorm room that we shared together before I left—and as my name was still on the rooming sheet, I decided to spend the night there yesterday, just to give me a break from the overwhelming attention outside my parents' house.

But the change in scenery didn't keep me from feeling slightly uneasy as I looked over the crowd before me. Because if I didn't have enough to think about for my speech in a few minutes, I also had to deal with the wicked startlingly memory of the extremely disconcerting dream I had last night.

I had hoped that those unsettling nightly occurrences were a thing of the past. But as soon as I fell asleep in the dorm room that I *thought* I would now be safe in, I instead woke up in a rapid sweat from an unusually intense vision that I convinced myself was just a dream.

Because in it, I was being held under water in some liquid-filled contraption. And some secret-ops agency wanted to know something that I couldn't remember— something I didn't *want* to remember. I had a feeling that it was something just too painful to recall.

But they're desperate to know—this agency, because for some reason they're afraid of me. Only, I can't seem to figure out why.

Weird.

I was actually pretty surprised that Callum wasn't in my dream last night—because he was the first person I thought about when I woke up from it. I was thankful that he picked up on the first ring when I called his cellphone at almost 3 o'clock this morning.

"Kay! Kay! Where are you?" He sounded frantic and relieved at the same time.

"I'm here Callum—at the dorm." Callum had seen my return when it was broadcast on the news. "There were too many people outside my family's apartment, so I decided to stay with Beth tonight."

"Can I come over? Can I see you now—like *right* now?"

I wanted to tell him yes. Instead, I tried to keep my composure over the phone, but I had to keep putting it down so that I could take breaks to cry. Hearing his voice again was more overwhelming than dealing with the press, the trauma, the reunions and the loss of a village family I'd never get to see again. I responded to him as calmly as I could. "I thought about you every day Callum."

"And I you, Kay." There was a brief pause. "I love you Kay. You do know that? That that'll never change? I've always loved you. I'll love you until I'm a 100 years old, until the day I die—even after, I'd still make sure you felt it Kay. That you'll always be protected by it. Please, please know that."

That's when I fell apart. I tried to say, "I love you," but I was so choked up I could barely speak.

Callum continued for me.

"I heard about the press conference tomorrow. I'll be there, okay? I'll be the first one there."

And he was. He was sitting in the front row now, and seeing his face was the only thing that made me feel I could get through this.

The Dean walked to my side after the stagehand finished adjusting the microphone for me. She tapped on it a few times before speaking.

"Attention ladies and gentleman. Press. We will begin now if everyone will kindly take their seats." The auditorium quickly quieted down, and I nervously stepped up to the podium—the Dean patting my hand for encouragement.

As many times as I used to picture working press conferences with a room full of journalists, I definitely never once thought it would be under these circumstances. Still, I took in a deep breath and kept my eyes on Callum—closing my eyes only briefly before speaking.

"Hello everyone. I um…well, thanks for coming." Don't babble Kay. Cut to the chase—you'll get through this faster. I took in another deep breath.

"Well, you may be wondering why I've gathered you all here today. I mean, I know I've been missing for a while, and my reappearance is sort of pretty big news right now. But, that's not why I wanted to speak to you."

I looked over at Beth who wasn't sitting far from Callum. She nodded me on.

"You see everyone, while I was away, I met some pretty incredible people, and they taught me a lot of things I didn't know before my time in Africa.

I have to admit, a lot of what I learned was about myself, and the kind of person I could become—a maturity I learned that I don't know I would have ever realized on my own." I thought about Erec, and how he inspired me to go beyond my comfort zone. I thought about Grandpa, and how he taught me to see beyond the obvious. I also thought about Tuki, and how she inspired me to be an inspiration to others.

I took out the little piece of paper that I'd written exactly what I wanted to say on, and put on my reading glasses to make sure that I didn't miss anything important.

But just as I opened my mouth to read the first word, the lights in the auditorium went out. Everyone began to complain because no one could see anything—except me.

Yes. I saw it before I felt it. I don't mean that I physically saw it because she was standing behind me when she did it.

No—what I saw was it *all*—every vision I'd ever had of it. The vision in class when she attacked me; the vision at the airport when she lunged at me; even the spear no one else saw go through me back on the Assegai field. Each of these visions had come to warn me, to prepare me. But despite how hard Grandfather had tried to help, I never fully understood what these things were trying to tell me—the revelation had come too late.

Because in the middle of my speech on a sunny July afternoon, I felt the piercing tear of an ivory dagger go through my back, and exit through my stomach.

I did not have to see her face to know whom it was. I only knew of one person who could be filled with so much hate, that she would leave the only home she ever knew to be the downfall of the one she believed had not only brought death to her desired king, but who had also brought death to the sister who was once her most trusted advisor.

If only Zaina had returned home, she would have known that all was well there in the end.

The barrage of flashes commenced then as my limp body finally hit the floor. And although I couldn't see through the blinding lights that rushed towards me, I can tell you what I did see.

It was every lesson I ever learned, every friend I ever loved and every person I ever helped during my time in

Ipharadisi. And because of it, I was not afraid now. I'd done something with my life that no one in the world could take away, and for that I was satisfied.

My parents hadn't arrived to the auditorium yet, and I was thankful that they didn't have to suffer witnessing the loss of their only child. But Beth was here, and so was Callum. And Callum, who was the first to run to the stage, kissed my forehead and held my hand as I died.

Thus was the end of a life well lived, by Nanyamka "Kay" Apiyo Morowa.

1:21 PM

News Anchor:

"Good afternoon, we interrupt your regular scheduled programming to bring you startling news out of the New York Metropolitan area.

Nanyamka Apiyo Morowa, a third-year journalism student at New York University, was violently stabbed during a press conference just minutes ago.

You may remember, this was the same young woman who went missing last December, after she disappeared during an academic-based trip to South Africa.

Police are currently searching for her attacker, but no suspect has yet been found."

2:21 PM

News anchor:

"We're now live at NYU hospital, where
the young woman who was attacked
earlier during a live press conference,
is reported to be in critical
condition.

I'm being told family members are in
route to the hospital now. As you can
see, we're now looking at footage of
Ms. Morowa as she was being rushed into
the hospital just minutes ago.

There also appears to be a young man by
the side of Ms. Morowa's stretcher.
He's clearly visibly upset, but we
haven't been able to identify who he is
as of yet.

More updates to follow."

3:21 PM

News anchor:

"It's an incredibly somber afternoon as we're forced to interrupt your regular scheduled programming to bring you a devastating update on the startling attack we reported on earlier today.

We have just received confirmation that the young woman, Nanyamka Apiyo Morowa, was pronounced dead by medical staff at the NYU hospital shortly after being brought in. Doctors say they did everything they could, but the young woman's injuries were just too extensive.

Our deepest condolences of course go out to the entire Morowa family.

What a tragic loss to the NYU and New York City communities."

ONE YEAR LATER

News Anchor:

"It's been one year since the unsolved killing of Nanyamka Apiyo Morowa: the talented young NYU student who went missing seven months prior to being fatally wounded just days after her return back to New York.

Friends and family attended a memorial service for the slain student today. It was held in the Tishman auditorium of the NYU campus in honor of her memory.

Those who knew Nanyamka brought flowers and shared stories of their beloved friend and classmate.

Nanyamka Apiyo Morowa continues to be sorely missed."

I watched my parents grieving on television, and part of me grieved with them. It'd been one year since my own sister drove an ivory dagger through my body, killing me instantly.

And now Beth, my mom, my dad—even Callum, all thought I was dead. And they could never, ever know the truth—that somewhere, somehow, I was still alive and...

DIFFERENT.

Can't wait to find out what happens next?

Spread the word!

Tell your friends and family to pick up a copy of "The Phoenix Rising – Destiny Calls" and be part of the effort to get out the sequel!

ABOUT THE AUTHOR

After graduating from Brooklyn Technical High School in New York City, Phenice Arielle went on to major in journalism at the Pennsylvania State University. She has done several entertainment features for local newspapers, and is also credited for her work as an award-nominated singer-songwriter.

For book extras, and to stay in the loop about the upcoming sequel to Destiny Calls, please visit ThePhoenixRisingBook.Com

Follow @PheniceArielle to be the first to know when the Sequel is available!

http://www.Twitter.com/PheniceArielle

Made in the USA
Lexington, KY
09 July 2013